The White People and other stories

Vol. 2 of the Best Weird Tales of Arthur Machen

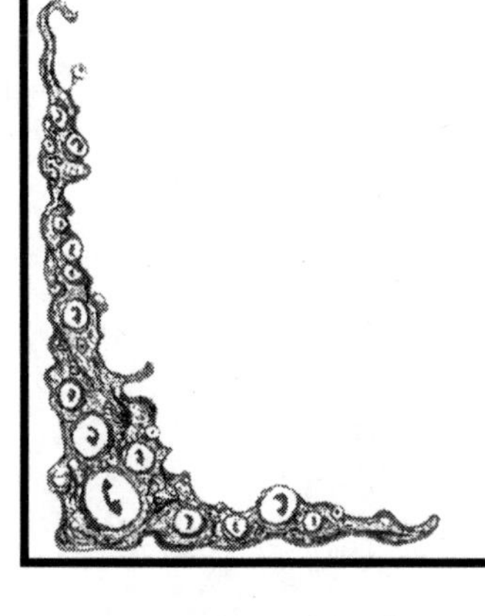

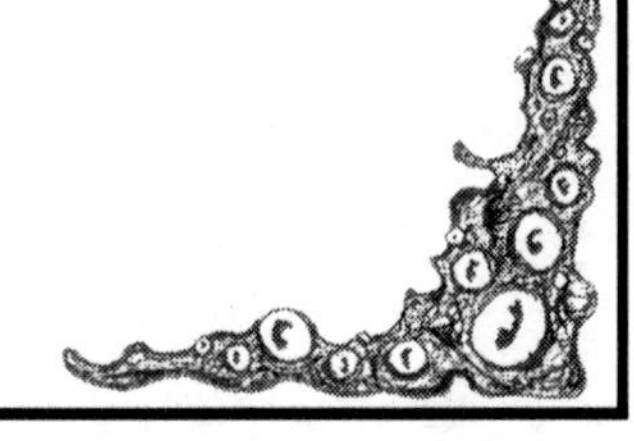

More Titles from Chaosium

Call of Cthulhu® Fiction

The Antarktos Cycle
The Book of Eibon
The Disciples of Cthulhu, 2nd Ed.
The Ithaqua Cycle
The Necronomicon, 2nd Ed.
Singers of Strange Songs
Song of Cthulhu
Tales Out of Innsmouth
Lin Carter's The Xothic Legend Cycle
R. W. Chambers' The Yellow Sign (his complete weird fiction)
Arthur Machen's The Three Impostors and Other Stories

Miskatonic University® Archives

The Book of Dzyan

The White People and Other Stories

The Best Weird Tales of Arthur Machen, Volume 2

EDITED AND INTRODUCED BY S. T. JOSHI

A Chaosium Book
2003

The White People and Other Stories is published by Chaosium, Inc.

The White People and Other Stories is an original omnibus publication by Chaosium, Inc. "The Red Hand" was originally published in *Chapman's Magazine* (December 1895). "The Rose Garden" was originally published in *The Neolith* (August 1908). "Psychology," "Nature," and "The Holy Things" were originally published under the general title "Fragments of Paper" in *The Academy* (January 4, 1908). "The Turanians," "The Idealist," "Witchcraft," "The Ceremony," "Torture," and "Midsummer" were originally published in *Ornaments in Jade* (New York: Alfred A. Knopf, 1924). "The White People" was originally published in *Horlick's Magazine* (January 1904). "A Fragment of Life" was originally published in *Horlick's Magazine* (February, March, April, and May 1904), and in revised form in *The House of Souls* (London: E. Grant Richards, 1906). "Introduction" was originally published as "Introduction to *The Angels of Mons*" in *The Angels of Mons: The Bowmen and Other Legends of the War* (London: Simpkin, Marshall, Hamilton, Kent & Co., 1915). "The Bowmen" was originally published in *The Evening News* (London, September 29, 1914). "The Soldiers' Rest" was originally published in *The Evening News* (London, October 20, 1914). "The Monstrance" and "The Dazzling Light" were originally published in *The Angels of Mons: The Bowmen and Other Legends of the War* (London: Simpkin, Marshall, Hamilton, Kent & Co., 1915). "The Great Return" was originally serialized in *The Evening News* (London, October 21 to November 16, 1915). "Out of the Earth" was originally published in *T. P.'s Weekly* (November 27, 1915). "The Coming of the Terror" was originally published in *Century Magazine* (October 1917). "The Happy Children" was first published in *The Masterpiece Library of Short Stories*, edited by Sir J. A. Hammerton (London: Educational Book Company, 1920).

Cover art ©2003 by Harry Fassl. Cover layout by Charlie Krank. Interior layout and copy editing by David Mitchell. Additional copy editing by S. T. Joshi. Editor-in-chief Lynn Willis.

Our web site is updated regularly; see **www.chaosium.com**.

This book is printed on 100% acid-free paper.

FIRST EDITION

10 9 8 7 6 5 4

Chaosium Publication 6035. Published in May 2003.

ISBN 1-56882-172-7

Printed in the U.S.A.

Contents

Introduction

The final years of Machen's "great decade" of fiction writing—the period between 1887 and 1901 when, thanks to a timely inheritance, he was able to devote his energies entirely to his art without thought of monetary recompense—produced several of the works for which Machen is known today. Even excluding the marginally weird novel *The Hill of Dreams* (written in 1897 but not published until 1907), which H. P. Lovecraft memorably described as a "memorable epic of the sensitive aesthetic mind," we are faced with such works as "The Red Hand" (1897), the prose poems collected in *Ornaments in Jade* (1924), "The White People" (the second-greatest horror tale ever written, according to Lovecraft, next to Algernon Blackwood's "The Willows"), and the unclassifiable short novel *A Fragment of Life.* Had Machen written nothing else, these works alone would be sufficient to grant him a place in weird literature—or in literature as a whole.

"The Red Hand" (written in 1895) is a pendant to *The Three Impostors,* resurrecting the two central figures in that novel, Phillipps and Dyson, as they continue their intellectual dispute over the nature of reality while becoming involved in what proves to be an exceptionally clever supernatural detective story. Dyson, the mystic (hence the stand-in for Machen), evokes a "theory of improbability" to account for the remarkable series of coincidences that leads him to the solution of the case; but this is less interesting than the overall philosophical thrust of the tale, in which Machen utilizes the tools of rationalism (specifically, the forensic analysis of evidence in regard to the murder at the heart of the case) to undermine rationalism and thereby to "prove" to his satisfaction that the matter can only be accounted for by appealing to the supernatural—in this case, the continued existence of "little people." It is not surprising that Lovecraft quoted a passage from this story ("There are sacraments of evil as well as of good about us . . .") as the epigraph to "The Horror at Red Hook" (1925), since that tale was itself a precursor to "The Call of Cthulhu" and other works where much the same sort of rationalism is used to establish the unshakable reality of Cthulhu and Yog-Sothoth.

Of the prose-poems in *Ornaments in Jade* it is difficult to speak in detail. These delicate vignettes may in some sense be pendants to *The Hill of Dreams*—not in terms of plot, but in terms of style and substance. Upon publication of *The Three Impostors,* Machen was heavily criticized for too closely imitating the jaunty style of Robert Louis Stevenson; and, as he himself testifies, he "resolved to try to amend my ways":

> I was to start afresh, then, from the beginning to turn over a new leaf, both as regards matter and manner. No more white powders, no more of the calyx principis inferorum, no more hanky-panky with the Great God Pan, or the Little People or any people of that dubious sort; and—this was the hard part of it—no more of the measured, rounded Stevensonian cadence, which I had learned to use with some faculty and more facility.[1]

The task was agonizing—*The Hill of Dreams* took eighteen months and several drafts to complete—but in the end it was accomplished: Machen had evolved his own style, a style of impeccable fluidity, elegance, and, above all, *sincerity.* The prose-poems in *Ornaments in Jade*—comparable only to those of Clark Ashton Smith as the finest in English—complete Machen's transformation from clever imitator to independent artist. If there is any dominant theme that unites them, it is the constant contrast between mundane modernity and the hoary past—a past that is simultaneously terrifying in its primitivism and awesome in its suggestions of intimate, symbolic connexions with the essence of life and Nature. However brutalized modern people are by the dominant materialism of the age, their sense of spirituality can well up in spite of themselves in the practice of ancient rituals.

As for "The White People," in a sense it returns to the theme of "The Great God Pan" (1890) in its emphasis on illicit sex. For Machen, the orthodox Anglo-Catholic, sexual aberrations represented a kind of violation of the entire fabric of the universe. This is the substance of the remarks by Ambrose at the beginning of the tale, especially his comment that sin is "the attempt to penetrate into another and higher sphere in a *forbidden* [my italics] manner" and "the effort to gain the ecstasy and knowledge that pertain alone to angels . . ." This story—in which a young girl unwittingly reveals in her diary her inculcation into a witch-cult and, evidently, her impregnation by some nameless entity—transmogrifies illicit sex into a cosmic sin that will either lift us up into the ranks of the angels or plunge us down into the company of demons. And yet, Machen's exposition of the details of the matter (especially the sexual element) are so indirect that many readers have been puzzled as to the exact nature of the scenario. One such reader was the young J. Vernon Shea, who asked his friend H. P. Lovecraft to elucidate the tale. Lovecraft did so, concluding: "On account of a sympathetic action like that described in the prologue, the now-adolescent child—though without contact with any creative element—became pregnant with a Horror, to whose birth (knowing what she did of dark tradition) she could not look forward without a stark frenzy far beyond the fear of mere disgrace. Thus she

[1]Arthur Machen, "Introduction" to *The Hill of Dreams* (New York: Knopf, 1923), pp. vi–vii

killed herself."[2] In the absence of contrary evidence, this interpretation must be accepted. Machen's single sentence at the end ("She had poisoned herself—in time") is the only clue this repressed Victorian writer can provide to the sexual anomalies of the situation.

And yet, Lovecraft was manifestly inspired not by the mechanics of the plot of "The White People," but by its magnificent allusiveness and subtlety. The diary in which the girl tells unwittingly of her initiation into the witch-cult is a masterstroke: *we* know what is happening, but *she* in her naïveté does not. Lovecraft used the technique in smaller compass in Wilbur Whateley's diary entries in "The Dunwich Horror" (1928). And those chilling hints of nameless rituals that the girl provides ("I must not write down . . . the way to make the Aklo letters, or the Chian language, or the great beautiful Circles, nor the Mao Games, nor the chief songs") also seized Lovecraft's imagination, and he presents a very similar kind of telling-by-not-telling in "The Whisperer in Darkness": "I learned whence Cthulhu *first* came, and why half the great temporary stars of history had flared forth. I guessed . . . the secret behind the Magellanic Clouds and globular nebulae, and the black truth veiled by the immemorial allegory of Tao." And recall the laconic statement in "The Shadow Out of Time" (1934–35): "What was hinted in the speech of post-human entities of the fate of mankind produced such an effect upon me that I will not set it down here."

A Fragment of Life is an altogether different proposition. If this short novel is only on the very edge of the weird, it deserves far wider recognition as one of Machen's most finished works. The exquisitely gradual way in which the stolid bourgeois couple, Edward and Mary Darnell, slowly awaken to their sense of wonder and abandon London for their native Wales is one of Machen's great literary accomplishments. Amidst all the mundane details of the small-scale social life of the Darnells, we receive small hints that their love of beauty has not been entirely destroyed, as it has for so many who live too fully in the modern world. Machen delivers an unanswerable criticism of the narrowing of vision that such a life engenders: "So, day after day, he lived in the grey phantasmal world, akin to death, that has, somehow, with most of us, made good its claim to be called life." And yet, something so simple as birdsong heard by Edward ("That night was the night I thought I heard the nightingale . . . and the sky was such a wonderful deep blue") provides an anticipation of the coming change. Mary, too, although seemingly more hard-headedly practical than Edward, senses the alteration in her being ("one would have almost said that they were the eyes of one who longed and half expected to be initiated into the mysteries, who

[2] H. P. Lovecraft, Letter to J. Vernon Shea (December 9, 1931); *Selected Letters 1929–1931*, ed. August Derleth and Donald Wandrei (Sauk City, WI: Arkham House, 1971), p. 439.

knew not what great wonder was to be revealed"). The entire novel is a kind of instantiation of the critical theories in Machen's idiosyncratic treatise, *Hieroglyphics: A Note upon Ecstasy in Literature* (1902), in which he criticized such writers as Jane Austen and George Eliot for being too closely tied to mundane reality and failing to include that modicum of "ecstasy" which ought, in Machen's eyes, to inform all literature. We may well believe that Machen was insufficiently attuned to the "ecstasy" that is in fact present in the work of the social realists he disdains, but we can hardly gainsay that he himself has flawlessly embodied his own principles in *A Fragment of Life.*

After writing this novel (which was itself worked on sporadically over five years, 1899–1904), Machen appeared to lose focus as far as fiction writing was concerned. In 1907 he wrote the curious novel *The Secret Glory* (not published until 1922), but that was the extent of his creative output between 1904 and 1914. With his inheritance gone, Machen was forced to produce mountains of journalism; the book publications of his fiction—specifically *The House of Souls* (1906) and *The Hill of Dreams* (1907)—brought him fleeting attention, but not much in the way of income. It was only in 1914 that he resumed fiction writing—but he did so in a peculiar way.

Machen had, since 1910, been serving on the staff of one of the leading newspapers in London, the *Evening News,* as reporter and columnist. (In one of his articles of 1916, oddly enough, he reviewed Clark Ashton Smith's first volume, *The Star-Treader and Other Poems* [1912].) At least two of the four stories that comprised *The Bowmen and Other Legends of the War* (1915)—"The Bowmen" (September 29, 1914) and "The Soldiers' Rest" (October 20, 1914)—appeared in the *Evening News.* The well-known story of how "The Bowmen"—a tale about the ghosts of mediæval British soldiers who come to the aid of a beleaguered British unit at the battle of Mons in late August 1914—came to be regarded as a real occurrence, with angels rescuing the soldiers and supposedly first-hand accounts by the soldiers themselves testifying to the miracle—need not be discussed in detail; Machen himself recounts the matter in the introduction to *The Bowmen and Other Legends of the War,* included here. His repeated protestations that the story was entirely a product of his imagination went for naught; the outbreak of the European war—which commenced less than two months prior to the publication of "The Bowmen"—was so traumatic that the emergence of such legendry was inevitable. Machen himself alludes to Kipling's "The Lost Legion" as a central literary influence on the tale, although other literary sources reaching back to Herodotus' *Histories* have recently been postulated.[3] But what is more significant is Machen's own attempt to pull off a kind of hoax with

[3]See Phillip Ellis, "Spectral Soldiers: Possible Literary Antecedents for 'The Bowmen,'" *Studies in Weird Fiction* No. 24 (Winter 1999): 5–10.

"The Bowmen." The mere fact that it was published in the newspaper—even though newspapers at this time published more fiction than they do now—and the fact that it was written with the plain-spoken sobriety expected of factual articles, suggest that Machen is not wholly blameless in the subsequent furor caused by his little tale.

Much the same could be said for "The Great Return," which also appeared in the *Evening News* (October 21–November 16, 1915) and was subsequently published in book form by a religious publisher, the Faith Press. Here Machen seeks no more than to present—in the most orthodox repertorial manner—a series of curious incidents in Wales that, to his mind, suggest the actual rediscovery of the Holy Grail. Once again, as in "The Red Hand," although in a somewhat cruder way, Machen seeks to use the tools of rationalism to undermine rationalism: here the outwardly skeptical newspaper reporter—who is none other than Machen himself, with no attempt made to establish a distance between author and persona—becomes gradually convinced of the reality of the phenomena described. Machen is content to present a scenario whereby something miraculous might have happened: this is sufficient for his current purpose of attacking the godless materialism of his age.

The European war was obviously a highly disturbing event to Machen. Already alienated from his time by his own religious mysticism, so much in contrast with the prevailing scientific rationalism of the later nineteenth century, he found his own faith shaken by a war in which Christians were killing other Christians with great gusto. Toward the end of the conflict he wrote a series of sophistical articles attempting to justify the ways of God to man; they were collected as *War and the Christian Faith* (1918). But a much more interesting response to the war came in the story known as "The Coming of the Terror," the only horror tale by Machen that has never been reprinted from its original appearance.

The story itself, of course, is better known as the short novel, *The Terror* (1917), which was itself serialized in the *Evening News* (October 16–31, 1916). The abridged version in the *Century Magazine* (October 1917) reduced the 40,000 words of the original to a mere 10,000 words; Machen himself testified that the abridgment was made "with a skill that was really remarkable."[4] Once again we are faced with a repertorial account—sober, factual, even a bit bland—but again the purpose is to demonstrate that "science deals only with surfaces" and that the true causes for the revolt of animals against the domination of mankind lie much deeper. Machen unfortunately rejects the notion that the animals' attacks were a product of a "contagion of hate"

[4]Arthur Machen, note to Henry Danielson, *Arthur Machen: A Bibliography* (London: Henry Danielson, 1923), p. 47.

caused by the war—a perfectly plausible and aesthetically satisfying motivation—and opts instead for the lame explanation that man has discarded the "grace of spirituality" that purportedly separates us from the beasts. But up to this point, the tale achieves notable heights of inexplicable terror that Machen attained only in his best tales.

The subsequent literary career of Arthur Machen is a slow decline into harmless verbosity. His later tales were gathered in two undistinguished collections, *The Cosy Room* (1936) and *The Children of the Pool* (1936). Of the horror novel *The Green Round* (1933), Lovecraft's charitable comment is the best that can be said of it: "It is really extremely interesting—with something of that persistent sense of unreal worlds impinging on the real world which many imaginative persons possess. In the casualness & unexplainedness of the phenomena represented, it recalls some of Machen's queer prefaces to his earlier books. However—it is marred by a certain rambling diffuseness, tameness, & over-use of typical stylistic mannerisms!"[5] None of these works add anything to Machen's overall reputation as a horror writer. All that one need read of Arthur Machen in the weird vein are contained in these two Chaosium volumes of his tales; if one adds *The Hill of Dreams, Hieroglyphics,* his three splendid autobiographies (*Far Off Things* [1922], *Things Near and Far* [1923], and *The London Adventure* [1924]), and a small selection of his prodigal output of essays and journalism, one will have absorbed the best that Machen produced in a lifetime of unstinted literary labor. And that best is very good indeed.

—S. T. JOSHI

[5]H. P. Lovecraft, Letter to Elizabeth Toldridge (March 29, 1934); *Selected Letters 1932–1934,* ed. August Derleth and James Turner (Sauk City, WI: Arkham House, 1976), p. 397.

The Red Hand

I. The Problem of the Fish-Hooks

"THERE can be no doubt whatever," said Mr. Phillipps, "that my theory is the true one; these flints are prehistoric fish-hooks."

"I dare say; but you know that in all probability the things were forged the other day with a door-key."

"Stuff!" said Phillipps; "I have some respect, Dyson, for your literary abilities, but your knowledge of ethnology is insignificant, or rather non-existent. These fish-hooks satisfy every test; they are perfectly genuine."

"Possibly, but as I said just now, you go to work at the wrong end. You neglect the opportunities that confront you and await you, obvious, at every corner; you positively shrink from the chance of encountering primitive man in this whirling and mysterious city, and you pass the weary hours in your agreeable retirement of Red Lion Square fumbling with bits of flint, which are, as I said, in all probability, rank forgeries."

Phillipps took one of the little objects, and held it up in exasperation.

"Look at that ridge," he said. "Did you ever see such a ridge as that on a forgery?"

Dyson merely grunted and lit his pipe, and the two sat smoking in rich silence, watching through the open window the children in the square as they flitted to and fro in the twilight of the lamps, as elusive as bats flying on the verge of a dark wood.

"Well," said Phillipps at last, "it is really a long time since you have been round. I suppose you have been working at your old task."

"Yes," said Dyson, "always the chase of the phrase. I shall grow old in the hunt. But it is a great consolation to meditate on the fact that there are not a dozen people in England who know what style means."

"I suppose not; for the matter of that, the study of ethnology is far from popular. And the difficulties! Primitive man stands dim and very far off across the great bridge of years."

"By the way," he went on after a pause, "what was that stuff you were talking just now about shrinking from the chance of encountering primitive man at the corner, or something of the kind? There are certainly people about here whose ideas are very primitive."

"I wish, Phillipps, you would not rationalize my remarks. If I recollect the phrase correctly, I hinted that you shrank from the chance of encountering primitive man in this whirling and mysterious city, and I meant exactly what I said. Who can limit the age of survival? The troglodyte and the lake-dweller, perhaps representatives of yet darker races, may very probably be lurking in our midst, rubbing shoulders with frock-coated and finely-draped humanity, ravening like wolves at heart and boiling with the foul passions of the swamp and the black cave. Now and then as I walk in Holborn or Fleet Street I see a face which I pronounce abhorred, and yet I could not give a reason for the thrill of loathing that stirs within me."

"My dear Dyson, I refuse to enter myself in your literary 'trying-on' department. I know that survivals do exist, but all things have a limit, and your speculations are absurd. You must catch me your troglodyte before I will believe in him."

"I agree to that with all my heart," said Dyson, chuckling at the ease with which he had succeeded in "drawing" Phillips. "Nothing could be better. It's a fine night for a walk," he added, taking up his hat.

"What nonsense you are talking, Dyson!" said Phillipps. "However, I have no objection to taking a walk with you: as you say, it is a pleasant night."

"Come along then," said Dyson, grinning, "but remember our bargain."

The two men went out into the square, and threading one of the narrow passages that serve as exits, struck towards the north-east. As they passed along a flaring causeway they could hear at intervals between the clamour of the children and the triumphant *Gloria* played on a piano-organ the long deep hum and roll of the traffic in Holborn, a sound so persistent that it echoed like the turning of everlasting wheels. Dyson looked to right and left and conned the way, and presently they were passing through a more peaceful quarter, touching on deserted squares and silent streets black as midnight. Phillipps had lost all count of direction, and as by degrees the region of faded respectability gave place to the squalid, and dirty stucco offended the eye of the artistic observer, he merely ventured the remark that he had never seen a neighbourhood more unpleasant or more commonplace.

"More mysterious, you mean," said Dyson. "I warn you, Phillipps, we are now hot upon the scent."

They dived yet deeper into the maze of brickwork; some time before they had crossed a noisy thoroughfare running east and west, and now the quarter seemed all amorphous, without character; here a decent house with sufficient garden, here a faded square, and here factories surrounded by high, blank walls, with blind passages and dark corners; but all ill-lighted and unfrequented and heavy with silence.

Presently, as they paced down a forlorn street of two-story houses, Dyson caught sight of a dark and obscure turning.

"I like the look of that," he said; "it seems to me promising." There was a street lamp at the entrance, and another, a mere glimmer, at the further end. Beneath the lamp, on the pavement, an artist had evidently established his academy in the daytime, for the stones were all a blur of crude colours rubbed into each other, and a few broken fragments of chalk lay in a little heap beneath the wall.

"You see people do occasionally pass this way," said Dyson, pointing to the ruins of the screever's work. "I confess I should not have thought it possible. Come, let us explore."

On one side of this by-way of communication was a great timber-yard, with vague piles of wood looming shapeless above the enclosing wall; and on the other side of the road a wall still higher seemed to enclose a garden, for there were shadows like trees, and a faint murmur of rustling leaves broke the silence. It was a moonless night, and clouds that had gathered after sunset had blackened, and midway between the feeble lamps the passage lay all dark and formless, and when one stopped and listened, and the sharp echo of reverberant footsteps ceased, there came from far away, as from beyond the hills, a faint roll of the noise of London. Phillipps was bolstering up his courage to declare that he had had enough of the excursion, when a loud cry from Dyson broke in upon his thoughts.

"Stop, stop for Heaven's sake, or you will tread on it! There! almost under your feet!" Phillipps looked down, and saw a vague shape, dark, and framed in surrounding darkness, dropped strangely on the pavement, and then a white cuff glimmered for a moment as Dyson lit a match, which went out directly.

"It's a drunken man," said Phillipps very coolly.

"It's a murdered man," said Dyson, and he began to call for police with all his might, and soon from the distance running footsteps echoed and grew louder, and cries sounded.

A policeman was the first to come up.

"What's the matter?" he said, as he drew to a stand, panting. "Anything amiss here?" for he had not seen what was on the pavement.

"Look!" said Dyson, speaking out of the gloom. "Look there! My friend and I came down this place three minutes ago, and that is what we found."

The man flashed his light on the dark shape and cried out.

"Why, it's murder," he said; "there's blood all about him, and a puddle of it in the gutter there. He's not dead long, either. Ah! there's the wound! It's in the neck."

Dyson bent over what was lying there. He saw a prosperous gentleman, dressed in smooth, well-cut clothes. The neat whiskers were beginning to grizzle a little; he might have been forty-five an hour before; and a handsome gold watch had half slipped out of his waistcoat pocket. And there in the flesh of the neck, between chin and ear, gaped a great wound, clean cut, but all clotted with dry blood, and the white of the cheeks shone like a lighted lamp above the red.

Dyson turned, and looked curiously about him; the dead man lay across the path with his head inclined towards the wall, and the blood from the wound streamed away across the pavement, and lay a dark puddle, as the policeman had said, in the gutter. Two more policemen had come up, the crowd gathered, humming from all quarters, and the officers had as much as they could do to keep the curious at a distance. The three lanterns were flashing here and there, searching for more evidence, and in the gleam of one of them Dyson caught sight of an object in the road, to which he called the attention of the policeman nearest to him.

"Look, Phillipps," he said, when the man had secured it and held it up. "Look, that should be something in your way!"

It was a dark flinty stone, gleaming like obsidian, and shaped to a broad edge something after the manner of an adze. One end was rough, and easily grasped in the hand, and the whole thing was hardly five inches long. The edge was thick with blood.

"What is that, Phillipps?" said Dyson; and Phillipps looked hard at it.

"It's a primitive flint knife," he said. "It was made about ten thousand years ago. One exactly like this was found near Aubury, in Wiltshire, and all the authorities gave it that age."

The policeman stared astonished at such a development of the case; and Phillipps himself was all aghast at his own words. But Mr. Dyson did not notice him. An inspector who had just come up and was listening to the outlines of the case, was holding a lantern to the dead man's head. Dyson, for his part, was staring with a white heat of curiosity at something he saw on the wall, just above where the man was lying; there were a few rude marks done in red chalk.

"This is a black business," said the inspector at length; "does anybody know who it is?"

A man stepped forward from the crowd. "I do, governor," he said, "he's a big doctor, his name's Sir Thomas Vivian; I was in the 'orspital abart six months ago, and he used to come round; he was a very kind man."

"Lord," cried the inspector, "this is a bad job indeed. Why, Sir Thomas Vivian goes to the Royal Family. And there's a watch worth a hundred guineas in his pocket, so it isn't robbery."

Dyson and Phillipps gave their cards to the authorities, and moved off, pushing with difficulty through the crowd that was still gathering, gathering fast; and the alley that had been lonely and desolate now swarmed with white staring faces and hummed with the buzz of rumour and horror, and rang with the commands of the officers of police. The two men, once free from this swarming curiosity, stepped out briskly, but for twenty minutes neither spoke a word.

"Phillipps," said Dyson, as they came into a small but cheerful street, clean and brightly lit, "Phillipps, I owe you an apology. I was wrong to have spoken as I did to-night. Such infernal jesting," he went on, with heat, "as if there were no wholesome subjects for a joke. I feel as if I had raised an evil spirit."

"For Heaven's sake say nothing more," said Phillipps, choking down horror with visible effort. "You told the truth to me in my room; the troglodyte, as you said, is still lurking about the earth, and in these very streets around us, slaying for mere lust of blood."

"I will come up for a moment," said Dyson when they reached Red Lion Square, "I have something to ask you. I think there should be nothing hidden between us at all events."

Phillipps nodded gloomily, and they went up to the room, where everything hovered indistinct in the uncertain glimmer of the light from without. When the candle was lighted and the two men sat facing each other, Dyson spoke.

"Perhaps," he began, "you did not notice me peering at the wall just above the place where the head lay. The light from the inspector's lantern was shining full on it, and I saw something that looked queer to me, and I examined it closely. I found that some one had drawn in red chalk a rough outline of a hand—a human hand—upon the wall. But it was the curious position of the fingers that struck me; it was like this"; and he took a pencil and a piece of paper and drew rapidly, and then handed what he had done to Phillipps. It was a rough sketch of a hand seen from the back, with the fingers clenched, and the top of the thumb protruded between the first and second fingers, and pointed downwards, as if to something below.

"It was just like that," said Dyson, as he saw Phillipps's face grow still whiter. "The thumb pointed down as if to the body; it seemed almost a live hand in ghastly gesture. And just beneath there was a small mark with the powder of the chalk lying on it—as if some one had commenced a stroke and had broken the chalk in his hand. I saw the bit of chalk lying on the ground. But what do you make of it?"

"It's a horrible old sign," said Phillipps—"one of the most horrible signs connected with the theory of the evil eye. It is used still in Italy, but there can be no doubt that it has been known for ages. It is one of the survivals; you must look for the origin of it in the black swamp whence man first came."

Dyson took up his hat to go.

"I think, jesting apart," said he, "that I kept my promise, and that we were and are hot on the scent, as I said. It seems as if I had really shown you primitive man, or his handiwork at all events."

II. Incident of the Letter

ABOUT a month after the extraordinary and mysterious murder of Sir Thomas Vivian, the well-known and universally respected specialist in heart disease, Mr. Dyson called again on his friend Mr. Phillipps, whom he found, not, as usual, sunk deep in painful study, but reclining in his easy-chair in an attitude of relaxation. He welcomed Dyson with cordiality.

"I am very glad you have come," he began; "I was thinking of looking you up. There is no longer the shadow of doubt about the matter."

"You mean the case of Sir Thomas Vivian?"

"Oh, no, not at all. I was referring to the problem of the fish-hooks. Between ourselves, I was a little too confident when you were here last, but since then other facts have turned up; and only yesterday I had a letter from a distinguished F. R. S. which quite settles the affair. I have been thinking what I should tackle next; and I am inclined to believe that there is a good deal to be done in the way of so-called undecipherable inscriptions."

"Your line of study pleases me," said Dyson. "I think it may prove useful. But in the meantime, there was surely something extremely mysterious about the case of Sir Thomas Vivian."

"Hardly, I think. I allowed myself to be frightened that night; but there can be no doubt that the facts are patient of a comparatively commonplace explanation."

"Really! What is your theory then?"

"Well, I imagine that Vivian must have been mixed up at some period of his life in an adventure of a not very creditable description, and that he was murdered out of revenge by some Italian whom he had wronged."

"Why Italian?"

"Because of the hand, the sign of the *mano in fica.* That gesture is now only used by Italians. So you see that what appeared the most obscure feature in the case turns out to be illuminant."

"Yes, quite so. And the flint knife?"

"That is very simple. The man found the thing in Italy, or possibly stole it from some museum. Follow the line of least resistance, my dear fellow, and you will see there is no need to bring up primitive man from his secular grave beneath the hills."

"There is some justice in what you say," said Dyson. "As I understand you, then, you think that your Italian, having murdered Vivian, kindly chalked up that hand as a guide to Scotland Yard?"

"Why not? Remember a murderer is always a madman. He may plot and contrive nine-tenths of his scheme with the acuteness and the grasp of a chess-player or a pure mathematician; but somewhere or other his wits leave him and he behaves like a fool. Then you must take into account the insane pride or vanity of the criminal; he likes to leave his mark, as it were, upon his handiwork."

"Yes, it is all very ingenious; but have you read the reports of the inquest?"

"No, not a word. I simply gave my evidence, left the court, and dismissed the subject from my mind."

"Quite so. Then if you don't object I should like to give you an account of the case. I have studied it rather deeply, and I confess it interests me extremely."

"Very good. But I warn you I have done with mystery. We are to deal with facts now."

"Yes, it is fact that I wish to put before you. And this is fact the first. When the police moved Sir Thomas Vivian's body they found an open knife beneath him. It was an ugly-looking thing such as sailors carry, with a blade that the mere opening rendered rigid, and there the blade was all ready, bare and gleaming, but without a trace of blood on it, and the knife was found to be quite new; it had never been used. Now, at the first glance it looks as if your imaginary Italian were just the man to have such a tool. But consider a moment. Would he be likely to buy a new knife expressly to commit murder? And, secondly, if he had such a knife, why didn't he use it, instead of that very odd flint instrument?

"And I want to put this to you. You think the murderer chalked up the hand after the murder as a sort of 'melodramatic Italian assassin his mark' touch. Passing over the question as to whether the real criminal ever does such a thing, I would point out that, on the medical evidence, Sir Thomas Vivian hadn't been dead for more than an hour. That would place the stroke at about a quarter to ten, and you know it was perfectly dark when we went out at 9.30. And that passage was singularly gloomy and ill-lighted, and the hand was drawn roughly, it is true, but correctly and without the bungling of strokes and the bad shots that are inevitable when one tries to draw in the dark or with shut eyes. Just try to draw such a simple figure as a square without looking at the paper, and then ask me to conceive that your Italian, with the rope waiting for his neck, could draw the hand on the wall so firmly and truly, in the black shadow of that alley. It is absurd. By consequence, then, the hand was drawn early in the evening, long before any murder was committed; or else—mark this, Phillipps—it was drawn by some one to whom darkness and gloom were familiar and habitual; by some one to whom the common dread of the rope was unknown!

"Again: a curious note was found in Sir Thomas Vivian's pocket. Envelope and paper were of a common make, and the stamp bore the West Central postmark. I will come to the nature of the contents later on, but it is the question of the handwriting that is so remarkable. The address on the outside was neatly written in a small clear hand, but the letter itself might have been written by a Persian who had learnt the English script. It was upright, and the letters were curiously contorted, with an affectation of dashes and backward curves which really reminded me of an Oriental manuscript, though it was all perfectly legible. But—and here comes the poser—on searching the dead man's waistcoat pockets a small memorandum book was found; it was almost filled with pencil jottings. These memoranda related chiefly to matters of a private as distinct from a professional nature; there were appointments to meet friends, notes of theatrical first-nights, the address of a good hotel in Tours, and the title of a new novel—nothing in any way intimate. And the whole of these jottings were written in a hand nearly identical with the writing of the note found in the dead man's coat pocket! There was just enough difference between them to enable the expert to swear that the two were not written by the same person. I will just read you so much of Lady Vivian's evidence as bears on this point of the writing; I have the printed slip with me. Here you see she says: 'I was married to my late husband seven years ago; I never saw any letter addressed him in a hand at all resembling that on the envelope produced, nor have I ever seen writing like that in the letter before me. I never saw my late husband using the memorandum book, but I am sure he did write everything in it; I am certain of that because we stayed last May at the Hotel du Faisan, Rue Royale, Tours, the address of which is given in the book; I remember his getting the novel *A Sentinel* about six weeks ago. Sir Thomas Vivian never liked to miss the first-nights at the theatres. His usual hand was perfectly different from that used in the notebook.'

"And now, last of all, we come back to the note itself. Here it is in facsimile. My possession of it is due to the kindness of Inspector Cleeve, who is pleased to be amused at my amateur inquisitiveness. Read it, Phillipps; you tell me you are interested in obscure inscriptions; here is something for you to decipher."

Mr. Phillipps, absorbed in spite of himself in the strange circumstances Dyson had related, took the piece of paper, and scrutinized it closely. The handwriting was indeed bizarre in the extreme, and, as Dyson had noted, not unlike the Persian character in its general effect, but it was perfectly legible.

"Read it aloud," said Dyson, and Phillipps obeyed.

"'Hand did not point in vain. The meaning of the stars is no longer obscure. Strangely enough, the black heaven vanished, or was stolen yesterday, but that does not matter in the least, as I have a celestial globe. Our old orbit remains unchanged; you have not forgotten the number of my sign, or will you appoint some other house? I have been on the other side of the moon, and can bring something to show you.'"

"And what do you make of that?" said Dyson.

"It seems to me mere gibberish," said Phillipps; "you suppose it has a meaning?"

"Oh, surely; it was posted three days before the murder; it was found in the murdered man's pocket; it is written in a fantastic hand which the murdered man himself used for his private memoranda. There must be purpose under all this, and to my mind there is something ugly enough hidden under the circumstances of this case of Sir Thomas Vivian."

"But what theory have you formed?"

"Oh, as to theories, I am still in a very early stage; it is too soon to state conclusions. But I think I have demolished your Italian. I tell you, Phillipps, again, the whole thing has an ugly look to my eyes. I cannot do as you do, and fortify myself with cast-iron propositions to the effect that this or that doesn't happen, and never has happened. You note that the first word in the letter is 'hand.' That seems to me, taken with what we know about the hand on the wall, significant enough, and what you yourself told me of the history and meaning of the symbol, its connection with a world-old belief and faiths of dim far-off years, all this speaks of mischief, for me at all events. No; I stand pretty well to what I said to you half in joke that night before we went out. There are sacraments of evil as well as of good about us, and we live and move to my belief in an unknown world, a place where there are caves and shadows and dwellers in twilight. It is possible that man may sometimes return on the track of evolution, and it is my belief that an awful lore is not yet dead."

"I cannot follow you in all this," said Phillipps; "it seems to interest you strangely. What do you propose to do?"

"My dear Phillipps," replied Dyson, speaking in a lighter tone, "I am afraid I shall have to go down a little in the world. I have a prospect of visits to the pawnbrokers before me, and the publicans must not be neglected. I must cultivate a taste for four ale; shag tobacco I already love and esteem with all my heart."

III. Search for the Vanished Heaven

FOR many days after the discussion with Phillipps, Mr. Dyson was resolute in the line of research he had marked out for himself. A fervent curiosity and an innate liking for the obscure were great incentives, but especially in this case of Sir Thomas Vivian's death (for Dyson began to boggle a little at the word "murder") there seemed to him an element that was more than curious. The sign of the red hand upon the wall, the tool of flint that had given death, the almost identity between the handwriting of the note and the fantastic script reserved religiously, as it appeared, by the doctor for trifling jottings, all these diverse and variegated threads joined to weave in his mind a strange and shadowy picture, with ghastly shapes dominant and deadly, and yet ill-defined, like the giant figures wavering in an ancient tapestry. He thought he had a clue to the meaning of the note, and in his resolute search for the "black heaven," which had vanished, he beat furiously about the alleys and obscure streets of central London, making himself a familiar figure to the pawnbroker, and a frequent guest at the more squalid pot-houses.

For a long time he was unsuccessful, and he trembled at the thought that the "black heaven" might be hid in the coy retirements of Peckham, or lurk perchance in distant Willesden, but finally, improbability, in which he put his trust, came to the rescue. It was a dark and rainy night, with something in the unquiet and stirring gusts that savoured of approaching winter, and Dyson, beating up a narrow street not far from the Gray's Inn Road, took shelter in an extremely dirty "public," and called for beer, forgetting for the moment his preoccupations, and only thinking of the sweep of the wind about the tiles and the hissing of the rain through the black and troubled air. At the bar there gathered the usual company: the frowsy women and the men in shiny black, those who appeared to mumble secretly together, others who wrangled in interminable argument, and a few shy drinkers who stood apart, each relishing his dose, and the rank and biting flavour of cheap spirit. Dyson was wondering at the enjoyment of it all, when suddenly there came a sharper accent. The folding-doors swayed open, and a middle-aged woman staggered towards the bar, and clutched the pewter rim as if she stepped a deck in a roaring gale. Dyson glanced at her attentively as a pleasing specimen of her class; she was decently dressed in black, and carried a black bag of somewhat rusty leather, and her intoxication was apparent and far advanced. As she swayed at the bar, it was evidently all she could do to stand upright, and the barman, who had looked at her with disfavour, shook his head in reply to her thick-voiced demand for a drink. The woman glared at him, transformed in a moment to a fury, with bloodshot eyes, and poured forth a torrent of execration, a stream of blasphemies and early English phraseology.

"Get out of this," said the man; "shut up and be off, or I'll send for the police."

"Police, you —," bawled the woman, "I'll — well give you something to fetch the police for!" and with a rapid dive into her bag she pulled out some object which she hurled furiously at the barman's head.

The man ducked down, and the missile flew over his head and smashed a bottle to fragments, while the woman with a peal of horrible laughter rushed to the door, and they could hear her steps pattering fast over the wet stones.

The barman looked ruefully about him.

"Not much good going after her," he said, "and I'm afraid what she's left won't pay for that bottle of whisky." He fumbled amongst the fragments of broken glass, and drew out something dark, a kind of square stone it seemed, which he held up.

"Valuable cur'osity," he said, "any gent like to bid?"

The habitués had scarcely turned from their pots and glasses during these exciting incidents; they gazed a moment, fishily, when the bottle smashed, and that was all, and the mumble of the confidential was resumed and the jangle of the quarrelsome, and the shy and solitary sucked in their lips and relished again the rank flavour of the spirit.

Dyson looked quickly at what the barman held before him.

"Would you mind letting me see it?" he said; "it's a queer-looking thing, isn't it?"

It was a small black tablet, apparently of stone, about four inches long by two and a half broad, and as Dyson took it he felt rather than saw that he touched the secular with his flesh. There was some kind of carving on the surface, and, most conspicuous, a sign that made Dyson's heart leap.

"I don't mind taking it," he said quietly. "Would two shillings be enough?"

"Say half a dollar," said the man, and the bargain was concluded. Dyson drained his pot of beer, finding it delicious, and lit his pipe, and went out deliberately soon after. When he reached his apartment he locked the door, and placed the tablet on his desk, and then fixed himself in his chair, as resolute as an army in its trenches before a beleaguered city. The tablet was full under the light of the shaded candle, and scrutinizing it closely, Dyson saw first the sign of the hand with the thumb protruding between the fingers; it was cut finely and firmly on the dull black surface of the stone, and the thumb pointed downward to what was beneath.

"It is a mere ornament," said Dyson to himself, "perhaps symbolical ornament, but surely not an inscription, or the signs of any words ever spoken."

The hand pointed to a series of fantastic figures, spirals and whorls of the finest, most delicate lines, spaced at intervals over the remaining surface of the tablet. The marks were as intricate and seemed almost as much as without design as the pattern of a thumb impressed on a pane of glass.

"Is it some natural marking?" thought Dyson; "there have been queer designs, likenesses of beasts and flowers, in stones with which man's hand had nothing to do"; and he bent over the stone with a magnifier, only to be convinced that no hazard of nature could have delineated those varied labyrinths of line. The whorls were different sizes; some were less than the twelfth of an inch in diameter, and the largest was a little smaller than a sixpence, and under the glass the regularity and accuracy of the cutting were evident, and in the smaller spirals the lines were graduated at intervals of a hundredth of an inch. The whole thing had a marvellous and fantastic look, and gazing at the mystic whorls beneath the hand, Dyson became subdued with an impression of vast and far-off ages, and of a living being that had touched the stone with enigmas before the hills were formed, when the hard rocks still boiled with fervent heat.

"The 'black heaven' is found again," he said, "but the meaning of the stars is likely to be obscure for everlasting so far as I am concerned."

London stilled without, and a chill breath came into the room as Dyson sat gazing at the tablet shining duskily under the candlelight; and at last, as he closed the desk over the ancient stone, all his wonder at the case of Sir Thomas Vivian increased tenfold, and he thought of the well-dressed prosperous gentleman lying dead mystically beneath the sign of the hand, and the insupportable conviction seized him that between the death of this fashionable West-end doctor and the weird spirals of the tablet there were most secret and unimaginable links.

For days he sat before his desk gazing at the tablet, unable to resist its loadstone fascination, and yet quite helpless, without ever the hope of solving the symbols so secretly inscribed. At last, desperate, he called in Mr. Phillipps in consultation, and told in brief the story of the finding of the stone.

"Dear me!" said Phillipps, "this is extremely curious; you have had a find indeed. Why it looks to me even more ancient than the Hittite seal. I confess the character, if it is a character, is entirely strange to me. These whorls are really very quaint."

"Yes, but I want to know what they mean. You must remember this tablet is the 'black heaven' of the letter found in Sir Thomas Vivian's pocket; it bears directly on his death."

"Oh, no, that is nonsense! This is, no doubt, an extremely ancient tablet, which has been stolen from some collection. Yes, the hand makes an odd coincidence, but only a coincidence after all."

"My dear Phillipps, you are a living example of the truth of the axiom that extreme scepticism is mere credulity. But can you decipher the inscription?"

"I undertake to decipher anything," said Phillipps. "I do not believe in the insoluble. These characters are curious, but I cannot fancy them to be inscrutable."

"Then take the thing away with you and make what you can of it. It has begun to haunt me; I feel as if I had gazed too long into the eyes of the Sphinx."

Phillipps departed with the tablet in an inner pocket. He had not much doubt of success, for he had evolved thirty-seven rules for the solution of inscriptions. Yet when a week had passed and he called to see Dyson there was no vestige of triumph on his features. He found his friend in a state of extreme irritation, pacing up and down in the room like a man in a passion. He turned with a start as the door opened.

"Well," said Dyson, "you have got it? What is it all about?"

"My dear fellow, I am sorry to say I have completely failed. I have tried every known device in vain. I have even been so officious as to submit it to a friend at the Museum, but he, though a man of prime authority on the subject, tells me that he is quite at fault. It must be some wreckage of a vanished race, almost, I think—a fragment of another world than ours. I am not a superstitious man, Dyson, and you know that I have no truck with even the noble delusions, but I confess I yearn to be rid of this small square of blackish stone. Frankly, it has given me an ill week; it seems to me troglodytic and abhorred."

Phillipps drew out the tablet and laid it on the desk before Dyson.

"By the way," he went on, "I was right at all events in one particular; it has formed part of some collection. There is a piece of grimy paper on the back that must have been a label."

"Yes, I noticed that," said Dyson, who had fallen into deepest disappointment; "no doubt the paper is a label. But as I don't much care where the tablet originally came from, and only wish to know what the inscription means, I paid no attention to the paper. The thing is a hopeless riddle, I suppose, and yet it must surely be of the greatest importance."

Phillipps left soon after, and Dyson, still despondent, took the tablet in his hand and carelessly turned it over. The label had so grimed that it seemed merely a dull stain, but as Dyson looked at it idly, and yet attentively, he could see pencil-marks, and he bent over it eagerly, with his glass to his eye. To his annoyance, he found that part of the paper had been torn away, and he could only with difficulty make out odd words and pieces of words. First he read something that looked like "inroad," and then beneath, "stony-hearted step—" and a tear cut off the rest. But in an instant a solution suggested itself, and he chuckled with huge delight.

"Certainly," he said aloud, "this is not only the most charming but the most convenient quarter in all London; here I am, allowing for the accidents of side streets, perched on a tower of observation."

He glanced triumphantly out of the window across the street to the gate of the British Museum. Sheltered by the boundary wall of that agreeable institution, a "screever," or artist in chalks, displayed his brilliant impressions on the pavement, soliciting the approval and the coppers of the gay and serious.

"This," said Dyson, "is more than delightful! An artist is provided to my hand."

IV. The Artist of the Pavement

MR. PHILLIPPS, in spite of all disavowals—in spite of the wall of sense of whose enclosure and limit he was wont to make his boast—yet felt in his heart profoundly curious as to the case of Sir Thomas Vivian. Though he kept a brave face for his friend, his reason could not decently resist the conclusion that Dyson had enunciated, namely, that the whole affair had a look both ugly and mysterious. There was the weapon of a vanished race that had pierced the great arteries; the red hand, the symbol of a hideous faith, that pointed to the slain man; and then the tablet which Dyson declared he had expected to find, and had certainly found, bearing the ancient impress of the hand of malediction, and a legend written beneath in a character compared with which the most antique cuneiform was a thing of yesterday. Besides all this, there were other points that tortured and perplexed. How to account for the bare knife found unstained beneath the body? And the hint that the red hand upon the wall must have been drawn by some one whose life was passed in darkness thrilled him with a suggestion of dim and infinite horror. Hence he was in truth not a little curious as to what was to come, and some ten days after he had returned the tablet he again visited the "mystery-man," as he privately named his friend.

Arrived in the grave and airy chambers in Great Russell Street, he found the moral atmosphere of the place had been transformed. All Dyson's irritation had disappeared, his brow was smoothed with complacency, and he sat at a table by the window gazing out into the street with an expression of grim enjoyment, a pile of books and papers lying unheeded before him.

"My dear Phillipps, I am delighted to see you! Pray excuse my moving. Draw your chair up here to the table, and try this admirable shag tobacco."

"Thank you," said Phillipps, "judging by the flavour of the smoke, I should think it is a little strong. But what on earth is all this? What are you looking at?"

"I am on my watch-tower. I assure you that the time seems short while I contemplate this agreeable street and the classic grace of the Museum portico."

"Your capacity for nonsense is amazing," replied Phillipps, "but have you succeeded in deciphering the tablet? It interests me."

"I have not paid much attention to the tablet recently," said Dyson. "I believe the spiral character may wait."

"Really! And how about the Vivian murder?"

"Ah, you do take an interest in that case? Well, after all, we cannot deny that it was a queer business. But is not 'murder' rather a coarse word? It smacks a little, surely, of the police poster. Perhaps I am a trifle decadent, but I cannot help believing in the splendid word; 'sacrifice,' for example, is surely far finer than 'murder.'"

"I am all in the dark," said Phillipps. "I cannot even imagine by what track you are moving in this labyrinth."

"I think that before very long the whole matter will be a good deal clearer for us both, but I doubt whether you will like hearing the story."

Dyson lit his pipe afresh and leant back, not relaxing, however, in his scrutiny of the street. After a somewhat lengthy pause, he startled Phillipps by a loud breath of relief as he rose from the chair by the window and began to pace the floor.

"It's over for the day," he said, "and, after all, one gets a little tired."

Phillipps looked with inquiry into the street. The evening was darkening, and the pile of the Museum was beginning to loom indistinct before the lighting of the lamps, but the pavements were thronged and busy. The artist in chalks across the way was gathering together his materials, and blurring all the brilliance of his designs, and a little lower down there was the clang of shutters being placed in position. Phillipps could see nothing to justify Mr. Dyson's sudden abandonment of his attitude of surveillance, and grew a little irritated by all these thorny enigmas.

"Do you know, Phillipps," said Dyson, as he strolled at ease up and down the room, "I will tell you how I work. I go upon the theory of improbability. The theory is unknown to you? I will explain. Suppose I stand on the steps of St. Paul's and look out for a blind man lame of the left leg to pass me, it is evidently highly improbable that I shall see such a person by waiting for an hour. If I wait two hours the improbability is diminished, but is still enormous, and a watch of a whole day would give little expectation of success. But suppose I take up the same position day after day, and week after week, don't you perceive that the improbability is lessening constantly—growing smaller day after day? Don't you see that two lines which are not parallel are gradually approaching one another, drawing nearer and nearer to a point of meeting, till at last they do meet, and improbability has vanished altogether? That is how I found the black tablet: I acted on the theory of improbability. It is the only scientific principle I know of which can enable one to pick out an unknown man from amongst five million."

"And you expect to find the interpreter of the black tablet by this method?"

"Certainly."

"And the murderer of Sir Thomas Vivian also?"

"Yes, I expect to lay my hands on the person concerned in the death of Sir Thomas Vivian in exactly the same way."

The rest of the evening, after Phillipps had left, was devoted by Dyson to sauntering in the streets, and afterwards, when the night grew late, to his literary labours, or the chase of the phrase, as he called it. The next morning the station by the window was again resumed. His meals were brought to him at the table, and he ate with his eyes on the street. With briefest intervals, snatched reluctantly from time to time, he persisted in his survey throughout the day, and only at dusk, when the shutters were put up and the "screever" ruthlessly deleted all his labor of the day, just before the gas-lamps began to star the shadows, did he feel at liberty to quit his post. Day after day this ceaseless glance upon the street continued, till the landlady grew puzzled and aghast at such a profitless pertinacity.

But at last, one evening, when the play of lights and shadows was scarce beginning, and the clear cloudless air left all distinct and shining, there came the moment. A man of middle age, bearded and bowed, with a touch of grey about the ears, was strolling slowly along the northern pavement of Great Russell Street from the eastern end. He looked up at the Museum as he went by, and then glanced involuntarily at the art of the "screever," and at the artist himself, who sat beside his pictures, hat in hand. The man with the beard stood still an instant, swaying slightly to and fro as if in thought, and Dyson saw his fists shut tight, and his back quivering, and the one side of his face in view twitched and grew contorted with the indescribable torment of approaching epilepsy. Dyson drew a soft hat from his pocket, and dashed the door open, taking the stair with a run.

When he reached the street the person he had seen so agitated had turned about, and, regardless of observation, was racing wildly towards Bloomsbury Square, with his back to his former course.

Mr. Dyson went up to the artist of the pavement, and gave him some money, observing quietly, "You needn't trouble to draw that thing again." Then he too turned about, and strolled idly down the street in the opposite direction to that taken by the fugitive. So the distance between Dyson and the man with the bowed head grew steadily greater.

V. Story of the Treasure House

"THERE are many reasons why I chose your rooms for the meeting in preference to my own. Chiefly, perhaps, because I thought the man would be more at his ease on neutral ground."

"I confess, Dyson," said Phillipps, "that I feel both impatient and uneasy. You know my standpoint: hard matter of fact, materialism if you like, in its crudest form. But there is something about all this affair of Vivian that makes me a little restless. And how did you induce the man to come?"

"He has an exaggerated opinion of my powers. You remember what I said about the doctrine of improbability? When it does work out, it gives results which seem very amazing to a person who is not in the secret. That is eight striking, isn't it? And there goes the bell."

They heard footsteps on the stair, and presently the door opened, and a middle-aged man, with a bowed head, bearded, and with a good deal of grizzling hair about his ears, came into the room. Phillipps glanced at his features, and recognized the lineaments of terror.

"Come in, Mr. Selby," said Dyson. "This is Mr. Phillipps, my intimate friend and our host for this evening. Will you take anything? Then perhaps we had better hear your story—a very singular one, I am sure."

The man spoke in a voice hollow and a little quavering, and a fixed stare that never left his eyes seemed directed to something awful that was to remain before him by day and night for the rest of his life.

"You will, I am sure, excuse preliminaries," he began; "what I have to tell is best told quickly. I will say, then, that I was born in a remote part of the west of England, where the very outlines of the woods and hills, and the winding of the streams in the valleys, are apt to suggest the mystical to any one strongly gifted with imagination. When I was quite a boy there were certain huge and rounded hills, certain depths of hanging wood, and secret valleys bastioned round on every side that filled me with fancies beyond the bourne of rational expression, and as I grew older and began to dip into my father's books, I went by instinct, like the bee, to all that would nourish fantasy. Thus, from a course of obsolete and occult reading, and from listening to certain wild legends in which the older people still secretly believe, I grew firmly convinced of the existence of treasure, the hoard of a race extinct for ages, still hidden beneath the hills, and my every thought was directed to the discovery of the golden heaps that lay, as I fancied, within a few feet of the green turf. To one spot, in especial, I was drawn as if by enchantment; it was a tumulus, the domed memorial of some forgotten people, crowning the crest of a vast mountain range; and I have often lingered there on summer evenings, sitting on the great block of limestone at the summit, and looking out far over the yellow sea towards the Devonshire coast. One day as I dug heedlessly with the ferrule of my stick at the mosses and lichens which grew rank over the stone, my eye was caught by what seemed a pattern beneath the growth of green; there was a curving line, and marks that did not look altogether the work of nature. At first I thought I had bared some rare fossil, and I took out my out my knife and scraped away at the moss till a square foot was uncovered. Then I saw two signs which startled me; first, a closed hand, pointing downwards, the thumb protruding between the fingers, and beneath the hand a whorl or spiral, traced with exquisite accuracy in the hard surface of the rock. Here, I persuaded myself, was an index to the great secret, but I chilled at the recollection of the fact that some antiquarians had tunnelled the tumulus through and through, and had been a good deal surprised at not finding so much as an arrowhead within. Clearly, then, the signs on the limestone had no local significance; and I made up my mind that I must search abroad. By sheer accident I was in a measure successful in my quest. Strolling by a cottage, I saw some children playing by the roadside; one was holding up some object in his hand, and the rest were going through one of the many forms of elaborate pretence which make up a great part of the mystery of a child's life. Something in the object held by the little boy attracted me, and I asked him to let me see it. The plaything of these children consisted of an oblong tablet of black stone; and on it was inscribed the hand pointing downwards, just as I had seen it on the rock, while beneath, spaced over the tablet, were a number of whorls and spirals, cut, as it seemed to me, with the utmost care and nicety. I bought the toy for a couple of shillings; the woman of the house told me it had been lying about for years; she thought her husband had found it one day in the brook which ran in front of the cottage; it was a very hot summer, and the stream was almost dry, and he saw it amongst the stones. That day I tracked the brook to a well of water gushing up cold and clear at the head of a lonely glen in the mountains. That was twenty years ago, and I only succeeded in deciphering the mysterious inscription last August. I must not trouble you with irrelevant details of my life; it is enough for me to say that I was forced, like many another man, to leave my old home and come to London. Of money I had very little, and I was glad to find a cheap room in a squalid street off the Gray's Inn Road. The late Sir Thomas Vivian, then far poorer and more wretched than myself, had a garret in the same house, and before many months we became intimate friends, and I had confided to him the object of my life. I had at first great difficulty in persuading him that I was not giving my days and my nights to an inquiry altogether hopeless and chimerical; but when he was convinced he grew keener than myself, and glowed at the thought of the riches which were to be the prize of some ingenuity and patience. I liked the man intensely, and pitied his case; he had a strong desire to enter the medical profession, but he lacked the means to pay the smallest fees, and indeed he was, not once or twice, but often reduced to the very verge of starvation. I freely and solemnly promised that, under whatever chances, he should share in my heaped fortune when it came, and this promise to one who had always been poor, and yet thirsted for wealth and pleasure in a manner unknown to me, was the strongest incentive. He threw himself into the task with eager interest, and applied a very acute intellect and unwearied patience to the solution of the characters on the tablet. I, like other ingenious young men, was curious in the matter of handwriting, and I had invented or adapted a fantastic script which I used occasionally, and which took Vivian so strongly that he was at the pains to imitate it. It was arranged between us that if we were ever parted, and had occasion to write on the affair that was so close to our hearts, this queer hand of my invention was to be used, and we also contrived a semi-cypher for the same purpose. Meanwhile we exhausted ourselves in efforts to get at the heart of the mystery, and after a couple of years had gone by I could see that Vivian began to sicken a little of the adventure, and one night he told me with some emotion that he feared both our lives were being passed away in idle and hopeless endeavor. Not many months afterwards he was so happy as to receive a considerable legacy from an aged and distant relative whose very existence had been almost forgotten by him; and with money at the bank, he became at once a stranger to me. He had passed his preliminary examination many years before, and he forthwith decided to enter at St. Thomas's Hospital, and he told me that he must look out for a more convenient lodging. As we said good-bye, I reminded him of the promise I had given, and solemnly renewed it; but Vivian laughed with something between pity and contempt in his voice and expression as he thanked me. I need not dwell on the long struggle and misery of my existence, now doubly lonely; I never wearied or despaired of final success, and every day saw me at work, the tablet before me, and only at dusk would I go out and take my daily walk along Oxford Street, which attracted me I think by the noise and motion and glitter of lamps.

"This walk grew with me to a habit; every night, and in all weathers, I crossed the Gray's Inn Road and struck westward, sometimes choosing a northern track, by the Euston Road and Tottenham Court Road, sometimes I went by Holborn, and sometimes by the way of Great Russell Street. Every night I walked for an hour to and fro on the northern pavement of Oxford Street, and the tale of De Quincey and his name for the street, 'Stony-hearted step-mother,' often recurred to my memory. Then I would return to my grimy den and spend hours more in endless analysis of the riddle before me.

"The answer came to me one night a few weeks ago; it flashed into my brain in a moment, and I read the inscription, and saw that after all I had not wasted my days. 'The place of the treasure house of them that dwell below,' were the first words I read, and then followed minute indications of the spot in my own country where the great works of gold were to be kept for ever. Such a track was to be followed, such a pitfall avoided; here the way narrowed almost to a fox's hole, and there it broadened, and so at last the chamber would be reached. I determined to lose no time in verifying my discovery—not that I doubted at that great moment, but I would not risk even the smallest chance of disappointing my old friend Vivian, now a rich and prosperous man. I took the train for the West, and one night, with chart in hand, traced out the passage of the hills, and went so far that I saw the gleam of gold before me. I would not go on; I resolved that Vivian must be with me; and I only brought away a strange knife of flint which lay on the path, as confirmation of what I had to tell. I returned to London, and was a good deal vexed to find the stone tablet had disappeared from my rooms. My landlady, an inveterate drunkard, denied all knowledge of the fact, but I have little doubt she had stolen the thing for the sake of the glass of whisky it might fetch. However, I knew what was written on the tablet by heart, and I had also made an exact facsimile of the characters, so the loss was not severe. Only one thing annoyed me: when I first came into possession of the stone, I had pasted a piece of paper on the back and had written down the date and place of finding, and later on I had scribbled a word or two, a trivial sentiment, the name of my street, and such-like idle pencillings on the paper; and these memories of days that had seemed so hopeless were dear to me: I had thought they would help to remind me in the future of the hours when I had hoped against despair. However, I wrote at once to Sir Thomas Vivian, using the handwriting I have mentioned and also the quasi-cypher. I told him of my success, and after mentioning the loss of the tablet and the fact that I had a copy of the inscription, I reminded him once more of my promise, and asked him either to write or call. He replied that he would see me in a certain obscure passage in Clerkenwell well known to us both in the old days, and at seven o'clock one evening I went to meet him. At the corner of this by-way, as I was walking to and fro, I noticed the blurred pictures of some street artist, and I picked up a piece of chalk he had left behind him, not much thinking what I was doing. I paced up and down the passage, wondering a good deal, as you may imagine, as to what manner of man I was to meet after so many years of parting, and the thoughts of the buried time coming thick upon me, I walked mechanically without raising my eyes from the ground. I was startled out of my reverie by an angry voice and a rough inquiry why I didn't keep to the right side of the pavement, and looking up I found I had confronted a prosperous and important gentleman, who eyed my poor appearance with a look of great dislike and contempt. I knew directly it was my old comrade, and when I recalled myself to him, he apologized with some show of regret, and began to thank me for my kindness, doubtfully, as if he hesitated to commit himself, and, as I could see, with the hint of a suspicion as to my sanity. I would have engaged him at first in reminiscences of our friendship, but I found Sir Thomas viewed those days with a good deal of distaste, and replying politely to my remarks, continually edged in 'business matters,' as he called them. I changed my topics, and told him in greater detail what I have told you. Then I saw his manner suddenly change; as I pulled out the flint knife to prove my journey 'to the other side of the moon,' as we called it in our jargon, there came over him a kind of choking eagerness, his features were somewhat discomposed, and I thought I detected a shuddering horror, a clenched resolution, and the efforts to keep quiet succeed one another in a manner that puzzled me. I had occasion to be a little precise in my particulars, and it being still light enough, I remembered the red chalk in my pocket, and drew the hand on the wall. 'Here, you see, is the hand,' I said, as I explained its true meaning, 'note where the thumb issues from between the first and second fingers,' and I would have gone on, and had applied the chalk to the wall to continue my diagram, when he struck my hand down, much to my surprise. 'No, no,' he said, 'I do not want all that. And this place is not retired enough; let us walk on, and do you explain everything to me minutely.' I complied readily enough, and he led me away, choosing the most unfrequented by-ways, while I drove in the plan of the hidden house word by word. Once or twice as I raised my eyes I caught Vivian looking strangely about him; he seemed to give a quick glint up and down, and glance at the houses; and there was a furtive and anxious air about him that displeased me. 'Let us walk on to the north,' he said at length, 'we shall come to some pleasant lanes where we can discuss these matters, quietly; my night's rest is at your service.' I declined, on the pretext that I could not dispense with my visit to Oxford Street, and went on till he understood every turning and winding and the minutest detail as well as myself. We had returned on our footsteps, and stood again in the dark passage, just where I had drawn the red hand on the wall, for I recognized the vague shape of the trees whose branches hung above us. 'We have come back to our starting-point,' I said; 'I almost think I could put my finger on the wall where I drew the hand. And I am sure you could put your finger on the mystic hand in the hills as well as I. Remember between stream and stone.'

"I was bending down, peering at what I thought must be my drawing, when I heard a sharp hiss of breath, and started up, and saw Vivian with his arm uplifted and a bare blade in his hand, and death threatening in his eyes. In sheer self-defence I caught at the flint weapon in my pocket, and dashed at him in blind fear of my life, and the next instant he lay dead upon the stones.

"I think that is all," Mr. Selby continued after a pause, "and it only remains for me to say to you, Mr. Dyson, that I cannot conceive what means enabled you to run me down."

"I followed many indications," said Dyson, "and I am bound to disclaim all credit for acuteness, as I have made several gross blunders. Your celestial cypher did not, I confess, give me much trouble; I saw at once that terms of astronomy were substituted for common words and phrases. You had lost something black, or something black had been stolen from you; a celestial globe is a copy of the heavens, so I knew you meant you had a copy of what you had lost. Obviously, then, I came to the conclusion that you had lost a black object with characters or symbols written or inscribed on it, since the object in question certainly contained valuable information, and all information must be written or pictured. 'Our old orbit remains unchanged'; evidently our old course or arrangement. 'The number of my sign' must mean the number of my house, the allusion being to the signs of the zodiac. I need not say that 'the other side of the moon' can stand for nothing but some place where no one else has been; and 'some other house' is some other place of meeting, the 'house' being the old term 'house of the heavens.' Then my next step was to find the 'black heaven' that had been stolen, and by a process of exhaustion I did so."

"You have got the tablet?"

"Certainly. And on the back of it, on the slip of paper you have mentioned, I read 'inroad,' which puzzled me a good deal, till I thought of Gray's Inn Road; you forgot the second *n*. 'Stony-hearted step—' immediately suggested the phrase of De Quincey you have alluded to; and I made the wild but correct shot, that you were a man who lived in or near the Gray's Inn Road, and had the habit of walking in Oxford Street, for you remember how the opium eater dwells on his wearying promenades along that thoroughfare? On the theory of improbability, which I have explained to my friend here, I concluded that occasionally, at all events, you would choose the way Guilford Street, Russel Square, and Great Russell Street, and I knew that if I watched long enough I should see you. But how was I to recognize my man? I noticed the screever opposite my rooms, and got him to draw every day a large hand, in the gesture so familiar to us all, upon the wall behind him. I thought that when the unknown person did pass he would certainly betray some emotion at the sudden vision of the sign, to him the most terrible of symbols. You know the rest. Ah, as to catching you an hour later, that was, I confess, a refinement. From the fact of your having occupied the same rooms for so many years, in a neighbourhood moreover where lodgers are migratory to excess, I drew the conclusion that you were a man of fixed habit, and I was sure that after you had got over your fright you would return for the walk down Oxford Street. You did, by way of New Oxford Street, and I was waiting at the corner."

"Your conclusions are admirable," said Mr. Selby. "I may tell you that I had my stroll down Oxford Street the night Sir Thomas Vivian died. And I think that is all I have to say."

"Scarcely," said Dyson. "How about the treasure?"

"I had rather we did not speak of that," said Mr. Selby, with a whitening of the skin about the temples.

"Oh, nonsense, sir, we are not blackmailers. Besides, you know you are in our power."

"Then, as you put it like that, Mr. Dyson, I must tell you I returned to the place. I went on a little farther than before."

The man stopped short; his mouth began to twitch, his lips moved apart, and he drew in quick breaths, sobbing.

"Well, well," said Dyson, "I dare say you have done comfortably."

"Comfortably," Selby went on constraining himself with an effort, "yes, so comfortably that hell burns hot within me for ever. I only brought one thing away from that awful house within the hills; it was lying just beyond the spot where I found the flint knife."

"Why did you not bring more?"

The whole bodily frame of the wretched man visibly shrank and wasted; his face grew yellow as tallow, and the sweat dropped from his brows. The spectacle was both revolting and terrible, and when the voice came, it sounded like the hissing of a snake.

"Because the keepers are still there, and I saw them, and because of this," and he pulled out a small piece of curious gold-work and held it up.

"There," he said, "that is the Pain of the Goat."

Phillipps and Dyson cried out together in horror at the revolting obscenity of the thing.

"Put it away, man; hide it, for Heaven's sake, hide it!"

"I brought that with me; that is all," he said. "You do not wonder that I did not stay long in a place where those who live are a little higher than the beasts, and where what you have seen is surpassed a thousandfold?"

"Take this," said Dyson, "I brought it with me in case it might be useful"; and he drew out the black tablet, and handed it to the shaking, horrible man.

"And now," said Dyson, "Will you go out?"

* * *

The two friends sat silent a little while, facing one another with restless eyes and lips that quivered.

"I wish to say that I believe him," said Phillipps.

"My dear Phillipps," said Dyson as he threw the windows wide open, "I do not know that, after all, my blunders in this queer case were so very absurd." ❋

Ornaments in Jade

The Rose Garden

AND afterwards she went very softly, and opened the window and looked out. Behind her, the room was in a mystical semi-darkness; chairs and tables were hovering, ill-defined shapes; there was but the faintest illusory glitter from the talc moons in the rich Indian curtain which she had drawn across the door. The yellow silk draperies of the bed were but suggestions of colour, and the pillow and the white sheets glimmered as a white cloud in a far sky at twilight.

She turned from the dusky room, and with dewy tender eyes gazed out across the garden towards the lake. She could not rest nor lay herself down to sleep; though it was late, and half the night had passed, she could not rest. A sickle moon was slowly drawing upwards through certain filmy clouds that stretched in a long band from east to west, and a pallid light began to flow from the dark water, as if there also some vague planet were rising. She looked with eyes insatiable for wonder; and she found a strange eastern effect in the bordering of reeds, in their spearlike shapes, in the liquid ebony that they shadowed, in the fine inlay of pearl and silver as the moon shone free; a bright symbol in the steadfast calm of the sky.

There were faint stirring sounds heard from the fringe of reeds, and now and then the drowsy, broken cry of the waterfowl, for they knew that the dawn was not far off. In the centre of the lake was a carved white pedestal, and on it shone a white boy, holding the double flute to his lips.

Beyond the lake the park began, and sloped gently to the verge of the wood, now but a dark cloud beneath the sickle moon. And then beyond, and farther still, undiscovered hills, grey bands of cloud, and the steep pale height of the heaven. She gazed on with her tender eyes, bathing herself, as it were, in the deep rest of the night, veiling her soul with the half-light and the half-shadow, stretching out her delicate hands into the coolness of the misty silvered air, wondering at her hands.

And then she turned from the window, and made herself a divan of cushions on the Persian carpet, and half sat, half lay there, as motionless, as ecstatic as a poet dreaming under roses, far in Ispahan. She had gazed out, after all, to assure herself that sight and the eyes showed nothing but a glimmering veil, a gauze of curious lights and figures: that in it there was no reality nor substance. He had always told her that there was only one existence, one science, one religion, that the external world was but a variegated shadow which might either conceal or reveal the truth; and now she believed.

He had shewn her that bodily rapture might be the ritual and expression of the ineffable mysteries, of the world beyond sense, that must be entered by the way of sense; and now she believed. She had never much doubted any of his words, from the moment of their meeting a month before. She had looked up as she sat in the arbour, and her father was walking down through the avenue of roses, bringing to her the stranger, thin and dark, with a pointed beard and melancholy eyes. He murmured something to himself as they shook hands; she heard the rich, unknown words that sounded as the echo of far music. Afterwards he had told her what those words signified:

"How say ye that I was lost? I wandered among roses.
Can he go astray that enters the rose garden?
The Lover in the house of the Beloved is not forlorn.
I wandered among roses. How say ye that I was lost?"

His voice, murmuring the strange words, had persuaded her, and now she had the rapture of the perfect knowledge. She had looked out into the silvery uncertain night in order that she might experience the sense that for her these things no longer existed. She was not any more a part of the garden, or of the lake, or of the wood, or of the life that she had led hitherto. Another line that he had quoted came to her:

"The kingdom of I and We forsake and your home in
annihilation make."

It had seemed at first almost nonsense—if it had been possible for him to talk nonsense; but now she was filled and thrilled with the meaning of it. Herself was annihilated; at his bidding she had destroyed all her old feelings and emotions, her likes and dislikes, all the inherited loves and hates that her father and mother had given her; the old life had been thrown utterly away.

It grew light, and when the dawn burned she fell asleep, murmuring:

"How say ye that I was lost?" ❋

The Turanians

THE smoke of the tinkers' camp rose a thin pale blue from the heart of the wood.

Mary had left her mother at work on "things," and had gone out with a pale and languid face into the hot afternoon. She had talked of walking across the fields to the Green, and of having a chat with the doctor's daughter, but she had taken the other path that crept down towards the hollow and the dark thickets of the wood.

After all, she had felt too lazy to rouse herself, to make the effort of conversation, and the sunlight scorched the path that was ruled straight from stile to stile across the brown August fields, and she could see, even from far away, how the white dust clouds were smoking on the road by the Green. She hesitated, and at last went down under the far-spreading oak-trees, by a winding way of grass that cooled her feet.

Her mother, who was very kind and good, used to talk to her sometimes on the evils of "exaggeration," on the necessity of avoiding phrases violently expressed, words of too fierce an energy. She remembered how she had run into the house a few days before and had called her mother to look at a rose in the garden that "burnt like a flame." Her mother had said the rose was very pretty, and a little later had hinted her doubts as to the wisdom of "such very strong expressions."

"I know, my dear Mary," she had said, "that in your case it isn't affectation. You really *feel* what you say, don't you? Yes; but is it nice to feel like that? Do you think that it's quite *right,* even?"

The mother had looked at the girl with a curious wistfulness, almost as if she would say something more, and sought for the fit words, but could not find them. And then she merely remarked:

"You haven't seen Alfred Moorhouse since the tennis party, have you? I must ask him to come next Tuesday; you like him?"

The daughter could not quite see the link between her fault of "exaggeration" and the charming young barrister, but her mother's warning recurred to her as she strayed down the shadowed path, and felt the long dark grass cool and refreshing about her feet. She would not have put this sensation into words, but she thought it was as though her ankles were gently, sweetly kissed as the rich grass touched them, and her mother would have said it was not right to think such things.

And what a delight there was in the colours all about her! It was as though she walked in a green cloud; the strong sunlight was filtered through the leaves, reflected from the grass, and made all visible things, the tree-stems, the flowers, and her own hands seem new, transformed into another likeness. She had walked by the wood-path over and over again, but to-day it had become full of mystery and hinting, and every turn brought a surprise.

To-day the mere sense of being alone under the trees was an acute secret joy, and as she went down deeper and the wood grew dark about her, she loosened her brown hair, and when the sun shone over the fallen tree she saw her hair was not brown but bronze and golden, glowing on her pure white dress.

She stayed by the well in the rock, and dared to make the dark water her mirror, looking to right and left with shy glances and listening for the rustle of parted boughs, before she would match her gold with luminous ivory. She saw wonders in a glass as she leaned over the shadowed mysterious pool, and smiled at the smiling nymph, whose lips parted as if to whisper secrets.

As she went on her way, the thin blue smoke rose from a gap in the trees, and she remembered her childish dread of "the gipsies." She walked a little farther, and laid herself to rest on a smooth patch of turf, and listened to the strange intonations that sounded from the camp. "Those horrible people" she had heard the yellow folk called, but she found now a pleasure in voices that sang and, indistinctly heard, were almost chanting, with a rise and fall of notes and a wild wail, and the solemnity of unknown speech. It seemed a fit music for the unknown woodland, in harmony with the drip of the well, and the birds' sharp notes, and the rustle and hurry of the wood creatures.

She rose again and went on till she could see the red fire between the boughs; and the voices thrilled into an incantation. She longed to summon up courage, and talk to these strange wood-folk, but she was afraid to burst into the camp. So she sat down under a tree and waited, hoping that one of them might happen to come her way.

There were six or seven men, as many women, and a swarm of fantastic children, lolling and squatting about the fire, gabbling to one another in their singsong speech. They were people of curious aspect, short and squat, high-cheekboned, with dingy yellow skin and long almond eyes; only in one or two of the younger men there was a suggestion of a wild, almost faunlike grace, as of creatures who always moved between the red fire and the green leaf. Though everybody called them gipsies, they were in reality Turanian metal-workers, degenerated into wandering tinkers; their ancestors had fashioned the bronze battle-axes, and they mended pots and kettles. Mary waited under the tree, sure that she had nothing to fear, and resolved not to run away if one of them appeared.

The sun sank into a mass of clouds and the air grew close and heavy; a mist steamed up about the trees, a blue mist like the smoke of a wood-fire. A strange smiling face peered out from between the leaves, and the girl knew that her heart leapt as the young man walked towards her.

The Turanians moved their camp that night. There was a red glint, like fire, in the vast shadowy west, and then a burning paten floated up from a wild hill. A procession of weird bowed figures passed across the crimson disk, one stumbling after another in long single file, each bending down beneath his huge shapeless pack, and the children crawled last, goblinlike, fantastic.

The girl was lying in her white room, caressing a small green stone, a curious thing cut with strange devices, awful with age. She held it close to the luminous ivory, and the gold poured upon it.

She laughed for joy, and murmured and whispered to herself, asking herself questions in the bewilderment of her delight. She was afraid to say anything to her mother. ❋

The Idealist

"DID you notice Symonds while Beever was telling that story just now?" said one clerk to the other.

"No. Why? Didn't he like it?"

The second clerk had been putting away his papers and closing his desk in a grave and business-like manner, but when Beever's story was recalled to him he began to bubble anew, tasting the relish of the tale for a second time.

"He's a fair scorcher, old Beever," he remarked between little gasps of mirth. "But didn't Symonds like it?"

"Like it? He looked disgusted, I can tell you. Made a face, something in this style:" and the man drew his features into a design of sour disapproval, as he gave his hat the last polish with his coatsleeve.

"Well, I'm off now," he said. "I want to get home early, as there's tart for tea," and he fashioned another grimace, an imitation of his favourite actor's favourite contortion.

"Well, good-bye," said his friend. "You are a hot 'un, you are. You're worse than Beever. See you on Monday. What will Symonds say?" and he shouted after him as the door swung to and fro.

Charles Symonds, who had failed to see the humour of Mr. Beever's tale, had left the office a few minutes earlier and was now pacing slowly westward, mounting Fleet Street. His fellow clerk had not been much amiss in his observation. Symonds had heard the last phrases of Beever's story, and unconsciously had looked half round towards the group, angry and disgusted at their gross and stupid merriment. Beever and his friends seemed to him guilty of sacrilege; he likened them to plough-boys pawing and deriding an exquisite painted panel, blaring out their contempt and brutal ignorance. He could not control his features; in spite of himself he looked loathing at the three yahoos. He would have given anything if he could have found words and told them what he thought, but even to look displeasure was difficult. His shyness was a perpetual amusement to the other clerks, who often did little things to annoy him, and enjoyed the spectacle of Symonds inwardly raging and burning like Etna, but too hopelessly diffident to say a word. He would turn dead man's white, and grind his teeth at an insult, and pretend to join in the laugh, and pass it off as a joke. When he was a boy his mother was puzzled by him, not knowing whether he were sullen or insensible, or perhaps very good-tempered.

He climbed Fleet Street, still raw with irritation, partly from a real disgust at the profane coarseness of the clerks, and partly from a feeling that they talked so because they knew he hated such gross farces and novels. It was hideous to live and work with such foul creatures, and he glanced back fury at the City, the place of the stupid, the blatant, the intolerable.

He passed into the rush and flood of the Strand, into the full tide of a Saturday afternoon, still meditating the outrage, and constructing a cutting sentence for future use, heaping up words which should make Beever tremble. He was quite aware that he would never utter one of those biting phrases, but the pretence soothed him, and he began to remember other things. It was in late November and the clouds were already gathering for the bright solemnity of the sunset, flying to their places before the wind. They curled into fantastic shapes, high up there in the wind's whirlpool, and Symonds, looking towards the sky, was attracted by two grey writhing clouds that drew together in the west, in the far perspective of the Strand. He saw them as if they had been living creatures, noting every change and movement and transformation, till the shaking winds made them one and drove a vague form away to the south.

The curious interest he had taken in the cloud shapes had driven away the thought of the office, of the fetid talk which he so often heard. Beever and his friends ceased to exist, and Symonds escaped to his occult and private world which no one had ever divined. He lived far away down in Fulham, but he let the buses rock past him, and walked slowly, endeavouring to prolong the joys of anticipation. Almost with a visible gesture he drew himself apart, and went solitary, his eyes downcast, and gazing not on the pavement but on certain clear imagined pictures.

He quickened his steps as he passed along the northern pavement of Leicester Square, hurrying to escape the sight of the enamelled strange spectra who were already beginning to walk and stir abroad, issuing from their caves and waiting for the gas-light. He scowled as he looked up and chanced to see on a hoarding an icon with raddled cheeks and grinning teeth, at which some young men were leering; and one was recalling this creature's great song:

"And that's the way they do it.
How d'ye fink it's done?
Oh, *that's* the way they do it.
Doesn't it taike the bun?"

Symonds scowled at the picture of her, remembering how Beever had voted her "good goods," how the boys bellowed the chorus under his windows of Saturday nights. Once he had opened the window as they passed by, and had sworn at them and cursed them, in a whisper, lest he should be overheard.

He peered curiously at the books in a Piccadilly shop; now and then when he could save a few pounds he had made purchases there, but the wares which the bookseller dealt in were expensive, and he was obliged to be rather neatly dressed at the office, and he had other esoteric expenses. He had made up his mind to learn Persian and he hesitated as to whether he should turn back now, and see if he could pick up a grammar in Great Russell Street at a reasonable price. But it was growing dark, and the mists and shadows that he loved were gathering and inviting him onwards to those silent streets near the river.

When he at last diverged from the main road he made his way by a devious and eccentric track, threading an intricate maze of streets which to most people would have been dull and gloomy and devoid of interest. But to Symonds these backwaters of London were as bizarre and glowing as a cabinet of Japanese curios; he found here his delicately chased bronzes, work in jade, the flush and flame of extraordinary colours. He delayed at a corner, watching a shadow on a lighted blind, watching it fade and blacken and fade, conjecturing its secrets, inventing dialogue for this drama in *Ombres Chinoises*. He glanced up at another window, and saw a room vivid, in a hard yellow light of flaming gas, and lurked in the shelter of an old elm till he was perceived and the curtains were drawn hastily. On the way he had chosen, it was his fortune to pass many well-ordered decent streets, by villas detached and semi-detached, half hidden behind flowering-shrubs and evergreens. At this hour, on a Saturday in

November, few were abroad, and Symonds was often able, crouching down by the fence, to peer into a lighted room, to watch persons who thought themselves utterly unobserved. As he came near to his home he went through meaner streets, and he stopped at a corner, observing two children at play, regarding them with the minute scrutiny of an entomologist at the microscope. A woman who had been out shopping crossed the road and drove the children home, and Symonds moved on, hastily, but with a long sigh of enjoyment.

His breath came quick, in gusts, as he drew out his latch-key. He lived in an old Georgian house, and he raced up the stairs, and locked the door of the great lofty room in which he lived. The evening was damp and chilly, but the sweat streamed down his face. He struck a match, and there was a strange momentary vision of the vast room, almost empty of furniture, a hollow space bordered by grave walls and the white glimmer of the corniced ceiling.

He lit a candle, opened a large box that stood in a corner, and set to work. He seemed to be fitting together some sort of lay figure; a vague hint of the human shape increased under his hands. The candle sparkled at the other end of the room, and Symonds was sweating over his task in a cavern of dark shadow. His nervous shaking fingers fumbled over that uncertain figure, and then he began to draw out incongruous monstrous things. In the dusk, white silk shimmered, laces and delicate frills hovered for a moment, as he bungled over the tying of knots, the fastening of bands. The old room grew rich, heavy, vaporous with subtle scents; the garments that were passing through his hands had been drenched with fragrance. Passion had contorted his face; he grinned stark in the candlelight.

When he had finished the work he drew it with him to the window, and lighted three more candles. In his excitement, for that night he forgot the effect of *Ombres Chinoises,* and those who passed and happened to look up at the white staring blind found singular matter for speculation. ❋

Witchcraft

"RATHER left the others behind, haven't we, Miss Custance?" said the captain, looking back to the gate and the larchwood.

"I'm afraid we have, Captain Knight. I hope you don't mind very much, do you?"

"Mind? Delighted, you know. Sure this damp air isn't bad for you, Miss Custance?"

"Oh, d'you think it's damp? I like it. Ever since I can remember I've enjoyed these quiet autumn days. I won't hear of father's going anywhere else."

"Charmin' place, the Grange. Don't wonder you like comin' down here."

Captain Knight glanced back again and suddenly chuckled.

"I say, Miss Custance," he said, "I believe the whole lot's lost their way. Don't see a sign of them. Didn't we pass another path on the left?"

"Yes, and don't you remember you wanted to turn off?"

"Yes, of course. I thought it looked more possible, don't you know. That's where they must have gone. Where does it lead?"

"Oh, nowhere exactly. It dwindles and twists about a lot, and I'm afraid the ground is rather marshy."

"You don't say so?" The captain laughed out loud. "How awfully sick Ferris will be. He hates crossing Piccadilly if there's a bit of mud about."

"Poor Mr. Ferris!" And the two went on, picking their way on the rough path, till they came in sight of a little old cottage sunken alone in a hollow amongst the woods.

"Oh, you must come and see Mrs. Wise," said Miss Custance. "She's such a dear old thing, I'm sure you'd fall in love with her. And she'd never forgive me if she heard afterwards that we'd passed so close without coming in. Only for five minutes, you know."

"Certainly, Miss Custance. Is that the old lady there at the door?"

"Yes. She's always been so good to us children, and I know she'll talk of our coming to see her for months. You don't mind, do you?"

"I shall be charmed, I'm sure," and he looked back once more to see if there were any appearance of Ferris and his party.

"Sit down, Miss Ethel, sit down, please, miss," said the old woman when they went in. "And please to sit down here, sir, will you be so kind?"

She dusted the chairs, and Miss Custance enquired after the rheumatism and the bronchitis, and promised to send something from the Grange. The old woman had good country manners, and spoke well, and now and then politely tried to include Captain Knight in the conversation. But all the time she was quietly looking at him.

"Yes, sir, I be a bit lonely at times," she said when her visitors rose. "I do miss Nathan sorely; you can hardly hardly remember my husband, can you, Miss Ethel? But I have the Book, sir, and good friends too."

* * *

A couple of days later Miss Custance came alone to the cottage. Her hand trembled as she knocked at the door.

"Is it done?" she asked, when the old woman appeared.

"Come in, miss," said Mrs. Wise, and she shut the door, and put up the wooden bolt. Then she crept to the hearth, and drew out something from a hiding-place in the stones.

"Look at that," she said, showing it to the young lady. "Isn't it a picture?"

Miss Custance took the object into her fine delicate hands, and glanced at it, and then flushed scarlet.

"How horrible!" she exclaimed. "What did you do that for? You never told me."

"It's the only way, miss, to get what you want."

"It's a loathsome thing. I wonder you're not ashamed of yourself."

"I be as much ashamed as you be, I think," said Mrs. Wise, and she leered at the pretty, shy-faced girl. Their eyes met and their eyes laughed at one another.

"Cover it up, please, Mrs. Wise; I needn't look at it now, at all events. But are you sure?"

"There's never been a mishap since old Mrs. Cradoc taught me, and she's been dead for sixty year and more. She used to tell of her grandmother's days when there were meetings in the wood over there."

"And you're quite sure?"

"You do as I tell you. You must take it like this"; and the old woman whispered her instructions, and would have put out a hand in illustration, but the girl pushed it away.

"I understand now, Mrs. Wise. No, don't do that. I quite see what you mean. Here's the money."

"And whatever you do, don't you forget the ointment as I told you," said Mrs. Wise.

* * *

"I've been to read to poor old Mrs. Wise," Ethel said that evening to Captain Knight. "She's over eighty and her eyesight is getting very bad."

"Very good of you, Miss Custance, I'm sure," said Captain Knight, and he moved away to the other end of the drawing-room, and began to talk to a girl in yellow, with whom he had been exchanging smiles at a distance, ever since the men came in from the dining-room.

That night, when she was alone in her room, Ethel followed Mrs. Wise's instructions. She had hidden the object in a drawer, and as she drew it out, she looked about her, though the curtains were drawn close.

She forgot nothing, and when it was done she listened. ❋

The Ceremony

FROM her childhood, from those early and misty days which began to seem unreal, she recollected the grey stone in the wood.

It was something between the pillar and the pyramid in shape, and its grey solemnity amidst the leaves and the grass shone and shone from those early years, always with some hint of wonder. She remembered how, when she was quite a little girl, she had strayed one day, on a hot afternoon, from her nurse's side, and only a little way in the wood the grey stone rose from the grass, and she cried out and ran back in panic terror.

"What a silly little girl," the nurse had said. "It's only the — stone." She had quite forgotten the name that the servant had given, and she was always ashamed to ask as she grew older.

But always that hot day, that burning afternoon of her childhood when she had first looked consciously on the grey image in the wood, remained not a memory but a sensation. The wide wood swelling like the sea, the tossing of the bright boughs in the sunshine, the sweet smell of the grass and flowers, the beating of the summer wind upon her cheek, the gloom of the underglade rich, indistinct, gorgeous, significant as old tapestry; she could feel it and see it all, and the scent of it was in her nostrils. And in the midst of the picture, where the strange plants grew gross in shadow, was the old grey shape of the stone.

But there were in her mind broken remnants of another and far earlier impression. It was all uncertain, the shadow of a shadow, so vague that it might well have been a dream that had mingled with the confused waking thoughts of a little child. She did not know that she remembered, she rather remembered the memory. But again it was a summer day, and a woman, perhaps the same nurse, held her in her arms, and went through the wood. The woman carried bright flowers in one hand; the dream had in it a glow of bright red, and the perfume of cottage roses. Then she saw herself put down for a moment on the grass, and the red colour stained the grim stone, and there was nothing else—except that one night she woke up and heard the nurse sobbing.

She often used to think of the strangeness of very early life; one came, it seemed, from a dark cloud, there was a glow of light, but for a moment, and afterwards the night. It was as if one gazed at a velvet curtain, heavy, mysterious, impenetrable blackness, and then, for the twinkling of an eye, one spied through a pin-hole a storied town that flamed, with fire about its walls and pinnacles. And then again the folding darkness, so that sight became illusion, almost in the seeing. So to her was that earliest, doubtful vision of the grey stone, of the red colour spilled upon it, with the incongruous episode of the nursemaid, who wept at night.

But the later memory was clear; she could feel, even now, the inconsequent terror that sent her away shrieking, running to the nurse's skirts. Afterwards, through the days of girlhood, the stone had taken its place amongst the vast array of unintelligible things which haunt every child's imagination. It was part of life, to be accepted and not questioned; her elders spoke of many things which she could not understand, she opened books and was dimly amazed, and in the Bible there were many phrases which seemed strange. Indeed, she was often puzzled by her parents' conduct, by their looks at one another, by their half-words, and amongst all these problems which she hardly recognized as problems, was the grey ancient figure rising from dark grass.

Some semi-conscious impulse made her haunt the wood where shadow enshrined the stone. One thing was noticeable; that all through the summer months the passers-by dropped flowers there. Withered blossoms were always on the ground, amongst the grass, and on the stone fresh blooms constantly appeared. From the daffodil to the Michaelmas daisy there was marked the calendar of the cottage gardens, and in the winter she had seen sprays of juniper and box, mistletoe and holly. Once she had been drawn through the bushes by a red glow, as if there had been a fire in the wood, and when she came to the place, all the stone shone and all the ground about it was bright with roses.

In her eighteenth year she went one day into the wood, carrying with her a book that she was reading. She hid herself in a nook of hazel, and her soul was full of poetry, when there was a rustling, the rapping of parted boughs returning to their place. Her concealment was but a little way from the stone, and she peered through the net of boughs, and saw a girl timidly approaching. She knew her quite well; it was Annie Dolben, the daughter of a labourer, lately a promising pupil at Sunday school. Annie was a nice-mannered girl, never failing in her curtsy, wonderful for her knowledge of the Jewish Kings. Her face had taken an expression that whispered, that hinted strange things; there was a light and a glow behind the veil of flesh. And in her hand she bore lilies.

The lady hidden in hazels watched Annie come close to the grey image; for a moment her whole body palpitated with expectation, almost the sense of what was to happen dawned upon her. She watched Annie crown the stone with flowers, she watched the amazing ceremony that followed.

And yet, in spite of all her blushing shame, she herself bore blossoms to the wood a few months later. She laid white hothouse lilies upon the stone, and orchids of dying purple, and crimson exotic flowers. Having kissed the grey image with devout passion, she performed there all the antique immemorial rite. ❋

Psychology

MR. DALE, who had quiet rooms in a western part of London, was very busily occupied one day with a pencil and little scraps of paper. He would stop in the middle of his writing, of his monotonous tramp from door to window, jot down a line of hieroglyphics, and turn again to his work. At lunch he kept his instruments on the table beside him, and a little notebook accompanied him on his evening walk about the Green. Sometimes he seemed to experience a certain difficulty in the act of writing, as if the heat of shame or even incredulous surprise held his hand, but one by one the fragments of paper fell into the drawer, and a full feast awaited him at the day's close.

As he lit his pipe at dusk, he was standing by the window and looking out into the street. In the distance cab-lights flashed to and fro, up and down the hill, on the main road. Across the way he saw the long line of sober grey houses, cheerfully lit up for the most part, displaying against the night the dining-room and the evening meal. In one house, just opposite, there was brighter illumination, and the open windows showed a modest dinner-party in progress, and here and there a drawing-room on the first floor glowed ruddy, as the tall shaded lamp was lit. Everywhere Dale saw a quiet and comfortable respectability; if there were no gaiety there was no riot, and he thought himself fortunate to have got "rooms" in so sane and meritorious a street.

The pavement was almost deserted. Now and again a servant would dart out from a side door and scurry off in the direction of the shops, returning in a few minutes in equal haste. But foot passengers were rare, and only at long intervals a stranger would drift from the highway and wander with slow speculation down Abingdon Road, as if he had passed its entrance a thousand times and had at last been piqued with curiosity and the desire of exploring the unknown. All the inhabitants of the quarter prided themselves on their quiet and seclusion, and many of them did not so much as dream that if one went far enough the road degenerated and became abominable, the home of the hideous, the mouth of a black purlieu. Indeed stories, ill and malodorous, were told of the streets parallel, to east and west, which perhaps communicated with the terrible sink beyond, but those who lived at the good end of Abingdon Road knew nothing of their neighbours.

Dale leant far out of his window. The pale London sky deepened to violet as the lamps were lit, and in the twilight the little gardens before the houses shone, seemed as if they grew more clear. The golden laburnum but reflected the last bright yellow veil that had fallen over the sky after sunset, the white hawthorn was a gleaming splendour, the red may a flameless fire in the dusk. From the open window, Dale could note the increasing cheerfulness of the diners opposite, as the moderate cups were filled and emptied; blinds in the higher stories brightened up and down the street when the nurses came up with the children. A gentle breeze that smelt of grass and woods and flowers, fanned away the day's heat from the pavement stones, rustled through the blossoming boughs, and sank again, leaving the road to calm.

All the scene breathed the gentle domestic peace of the stories; there were regular lives, dull duties done, sober and common thoughts on every side. He felt that he needed not to listen at the windows, for he could divine all the talk, and guess the placid and usual channels in which the conversation flowed. Here there were no spasms, nor raptures, nor the red storms of romance, but a safe rest; marriage and birth and begetting were no more here than breakfast and lunch and afternoon tea.

And then he turned away from the placid transparency of the street, and sat down before his lamp and the papers he had so studiously noted. A friend of his, an "impossible" man named Jenyns, had been to see him the night before, and they had talked about the psychology of the novelists, discussing their insight, and the depth of their probe.

"It is all very well as far as it goes," said Jenyns. "Yes, it is perfectly accurate. Guardsmen do like chorus-girls, the doctor's daughter is fond of the curate, the grocer's assistant of the Baptist persuasion has sometimes religious difficulties, 'smart' people no doubt think a great deal about social events and complications: the Tragic Comedians felt and wrote all that stuff, I dare say. But do you think that is all? Do you call a description of the gilt tools on the morocco here an exhaustive essay on Shakespeare?"

"But what more is there?" said Dale. "Don't you think, then, that human nature has been fairly laid open? What more?"

"Songs of the frantic lupanar delirium of the madhouse. Not extreme wickedness, but the insensate, the unintelligible, the lunatic passion and idea, the desire that must come from some other sphere that we cannot even faintly imagine. Look for yourself; it is easy."

Dale looked now at the ends and scraps of paper. On them he had carefully registered all the secret thoughts of the day, the crazy lusts, the senseless furies, the foul monsters that his heart had borne, the maniac phantasies that he had harboured. In every note he found a rampant madness, the equivalents in thought of mathematical absurdity, of two-sided triangles, of parallel straight lines which met.

"And we talk of absurd dreams," he said to himself. "And these are wilder than the wildest visions. And our sins; but these are the sins of nightmare.

"And every day," he went on, "we lead two lives, and the half of our soul is madness, and half heaven is lit by a black sun. I say I am a man, but who is the other that hides in me?" ❋

Torture

"I REALLY do not know what to do with him," said the father. "He seems absolutely stupid."

"Poor boy!" said his mother, "I am afraid he is not well. He doesn't look in good health."

"But what's the matter with him? He eats well enough; he had two helpings of meat, and two of pudding to-day at dinner, and a quarter of an hour afterwards he was munching some sweet stuff. His appetite's all right, you see, anyhow."

"But he's very pale. He makes me feel anxious."

"And he makes me feel anxious. Look at this letter from Wells, the head master. Here you see he says: 'It seems almost impossible to get him to play games; he has had two or three thrashings, as I hear, for shirking cricket. And his form master gives me a very bad account of his work during the term, so that I fear the school is doing him little if any good.' And you see, Mary, it isn't as if he were a little boy; he was fifteen last April. It's getting serious, you know."

"What d'you think we had better do?"

"I wish I knew. Look at him here. He's only been home for a week, and you'd think he'd be in the best of spirits, enjoying himself with the squire's boys, and singing and racketing about all over the place. And you know the way he has been going on, almost from the day he came back; lounging and crawling from the house to the garden and back again, staying in bed half the day, and coming down with his eyes half open. I must insist on that being put a stop to, at all events. I shall trust to you to get him up at a proper time."

"Very well, dear. I thought he looked so tired."

"But he does nothing to make him tired! I wouldn't mind so much if the fellow were bookish, but you see what Wells says on that score. Why, I can't even get him to read a story-book. I declare his face is enough to make one angry. One can see he's totally devoid of any interest in anything."

"I am afraid he's unhappy, Robert."

"Unhappy! A schoolboy unhappy! Well, I wish you'd see what you can do. I find it perfectly useless to talk to him myself."

It was curious, but the father was quite right in laughing at the notion of his son's unhappiness. Harry was, in his quiet way, in the best of spirits. It was perfectly true that he hated cricket, and, the head master might have added, he hated other boys. He cared nothing for printed matter of any kind, whether fact or fiction, and he found *Treasure Island* as dull as Cicero. But all through the past term he had been pondering an idea; it had been with him in the early mornings in the dormitory, in schooltime and in playtime, and he watched with it at night, long after the other boys had gone to sleep. Before the coming of the idea he had found his existence unhappy enough. He had a puffy, unwholesome face and sandy hair, and his great wide mouth was made the subject of many jests. He was unpopular because he did not like games, and because he would not bathe unless he were flung into the water, and he was always in trouble over his lessons, which he could not understand. He burst out crying one night in the middle of preparation, and of course he would not say what was the matter. The fact was that he had been trying to extract the meaning from some weary nonsense about triangles, known by the absurd name of Euclid, and he had found it utterly impossible to learn the rabid stuff by heart. The impossibility of it, and the hopeless cloud in his mind, and the terror of the thrashing he would get in the morning, broke him down; the "blubbering idiot," as they said.

Those were unhappy times, but that very night his idea came to him, and the holidays became indeed desirable, and ten times desirable. Every day and all the day he elaborated and re-elaborated his great thought, and though he was as stupid, unpopular, and unprofitable as ever, he was no longer wretched.

When he got home at the end of term he lost no time in setting about his task. It was true that he was sleepy and heavy in the mornings, but that was because he worked till late at night. He found it impossible to do much in the day-time; his parents spied out his ways, and he knew that he was much too dull to invent lies and explanations. The day after his return his father had come across him as he slunk into a dark corner of the shrubbery with something hidden under his coat. He could only stand and look hopeless, idiotic, when an empty beer bottle was drawn forth; he could not say what he was doing or what he wanted with a green glass bottle. His father had left him, telling him not to play the fool, and he felt that he was always watched. When he took the cord from the back-kitchen one of the maids was peering after him down the passage, and his mother found him trying to bind a large log of wood to the trunk of one of the trees. She wanted to know what he was doing, and whether he could not find some more sensible amusement, and he stared at her with his heavy white face. He knew that he was under observation, and so he worked at night. The two servant girls who slept in the next room often awoke, fancying they heard a queer sort of noise, a "chink-chink," as one of them described the sensation, but they could not make out what it was.

And at last he was ready. He was "loafing about" one afternoon, and he happened to meet Charlotte Emery, a little girl of twelve, the daughter of a neighbour. Harry flushed to a dull burning red.

"Come for a walk with me to the Beeches?" he said. "I wish you would."

"Oh, I mustn't, Harry. Mother wouldn't like it."

"Do come. I've got a new game; grand fun."

"Is it really? What sort of game is it?"

"I can't show you here. Just walk on towards the Beeches, and I'll follow you directly. I knew you would."

Harry ran full tilt to the hiding-place where he had bestowed his apparatus. He soon overtook Charlotte, and the two went off together towards the Beeches, a lonely wooded hill, a mile away. The boy's father would have been astonished if he could have seen him; Harry was glowing and burning with that dull red colour, but he laughed as he walked beside Charlotte.

When they were alone together in the wood, Charlotte said:

"Now you must show me the game. You promised."

"I know. But you must do just as I tell you."

"Yes, I will."

"Even if it hurts?"

"Yes. But you wouldn't hurt me, Harry. I like you."

The boy stared at her, gazed with his dull, fishy, light blue eyes; his white, unwholesome face glared at her almost in terror. She was a dark girl, olive-skinned, with black eyes and black hair, and the scent of her hair had already half-intoxicated him, as they walked close together.

"You like me," he said at last, stuttering.

"Yes, I like you very much. I love you, Harry dear. Won't you give me a kiss?" And she put her arm round his neck, round the neck of the ugly, pasty schoolboy. The leaden marks under his eyes seemed to grow darker.

He dropped the parcel that he held under one arm. It broke open and the contents fell to the ground. There were three or four fantastic instruments, ugly little knives made of green bottle-glass, clumsily set into wooden handles. He had stolen a broom for this purpose. And there were some lengths of rope, fitted with running nooses. It was the idea that he had so long cherished.

But he threw himself full length upon the grass, and burst into tears—the "blubbering idiot." ❋

Midsummer

THE old farm-house on the hill flushed rose in the afterglow, and then, as the dusk began to mount from the brook, faded and yet grew brighter, its whitewashed walls gleaming as though light flowed from them, as the moon gleams when the red clouds turn to grey.

The ancient hawthorn tree at the barn-end became a tall black stem and its leaves and boughs a black mass against the pale uncertain blue of the twilight sky. Leonard looked up with a great sigh of relief. He was perched on the stile by the bridge, and as the wind fell, the ripple of the water swelled into a sweeter song, and there was no other sound to be heard. His pipe was finished, and though he knew that his rooms up at the farm looked out on the red rose and the white, he could not make up his mind to leave the view of the shimmering unearthly walls, and the melody of clear running water.

The contrast of it all with London was almost too immense, hardly realized or credible. A few hours before, and his ears seemed bursting with the terrible battle of the streets, with the clangour and jangle of great waggons thundering over the stones, with the sharp rattle of hansoms, the heavy rumble of swaying omnibuses. And during the journey his eyes still saw the thronging crowds, the turbid, furious streams of men that pushed eastward and westward, hurrying and jostling one another, wearying the brain with their constant movement, the everlasting flux and reflux of white faces. And the air, a hot smoke, a faint sick breath as though from a fever-stricken city; the sky, all grey heat that beat upon weary men, as they looked up through the cloud of dust that went before and followed them.

And now he was soothed in the deep silence and soothed by the chanting water, his eyes saw the valley melting into soft shadow, and in his nostrils was the ineffable incense of a summer night, that as a medicine allayed all the trouble and pain of body and mind. He wet his hands in the dew of the long grass and bathed his forehead, as if all the defilement and anguish of the streets should thus be washed utterly away.

He tried to analyse the scent of the night. The green leaves that overshadowed the brook and made the water dark at noon, gave out their odour, and the deep meadow grass was fragrant, a gale of scent breathed from the huge elder-bush that lit up the vague hill-side, hanging above the well. But the meadow-sweet was bursting into blossom at his feet, and ah! the wild red roses drooped down from dreamland.

At last he began to climb the hillside towards those white magic walls that had charmed him. His two rooms were at the end of the long low farm-house, and though there was a passage leading to the big kitchen, Leonard's sitting-room opened immediately on the garden, on the crimson roses. He could go and come as he pleased without disturbing the household, or as the pleasant farmer had expressed it, he had a home of his own. He entered and locked the door, and lit the two candles that stood in bright brass candlesticks on the mantelpiece. The room had a low ceiling crossed by a whitewashed beam, the walls were bulging and uneven, decked with samplers, with faded prints, and in a corner stood a glass cupboard, displaying quaint flowery china of some forgotten local pattern.

The room was as quiet, as full of peace, as the air and the night, and Leonard knew that here, at the old bureau, he would find the treasure he had been long vainly seeking. He was tired, but he did not feel inclined to go to bed. He lit his pipe again, and began to arrange his papers, and idly sat down at the bureau, thinking of the task, or rather of the delight, before him. An idea flashed suddenly into his mind, and he began to write hurriedly, in an ecstasy, afraid lest he should lose what he had so happily found.

At midnight his window was still bright on the hill, and he laid down his pen with a sigh of pleasure at the accomplished work. And now he could not go to bed; he felt he must wander into the night, and summon sleep from the velvet air, from the scent of darkness, from the dew. He gently unlocked and locked the door, and walked slowly between the Persian roses, and climbed the stone stile in the garden wall. The moon was mounting to a throne, in full splendour; below, at a little distance, there seemed the painted scene of a village, and higher, beyond the farm-house, a great wood began. And as he thought of the green retreats he had glanced at in the sunlit evening, he was filled with a longing for the wood-world at night, with a desire for its darkness, for the mystery of it beneath the moon. He followed the path he had noted, till on the wood's verge he looked back and found that the shape of the farm-house had or fallen into the night and vanished.

He entered the shadow, treading softly, and let the track lead him away from the world. The night became full of whisperings, of dry murmuring noises; it seemed soon as if a stealthy host were beneath the trees, every man tracking another. Leonard quite forgot his work, and its triumph, and felt as though his soul were astray in a new dark sphere that dreams had foretold. He had come to a place remote, without form or colour, made alone of shadow and overhanging gloom. Unconsciously he wandered from the path, and for a time he fought his way through the undergrowth, struggling with interlacing boughs and brambles that dragged back his feet.

At last he got free, and found that he had penetrated into a broad avenue, piercing, it seemed, through the heart of the wood. The moon shone bright from above the tree-tops, and gave a faint green colour to the track which ascended to an open glade; a great amphitheatre amidst the trees. He was tired, and lay down in the darkness beside the turfy road, and wondered whether he had lit on some forgotten way, on some great path that the legions had trodden. And as he lay there watching, gazing at the pale moonlight, he saw a shadow advancing on the grass before him.

"A breath of wind must be stirring some bough behind me," he thought, but in the instant a woman went by, and then the shadows and white women followed thick.

Leonard gripped hard at a stick he was carrying, and drove his nails into the flesh. He saw the farmer's daughter, the girl who had waited on him a few hours before, and behind her came girls with like faces, no doubt the quiet modest girls of the English village, of the English farm-house.

For a moment they fronted him, shameless, unabashed before one another, and then they had passed.

He had seen their smiles, he had seen their gestures, and things that he had thought the world had long forgotten.

The white writhing figures passed up towards the glade, and the boughs hid them, but he never doubted as to what he had seen. ❋

Nature

"AND there was a broad level by the river," Julian went on, telling the story of his holiday. "A broad level of misty meadows, divided by low banks, between the hills and the river. They say the Roman world is lost beneath the turf, that a whole city sleeps there, gold and marble and amber all buried for ever."

"You did not see anything?"

"No, I suppose not. I used to get up early, and go out, and leave the little modern village behind me, hidden in the hot haze. And then I would stand in the misty meadows, and watch the green turf shimmer and lighten, as the grey halo rolled away. Oh! the silence. There was no sound except the lapping of the river, the wash of the water on the reeds.

"The banks are yellow mud," he went on, "but in the early morning, as the sun began to shine in the mist, they pearled and grew like silver. There was a low mound that hid something, and on it an old thorn tree bent towards the east; it was a little way from the tide's brim. I stood there and saw the woods swell out of the haze in the early morning, and that white sun seemed to encompass the town with gleaming walls. If I had stayed still, I think I should have seen the glittering legion and the eagles, I should have heard the sonorous trumpets pealing from the walls."

"I expect you have seen and heard more than that," said his friend. "I always told you that the earth too, and the hills, and even the old walls are a language, hard to translate."

"And I came upon a place that made me think of that," said Julian. "It was far from the town; I lost my way amongst those rolling hills, and strayed by footpaths from field to wood, and all that I saw of man was here and there a blue smoke that crawled up from the earth, from the tree, it might be, or the brook, for I could see no house. I went on, always with the sense that I was following an unknown object, and, suddenly, a shape rose from forgotten dreams. An old farm-house, built of grey, silvering stones; a long barn wavering and dipping down to a black pool, pine trees overhanging the roof. It was all dim, as if it had been seen reflected in water. I went a little nearer, and I found that I was lifted free of the maze of hills. I fronted the mountain, looking across a deep broad valley, and all the year the mountain winds must blow upon the porch; they look from their deep windows and see the fleeting of the clouds and the sun, on that vast green hillside. Yellow flowers were shaking in the garden, for even on that still day the mountain wind swept across the valley. But those grey glistening walls! A light flowed from them, and they spoke of something beyond thought.

"I visited, too, the river valley, passing out to the north. The town was soon hidden behind trees, behind a curtain of Lombardy poplars, whispering of Italy, of the vine, the olive garden. The curving lane led me beneath orchards, their under-boughs dark-green, almost black, in the shadow, and the road winding between orchard and river led me into the long valley, where the forest is as a cloud upon the hill. I watched the yellow tide cease, and the water flow clear, and the breath of the wind was unearthly. It was there that I saw the burning pools."

"You stayed for the sunset?"

"Yes, I stayed all day within the valley. The sky was grey, but not cloudy; rather it was a glowing of silver light that made the earth seem dim and yet shining. Indeed, I say that though the sun was hidden, you would have dreamed that white moons were floating through the air, for now and again I saw the misty hillside pale and lighten, and a tree would appear suddenly in midforest, and glitter as if it blossomed. Yes, and in the calm meadows by the riverside there were little points of brightness, as if tongues of white fire sparkled in the grey grass."

"And the river itself?"

"It was all the day a hieroglyphic, winding in esses beneath those haunting banks, colourless, and yet alight like all the world around. At last, in the evening, I sat down beneath a wych-elm on the slope, where I breathed the scent and knew the heavy stillness of the wood. Then a strong wind blew, high up in heaven, and the grey veil vanished. The sky was clear pale blue; in the west there was exhibited an opal burning green, and beneath a purple wall. Then, in the middle of the purple, a rent opened; there was a red glint, and red momentary rays, as if rose-hot metal were beaten and dinted on the anvil, and the sparks fled abroad. So the sun sank.

"I thought I would wait and see all the valley, the river, and the level, and the woods sink into twilight, become sombre, formless. The light went out from the river, the water paled as it flowed between the sad reeds and grasses. I heard a harsh melancholy cry, and above, in the dusky air, a flight of great birds passed seaward in changing, hieroglyphic order. The keen line of the hills by sunset home seemed to melt away, to become vague.

"Then I saw the sky was blossoming in the north. Rose gardens appeared there, with golden hedges, and bronze gates, and the great purple wall caught fire as it grew leaden. The earth was lit again, but with unnatural jewelled colours; the palest light was sardonyx, the darkness was amethyst. And then the valley was aflame. Fire in the wood, the fire of a sacrifice beneath the oaks. Fire in the level fields, a great burning in the north, and vehement flame to the south, above the town. And in the still river the very splendour of fire, yes, as if all precious things were cast into its furnace pools, as if gold and roses and jewels became flame."

"And then?"

"Then, the shining of the evening star."

"And you," said his friend, "perhaps without knowing, have told me the story of a wonderful and incredible passion."

Julian stared at him, in amazement.

"You are quite right," he said at length. ❋

The Holy Things

THE sky was blue above Holborn, and only one little cloud, half white, half golden, floated on the wind's way from west to east. The long aisle of the street was splendid in the full light of the summer, and away in the west, where the houses seemed to meet and join, it was as a rich tabernacle, mysterious, the carven house of holy things.

A man came into the great highway from a quiet court. He had been sitting under plane-tree shade for an hour or more, his mind racked with perplexities and doubts, with the sense that all was without meaning or purpose, a tangle of senseless joys and empty sorrows. He had stirred in it and fought and striven, and now disappointment and success were alike tasteless. To struggle was weariness, to attain was weariness, to do nothing was weariness. He had felt, a little while before, that from the highest to the lowest things of life there was no choice, there was not one thing that was better than another: the savour of the cinders was no sweeter than the savour of the ashes. He had done work which some men liked and others disliked, and liking and disliking were equally tiresome to him. His poetry or his pictures or whatever it was that he worked at had utterly ceased to interest him, and he had tried to be idle, and found idleness as impossible as work. He had lost the faculty for making and he had lost the power of resting; he dozed in the day-time and started up and cried at night. Even that morning he had doubted and hesitated, wondering whether to stay indoors or to go out, sure that in either plan there was an infinite weariness and disgust.

When he at last went abroad he let the crowd push him into the quiet court, and at the same time cursed them in a low voice for doing so; he tried to persuade himself that he had meant to go somewhere else. When he sat down he desperately endeavoured to rouse himself, and as he knew that all the strong interests are egotistic, he made an effort to grow warm over the work he had done, to find a glow of satisfaction in the thought that he had accomplished something. It was nonsense; he had found out a clever trick and had made the most of it, and it was over. Besides, how would it interest him if afterwards he was praised when he was dead? And what was the use of trying to invent some new tricks? It was folly; and he ground his teeth as a new idea came into his mind and was rejected. To get drunk always made him so horribly ill, and other things were more foolish and tiresome than poesy or painting, whichever it was.

He could not even rest on the uncomfortable bench, beneath the dank, stinking plane tree. A young man and a girl came up and sat next to him, and the girl said, "Oh, isn't it beautiful to-day?" and then they began to jabber to one another—the blasted fools! He flung himself from the seat and went out into Holborn.

As far as one could see, there were two processions of omnibuses, cabs, and vans that went east and west and west and east. Now the long line would move on briskly, now it stopped. The horses' feet rattled and pattered on the asphalt, the wheels ground and jarred, a bicyclist wavered in and out between the serried ranks, jangling his bell. The foot passengers went to and fro on the pavement, with an endless change of unknown faces; there was an incessant hum and murmur of voices. In the safety of a blind passage an Italian whirled round the handle of his piano-organ; the sound of it swelled and sank as the traffic surged and paused, and now and then one heard the shrill voices of the children who danced and shrieked in time to the music. Close to the pavement a coster pushed his barrow, and proclaimed flowers in an odd intonation, reminding one of the Gregorian chant. The cyclist went by again with his jangling insistent bell, and a man who stood by the lamp-post set fire to his pastille ribbon, and let the faint blue smoke rise into the sun. Away in the west, where the houses seemed to meet, the play of sunlight on the haze made, as it were, golden mighty shapes that paused and advanced, and paused again.

He had viewed the scene hundreds of times, and for a long while had found it a nuisance and a weariness. But now as he walked stupidly, slowly, along the southern side of Holborn, a change fell. He did not in the least know what it was, but there seemed to be a strange air, and a new charm that soothed his mind.

When the traffic was stopped, to his soul there was a solemn hush that summoned remnants of a far-off memory. The voices of the passengers sank away, the street was endued with a grave and reverent expectation. A shop that he passed had a row of electric lamps burning above the door, and the golden glow of them in the sunlight was, he felt, significant. The grind and jar of the wheels, as the procession moved on again, gave out a chord of music, the opening of some high service that was to be done, and now, in an ecstasy, he was sure that he heard the roll and swell and triumph of the organ, and shrill sweet choristers began to sing. So the music sank and swelled and echoed in the vast aisle—in Holborn.

What could these lamps mean, burning in the bright sunlight? The music was hushed in a grave close, and in the rattle of traffic he heard the last deep sonorous notes shake against the choir walls—he had passed beyond the range of the Italian's instrument. But then a rich voice began alone, rising and falling in monotonous but awful modulations, singing a longing triumphant song, bidding the faithful lift up their hearts, be joined in heart with the Angels and Archangels, with the Thrones and Dominations. He could see no longer, he could not see the man who passed close beside him, pushing his barrow, and calling flowers.

Ah! He could not be mistaken, he was sure now. The air was blue with incense, he smelt the adorable fragrance. The time had almost come. And then the silvery, reiterated, instant summons of a bell; and again, and again.

The tears fell from his eyes, in his weeping the tears poured a rain upon his cheeks. But he saw in the distance, in the far distance, the carven tabernacle, golden mighty figures moving slowly, imploring arms stretched forth.

There was a noise of a great shout; the choir sang in the tongue of his boyhood that he had forgotten:

SANT . . . SANT . . . SANT

Then the silvery bell tinkled anew; and again, and again. He looked and saw the Holy, White, and Shining Mysteries exhibited—in Holborn. ❋

The White People

Prologue

"SORCERY and sanctity," said Ambrose, "these are the only realities. Each is an ecstasy, a withdrawal from the common life."

Cotgrave listened, interested. He had been brought by a friend to this mouldering house in a northern suburb, through an old garden to the room where Ambrose the recluse dozed and dreamed over his books.

"Yes," he went on, "magic is justified of her children. There are many, I think, who eat dry crusts and drink water, with a joy infinitely sharper than anything within the experience of the 'practical' epicure."

"You are speaking of the saints?"

"Yes, and of the sinners, too. I think you are falling into the very general error of confining the spiritual world to the supremely good; but the supremely wicked, necessarily, have their portion in it. The merely carnal, sensual man can no more be a great sinner than he can be a great saint. Most of us are just indifferent, mixed-up creatures; we muddle through the world without realizing the meaning and the inner sense of things, and, consequently, our wickedness and our goodness are alike second-rate, unimportant."

"And you think the great sinner, then, will be an ascetic, as well as the great saint?"

"Great people of all kinds forsake the imperfect copies and go to the perfect originals. I have no doubt but that many of the very highest among the saints have never done a 'good action' (using the words in their ordinary sense). And, on the other hand, there have been those who have sounded the very depths of sin, who all their lives have never done an 'ill deed.'"

He went out of the room for a moment, and Cotgrave, in high delight, turned to his friend and thanked him for the introduction.

"He's grand," he said. "I never saw that kind of lunatic before."

Ambrose returned with more whisky and helped the two men in a liberal manner. He abused the teetotal sect with ferocity, as he handed the seltzer, and pouring out a glass of water for himself, was about to resume his monologue, when Cotgrave broke in—

"I can't stand it, you know," he said, "your paradoxes are too monstrous. A man may be a great sinner and yet never do anything sinful! Come!"

"You're quite wrong," said Ambrose. "I never make paradoxes; I wish I could. I merely said that a man may have an exquisite taste in Romanée Conti, and yet never have even smelt four ate. That's all, and it's more like a truism than a paradox, isn't it? Your surprise at my remark is due to the fact that you haven't realized what sin is. Oh, yes, there is a sort of connexion between Sin with the capital letter, and actions which are commonly called sinful: with murder, theft, adultery, and so forth. Much the same connexion that there is between the A, B, C and fine literature. But I believe that the misconception—it is all but universal—arises in great measure from our looking at the matter through social spectacles. We think that a man who does evil to *us* and to his neighbours must be very evil. So he is, from a social standpoint; but can't you realize that Evil in its essence is a lonely thing, a passion of the solitary, individual soul? Really, the average murderer, *quâ* murderer, is not by any means a sinner in the true sense of the word. He is simply a wild beast that we have to get rid of to save our own necks from his knife. I should class him rather with tigers than with sinners."

"It seems a little strange."

"I think not. The murderer murders not from positive qualities, but from negative ones; he lacks something which non-murderers possess. Evil, of course, is wholly positive—only it is on the wrong side. You may believe me that sin in its proper sense is very rare; it is probable that there have been far fewer sinners than saints. Yes, your standpoint is all very well for practical, social purposes; we are naturally inclined to think that a person who is very disagreeable to us must be a very great sinner! It is very disagreeable to have one's pocket picked, and we pronounce the thief to be a very great sinner. In truth, he is merely an undeveloped man. He cannot be a saint, of course; but he may be, and often is, an infinitely better creature than thousands who have never broken a single commandment. He is a great nuisance to *us,* I admit, and we very properly lock him up if we catch him; but between his troublesome and unsocial action and evil—Oh, the connexion is of the weakest."

It was getting very late. The man who had brought Cotgrave had probably heard all this before, since he assisted with a bland and judicious smile, but Cotgrave began to think that his "lunatic" was turning into a sage.

"Do you know," he said, "you interest me immensely? You think, then, that we do not understand the real nature of evil?"

"No, I don't think we do. We over-estimate it and we under-estimate it. We take the very numerous infractions of our social 'bye-laws'—the very necessary and very proper regulations which keep the human company together—and we get frightened at the prevalence of 'sin' and 'evil.' But this is really nonsense. Take theft, for example. Have you any *horror* at the thought of Robin Hood, of the Highland caterans of the seventeenth century, of the moss-troopers, of the company promoters of our day?

"Then, on the other hand, we underrate evil. We attach such an enormous importance to the 'sin' of meddling with our pockets (and our wives) that we have quite forgotten the awfulness of real sin."

"And what is sin?" said Cotgrave.

"I think I must reply to your question by another. What would your feelings be, seriously, if your cat or your dog began to talk to you, and to dispute with you in human accents? You would be overwhelmed with horror. I am sure of it. And if the roses in your garden sang a weird song, you would go mad. And suppose the stones in the road began to swell and grow before your eyes, and if the pebble that you noticed at night had shot out stony blossoms in the morning?

"Well, these examples may give you some notion of what sin really is."

"Look here," said the third man, hitherto placid, "you two seem pretty well wound up. But I'm going home. I've missed my tram, and I shall have to walk."

Ambrose and Cotgrave seemed to settle down more profoundly when the other had gone out into the early misty morning and the pale light of the lamps.

"You astonish me," said Cotgrave. "I had never thought of that. If that is really so, one must turn everything upside down. Then the essence of sin really is—"

"In the taking of heaven by storm, it seems to me," said Ambrose. "It appears to me that it is simply an attempt to penetrate into another and a higher sphere in a forbidden manner. You can understand why it is so rare. They are few, indeed, who wish to penetrate into other spheres, higher or lower, in ways allowed or forbidden. Men, in the mass, are amply content with life as they find it. Therefore there are few saints, and sinners (in the proper sense) are fewer still, and men of genius, who partake sometimes of each character, are rare also. Yes; on the whole, it is, perhaps, harder to be a great sinner than a great saint."

"There is something profoundly unnatural about sin? Is that what you mean?"

"Exactly. Holiness requires as great, or almost as great, an effort; but holiness works on lines that *were* natural once; it is an effort to recover the ecstasy that was before the Fall. But sin is an effort to gain the ecstasy and the knowledge that pertain alone to angels, and in making this effort man becomes a demon. I told you that the mere murderer is not *therefore* a sinner; that is true, but the sinner is sometimes a murderer. Gilles de Raiz is an instance. So you see that while the good and the evil are unnatural to man as he now is—to man the social, civilized being—evil is unnatural in a much deeper sense than good. The saint endeavours to recover a gift which he has lost; the sinner tries to obtain something which was never his. In brief, he repeats the Fall."

"But are you a Catholic?" said Cotgrave.

"Yes; I am a member of the persecuted Anglican Church."

"Then, how about those texts which seem to reckon as sin that which you would set down as a mere trivial dereliction?"

"Yes; but in one place the word 'sorcerers' comes in the same sentence, doesn't it? That seems to me to give the key-note. Consider: can you imagine for a moment that a false statement which saves an innocent man's life is a sin? No; very good, then, it is not the mere liar who is excluded by those words; it is, above all, the 'sorcerers' who use the material life, who use the failings incidental to material life as instruments to obtain their infinitely wicked ends. And let me tell you this: our higher senses are so blunted, we are so drenched with materialism, that we should probably fail to recognize real wickedness if we encountered it."

"But shouldn't we experience a certain horror—a terror such as you hinted we would experience if a rose tree sang—in the mere presence of an evil man?"

"We should if we were natural: children and women feel this horror you speak of, even animals experience it. But with most of us convention and civilization and education have blinded and deafened and obscured the natural reason. No, sometimes we may recognize evil by its hatred of the good—one doesn't need much penetration to guess at the influence which dictated, quite unconsciously, the 'Blackwood' review of Keats—but this is purely incidental; and, as a rule, I suspect that the Hierarchs of Tophet pass quite unnoticed, or, perhaps, in certain cases, as good but mistaken men."

"But you used the word 'unconscious' just now, of Keats' reviewers. Is wickedness ever unconscious?"

"Always. It must be so. It is like holiness and genius in this as in other points; it is a certain rapture or ecstasy of the soul; a transcendent effort to surpass the ordinary bounds. So, surpassing these, it surpasses also the understanding, the faculty that takes note of that which comes before it. No, a man may be infinitely and horribly wicked and never suspect it. But I tell you, evil in this, its certain and true sense, is rare, and I think it is growing rarer."

"I am trying to get hold of it all," said Cotgrave. "From what you say, I gather that the true evil differs generically from that which we call evil?"

"Quite so. There is, no doubt, an analogy between the two; a resemblance such as enables us to use, quite legitimately, such terms as the 'foot of the mountain' and the 'leg of the table.' And, sometimes, of course, the two speak, as it were, in the same language. The rough miner, or 'puddler,' the untrained, undeveloped 'tiger-man,' heated by a quart or two above his usual measure, comes home and kicks his irritating and injudicious wife to death. He is a murderer. And Gilles de Raiz was a murderer. But you see the gulf that separates the two? The 'word,' if I may so speak, is accidentally the same in each case, but the 'meaning' is utterly different. It is flagrant 'Hobson Jobson' to confuse the two, or rather, it is as if one supposed that Juggernaut and the Argonauts had something to do etymologically with one another. And no doubt the same weak likeness, or analogy, runs between all the 'social' sins and the real spiritual sins, and in some cases, perhaps, the lesser may be 'schoolmasters' to lead one on to the greater—from the shadow to the reality. If you are anything of a Theologian, you will see the importance of all this."

"I am sorry to say," remarked Cotgrave, "that I have devoted very little of my time to theology. Indeed, I have often wondered on what grounds theologians have claimed the title of Science of Sciences for their favourite study; since the 'theological' books I have looked into have always seemed to me to be concerned with feeble and obvious pieties, or with the kings of Israel and Judah. I do not care to hear about those kings."

Ambrose grinned.

"We must try to avoid theological discussion," he said. "I perceive that you would be a bitter disputant. But perhaps the 'dates of the kings' have as much to do with theology as the hobnails of the murderous puddler with evil."

"Then, to return to our main subject, you think that sin is an esoteric, occult thing?"

"Yes. It is the infernal miracle as holiness is the supernal. Now and then it is raised to such a pitch that we entirely fail to suspect its existence; it is like the note of the great pedal pipes of the organ, which is so deep that we cannot hear it. In other cases it may lead to the lunatic asylum, or to still stranger issues. But you must never confuse it with mere social misdoing. Remember how the Apostle, speaking of the 'other side,' distinguishes between 'charitable' actions and charity. And as one may give all one's goods to the poor, and yet lack charity; so, remember, one may avoid every crime and yet be a sinner."

"Your psychology is very strange to me," said Cotgrave, "but I confess I like it, and I suppose that one might fairly deduce from your premisses the conclusion that the real sinner might very possibly strike the observer as a harmless personage enough?"

"Certainly; because the true evil has nothing to do with social life or social laws, or if it has, only incidentally and accidentally. It is a lonely passion of the soul—or a passion of the lonely soul—whichever you like. If, by chance, we understand it, and grasp its full significance, then, indeed, it will fill us with horror and with awe. But this emotion is widely distinguished from the fear and the disgust with which we regard the ordinary criminal, since this latter is largely or entirely founded on the regard which we have for our own skins or purses. We hate a murderer, because we know that we should hate to be murdered, or to have any one that we like murdered. So, on the 'other side,' we venerate the saints, but we don't 'like' them as we like our friends. Can you persuade yourself that you would have 'enjoyed' St. Paul's company? Do you think that you and I would have 'got on' with Sir Galahad?

"So with the sinners, as with the saints. If you met a very evil man, and recognized his evil; he would, no doubt, fill you with horror and awe; but there is no reason why you should 'dislike' him. On the contrary, it is quite possible that if you could succeed in putting the sin out of your mind you might find the sinner capital company, and in a little while you might have to reason yourself back into horror. Still, how awful it is. If the roses and the lilies suddenly sang on this coming morning; if the furniture began to move in procession, as in De Maupassaut's tale!"

"I am glad you have come back to that comparison," said Cotgrave, "because I wanted to ask you what it is that corresponds in humanity to these imaginary feats of inanimate things. In a word—what is sin? You have given me, I know, an abstract definition, but I should like a concrete example."

"I told you it was very rare," said Ambrose, who appeared willing to avoid the giving of a direct answer. "The materialism of the age, which has done a good deal to suppress sanctity, has done perhaps more to suppress evil. We find the earth so very comfortable that we have no inclination either for ascents or descents. It would seem as if the scholar who decided to 'specialize' in Tophet, would be reduced to purely antiquarian researches. No palæontologist could show you a *live* pterodactyl."

"And yet you, I think, have 'specialized,' and I believe that your researches have descended to our modern times."

"You are really interested, I see. Well, I confess, that I have dabbled a little, and if you like I can show you something that bears on the very curious subject we have been discussing."

Ambrose took a candle and went away to a far, dim corner of the room. Cotgrave saw him open a venerable bureau that stood there, and from some secret recess he drew out a parcel, and came back to the window where they had been sitting.

Ambrose undid a wrapping of paper, and produced a green pocket-book.

"You will take care of it?" he said. "Don't leave it lying about. It is one of the choicer pieces in my collection, and I should be very sorry if it were lost."

He fondled the faded binding.

"I knew the girl who wrote this," he said. "When you read it, you will see how it illustrates the talk we have had to-night. There is a sequel, too, but I won't talk of that."

"There was an odd article in one of the reviews some months ago," he began again, with the air of a man who changes the subject. "It was written by a doctor—Dr. Coryn, I think, was the name. He says that a lady, watching her little girl playing at the drawing-room window, suddenly saw the heavy sash give way and fall on the child's fingers. The lady fainted, I think, but at any rate the doctor was summoned, and when he had dressed the child's wounded and maimed fingers he was summoned to the mother. She was groaning with pain, and it was found that three fingers of her hand, corresponding with those that had been injured on the child's hand, were swollen and inflamed, and later, in the doctor's language, purulent sloughing set in."

Ambrose still handled delicately the green volume.

"Well, here it is," he said at last, parting with difficulty, it seemed, from his treasure.

"You will bring it back as soon as you have read it," he said, as they went out into the hall, into the old garden, faint with the odour of white lilies.

There was a broad red band in the east as Cotgrave turned to go, and from the high ground where he stood he saw that awful spectacle of London in a dream.

The Green Book

The morocco binding of the book was faded, and the colour had grown faint, but there were no stains nor bruises nor marks of usage. The book looked as if it had been bought "on a visit to London" some seventy or eighty years ago, and had somehow been forgotten and suffered to lie away out of sight. There was an old, delicate, lingering odour about it, such an odour as sometimes haunts an ancient piece of furniture for a century or more. The end-papers, inside the binding, were oddly decorated with coloured patterns and faded gold. It looked small, but the paper was fine, and there were many leaves, closely covered with minute, painfully formed characters.

* * *

I found this book (the manuscript began) in a drawer in the old bureau that stands on the landing. It was a very rainy day and I could not go out, so in the afternoon I got a candle and rummaged in the bureau. Nearly all the drawers were full of old dresses, but one of the small ones looked empty, and I found this book hidden right at the back. I wanted a book like this, so I took it to write in. It is full of secrets. I have a great many other books of secrets I have written, hidden in a safe place, and I am going to write here many of the old secrets and some new ones; but there are some I shall not put down at all. I must not write down the real names of the days and months which I found out a year ago, nor the way to make the Aklo letters, or the Chian language, or the great beautiful Circles, nor the Mao Games, nor the chief songs. I may write something about all these things but not the way to do them, for peculiar reasons. And I must not say who the Nymphs are, or the Dôls, or Jeelo, or what voolas mean. All these are most secret secrets, and I am glad when I remember what they are, and how many wonderful languages I know, but there are some things that I call the secrets of the secrets of the secrets that I dare not think of unless I am quite alone, and then I shut my eyes, and put my hands over them and whisper the word, and the Alala comes. I only do this at night in my room or in certain woods that I know, but I must not describe them, as they are secret woods. Then there are the Ceremonies, which are all of them important, but some are more delightful than others—there are the White Ceremonies, and the Green Ceremonies, and the Scarlet Ceremonies. The Scarlet Ceremonies are the best, but there is only one place where they can be performed properly, though there is a very nice imitation which I have done in other places. Besides these, I have the dances, and the Comedy, and I have done the Comedy sometimes when the others were looking, and they didn't understand anything about it. I was very little when I first knew about these things.

When I was very small, and mother was alive, I can remember remembering things before that, only it has all got confused. But I remember when I was five or six I heard them talking about me when they thought I was not noticing. They were saying how queer I was a year or two before, and how nurse had called my mother to come and listen to me talking all to myself, and I was saying words that nobody could understand. I was speaking the Xu language, but I only remember a very few of the words, as it was about the little white faces that used to look at me when I was lying in my cradle. They used to talk to me, and I learnt their language and talked to them in it about some great white place where they lived, where the trees and the grass were all white, and there were white hills as high up as the moon, and a cold wind. I have often dreamed of it afterwards, but the faces went away when I was very little. But a wonderful thing happened when I was about five. My nurse was carrying me on her shoulder; there was a field of yellow corn, and we went through it, it was very hot. Then we came to a path through a wood, and a tall man came after us, and went with us till we came to a place where there was a deep pool, and it was very dark and shady. Nurse put me down on the soft moss under a tree, and she said: "She can't get to the pond now." So they left me there, and I sat quite still and watched, and out of the water and out of the wood came two wonderful white people, and they began to play and dance and sing. They were a kind of creamy white like the old ivory figure in the drawing-room; one was a beautiful lady with kind dark eyes, and a grave face, and long black hair, and she smiled such a strange sad smile at the other, who laughed and came to her. They played together, and danced round and round the pool, and they sang a song till I fell asleep. Nurse woke me up when she came back, and she was looking something like the lady had looked, so I told her all about it, and asked her why she looked like that. At first she cried, and then she looked very frightened, and turned quite pale. She put me down on the grass and stared at me, and I could see she was shaking all over. Then she said I had been dreaming, but I knew I hadn't. Then she made me promise not to say a word about it to anybody, and if I did I should be thrown into the black pit. I was not frightened at all, though nurse was, and I never forgot about it, because when I shut my eyes and it was quite quiet, and I was all alone, I could see them again, very faint and far away, but very splendid; and little bits of the song they sang came into my head, but I couldn't sing it.

I was thirteen, nearly fourteen, when I had a very singular adventure, so strange that the day on which it happened is always called the White Day. My mother had been dead for more than a year, and in the morning I had lessons, but they let me go out for walks in the afternoon. And this afternoon I walked a new way, and a little brook led me into a new country, but I tore my frock getting through some of the difficult places, as the way was through many bushes, and beneath the low branches of trees, and up thorny thickets on the hills, and by dark woods full of creeping thorns. And it was a long, long way. It seemed as if I was going on for ever and ever, and I had to creep by a place like a tunnel where a brook must have been, but all the water had dried up, and the floor was rocky, and the bushes had grown overhead till they met, so that it was quite dark. And I went on and on through that dark place; it was a long, long way. And I came to a hill that I never saw before. I was in a dismal thicket full of black twisted boughs that tore me as I went through them, and I cried out because I was smarting all over, and then I found that I was climbing, and I went up and up a long way, till at last the thicket stopped and I came out crying just under the top of a big bare place, where there were ugly grey stones lying all about on the grass, and here and there a little twisted, stunted tree came out from under a stone, like a snake. And I went up, right to the top, a long way. I never saw such big ugly stones before; they came out of the earth some of them, and some looked as if they had been rolled to where they were, and they went on and on as far as I could see, a long, long way. I looked out from them and saw the country, but it was strange. It was winter time, and there were black terrible woods hanging from the hills all round; it was like seeing a large room hung with black curtains, and the shape of the trees seemed quite different from any I had ever seen before. I was afraid. Then beyond the woods there were other hills round in a great ring, but I had never seen any of them; it all looked black, and everything had a voor over it. It was all so still and silent, and the sky was heavy and grey and sad, like a wicked voorish dome in Deep Dendo. I went on into the dreadful rocks. There were hundreds and hundreds of them. Some were like horrid-grinning men; I could see their faces as if they would jump at me out of the stone, and catch hold of me, and drag me with them back into the rock, so that I should always be there. And there were other rocks that were like animals, creeping, horrible animals, putting out their tongues, and others were like words that I could not say, and others like dead people lying on the grass. I went on among them, though they frightened me, and my heart was full of wicked songs that they put into it; and I wanted to make faces and twist myself about in the way they did, and I went on and on a long way till at last I liked the rocks, and they didn't frighten me any more. I sang the songs I thought of; songs full of words that must not be spoken or written down. Then I made faces like the faces on the rocks, and I twisted myself about like the twisted ones, and I lay down flat on the ground like the dead ones, and I went up to one that was grinning, and put my arms round him and hugged him. And so I went on and on through the rocks till I came to a round mound in the middle of them. It was higher than a mound, it was nearly as high as our house, and it was like a great basin turned upside down, all smooth and round and green, with one stone, like a post, sticking up at the top. I climbed up the sides, but they were so steep I had to stop or I should have rolled all the way down again, and I should have knocked against the stones at the bottom, and perhaps been killed. But I wanted to get up to the very top of the big round mound, so I lay down flat on my face, and took hold of the grass with my hands and drew myself up, bit by bit, till I was at the top. Then I sat down on the stone in the middle, and looked all round about. I felt I had come such a long, long way, just as if I were a hundred miles from home, or in some other country, or in one of the strange places I had read about in the *Tales of the Genie* and the *Arabian Nights,* or as if I had gone across the sea, far away, for years and I had found another world that nobody had ever seen or heard of before, or as if I had somehow flown through the sky and fallen on one of the stars I had read about where everything is dead and cold and grey, and there is no air, and the wind doesn't blow. I sat on the stone and looked all round and down and round about me. It was just as if I was sitting on a tower in the middle of a great empty town, because I could see nothing all around but the grey rocks on the ground. I couldn't make out their shapes any more, but I could see them on and on for a long way, and I looked at them, and they seemed as if they had been arranged into patterns, and shapes, and figures. I knew they couldn't be, because I had seen a lot of them coming right out of the earth, joined to the deep rocks below, so I looked again, but still I saw nothing but circles, and small circles inside big ones, and pyramids, and domes, and spires, and they seemed all to go round and round the place where I was sitting, and the more I looked, the more I saw great big rings of rocks, getting bigger and bigger, and I stared so long that it felt as if they were all moving and turning, like a great wheel, and I was turning, too, in the middle. I got quite dizzy and queer in the head, and everything began to be hazy and not clear, and I saw little sparks of blue light, and the stones looked as if they were springing and dancing and twisting as they went round and round and round. I was frightened again, and I cried out loud, and jumped up from the stone I was sitting on, and fell down. When I got up I was so glad they all looked still, and I sat down on the top and slid down the mound, and went on again. I danced as I went in the peculiar way the rocks had danced when I got giddy, and I was so glad I could do it quite well, and I danced and danced along, and sang extraordinary songs that came into my head. At last I came to the edge of that great flat hill, and there were no more rocks, and the way went again through a dark thicket in a hollow. It was just as bad as the other one I went through climbing up, but I didn't mind this one, because I was so glad I had seen those singular dances and could imitate them. I went down, creeping through the bushes, and a tall nettle stung me on my leg, and made me burn, but I didn't mind it, and I tingled with the boughs and the thorns, but I only laughed and sang. Then I got out of the thicket into a close valley, a little secret place like a dark passage that nobody ever knows of, because it was so narrow and deep and the woods were so thick round it. There is a steep bank with trees hanging over it, and there the ferns keep green all through the winter, when they are dead and brown upon the hill, and the ferns there have a sweet, rich smell like what oozes out of fir trees. There was a little stream of water running down this valley, so small that I could easily step across it. I drank the water with my hand, and it tasted like bright, yellow wine, and it sparkled and bubbled as it ran down over beautiful red and yellow and green stones, so that it seemed alive and all colours at once. I drank it, and I drank more with my hand, but I couldn't drink enough, so I lay down and bent my head and sucked the water up with my lips. It tasted much better, drinking it that way, and a ripple would come up to my mouth and give me a kiss, and I laughed, and drank again, and pretended there was a nymph, like the one in the old picture at home, who lived in the water and was kissing me. So I bent low down to the water, and put my lips softly to it, and whispered to the nymph that I would come again. I felt sure it could not be common water, I was so glad when I got up and went on; and I danced again and went up and up the valley, under hanging hills. And when I came to the top, the ground rose up in front of me, tall and steep as a wall, and there was nothing but the green wall and the sky. I thought of "for ever and for ever, world without end, Amen"; and I thought I must have really found the end of the world, because it was like the end of everything, as if there could be nothing at all beyond, except the kingdom of Voor, where the light goes when it is put out, and the water goes when the sun takes it away. I began to think of all the long, long way I had journeyed, how I had found a brook and followed it, and followed it on, and gone through bushes and thorny thickets, and dark woods full of creeping thorns. Then I had crept up a tunnel under trees, and climbed a thicket, and seen all the grey rocks, and sat in the middle of them when they turned round, and then I had gone on through the grey rocks and come down the hill through the stinging thicket and up the dark valley, all a long, long way. I wondered how I should get home again, if I could ever find the way, and if my home was there any more, or if it were turned and everybody in it into grey rocks, as in the *Arabian Nights.* So I sat down on the grass and thought what I should do next. I was tired, and my feet were hot with walking, and as I looked about I saw there was a wonderful well just under the high, steep wall of grass. All the ground round it was covered with bright, green, dripping moss; there was every kind of moss there, moss like beautiful little ferns, and like palms and fir trees, and it was all green as jewellery, and drops of water hung on it like diamonds. And in the middle was the great well, deep and shining and beautiful, so clear that it looked as if I could touch the red sand at the bottom, but it was far below. I stood by it and looked in, as if I were looking in a glass. At the bottom of the well, in the middle of it, the red grains of sand were moving and stirring all the time, and I saw how the water bubbled up, but at the top it was quite smooth, and full and brimming. It was a great well, large like a bath, and with the shining, glittering green moss about it, it looked like a great white jewel, with green jewels all round. My feet were so hot and tired that I took off my boots and stockings, and let my feet down into the water, and the water was soft and cold, and when I got up I wasn't tired any more, and I felt I must go on, farther and farther, and see what was on the other side of the wall. I climbed up it very slowly, going sideways all the time, and when I got to the top and looked over, I was in the queerest country I had seen, stranger even than the hill of the grey rocks. It looked as if earth-children had been playing there with their spades, as it was all hills and hollows, and castles and walls made of earth and covered with grass. There were two mounds like big beehives, round and great and solemn, and then hollow basins, and then a steep mounting wall like the ones I saw once by the seaside where the big guns and the soldiers were. I nearly fell into one of the round hollows, it went away from under my feet so suddenly, and I ran fast down the side and stood at the bottom and looked up. It was strange and solemn to look up. There was nothing but the grey, heavy sky and the sides of the hollow; everything else had gone away, and the hollow was the whole world, and I thought that at night it must be full of ghosts and moving shadows and pale things when the moon shone down to the bottom at the dead of the night, and the wind wailed up above. It was so strange and solemn and lonely, like a hollow temple of dead heathen gods. It reminded me of a tale my nurse had told me when I was quite little; it was the same nurse that took me into the wood where I saw the beautiful white people. And I remembered how nurse had told me the story one winter night, when the wind was beating the trees against the wall, and crying and moaning in the nursery chimney. She said there was, somewhere or other, a hollow pit, just like the one I was standing in, everybody was afraid to go into it or near it, it was such a bad place. But once upon a time there was a poor girl who said she would go into the hollow pit, and everybody tried to stop her, but she would go. And she went down into the pit and came back laughing, and said there was nothing there at all, except green grass and red stones, and white stones and yellow flowers. And soon after people saw she had most beautiful emerald earrings, and they asked how she got them, as she and her mother were quite poor. But she laughed, and said her earrings were not made of emeralds at all, but only of green grass. Then, one day, she wore on her breast the reddest ruby that any one had ever seen, and it was as big as a hen's egg, and glowed and sparkled like a hot burning coal of fire. And they asked how she got it, as she and her mother were quite poor. But she laughed, and said it was not a ruby at all, but only a red stone. Then one day she wore round her neck the loveliest necklace that any one had ever seen, much finer than the queen's finest, and it was made of great bright diamonds, hundreds of them, and they shone like all the stars on a night in June. So they asked her how she got it, as she and her mother were quite poor. But she laughed, and said they were not diamonds at all, but only white stones. And one day she went to the Court, and she wore on her head a crown of pure angel-gold, so nurse said, and it shone like the sun, and it was much more splendid than the crown the king was wearing himself, and in her ears she wore the emeralds, and the big ruby was the brooch on her breast, and the great diamond necklace was sparkling on her neck. And the king and queen thought she was some great princess from a long way off, and got down from their thrones and went to meet her, but somebody told the king and queen who she was, and that she was quite poor. So the king asked why she wore a gold crown, and how she got it, as she and her mother were so poor. And she laughed, and said it wasn't a gold crown at all, but only some yellow flowers she had put in her hair. And the king thought it was very strange, and said she should stay at the Court, and they would see what would happen next. And she was so lovely that everybody said that her eyes were greener than the emeralds, that her lips were redder than the ruby, that her skin was whiter than the diamonds, and that her hair was brighter than the golden crown. So the king's son said he would marry her, and the king said he might. And the bishop married them, and there was a great supper, and afterwards the king's son went to his wife's room. But just when he had his hand on the door, he saw a tall, black man, with a dreadful face, standing in front of the door, and a voice said—

Venture not upon your life,
This is mine own wedded wife.

Then the king's son fell down on the ground in a fit. And they came and tried to get into the room, but they couldn't, and they hacked at the door with hatchets, but the wood had turned hard as iron, and at last everybody ran away, they were so frightened at the screaming and laughing and shrieking and crying that came out of the room. But next day they went in, and found there was nothing in the room but thick black smoke, because the black man had come and taken her away. And on the bed there were two knots of faded grass and a red stone, and some white stones, and some faded yellow flowers. I remembered this tale of nurse's while I was standing at the bottom of the deep hollow; it was so strange and solitary there, and I felt afraid. I could not see any stones or flowers, but I was afraid of bringing them away without knowing, and I thought I would do a charm that came into my head to keep the black man away. So I stood right in the very middle of the hollow, and I made sure that I had none of those things on me, and then I walked round the place, and touched my eyes, and my lips, and my hair in a peculiar manner, and whispered some queer words that nurse taught me to keep bad things away. Then I felt safe and climbed up out of the hollow, and went on through all those mounds and hollows and walls, till I came to the end, which was high above all the rest, and I could see that all the different shapes of the earth were arranged in patterns, something like the grey rocks, only the pattern was different. It was getting late, and the air was indistinct, but it looked from where I was standing something like two great figures of people lying on the grass. And I went on, and at last I found a certain wood, which is too secret to be described, and nobody knows of the passage into it, which I found out in a very curious manner, by seeing some little animal run into the wood through it. So I went after the animal by a very narrow dark way, under thorns and bushes, and it was almost dark when I came to a kind of open place in the middle. And there I saw the most wonderful sight I have ever seen, but it was only for a minute, as I ran away directly, and crept out of the wood by the passage I had come by, and ran and ran as fast as ever I could, because I was afraid, what I had seen was so wonderful and so strange and beautiful. But I wanted to get home and think of it, and I did not know what might not happen if I stayed by the wood. I was hot all over and trembling, and my heart was beating, and strange cries that I could not help came from me as I ran from the wood. I was glad that a great white moon came up from over a round hill and showed me the way, so I went back through the mounds and hollows and down the close valley, and up through the thicket over the place of the grey rocks, and so at last I got home again. My father was busy in his study, and the servants had not told about my not coming home, though they were frightened, and wondered what they ought to do, so I told them I had lost my way, but I did not let them find out the real way I had been. I went to bed and lay awake all through the night, thinking of what I had seen. When I came out of the narrow way, and it looked all shining, though the air was dark, it seemed so certain, and all the way home I was quite sure that I had seen it, and I wanted to be alone in my room, and be glad over it all to myself, and shut my eyes and pretend it was there, and do all the things I would have done if I had not been so afraid. But when I shut my eyes the sight would not come, and I began to think about my adventures all over again, and I remembered how dusky and queer it was at the end, and I was afraid it must be all a mistake, because it seemed impossible it could happen. It seemed like one of nurse's tales, which I didn't really believe in, though I was frightened at the bottom of the hollow; and the stories she told me when I was little came back into my head, and I wondered whether it was really there what I thought I had seen, or whether any of her tales could have happened a long time ago. It was so queer; I lay awake there in my room at the back of the house, and the moon was shining on the other side towards the river, so the bright light did not fall upon the wall. And the house was quite still. I had heard my father come upstairs, and just after the clock struck twelve, and after the house was still and empty, as if there was nobody alive in it. And though it was all dark and indistinct in my room, a pale glimmering kind of light shone in through the white blind, and once I got up and looked out, and there was a great black shadow of the house covering the garden, looking like a prison where men are hanged; and then beyond it was all white; and the wood shone white with black gulfs between the trees. It was still and clear, and there were no clouds on the sky. I wanted to think of what I had seen but I couldn't, and I began to think of all the tales that nurse had told me so long ago that I thought I had forgotten, but they all came back, and mixed up with the thickets and the grey rocks and the hollows in the earth and the secret wood, till I hardly knew what was new and what was old, or whether it was not all dreaming. And then I remembered that hot summer afternoon, so long ago, when nurse left me by myself in the shade, and the white people came out of the water and out of the wood, and played, and danced, and sang, and I began to fancy that nurse told me about something like it before I saw them, only I couldn't recollect exactly what she told me. Then I wondered whether she had been the white lady, as I remembered she was just as white and beautiful, and had the same dark eyes and black hair; and sometimes she smiled and looked like the lady had looked, when she was telling me some of her stories, beginning with "Once on a time," or "In the time of the fairies." But I thought she couldn't be the lady, as she seemed to have gone a different way into the wood, and I didn't think the man who came after us could be the other, or I couldn't have seen that wonderful secret in the secret wood. I thought of the moon: but it was afterwards when I was in the middle of the wild land, where the earth was made into the shape of great figures, and it was all walls, and mysterious hollows, and smooth round mounds, that I saw the great white moon come up over a round hill. I was wondering about all these things, till at last I got quite frightened, because I was afraid something had happened to me, and I remembered nurse's tale of the poor girl who went into the hollow pit, and was carried away at last by the black man. I knew I had gone into a hollow pit too, and perhaps it was the same, and I had done something dreadful. So I did the charm over again, and touched my eyes and my lips and my hair in a peculiar manner, and said the old words from the fairy language, so that I might be sure I had not been carried away. I tried again to see the secret wood, and to creep up the passage and see what I had seen there, but somehow I couldn't, and I kept on thinking of nurse's stories. There was one I remembered about a young man who once upon a time went hunting, and all the day he and his hounds hunted everywhere, and they crossed the rivers and went into all the woods, and went round the marshes, but they couldn't find anything at all, and they hunted all day till the sun sank down and began to set behind the mountain. And the young man was angry because he couldn't find anything, and he was going to turn back, when just as the sun touched the mountain, he saw come out of a brake in front of him a beautiful white stag. And he cheered to his hounds, but they whined and would not follow, and he cheered to his horse, but it shivered and stood stock still, and the young man jumped off the horse and left the hounds and began to follow the white stag all alone. And soon it was quite dark, and the sky was black, without a single star shining in it, and the stag went away into the darkness. And though the man had brought his gun with him he never shot at the stag, because he wanted to catch it, and he was afraid he would lose it in the night. But he never lost it once, though the sky was so black and the air was so dark, and the stag went on and on till the young man didn't know a bit where he was. And they went through enormous woods where the air was full of whispers and a pale, dead light came out from the rotten trunks that were lying on the ground, and just as the man thought he had lost the stag, he would see it all white and shining in front of him, and he would run fast to catch it, but the stag always ran faster, so he did not catch it. And they went through the enormous woods, and they swam across rivers, and they waded through black marshes where the ground bubbled, and the air was full of will-o'-the-wisps, and the stag fled away down into rocky narrow valleys, where the air was like the smell of a vault, and the man went after it. And they went over the great mountains and the man heard the wind come down from the sky, and the stag went on and the man went after. At last the sun rose and the young man found he was in a country that he had never seen before; it was a beautiful valley with a bright stream running through it, and a great, big round hill in the middle. And the stag went down the valley, towards the hill, and it seemed to be getting tired and went slower and slower, and though the man was tired, too, he began to run faster, and he was sure he would catch the stag at last. But just as they got to the bottom of the hill, and the man stretched out his hand to catch the stag, it vanished into the earth, and the man began to cry; he was so sorry that he had lost it after all his long hunting. But as he was crying he saw there was a door in the hill, just in front of him, and he went in, and it was quite dark, but he went on, as he thought he would find the white stag. And all of a sudden it got light, and there was the sky, and the sun shining, and birds singing in the trees, and there was a beautiful fountain. And by the fountain a lovely lady was sitting, who was the queen of the fairies, and she told the man that she had changed herself into a stag to bring him there because she loved him so much. Then she brought out a great gold cup, covered with jewels, from her fairy palace, and she offered him wine in the cup to drink. And he drank, and the more he drank the more he longed to drink, because the wine was enchanted. So he kissed the lovely lady, and she became his wife, and he stayed all that day and all that night in the hill where she lived, and when he woke he found he was lying on the ground, close to where he had seen the stag first, and his horse was there and his hounds were there waiting, and he looked up, and the sun sank behind the mountain. And he went home and lived a long time, but he would never kiss any other lady because he had kissed the queen of the fairies, and he would never drink common wine any more, because he had drunk enchanted wine. And sometimes nurse told me tales that she had heard from her great-grandmother, who was very old, and lived in a cottage on the mountain all alone, and most of these tales were about a hill where people used to meet at night long ago, and they used to play all sorts of strange games and do queer things that nurse told me of, but I couldn't understand, and now, she said, everybody but her great-grandmother had forgotten all about it, and nobody knew where the hill was, not even her great-grandmother. But she told me one very strange story about the hill, and I trembled when I remembered it. She said that people always went there in summer, when it was very hot, and they had to dance a good deal. It would be all dark at first, and there were trees there, which made it much darker, and people would come, one by one, from all directions, by a secret path which nobody else knew, and two persons would keep the gate, and every one as they came up had to give a very curious sign, which nurse showed me as well as she could, but she said she couldn't show me properly. And all kinds of people would come; there would be gentle folks and village folks, and some old people and boys and girls, and quite small children, who sat and watched. And it would all be dark as they came in, except in one corner where some one was burning something that smelt strong and sweet, and made them laugh, and there one would see a glaring of coals, and the smoke mounting up red. So they would all come in, and when the last had come there was no door any more, so that no one else could get in, even if they knew there was anything beyond. And once a gentleman who was a stranger and had ridden a long way, lost his path at night, and his horse took him into the very middle of the wild country, where everything was upside down, and there were dreadful marshes and great stones everywhere, and holes underfoot, and the trees looked like gibbet-posts, because they had great black arms that stretched out across the way. And this strange gentleman was very frightened, and his horse began to shiver all over, and at last it stopped and wouldn't go any farther, and the gentleman got down and tried to lead the horse, but it wouldn't move, and it was all covered with a sweat, like death. So the gentleman went on all alone, going farther and farther into the wild country, till at last he came to a dark place, where he heard shouting and singing and crying, like nothing he had ever heard before. It all sounded quite close to him, but he couldn't get in, and so he began to call, and while he was calling, something came behind him, and in a minute his mouth and arms and legs were all bound up, and he fell into a swoon. And when he came to himself, he was lying by the roadside, just where he had first lost his way, under a blasted oak with a black trunk, and his horse was tied beside him. So he rode on to the town and told the people there what had happened, and some of them were amazed; but others knew. So when once everybody had come, there was no door at all for anybody else to pass in by. And when they were all inside, round in a ring, touching each other, some one began to sing in the darkness, and some one else would make a noise like thunder with a thing they had on purpose, and on still nights people would hear the thundering noise far, far away beyond the wild land, and some of them, who thought they knew what it was, used to make a sign on their breasts when they woke up in their beds at dead of night and heard that terrible deep noise, like thunder on the mountains. And the noise and the singing would go on and on for a long time, and the people who were in a ring swayed a little to and fro; and the song was in an old, old language that nobody knows now, and the tune was queer. Nurse said her great-grandmother had known some one who remembered a little of it, when she was quite a little girl, and nurse tried to sing some of it to me, and it was so strange a tune that I turned all cold and my flesh crept as if I had put my hand on something dead. Sometimes it was a man that sang and sometimes it was a woman, and sometimes the one who sang it did it so well that two or three of the people who were there fell to the ground shrieking and tearing with their hands. The singing went on, and the people in the ring kept swaying to and fro for a long time, and at last the moon would rise over a place they called the Tole Deol, and came up and showed them swinging and swaying from side to side, with the sweet thick smoke curling up from the burning coals, and floating in circles all around them. Then they had their supper. A boy and a girl brought it to them; the boy carried a great cup of wine, and the girl carried a cake of bread, and they passed the bread and the wine round and round, but they tasted quite different from common bread and common wine, and changed everybody that tasted them. Then they all rose up and danced, and secret things were brought out of some hiding place, and they played extraordinary games, and danced round and round and round in the moonlight, and sometimes people would suddenly disappear and never be heard of afterwards, and nobody knew what had happened to them. And they drank more of that curious wine, and they made images and worshipped them, and nurse showed me how the images were made one day when we were out for a walk, and we passed by a place where there was a lot of wet clay. So nurse asked me if I would like to know what those things were like that they made on the hill, and I said yes. Then she asked me if I would promise never to tell a living soul a word about it, and if I did I was to be thrown into the black pit with the dead people, and I said I wouldn't tell anybody, and she said the same thing again and again, and I promised. So she took my wooden spade and dug a big lump of clay and put it in my tin bucket, and told me to say if any one met us that I was going to make pies when I went home. Then we went on a little way till we came to a little brake growing right down into the road, and nurse stopped, and looked up the road and down it, and then peeped through the hedge into the field on the other side, and then she said, "Quick!" and we ran into the brake, and crept in and out among the bushes till we had gone a good way from the road. Then we sat down under a bush, and I wanted so much to know what nurse was going to make with the clay, but before she would begin she made me promise again not to say a word about it, and she went again and peeped through the bushes on every side, though the lane was so small and deep that hardly anybody ever went there. So we sat down, and nurse took the clay out of the bucket, and began to knead it with her hands, and do queer things with it, and turn it about. And she hid it under a big dock-leaf for a minute or two and then she brought it out again, and then she stood up and sat down, and walked round the clay in a peculiar manner, and all the time she was softly singing a sort of rhyme, and her face got very red. Then she sat down again, and took the clay in her hands and began to shape it into a doll, but not like the dolls I have at home, and she made the queerest doll I had ever seen, all out of the wet clay, and hid it under a bush to get dry and hard, and all the time she was making it she was singing these rhymes to herself, and her face got redder and redder. So we left the doll there, hidden away in the bushes where nobody would ever find it. And a few days later we went the same walk, and when we came to that narrow, dark part of the lane where the brake runs down to the bank, nurse made me promise all over again, and she looked about, just as she had done before, and we crept into the bushes till we got to the green place where the little clay man was hidden. I remember it all so well, though I was only eight, and it is eight years ago now as I am writing it down, but the sky was a deep violet blue, and in the middle of the brake where we were sitting there was a great elder tree covered with blossoms, and on the other side there was a clump of meadowsweet, and when I think of that day the smell of the meadowsweet and elder blossom seems to fill the room, and if I shut my eyes I can see the glaring blue sky, with little clouds very white floating across it, and nurse who went away long ago sitting opposite me and looking like the beautiful white lady in the wood. So we sat down and nurse took out the clay doll from the secret place where she had hidden it, and she said we must "pay our respects," and she would show me what to do, and I must watch her all the time. So she did all sorts of queer things with the little clay man, and I noticed she was all streaming with perspiration, though we had walked so slowly, and then she told me to "pay my respects," and I did everything she did because I liked her, and it was such an odd game. And she said that if one loved very much, the clay man was very good, if one did certain things with it, and if one hated very much, it was just as good, only one had to do different things, and we played with it a long time, and pretended all sorts of things. Nurse said her great-grandmother had told her all about these images, but what we did was no harm at all, only a game. But she told me a story about these images that frightened me very much, and that was what I remembered that night when I was lying awake in my room in the pale, empty darkness, thinking of what I had seen and the secret wood. Nurse said there was once a young lady of the high gentry, who lived in a great castle. And she was so beautiful that all the gentlemen wanted to marry her, because she was the loveliest lady that anybody had ever seen, and she was kind to everybody, and everybody thought she was very good. But though she was polite to all the gentlemen who wished to marry her, she put them off, and said she couldn't make up her mind, and she wasn't sure she wanted to marry anybody at all. And her father, who was a very great lord, was angry, though he was so fond of her, and he asked her why she wouldn't choose a bachelor out of all the handsome young men who came to the castle. But she only said she didn't love any of them very much, and she must wait, and if they pestered her, she said she would go and be a nun in a nunnery. So all the gentlemen said they would go away and wait for a year and a day, and when a year and a day were gone, they would come back again and ask her to say which one she would marry. So the day was appointed and they all went away; and the lady had promised that in a year and a day it would be her wedding day with one of them. But the truth was, that she was the queen of the people who danced on the hill on summer nights, and on the proper nights she would lock the door of her room, and she and her maid would steal out of the castle by a secret passage that only they knew of, and go away up to the hill in the wild land. And she knew more of the secret things than any one else, and more than any one knew before or after, because she would not tell anybody the most secret secrets. She knew how to do all the awful things, how to destroy young men, and how to put a curse on people, and other things that I could not understand. And her real name was the Lady Avelin, but the dancing people called her Cassap, which meant somebody very wise, in the old language. And she was whiter than any of them and taller, and her eyes shone in the dark like burning rubies; and she could sing songs that none of the others could sing, and when she sang they all fell down on their faces and worshipped her. And she could do what they called shib-show, which was a very wonderful enchantment. She would tell the great lord, her father, that she wanted to go into the woods to gather flowers, so he let her go, and she and her maid went into the woods where nobody came, and the maid would keep watch. Then the lady would lie down under the trees and begin to sing a particular song, and she stretched out her arms, and from every part of the wood great serpents would come, hissing and gliding in and out among the trees, and shooting out their forked tongues as they crawled up to the lady. And they all came to her, and twisted round her, round her body, and her arms, and her neck, till she was covered with writhing serpents, and there was only her head to be seen. And she whispered to them, and she sang to them, and they writhed round and round, faster and faster, till she told them to go. And they all went away directly, back to their holes, and on the lady's breast there would be a most curious, beautiful stone, shaped something like an egg, and coloured dark blue and yellow, and red, and green, marked like a serpent's scales. It was called a glame stone, and with it one could do all sorts of wonderful things, and nurse said her great-grandmother had seen a glame stone with her own eyes, and it was for all the world shiny and scaly like a snake. And the lady could do a lot of other things as well, but she was quite fixed that she would not be married. And there were a great many gentlemen who wanted to marry her, but there were five of them who were chief, and their names were Sir Simon, Sir John, Sir Oliver, Sir Richard, and Sir Rowland. All the others believed she spoke the truth, and that she would choose one of them to be her man when a year and a day was done; it was only Sir Simon, who was very crafty, who thought she was deceiving them all, and he vowed he would watch and try if he could find out anything. And though he was very wise he was very young, and he had a smooth, soft face like a girl's, and he pretended, as the rest did, that he would not come to the castle for a year and a day, and he said he was going away beyond the sea to foreign parts. But he really only went a very little way, and came back dressed like a servant girl, and so he got a place in the castle to wash the dishes. And he waited and watched, and he listened and said nothing, and he hid in dark places, and woke up at night and looked out, and he heard things and he saw things that he thought were very strange. And he was so sly that he told the girl that waited on the lady that he was really a young man, and that he had dressed up as a girl because he loved her so very much and wanted to be in the same house with her, and the girl was so pleased that she told him many things, and he was more than ever certain that the Lady Avelin was deceiving him and the others. And he was so clever, and told the servant so many lies, that one night he managed to hide in the Lady Avelin's room behind the curtains. And he stayed quite still and never moved, and at last the lady came. And she bent down under the bed, and raised up a stone, and there was a hollow place underneath, and out of it she took a waxen image, just like the clay one that I and nurse had made in the brake. And all the time her eyes were burning like rubies. And she took the little wax doll up in her arms and held it to her breast, and she whispered and she murmured, and she took it up and she laid it down again, and she held it high, and she held it low, and she laid it down again. And she said, "Happy is he that begat the bishop, that ordered the clerk, that married the man, that had the wife, that fashioned the hive, that harboured the bee, that gathered the wax that my own true love was made of." And she brought out of an aumbry a great golden bowl, and she brought out of a closet a great jar of wine, and she poured some of the wine into the bowl, and she laid her mannikin very gently in the wine, and washed it in the wine all over. Then she went to a cupboard and took a small round cake and laid it on the image's mouth, and then she bore it softly and covered it up. And Sir Simon, who was watching all the time, though he was terribly frightened, saw the lady bend down and stretch out her arms and whisper and sing, and then Sir Simon saw beside her a handsome young man, who kissed her on the lips. And they drank wine out of the golden bowl together, and they ate the cake together. But when the sun rose there was only the little wax doll, and the lady hid it again under the bed in the hollow place. So Sir Simon knew quite well what the lady was, and he waited and he watched, till the time she had said was nearly over, and in a week the year and a day would be done. And one night, when he was watching behind the curtains in her room, he saw her making more wax dolls. And she made five, and hid them away. And the next night she took one out, and held it up, and filled the golden bowl with water, and took the doll by the neck and held it under the water. Then she said—

Sir Dickon, Sir Dickon, your day is done,
You shall be drowned in the water wan.

And the next day news came to the castle that Sir Richard had been drowned at the ford. And at night she took another doll and tied a violet cord round its neck and hung it up on a nail. Then she said—

> Sir Rowland, your life has ended its span,
> High on a tree I see you hang.

And the next day news came to the castle that Sir Rowland had been hanged by robbers in the wood. And at night she took another doll, and drove her bodkin right into its heart. Then she said—

> Sir Noll, Sir Noll, so cease your life,
> Your heart is piercèd with the knife.

And the next day news came to the castle that Sir Oliver had fought in a tavern, and a stranger had stabbed him to the heart. And at night she took another doll, and held it to a fire of charcoal till it was melted. Then she said—

> Sir John, return, and turn to clay,
> In fire of fever you waste away.

And the next day news came to the castle that Sir John had died in a burning fever. So then Sir Simon went out of the castle and mounted his horse and rode away to the bishop and told him everything. And the bishop sent his men, and they took the Lady Avelin, and everything she had done was found out. So on the day after the year and a day, when she was to have been married, they carried her through the town in her smock, and they tied her to a great stake in the market-place, and burned her alive before the bishop with her wax image hung round her neck. And people said the wax man screamed in the burning of the flames. And I thought of this story again and again as I was lying awake in my bed, and I seemed to see the Lady Avelin in the market-place, with the yellow flames eating up her beautiful white body. And I thought of it so much that I seemed to get into the story myself, and I fancied I was the lady, and that they were coming to take me to be burnt with fire, with all the people in the town looking at me. And I wondered whether she cared, after all the strange things she had done, and whether it hurt very much to be burned at the stake. I tried again and again to forget nurse's stories, and to remember the secret I had seen that afternoon, and what was in the secret wood, but I could only see the dark and a glimmering in the dark, and then it went away, and I only saw myself running, and then a great moon came up white over a dark round hill. Then all the old stories came back again, and the queer rhymes that nurse used to sing to me; and there was one beginning "Halsy cumsy Helen musty," that she used to sing very softly when she wanted me to go to sleep. And I began to sing it to myself inside of my head, and I went to sleep.

The next morning I was very tired and sleepy, and could hardly do my lessons, and I was very glad when they were over and I had had my dinner, as I wanted to go out and be alone. It was a warm day, and I went to a nice turfy hill by the river, and sat down on my mother's old shawl that I had brought with me on purpose. The sky was grey, like the day before, but there was a kind of white gleam behind it, and from where I was sitting I could look down on the town, and it was all still and quiet and white, like a picture. I remembered that it was on that hill that nurse taught me to play an old game called "Troy Town," in which one had to dance, and wind in and out on a pattern in the grass, and then when one had danced and turned long enough the other person asks you questions, and you can't help answering whether you want to or not, and whatever you are told to do you feel you have to do it. Nurse said there used to be a lot of games like that that some people knew of, and there was one by which people could be turned into anything you liked, and an old man her great-grandmother had seen had known a girl who had been turned into a large snake. And there was another very ancient game of dancing and winding and turning, by which you could take a person out of himself and hide him away as long as you liked, and his body went walking about quite empty, without any sense in it. But I came to that hill because I wanted to think of what had happened the day before, and of the secret of the wood. From the place where I was sitting I could see beyond the town, into the opening I had found, where a little brook had led me into an unknown country. And I pretended I was following the brook over again, and I went all the way in my mind, and at last I found the wood, and crept into it under the bushes, and then in the dusk I saw something that made me feel as if I were filled with fire, as if I wanted to dance and sing and fly up into the air, because I was changed and wonderful. But what I saw was not changed at all, and had not grown old, and I wondered again and again how such things could happen, and whether nurse's stories were really true, because in the daytime in the open air everything seemed quite different from what it was at night, when I was frightened, and thought I was to be burned alive. I once told my father one of her little tales, which was about a ghost, and asked him if it was true, and he told me it was not true at all, and that only common, ignorant people believed in such rubbish. He was very angry with nurse for telling me the story, and scolded her, and after that I promised her I would never whisper a word of what she told me, and if I did I should be bitten by the great black snake that lived in the pool in the wood. And all alone on the hill I wondered what was true. I had seen something very amazing and very lovely, and I knew a story, and if I had really seen it, and not made it up out of the dark, and the black bough, and the bright shining that was mounting up to the sky from over the great round hill, but had really seen it in truth, then there were all kinds of wonderful and lovely and terrible things to think of, so I longed and trembled, and I burned and got cold. And I looked down on the town, so quiet and still, like a little white picture, and I thought over and over if it could be true. I was a long time before I could make up my mind to anything; there was such a strange fluttering at my heart that seemed to whisper to me all the time that I had not made it up out of my head, and yet it seemed quite impossible, and I knew my father and everybody would say it was dreadful rubbish. I never dreamed of telling him or anybody else a word about it, because I knew it would be of no use, and I should only get laughed at or scolded, so for a long time I was very quiet, and went about thinking and wondering; and at night I used to dream of amazing things, and sometimes I woke up in the early morning and held out my arms with a cry. And I was frightened, too, because there were dangers, and some awful thing would happen to me, unless I took great care, if the story were true. These old tales were always in my head, night and morning, and I went over them and told them to myself over and over again, and went for walks in the places where nurse had told them to me; and when I sat in the nursery by the fire in the evenings I used to fancy nurse was sitting in the other chair, and telling me some wonderful story in a low voice, for fear anybody should be listening. But she used to like best to tell me about things when we were right out in the country, far from the house, because she said she was telling me such secrets, and walls have ears. And if it was something more than ever secret, we had to hide in brakes or woods; and I used to think it was such fun creeping along a hedge, and going very softly, and then we would get behind the bushes or run into the wood all of a sudden, when we were sure that none was watching us; so we knew that we had our secrets quite all to ourselves, and nobody else at all knew anything about them. Now and then, when we had hidden ourselves as I have described, she used to show me all sorts of odd things. One day, I remember, we were in a hazel brake, overlooking the brook, and we were so snug and warm, as though it was April; the sun was quite hot, and the leaves were just coming out. Nurse said she would show me something funny that would make me laugh, and then she showed me, as she said, how one could turn a whole house upside down, without anybody being able to find out, and the pots and pans would jump about, and the china would be broken, and the chairs would tumble over of themselves. I tried it one day in the kitchen, and I found I could do it quite well, and a whole row of plates on the dresser fell off it, and cook's little work-table tilted up and turned right over "before her eyes," as she said, but she was so frightened and turned so white that I didn't do it again, as I liked her. And afterwards, in the hazel copse, when she had shown me how to make things tumble about, she showed me how to make rapping noises, and I learnt how to do that, too. Then she taught me rhymes to say on certain occasions, and peculiar marks to make on other occasions, and other things that her great-grandmother had taught her when she was a little girl herself. And these were all the things I was thinking about in those days after the strange walk when I thought I had seen a great secret, and I wished nurse were there for me to ask her about it, but she had gone away more than two years before, and nobody seemed to know what had become of her, or where she had gone. But I shall always remember those days if I live to be quite old, because all the time I felt so strange, wondering and doubting, and feeling quite sure at one time, and making up my mind, and then I would feel quite sure that such things couldn't happen really, and it began all over again. But I took great care not to do certain things that might be very dangerous. So I waited and wondered for a long time, and though I was not sure at all, I never dared to try to find out. But one day I became sure that all that nurse said was quite true, and I was all alone when I found it out. I trembled all over with joy and terror, and as fast as I could I ran into one of the old brakes where we used to go—it was the one by the lane, where nurse made the little clay man—and I ran into it, and I crept into it; and when I came to the place where the elder was, I covered up my face with my hands and lay down flat on the grass, and I stayed there for two hours without moving, whispering to myself delicious, terrible things, and saying some words over and over again. It was all true and wonderful and splendid, and when I remembered the story I knew and thought of what I had really seen, I got hot and I got cold, and the air seemed full of scent, and flowers, and singing. And first I wanted to make a little clay man, like the one nurse had made so long ago, and I had to invent plans and stratagems, and to look about, and to think of things beforehand, because nobody must dream of anything that I was doing or going to do, and I was too old to carry clay about in a tin bucket. At last I thought of a plan, and I brought the wet clay to the brake, and did everything that nurse had done, only I made a much finer image than the one she had made; and when it was finished I did everything that I could imagine and much more than she did, because it was the likeness of something far better. And a few days later, when I had done my lessons early, I went for the second time by the way of the little brook that had led me into a strange country. And I followed the brook, and went through the bushes, and beneath the low branches of trees, and up thorny thickets on the hill, and by dark woods full of creeping thorns, a long, long way. Then I crept through the dark tunnel where the brook had been and the ground was stony, till at last I came to the thicket that climbed up the hill, and though the leaves were coming out upon the trees, everything looked almost as black as it was on the first day that I went there. And the thicket was just the same, and I went up slowly till I came out on the big bare hill, and began to walk among the wonderful rocks. I saw the terrible voor again on everything, for though the sky was brighter, the ring of wild hills all around was still dark, and the hanging woods looked dark and dreadful, and the strange rocks were as grey as ever; and when I looked down on them from the great mound, sitting on the stone, I saw all their amazing circles and rounds within rounds, and I had to sit quite still and watch them as they began to turn about me, and each stone danced in its place, and they seemed to go round and round in a great whirl, as if one were in the middle of all the stars and heard them rushing through the air. So I went down among the rocks to dance with them and to sing extraordinary songs; and I went down through the other thicket, and drank from the bright stream in the close and secret valley, putting my lips down to the bubbling water; and then I went on till I came to the deep, brimming well among the glittering moss, and I sat down. I looked before me into the secret darkness of the valley, and behind me was the great high wall of grass, and all around me there were the hanging woods that made the valley such a secret place. I knew there was nobody here at all besides myself, and that no one could see me. So I took off my boots and stockings, and let my feet down into the water, saying the words that I knew. And it was not cold at all, as I expected, but warm and very pleasant, and when my feet were in it I felt as if they were in silk, or as if the nymph were kissing them. So when I had done, I said the other words and made the signs, and then I dried my feet with a towel I had brought on purpose, and put on my stockings and boots. Then I climbed up the steep wall, and went into the place where there are the hollows, and the two beautiful mounds, and the round ridges of land, and all the strange shapes. I did not go down into the hollow this time, but I turned at the end, and made out the figures quite plainly, as it was lighter, and I had remembered the story I had quite forgotten before, and in the story the two figures are called Adam and Eve, and only those who know the story understand what they mean. So I went on and on till I came to the secret wood which must not be described, and I crept into it by the way I had found. And when I had gone about halfway I stopped, and turned round, and got ready, and I bound the handkerchief tightly round my eyes, and made quite sure that I could not see at all, not a twig, nor the end of a leaf, nor the light of the sky, as it was an old red silk handkerchief with large yellow spots, that went round twice and covered my eyes, so that I could see nothing. Then I began to go on, step by step, very slowly. My heart beat faster and faster, and something rose in my throat that choked me and made me want to cry out, but I shut my lips, and went on. Boughs caught in my hair as I went, and great thorns tore me; but

I went on to the end of the path. Then I stopped, and held out my arms and bowed, and I went round the first time, feeling with my hands, and there was nothing. I went round the second time, feeling with my hands, and there was nothing. Then I went round the third time, feeling with my hands, and the story was all true, and I wished that the years were gone by, and that I had not so long a time to wait before I was happy for ever and ever.

Nurse must have been a prophet like those we read of in the Bible. Everything that she said began to come true, and since then other things that she told me of have happened. That was how I came to know that her stories were true and that I had not made up the secret myself out of my own head. But there was another thing that happened that day. I went a second time to the secret place. It was at the deep brimming well, and when I was standing on the moss I bent over and looked in, and then I knew who the white lady was that I had seen come out of the water in the wood long ago when I was quite little. And I trembled all over, because that told me other things. Then I remembered how sometime after I had seen the white people in the wood, nurse asked me more about them, and I told her all over again, and she listened, and said nothing for a long, long time, and at last she said, "You will see her again." So I understood what had happened and what was to happen. And I understood about the nymphs; how I might meet them in all kinds of places, and they would always help me, and I must always look for them, and find them in all sorts of strange shapes and appearances. And without the nymphs I could never have found the secret, and without them none of the other things could happen. Nurse had told me all about them long ago, but she called them by another name, and I did not know what she meant, or what her tales of them were about, only that they were very queer. And there were two kinds, the bright and the dark, and both were very lovely and very wonderful, and some people saw only one kind, and some only the other, but some saw them both. But usually the dark appeared first, and the bright ones came afterwards, and there were extraordinary tales about them. It was a day or two after I had come home from the secret place that I first really knew the nymphs. Nurse had shown me how to call them, and I had tried, but I did not know what she meant, and so I thought it was all nonsense. But I made up my mind I would try again, so I went to the wood where the pool was, where I saw the white people, and I tried again. The dark nymph, Alanna, came, and she turned the pool of water into a pool of fire. . . .

Epilogue

"That's a very queer story," said Cotgrave, handing back the green book to the recluse, Ambrose. "I see the drift of a good deal, but there are many things that I do not grasp at all. On the last page, for example, what does she mean by 'nymphs'?"

"Well, I think there are references throughout the manuscript to certain 'processes' which have been handed down by tradition from age to age. Some of these processes are just beginning to come within the purview of science, which has arrived at them—or rather at the steps which lead to them—by quite different paths. I have interpreted the reference to 'nymphs' as a reference to one of these processes."

"And you believe that there are such things?"

"Oh, I think so. Yes, I believe I could give you convincing evidence on that point. I am afraid you have neglected the study of alchemy? It is a pity, for the symbolism, at all events, is very beautiful, and moreover if you were acquainted with certain books on the subject, I could recall to your mind phrases which might explain a good deal in the manuscript that you have been reading."

"Yes; but I want to know whether you seriously think that there is any foundation of fact beneath these fancies. Is it not all a department of poetry; a curious dream with which man has indulged himself?"

"I can only say that it is no doubt better for the great mass of people to dismiss it all as a dream. But if you ask my veritable belief—that goes quite the other way. No; I should not say belief, but rather knowledge. I may tell you that I have known cases in which men have stumbled quite by accident on certain of these 'processes,' and have been astonished by wholly unexpected results. In the cases I am thinking of there could have been no possibility of 'suggestion' or sub-conscious action of any kind. One might as well suppose a schoolboy 'suggesting' the existence of Æschylus to himself, while he plods mechanically through the declensions.

"But you have noticed the obscurity," Ambrose went on, "and in this particular case it must have been dictated by instinct, since the writer never thought that her manuscripts would fall into other hands. But the practice is universal, and for most excellent reasons. Powerful and sovereign medicines, which are, of necessity, virulent poisons also, are kept in a locked cabinet. The child may find the key by chance, and drink herself dead; but in most cases the search is educational, and the phials contain precious elixirs for him who has patiently fashioned the key for himself."

"You do not care to go into details?"

"No, frankly, I do not. No, you must remain unconvinced. But you saw how the manuscript illustrates the talk we had last week?"

"Is this girl still alive?"

"No. I was one of those who found her. I knew the father well; he was a lawyer, and had always left her very much to herself. He thought of nothing but deeds and leases, and the news came to him as an awful surprise. She was missing one morning; I suppose it was about a year after she had written what you have read. The servants were called, and they told things, and put the only natural interpretation on them—a perfectly erroneous one.

"They discovered that green book somewhere in her room, and I found her in the place that she described with so much dread, lying on the ground before the image."

"It was an image?"

"Yes, it was hidden by the thorns and the thick undergrowth that had surrounded it. It was a wild, lonely country; but you know what it was like by her description, though of course you will understand that the colours have been heightened. A child's imagination always makes the heights higher and the depths deeper than they really are; and she had, unfortunately for herself, something more than imagination. One might say, perhaps, that the picture in her mind which she succeeded in a measure in putting into words, was the scene as it would have appeared to an imaginative artist. But it is a strange, desolate land."

"And she was dead?"

"Yes. She had poisoned herself—in time. No; there was not a word to be said against her in the ordinary sense. You may recollect a story I told you the other night about a lady who saw her child's fingers crushed by a window?"

"And what was this statue?"

"Well, it was of Roman workmanship, of a stone that with the centuries had not blackened, but had become white and luminous. The thicket had grown up about it and concealed it, and in the Middle Ages the followers of a very old tradition had known how to use it for their own purposes. In fact it had been incorporated into the monstrous mythology of the Sabbath. You will have noted that those to whom a sight of that shining whiteness had been vouchsafed by chance, or rather, perhaps, by apparent chance, were required to blindfold themselves on their second approach. That is very significant."

"And is it there still?"

"I sent for tools, and we hammered it into dust and fragments."

"The persistence of tradition never surprises me," Ambrose went on after a pause. "I could name many an English parish where such traditions as that girl had listened to in her childhood are still existent in occult but unabated vigour. No, for me, it is the 'story,' not the 'sequel,' which is strange and awful, for I have always believed that wonder is of the soul." ❋

A Fragment of Life

I

EDWARD Darnell awoke from a dream of an ancient wood, and of a clear well rising into grey film and vapour beneath a misty, glimmering heat; and as his eyes opened he saw the sunlight bright in the room, sparkling on the varnish of the new furniture. He turned and found his wife's place vacant, and with some confusion and wonder of the dream still lingering in his mind, he rose also, and began hurriedly to set about his dressing, for he had overslept a little, and the 'bus passed the corner at 9.15. He was a tall, thin man, dark-haired and dark-eyed, and in spite of the routine of the City, the counting of coupons, and all the mechanical drudgery that had lasted for ten years, there still remained about him the curious hint of a wild grace, as if he had been born a creature of the antique wood, and had seen the fountain rising from the green moss and the grey rocks.

The breakfast was laid in the room on the ground floor, the back room with the French windows looking on the garden, and before he sat down to his fried bacon he kissed his wife seriously and dutifully. She had brown hair and brown eyes, and though her lovely face was grave and quiet, one would have said that she might have awaited her husband under the old trees, and bathed in the pool hollowed out of the rocks.

They had a good deal to talk over while the coffee was poured out and the bacon eaten, and Darnell's egg brought in by the stupid, staring servant-girt of the dusty face. They had been married for a year, and they had got on excellently, rarely sitting silent for more than an hour, but for the past few weeks Aunt Marian's present had afforded a subject for conversation which seemed inexhaustible. Mrs. Darnell had been Miss Mary Reynolds, the daughter of an auctioneer and estate agent in Notting Hill, and Aunt Marian was her mother's sister, who was supposed rather to have lowered herself by marrying a coal merchant, in a small way, at Turnham Green. Marian had felt the family attitude a good deal, and the Reynoldses were sorry for many things that had been said, when the coal merchant saved money and took up land on building leases in the neighbourhood of Crouch End, greatly to his advantage, as it appeared. Nobody had thought that Nixon could ever do very much; but he and his wife had been living for years in a beautiful house at Barnet, with bow-windows, shrubs, and a paddock, and the two families saw but little of each other, for Mr. Reynolds was not very prosperous. Of course, Aunt Marian and her husband had been asked to Mary's wedding, but they had sent excuses with a nice little set of silver apostle spoons, and it was feared that nothing more was to be looked for. However, on Mary's birthday her aunt had written a most affectionate letter, enclosing a cheque for a hundred pounds from 'Robert' and herself, and ever since the receipt of the money the Darnells had discussed the question of its judicious disposal. Mrs. Darnell had wished to invest the whole sum in Government securities, but Mr. Darnell had pointed out that the rate of interest was absurdly low, and after a good deal of talk he had persuaded his wife to put ninety pounds of the money in a safe mine, which was paying five per cent. This was very well, but the remaining ten pounds, which Mrs. Darnell had insisted on reserving, gave rise to legends and discourses as interminable as the disputes of the schools.

At first Mr. Darnell had proposed that they should furnish the "spare" room. There were four bedrooms in the house: their own room, the small one for the servant, and two others overlooking the garden, one of which had been used for storing boxes, ends of rope, and odd numbers of *Quiet Days* and *Sunday Evenings,* besides some worn suits belonging to Mr. Darnell which had been carefully wrapped up and laid by, as he scarcely knew what to do with them. The other room was frankly waste and vacant, and one Saturday afternoon, as he was coming home in the 'bus, and while he revolved that difficult question of the ten pounds, the unseemly emptiness of the spare room suddenly came into his mind, and he glowed with the idea that now, thanks to Aunt Marian, it could be furnished. He was busied with this delightful thought all the way home, but when he let himself in, he said nothing to his wife, since he felt that his idea must be matured. He told Mrs. Darnell that, having important business, he was obliged to go out again directly, but that he should be back without fail for tea at half-past six; and Mary, on her side, was not sorry to be alone, as she was a little behind-hand with the household books. The fact was, that Darnell, full of the design of furnishing the spare bedroom, wished to consult his friend Wilson, who lived at Fulham, and had often given him judicious advice as to the laying out of money to the very best advantage. Wilson was connected with the Bordeaux wine trade, and Darnell's only anxiety was lest he should not be at home.

However, it was all right; Darnell took a tram along the Goldhawk Road, and walked the rest of the way, and was delighted to see Wilson in the front garden of his house, busy amongst his flower-beds.

"Haven't seen you for an age," he said cheerily, when he heard Darnell's hand on the gate; "come in. Oh, I forgot," he added, as Darnell still fumbled with the handle, and vainly attempted to enter. "Of course you can't get in; I haven't shown it you."

It was a hot day in June, and Wilson appeared in a costume which he had put on in haste as soon as he arrived from the City. He wore a straw hat with a neat pugaree protecting the back of his neck, and his dress was a Norfolk jacket and knickers in heather mixture.

"See," he said, as he let Darnell in; "see the dodge. You don't *turn* the handle at all. First of all push hard, and then pull. It's a trick of my own, and I shall have it patented. You see, it keeps undesirable characters at a distance—such a great thing in the suburbs. I feel I can leave Mrs. Wilson alone now; and, formerly, you have no idea how she used to be pestered."

"But how about visitors?" said Darnell. "How do they get in?"

"Oh, we put them up to it. Besides," he said vaguely, "there is sure to be somebody looking out. Mrs. Wilson is nearly always at the window. She's out now; gone to call on some friends. The Bennetts' At Home day, I think it is. This is the first Saturday, isn't it? You know J. W. Bennett, don't you? Ah, he's in the House; doing very well, I believe. He put me on to a very good thing the other day."

"But, I say," said Wilson, as they turned and strolled towards the front door, "what do you wear those black things for? You took hot. Look at me. Well, I've been gardening, you know, but I feel as cool as a cucumber. I dare say you don't know where to get these things? Very few men do. Where do you suppose I got 'em?"

"In the West End, I suppose," said Darnell, wishing to be polite.

"Yes, that's what everybody says. And it is a good cut. Well, I'll tell you, but you needn't pass it on to everybody. I got the tip from Jameson—you know him, 'Jim-jams,' in the China trade, 39 Eastbrook—and he said he didn't want everybody in the City to know about it. But just go to Jennings, in Old Wall, and mention my name, and you'll be all right. And what d'you think they cost?"

"I haven't a notion," said Darnell, who had never bought such a suit in his life.

"Well, have a guess."

Darnell regarded Wilson gravely.

The jacket hung about his body like a sack, the knickerbockers drooped lamentably over his calves, and in prominent positions the bloom of the heather seemed about to fade and disappear.

"Three pounds, I suppose, at least," he said at length.

"Well, I asked Dench, in our place, the other day, and he guessed four ten, and his father's got something to do with a big business in Conduit Street. But I only gave thirty-five and six. To measure? Of course; look at the cut, man."

Darnell was astonished at so low a price.

"And, by the way," Wilson went on, pointing to his new brown boots, "you know where to go for shoe-leather? Oh, I thought everybody was up to that! There's only one place. 'Mr. Bill,' in Gunning Street,—nine and six."

They were walking round and round the garden, and Wilson pointed out the flowers in the beds and borders. There were hardly any blossoms, but everything was neatly arranged.

"Here are the tuberous-rooted Glasgownias," he said, showing a rigid row of stunted plants; "those are Squintaceæ; this is a new introduction, Moldavia Semperflorida Andersonii; and this is Prattsia."

"When do they come out?" said Darnell.

"Most of them in the end of August or beginning of September," said Wilson briefly. He was slightly annoyed with himself for having talked so much about his plants, since he saw that Darnell cared nothing for flowers; and, indeed, the visitor could hardly dissemble vague recollections that came to him; thoughts of an old, wild garden, full of odours, beneath grey walls, of the fragrance of the meadowsweet beside the brook.

"I wanted to consult you about some furniture," Darnell said at last. "You know we've got a spare room, and I'm thinking of putting a few things into it. I haven't exactly made up my mind, but I thought you might advise me."

"Come into my den," said Wilson. "No; this way, by the back"; and he showed Darnell another ingenious arrangement at the side door whereby a violent high-toned bell was set pealing in the house if one did but touch the latch. Indeed, Wilson handled it so briskly that the bell rang a wild alarm, and the servant, who was trying on her mistress's things in the bedroom, jumped madly to the window and then danced a hysteric dance. There was plaster found on the drawing-room table on Sunday afternoon, and Wilson wrote a letter to the *Fulham Chronicle,* ascribing the phenomenon to "some disturbance of a seismic nature."

For the moment he knew nothing of the great results of his contrivance, and solemnly led the way towards the back of the house. Here there was a patch of turf, beginning to took a little brown, with a background of shrubs. In the middle of the turf, a boy of nine or ten was standing all alone, with something of an air.

"The eldest," said Wilson. "Havelock. Well, Lockie, what are ye doing now? And where are your brother and sister?"

The boy was not at all shy. Indeed, he seemed eager to explain the course of events.

"I'm playing at being Gawd," he said, with an engaging frankness. "And I've sent Fergus and Janet to the bad place. That's in the shrubbery. And they're never to come out any more. And they're burning for ever and ever."

"What d'you think of that?" said Wilson admiringly. "Not bad for a youngster of nine, is it? They think a lot of him at the Sunday-school. But come into my den."

The den was an apartment projecting from the back of the house. It had been designed as a back kitchen and washhouse, but Wilson had draped the "copper" in art muslin and had boarded over the sink, so that it served as a workman's bench.

"Snug, isn't it?" he said, as he pushed forward one of the two wicker chairs. "I think out things here, you know; it's quiet. And what about this furnishing? Do you want to do the thing on a grand scale?"

"Oh, not at all. Quite the reverse. In fact, I don't know whether the sum at our disposal will be sufficient. You see the spare room is ten feet by twelve, with a western exposure, and I thought if we *could* manage it, that it would seem more cheerful furnished. Besides, it's pleasant to be able to ask a visitor; our aunt, Mrs. Nixon, for example. But she is accustomed to have everything very nice."

"And how much do you want to spend?"

"Well, I hardly think we should be justified in going much beyond ten pounds. That isn't enough, eh?"

Wilson got up and shut the door of the back kitchen impressively.

"Look here," he said, "I'm glad you came to me in the first place. Now you'll just tell me where you thought of going yourself."

"Well, I had thought of the Hampstead Road," said Darnell in a hesitating manner.

"I just thought you'd say that. But I'll ask you, what is the good of going to those expensive shops in the West End? You don't get a better article for your money. You're merely paying for fashion."

"I've seen some nice things in Samuel's, though. They get a brilliant polish on their goods in those superior shops. We went there when we were married."

"Exactly, and paid ten per cent more than you need have paid. It's throwing money away. And how much did you say you had to spend? Ten pounds. Well, I can tell you where to get a beautiful bedroom suite, in the very highest finish, for six pound ten. What d'you think of that? China included, mind you; and a square of carpet, brilliant colours, will only cost you fifteen and six. Look here, go any Saturday afternoon to Dick's, in the Seven Sisters Road, mention my name, and ask for Mr. Johnston. The suite's in ash, 'Elizabethan' they call it. Six pound ten, including the china, with one of their 'Orient' carpets, nine by nine, for fifteen and six. Dick's."

Wilson spoke with some eloquence on the subject of furnishing. He pointed out that the times were changed, and that the old heavy style was quite out of date.

"You know," he said, "it isn't like it was in the old days, when people used to buy things to last hundreds of years. Why, just before the wife and I were married, an uncle of mine died up in the North and left me his furniture. I was thinking of furnishing at the time, and I thought the things might come in handy; but I assure you there wasn't a single article that I cared to give house-room to. All dingy, old mahogany; big bookcases and bureaus, and claw-legged chairs and tables. As I said to the wife (as she was soon afterwards), 'We don't exactly want to set up a chamber of horrors, do we?' So I sold off the lot for what I could get. I must confess I like a cheerful room."

Darnell said he had heard that artists liked the old-fashioned furniture.

"Oh, I dare say. The 'unclean cult of the sunflower,' eh? You saw that piece in the *Daily Post?* I hate all that rot myself. It isn't healthy, you know, and I don't believe the English people will stand it. But talking of curiosities, I've got something here that's worth a bit of money."

He dived into some dusty receptacle in a corner of the room, and showed Darnell a small, worm-eaten Bible, wanting the first five chapters of Genesis and the last leaf of the Apocalypse. It bore the date of 1753.

"It's my belief that's worth a lot," said Wilson. "Look at the worm-holes. And you see it's 'imperfect,' as they call it. You've noticed that some of the most valuable books are 'imperfect' at the sales?"

The interview came to an end soon after, and Darnell went home to his tea. He thought seriously of taking Wilson's advice, and after tea he told Mary of his idea and of what Wilson had said about Dick's.

Mary was a good deal taken by the plan when she had heard all the details. The prices struck her as very moderate. They were sitting one on each side of the grate (which was concealed by a pretty card-board screen, painted with landscapes), and she rested her cheek on her hand, and her beautiful dark eyes seemed to dream and behold strange visions. In reality she was thinking of Darnell's plan.

"It would be very nice in some ways," she said at last. "But we must talk it over. What I am afraid of is that it will come to much more than ten pounds in the long run. There are so many things to be considered. There's the bed. It would look shabby if we got a common bed without brass mounts. Then the bedding, the mattress, and blankets, and sheets, and counterpane would all cost something."

She dreamed again, calculating the cost of all the necessaries, and Darnell stared anxiously; reckoning with her, and wondering what her conclusion would be. For a moment the delicate colouring of her face, the grace of her form, and the brown hair, drooping over her ears and clustering in little curls about her neck, seemed to hint at a language which he had not yet learned; but she spoke again.

"The bedding would come to a great deal, I am afraid. Even if Dick's are considerably cheaper than Boon's or Samuel's. And, my dear, we must have some ornaments on the mantelpiece. I saw some very nice vases at eleven-three the other day at Wilkin and Dodd's. We should want six at least, and there ought to be a centre-piece. You see how it mounts up."

Darnell was silent. He saw that his wife was summing up against his scheme, and though he had set his heart on it, he could not resist her arguments.

"It would be nearer twelve pounds than ten," she said. "The floor would have to be stained round the carpet (nine by nine, you said?), and we should want a piece of linoleum to go under the washstand. And the walls would look very bare without any pictures."

"I thought about the pictures," said Darnell; and he spoke quite eagerly. He felt that here, at least, he was unassailable. "You know there's the *Derby Day* and the *Railway Station,* ready framed, standing in the corner of the box-room already. They're a bit old-fashioned, perhaps, but that doesn't matter in a bedroom. And couldn't we use some photographs? I saw a very neat frame in natural oak in the City, to hold half a dozen, for one and six. We might put in your father, and your brother James, and Aunt Marian, and your grandmother, in her widow's cap—and any of the others in the album. And then there's that old family picture in the hair-trunk—that might do over the mantelpiece."

"You mean your great-grandfather in the gilt frame? But that's *very* old-fashioned, isn't it? He looks so queer in his wig. I don't think it would quite go with the room, somehow."

Darnell thought a moment. The portrait was a "kit-cat" of a young gentleman, bravely dressed in the fashion of 1750, and he very faintly remembered some old tales that his father had told him about this ancestor—tales of the woods and fields, of the deep sunken lanes, and the forgotten country in the west.

"No," he said, "I suppose it is rather out of date. But I saw some very nice prints in the City, framed and quite cheap."

"Yes, but everything counts. Well, we will talk it over, as you say. You know we must be careful."

The servant came in with the supper, a tin of biscuits, a glass of milk for the mistress, and a modest pint of beer for the master, with a little cheese and butter. Afterwards Edward smoked two pipes of honeydew, and they went quietly to bed; Mary going first, and her husband following a quarter of an hour later, according to the ritual established from the first days of their marriage. Front and back doors were locked, the gas was turned off at the meter, and when Darnell got upstairs he found his wife already in bed, her face turned round on the pillow.

She spoke softly to him as he came into the room.

"It would be impossible to buy a presentable bed at anything under one pound eleven, and good sheets are dear, anywhere."

He slipped off his clothes and slid gently into bed, putting out the candle on the table. The blinds were all evenly and duly drawn, but it was a June night, and beyond the walls, beyond that desolate world and wilderness of grey Shepherd's Bush, a great golden moon had floated up through magic films of cloud, above the hill, and the earth was filled with a wonderful light between red sunset lingering over the mountain and that marvellous glory that shone into the woods from the summit of the hill. Darnell seemed to see some reflection of that wizard brightness in the room; the pale walls and the white bed and his wife's face lying amidst brown hair upon the pillow were illuminated, and listening he could almost hear the corn-crake in the fields, the fern-owl sounding his strange note from the quiet of the rugged place where the bracken grew, and, like the echo of a magic song, the melody of the nightingale that sang all night in the alder by the little brook. There was nothing that he could say, but he slowly stole his arm under his wife's neck, and played with the ringlets of brown hair. She never moved, she lay there gently breathing, looking up to the blank ceiling of the room with her beautiful eyes, thinking also, no doubt, thoughts that she could not utter, kissing her husband obediently when he asked her to do so, and he stammered and hesitated as he spoke.

They were nearly asleep, indeed Darnell was on the very eve of dreaming, when she said very softly—

"I am afraid, darling, that we could never afford it." And he heard her words through the murmur of the water, dripping from the grey rock, and falling into the clear pool beneath.

Sunday morning was always an occasion of idleness. Indeed, they would never have got breakfast if Mrs. Darnell, who had the instincts of the housewife, had not awoke and seen the bright sunshine, and felt that the house was too still. She lay quiet for five minutes, while her husband slept beside her, and listened intently, waiting for the sound of Alice stirring down below. A golden tube of sunlight shone through some opening in the Venetian blinds, and it shone on the brown hair that lay about her head on the pillow, and she looked steadily into the room at the "duchesse" toilet-table, the coloured ware of the washstand, and the two photogravures in oak frames, *The Meeting* and *The Parting,* that hung upon the wall. She was half dreaming as she listened for the servant's footsteps, and the faint shadow of a shade of a thought came over her, and she imagined dimly, for the quick moment of a dream, another world where rapture was wine, where one wandered in a deep and happy valley, and the moon was always rising red above the trees. She was thinking of Hampstead, which represented to her the vision of the world beyond the walls, and the thought of the heath led her away to Bank Holidays, and then to Alice. There was not a sound in the house; it might have been midnight for the stillness if the drawling cry of the Sunday paper had not suddenly echoed round the corner of Edna Road, and with it came the warning clank and shriek of the milkman with his pails.

Mrs. Darnell sat up, and wide awake, listened more intently. The girl was evidently fast asleep, and must be roused, or all the work of the day would be out of joint, and she remembered how Edward hated any fuss or discussion about household matters, more especially on a Sunday, after his long week's work in the City. She gave her husband an affectionate glance as he slept on, for she was very fond of him, and so she gently rose from the bed and went in her nightgown to call the maid.

The servant's room was small and stuffy, the night had been very hot, and Mrs. Darnell paused for a moment at the door, wondering whether the girl on the bed was really the dusty-faced servant who bustled day by day about the house, or even the strangely bedizened creature, dressed in purple, with a shiny face, who would appear on the Sunday afternoon, bringing in an early tea, because it was her "evening out." Alice's hair was black and her skin was pale, almost of the olive tinge, and she lay asleep, her head resting on one arm, reminding Mrs. Darnell of a queer print of a *Tired Bacchante* that she had seen long ago in a shop window in Upper Street, Islington. And a cracked bell was ringing; that meant five minutes to eight, and nothing done.

She touched the girl gently on the shoulder, and only smiled when her eyes opened, and waking with a start, she got up in sudden confusion. Mrs. Darnell went back to her room and dressed slowly while her husband still slept, and it was only at the last moment, as she fastened her cherry-coloured bodice, that she roused him, telling him that the bacon would be overdone unless he hurried over his dressing.

Over the breakfast they discussed the question of the spare room all over again. Mrs. Darnell still admitted that the plan of furnishing it attracted her, but she could not see how it could be done for the ten pounds, and as they were prudent people they did not care to encroach on their savings. Edward was highly paid, having (with allowances for extra work in busy weeks) a hundred and forty pounds a year, and Mary had inherited from an old uncle, her godfather, three hundred pounds, which had been judiciously laid out in mortgage at $4^1/_2$ per cent. Their total income, then, counting in Aunt Marian's present, was a hundred and fifty-eight pounds a year, and they were clear of debt, since Darnell had bought the furniture for the house out of money which he had saved for five or six years before. In the first few years of his life in the City his income had, of course, been smaller, and at first he had lived very freely, without a thought of laying by. The theatres and music-halls had attracted him, and scarcely a week passed without his going (in the pit) to one or the other; and he had occasionally bought photographs of actresses who pleased him. These he had solemnly burnt when he became engaged to Mary; he remembered the evening well; his heart had been so full of joy and wonder, and the landlady had complained bitterly of the mess in the grate when he came home from the City the next night. Still, the money was lost, as far as he could recollect, ten or twelve shillings; and it annoyed him all the more to reflect that if he had put it by, it would have gone far towards the purchase of an "Orient" carpet in brilliant colours. Then there had been other expenses of his youth: he had purchased threepenny and even fourpenny cigars, the latter rarely, but the former frequently, sometimes singly, and sometimes in bundles of twelve for half-a-crown. Once a meerschaum pipe had haunted him for six weeks; the tobacconist had drawn it out of a drawer with some air of secrecy as he was buying a packet of "Lone Star." Here was another useless expense, these American-manufactured tobaccos; his "Lone Star," "Long Judge," "Old Hank, "Sultry Clime," and the rest of them cost from a shilling to one and six the two-ounce packet; whereas now he got excellent loose honeydew for threepence halfpenny an ounce. But the crafty tradesman, who had marked him down as a buyer of expensive fancy goods, nodded with his air of mystery, and, snapping open the case, displayed the meerschaum before the dazzled eyes of Darnell. The bowl was carved in the likeness of a female figure, showing the head and *torso,* and the mouthpiece was of the very best amber—only twelve and six, the man said, and the amber alone, he declared, was worth more than that. He explained that he felt some delicacy about showing the pipe to any but a regular customer, and was willing to take a little under cost price and "cut the loss." Darnell resisted for the time, but the pipe troubled him, and at last he bought it. He was pleased to show it to the younger men in the office for a while, but it never smoked very well, and he gave it away just before his marriage, as from the nature of the carving it would have been impossible to use it in his wife's presence. Once, while he was taking his holidays at Hastings, he had purchased a malacca cane—a useless thing that had cost seven shillings—and he reflected with sorrow on the innumerable evenings on which he had rejected his landlady's plain fried chop, and had gone out to *flaner* among the Italian restaurants in Upper Street, Islington (he lodged in Holloway), pampering himself with expensive delicacies: cutlets and green peas, braised beef with tomato sauce, fillet steak and chipped potatoes, ending the banquet very often with a small wedge of Gruyère, which cost twopence. One night, after receiving a rise in his salary, he had actually drunk a quarter-flask of Chianti and had added the enormities of Benedictine, coffee, and cigarettes to an expenditure already disgraceful, and sixpence to the waiter made the bill amount to four shillings instead of the shilling that would have provided him with a wholesome and sufficient repast at home. Oh, there were many other items in this account of extravagance, and Darnell had often regretted his way of life, thinking that if he had been more careful, five or six pounds a year might have been added to their income.

And the question of the spare room brought back these regrets in an exaggerated degree. He persuaded himself that the extra five pounds would have given a sufficient margin for the outlay that he desired to make; though this was, no doubt, a mistake on his part. But he saw quite clearly that, under the present conditions, there must be no levies made on the very small sum of money that they had saved. The rent of the house was thirty-five, and rates and taxes added another ten pounds—nearly a quarter of their income for house-room. Mary kept down the housekeeping bills to the very best of her ability, but meat was always dear, and she suspected the maid of cutting surreptitious slices from the joint and eating them in her bedroom with bread and treacle in the dead of night, for the girl had disordered and eccentric appetites. Mr. Darnell thought no more of restaurants, cheap or dear; he took his lunch with him to the City, and joined his wife in the evening at high tea—chops, a bit of steak, or cold meat from the Sunday's dinner. Mrs. Darnell ate bread and jam and drank a little milk in the middle of the day; but, with the utmost economy, the effort to live within their means and to save for future contingencies was a very hard one. They had determined to do without change of air for at least three years, as the honeymoon at Walton-on-the-Naze had cost a good deal; and it was on this ground that they had, somewhat illogically, reserved the ten pounds, declaring that as they were not to have any holiday they would spend the money on something useful.

And it was this consideration of utility that was finally fatal to Darnell's scheme. They had calculated and recalculated the expense of the bed and bedding, the linoleum, and the ornaments, and by a great deal of exertion the total expenditure had been made to assume the shape of "something very little over ten pounds," when Mary said quite suddenly—

"But, after all, Edward, we don't really *want* to furnish the room at all. I mean it isn't necessary. And if we did so it might lead to no end of expense. People would hear of it and be sure to fish for invitations. You know we have relatives in the country, and they would be almost certain, the Mallings, at any rate, to give hints."

Darnell saw the force of the argument and gave way. But he was bitterly disappointed.

"It would have been very nice, wouldn't it?" he said with a sigh.

"Never mind, dear," said Mary, who saw that he was a good deal cast down. "We must think of some other plan that will be nice and useful too."

She often spoke to him in that tone of a kind mother, though she was by three years the younger.

"And now," she said, "I must get ready for church. Are you coming?"

Darnell said that he thought not. He usually accompanied his wife to morning service, but that day he felt some bitterness in his heart, and preferred to lounge under the shade of the big mulberry tree that stood in the middle of their patch of garden—relic of the spacious lawns that had once lain smooth and green and sweet, where the dismal streets now swarmed in a hopeless labyrinth.

So Mary went quietly and alone to church. St. Paul's stood in a neighbouring street, and its Gothic design would have interested a curious inquirer into the history of a strange revival. Obviously, mechanically, there was nothing amiss. The style chosen was "geometrical decorated," and the tracery of the windows seemed correct. The nave, the aisles, the spacious chancel, were reasonably proportioned; and, to be quite serious, the only feature obviously wrong was the substitution of a low "chancel wall" with iron gates for the rood screen with the loft and rood. But this, it might plausibly be contended, was merely an adaptation of the old idea to modern requirements, and it would have been quite difficult to explain why the whole building, from the mere mortar setting between the stones to the Gothic gas standards, was a mysterious and elaborate blasphemy. The canticles were sung to Joll in B flat, the chants were "Anglican," and the sermon was the gospel for the day, amplified and rendered into the more modern and graceful English of the preacher. And Mary came away.

After their dinner (an excellent piece of Australian mutton, bought in the "World Wide" Stores, in Hammersmith), they sat for some time in the garden, partly sheltered by the big mulberry tree from the observation of their neighbours. Edward smoked his honeydew, and Mary looked at him with placid affection.

"You never tell me about the men in your office," she said at length. "Some of them are nice fellows, aren't they?"

"Oh, yes, they're very decent. I must bring some of them round, one of these days."

He remembered with a pang that it would be necessary to provide whisky. One couldn't ask the guest to drink table beer at tenpence the gallon.

"Who are they, though?" said Mary. "I think they might have given you a wedding present."

"Well, I don't know. We never have gone in for that sort of thing. But they're very decent chaps. Well, there's Harvey; 'Sauce' they call him behind his back. He's mad on bicycling. He went in last year for the Two Miles Amateur Record. He'd have made it, too, if he could have got into better training.

"Then there's James, a sporting man. You wouldn't care for him. I always think he smells of the stable."

"How horrid!" said Mrs. Darnell, finding her husband a little frank, lowering her eyes as she spoke.

"Dickenson might amuse you," Darnell went on. "He's always got a joke. A terrible liar, though. When he tells a tale we never know how much to believe. He swore the other day he'd seen one of the governors buying cockles off a barrow near London Bridge, and Jones, who's just come, believed every word of it."

Darnell laughed at the humorous recollection of the jest.

"And that wasn't a bad yarn about Salter's wife," he went on. "Salter is the manager, you know. Dickenson lives close by, in Notting Hill, and he said one morning that he had seen Mrs. Salter, in the Portobello Road, in red stockings, dancing to a piano organ."

"He's a little coarse, isn't he?" said Mrs. Darnell. "I don't see much fun in that."

"Well, you know, amongst men it's different. You might like Wallis; he's a tremendous photographer. He often shows us photos he's taken of his children—one, a little girl of three, in her bath. I asked him how he thought she'd like it when she was twenty-three."

Mrs. Darnell looked down and made no answer.

There was silence for some minutes while Darnell smoked his pipe. "I say, Mary," he said at length, "what do you say to our taking a paying guest?"

"A paying guest! I never thought of it. Where should we put him?"

"Why, I was thinking of the spare room. The plan would obviate your objection, wouldn't it? Lots of men in the City take them, and make money of it too. I dare say it would add ten pounds a year to our income. Redgrave, the cashier, finds it worth his while to take a large house on purpose. They have a regular lawn for tennis and a billiard-room."

Mary considered gravely, always with the dream in her eyes. "I don't think we could manage it, Edward," she said; "it would be inconvenient in many ways." She hesitated for a moment. "And I don't think I should care to have a young man in the house. It is so very small, and our accommodation, as you know, is so limited."

She blushed slightly, and Edward, a little disappointed as he was, looked at her with a singular longing, as if he were a scholar confronted with a doubtful hieroglyph, either wholly wonderful or altogether commonplace. Next door children were playing in the garden, playing shrilly, laughing, crying, quarrelling, racing to and fro. Suddenly a clear, pleasant voice sounded from an upper window.

"Enid! Charles! Come up to my room at once!"

There was an instant sudden hush. The children's voices died away.

"Mrs. Parker is supposed to keep her children in great order," said Mary. "Alice was telling me about it the other day. She had been talking to Mrs. Parker's servant. I listened to her without any remark, as I don't think it right to encourage servants' gossip; they always exaggerate everything. And I dare say children often require to be corrected."

The children were struck silent as if some ghastly terror had seized them.

Darnell fancied that he heard a queer sort of cry from the house, but could not be quite sure. He turned to the other side, where an elderly, ordinary man with a grey moustache was strolling up and down on the further side of his garden. He caught Darnell's eye, and Mrs. Darnell looking towards him at the same moment, he very politely raised his tweed cap. Darnell was surprised to see his wife blushing fiercely.

"Sayce and I often go into the City by the same 'bus," he said, "and as it happens we've sat next to each other two or three times lately. I believe he's a traveller for a leather firm in Bermondsey. He struck me as a pleasant man. Haven't they got rather a good-looking servant?"

"Alice has spoken to me about her—and the Sayces," said Mrs. Darnell. "I understand that they are not very well thought of in the neighbourhood. But I must go in and see whether the tea is ready. Alice will be wanting to go out directly."

Darnell looked after his wife as she walked quickly away. He only dimly understood, but he could see the charm of her figure, the delight of the brown curls clustering about her neck, and he again felt that sense of the scholar confronted by the hieroglyphic. He could not have expressed his emotion, but he wondered whether he would ever find the key, and something told him that before she could speak to him his own lips must be unclosed. She had gone into the house by the back kitchen door, leaving it open, and he heard her speaking to the girl about the water being "really boiling." He was amazed, almost indignant with himself; but the sound of the words came to his ears as strange, heart-piercing music, tones from another, wonderful sphere. And yet he was her husband, and they had been married nearly a year; and yet, whenever she spoke, he had to listen to the sense of what she said, constraining himself, lest he should believe she was a magic creature, knowing the secrets of immeasurable delight.

He looked out through the leaves of the mulberry tree. Mr. Sayce had disappeared from his view, but he saw the light-blue fume of the cigar that he was smoking floating slowly across the shadowed air. He was wondering at his wife's manner when Sayce's name was mentioned, puzzling his head as to what could be amiss in the household of a most respectable personage, when his wife appeared at the dining-room window and called him in to tea. She smiled as he looked up, and he rose hastily and walked in, wondering whether he were not a little "queer," so strange were the dim emotions and the dimmer impulses that rose within him.

Alice was all shining purple and strong scent, as she brought in the teapot and the jug of hot water. It seemed that a visit to the kitchen had inspired Mrs. Darnell in her turn with a novel plan for disposing of the famous ten pounds. The range had always been a trouble to her, and when sometimes she went into the kitchen, and found, as she said, the fire "roaring halfway up the chimney," it was in vain that she reproved the maid on the ground of extravagance and waste of coal. Alice was ready to admit the absurdity of making up such an enormous fire merely to bake (they called it "roast") a bit of beef or mutton, and to boil the potatoes and the cabbage; but she was able to show Mrs. Darnell that the fault lay in the defective contrivance of the range, in an oven which "would not get hot." Even with a chop or a steak it was almost as bad; the heat seemed to escape up the chimney or into the room, and Mary had spoken several times to her husband on the shocking waste of coal, and the cheapest coal procurable was never less than eighteen shillings the ton. Mr. Darnell had written to the landlord, a builder, who had replied in an illiterate but offensive communication, maintaining the excellence of the stove and charging all the faults to the account of "your good lady," which really implied that the Darnells kept no servant, and that Mrs. Darnell did everything. The range, then, remained, a standing annoyance and expense. Every morning, Alice said, she had the greatest difficulty in getting the fire to light at all, and once lighted it "seemed as if it fled right up the chimney." Only a few nights before Mrs. Darnell had spoken seriously to her husband about it; she had got Alice to weigh the coals expended in cooking a cottage pie, the dish of the evening, and deducting what remained in the scuttle after the pie was done, it appeared that the wretched thing had consumed nearly twice the proper quantity of fuel.

"You remember what I said the other night about the range?" said Mrs. Darnell, as she poured out the tea and watered the leaves. She thought the introduction a good one, for though her husband was a most amiable man, she guessed that he had been just a little hurt by her decision against his furnishing scheme.

"The range?" said Darnell. He paused as he helped himself to the marmalade and considered for a moment. "No, I don't recollect. What night was it?"

"Tuesday. Don't you remember? You had 'overtime,' and didn't get home till quite late."

She paused for a moment, blushing slightly; and then began to recapitulate the misdeeds of the range, and the outrageous outlay of coal in the preparation of the cottage pie.

"Oh, I recollect now. That was the night I thought I heard the nightingale (people say there are nightingales in Bedford Park), and the sky was such a wonderful deep blue."

He remembered how he had walked from Uxbridge Road Station, where the green 'bus stopped, and in spite of the fuming kilns under Acton, a delicate odour of the woods and summer fields was mysteriously in the air, and he had fancied that he smelt the red wild roses, drooping from the hedge. As he came to his gate he saw his wife standing in the doorway, with a light in her hand, and he threw his arms violently about her as she welcomed him, and whispered something in her ear, kissing her scented hair. He had felt quite abashed a moment afterwards, and he was afraid that he had frightened her by his nonsense; she seemed trembling and confused. And then she had told him how they had weighed the coal.

"Yes, I remember now," he said. "It is a great nuisance, isn't it? I hate to throw away money like that."

"Well, what do you think? Suppose we bought a really good range with aunt's money? It would save us a lot, and I expect the things would taste much nicer."

Darnell passed the marmalade, and confessed that the idea was brilliant.

"It's much better than mine, Mary," he said quite frankly. "I am so glad you thought of it. But we must talk it over; it doesn't do to buy in a hurry. There are so many makes."

Each had seen ranges which looked miraculous inventions; he in the neighbourhood of the City; she in Oxford Street and Regent Street, on visits to the dentist. They discussed the matter at tea, and afterwards they discussed it walking round and round the garden, in the sweet cool of the evening.

"They say the 'Newcastle' will burn anything, coke even," said Mary.

"But the 'Glow' got the gold medal at the Paris Exhibition," said Edward.

"But what about the 'Eutopia' Kitchener? Have you seen it at work in Oxford Street?" said Mary. "They say their plan of ventilating the oven is quite unique."

"I was in Fleet Street the other day," answered Edward, and I was looking at the 'Bliss' Patent Stoves. They burn less fuel than any in the market—so the makers declare."

He put his arm gently round her waist. She did not repel him; she whispered quite softly—

"I think Mrs. Parker is at her window," and he drew his arm back slowly.

"But we will talk it over," he said. "There is no hurry. I might call at some of the places near the City, and you might do the same thing in Oxford Street and Regent Street and Piccadilly, and we could compare notes."

Mary was quite pleased with her husband's good temper. It was so nice of him not to find fault with her plan; "He's so good to me," she thought, and that was what she often said to her brother, who did not care much for Darnell. They sat down on the seat under the mulberry, close together, and she let Darnell take her hand, and as she felt his shy, hesitating fingers touch her in the shadow, she pressed them ever so softly, and as he fondled her hand, his breath was on her neck, and she heard his passionate, hesitating voice whisper, "My dear, my dear," as his lips touched her cheek. She trembled a little, and waited. Darnell kissed her gently on the cheek and drew away his hand, and when he spoke he was almost breathless.

"We had better go in now," he said. "There is a heavy dew, and you might catch cold."

A warm, scented gale came to them from beyond the walls. He longed to ask her to stay out with him all night beneath the tree, that they might whisper to one another, that the scent of her hair might inebriate him, that he might feel her dress still brushing against his ankles. But he could not find the words, and it was absurd, and she was so gentle that she would do whatever he asked, however foolish it might be, just because he asked her. He was not worthy to kiss her lips; he bent down and kissed her silk bodice, and again he felt that she trembled, and he was ashamed, fearing that he had frightened her.

They went slowly into the house, side by side, and Darnell lit the gas in the drawing-room, where they always sat on Sunday evenings. Mrs. Darnell felt a little tired and lay down on the sofa, and Darnell took the arm-chair opposite. For a while they, were silent and then Darnell said suddenly—

"What's wrong with the Sayces? You seemed to think there was something a little strange about them. Their maid looks quite quiet."

"Oh, I don't know that one ought to pay any attention to servants' gossip. They're not always very truthful."

"It was Alice told you, wasn't it?"

"Yes. She was speaking to me the other day, when I was in the kitchen in the afternoon."

"But what was it?"

"Oh, I'd rather not tell you, Edward. It's not pleasant. I scolded Alice for repeating it to me."

Darnell got up and took a small, frail chair near the sofa.

"Tell me," he said again, with an odd perversity. He did not really care to hear about the household next door, but he remembered how his wife's cheeks flushed in the afternoon, and now he was looking at her eyes.

"Oh, I really couldn't tell you, dear. I should feel ashamed."

"But you're my wife."

"Yes, but it doesn't make any difference. A woman doesn't like to talk about such things."

Darnell bent his head down. His heart was beating; he put his ear to her mouth and said, "Whisper."

Mary drew his head down still lower with her gentle hand, and her cheeks burned as she whispered—

"Alice says that—upstairs—they have only—one room furnished. The maid told her—herself."

With an unconscious gesture she pressed his head to her breast, and he in turn was bending her red lips to his own, when a violent jangle clamoured through the silent house. They sat up, and Mrs. Darnell went hurriedly to the door.

"That's Alice," she said. "She is always in in time. It has only just struck ten."

Darnell shivered with annoyance. His lips, he knew, had almost been opened. Mary's pretty handkerchief, delicately scented from a little flagon that a school friend had given her, lay on the floor, and he picked it up, and kissed it, and hid it away.

The question of the range occupied them all through June and far into July. Mrs. Darnell took every opportunity of going to the

West End and investigating the capacity of the latest makes, gravely viewing the new improvements and hearing what the shopmen had to say; while Darnell, as he said, "kept his eyes open" about the City. They accumulated quite a literature of the subject, bringing away illustrated pamphlets, and in the evenings it was an amusement to look at the pictures. They viewed with reverence and interest the drawings of great ranges for hotels and public institutions, mighty contrivances furnished with a series of ovens each for a different use, with wonderful apparatus for grilling, with batteries of accessories which seemed to invest the cook almost with the dignity of a chief engineer. But when, in one of the lists, they encountered the images of little toy "cottage" ranges, for four pounds, and even for three pounds ten, they grew scornful, on the strength of the eight or ten pound article which they meant to purchase—when the merits of the divers patents had been thoroughly thrashed out.

The "Raven" was for a long time Mary's favourite. It promised the utmost economy with the highest efficiency, and many times they were on the point of giving the order. But the "Glow" seemed equally seductive, and it was only £8. 5s. as compared with £9. 7s. 6d., and though the "Raven" was supplied to the Royal Kitchen, the "Glow" could show more fervent testimonials from continental potentates.

It seemed a debate without end, and it endured day after day till that morning, when Darnell woke from the dream of the ancient wood, of the fountains rising into grey vapour beneath the heat of the sun. As he dressed, an idea struck him, and he brought it as a shock to the hurried breakfast, disturbed by the thought of the City 'bus which passed the corner of the street at 9.15.

"I've got an improvement on your plan, Mary," he said, with triumph. "Look at that," and he flung a little book on the table.

He laughed. "It beats your notion all to fits. After all, the great expense is the coal. It's not the stove—at least that's not the real mischief. It's the coal is so dear. And here you are. Look at those oil stoves. They don't burn any coal, but the cheapest fuel in the world—oil; and for two pounds ten you can get a range that will do everything you want."

"Give me the book," said Mary, "and we will talk it over in the evening, when you come home. Must you be going?"

Darnell cast an anxious glance at the clock.

"Good-bye," and they kissed each other seriously and dutifully, and Mary's eyes made Darnell think of those lonely water-pools, hidden in the shadow of the ancient woods.

So, day after day, he lived in the grey phantasmal world, akin to death, that has, somehow, with most of us, made good its claim to be called life. To Darnell the true life would have seemed madness, and when, now and again, the shadows and vague images reflected from its splendour fell across his path, he was afraid, and took refuge in what he would have called the sane "reality" of common and usual incidents and interests. His absurdity was, perhaps, the more evident, inasmuch as "reality" for him was a matter of kitchen ranges, of saving a few shillings; but in truth the folly would have been greater if it had been concerned with racing, stables, steam yachts, and the spending of many thousand pounds.

But so went forth Darnell, day by day, strangely mistaking death for life, madness for sanity, and purposeless and wandering phantoms for true beings. He was sincerely of opinion that he was a City clerk, living in Shepherd's Bush—having forgotten the mysteries and the far-shining glories of the kingdom which was his by legitimate inheritance.

II

All day long a fierce and heavy heat had brooded over the City, and as Darnell neared home he saw the mist lying on all the damp lowlands, wreathed in coils about Bedford Park to the south, and mounting to the west, so that the tower of Acton Church loomed out of a grey lake. The grass in the squares and on the lawns which he overlooked as the 'bus lumbered wearily along was burnt to the colour of dust. Shepherd's Bush Green was a wretched desert, trampled brown, bordered with monotonous poplars, whose leaves hung motionless in air that was still, hot smoke. The foot passengers struggled wearily along the pavements, and the reek of the summer's end mingled with the breath of the brickfields made Darnell gasp, as if he were inhaling the poison of some foul sick-room.

He made but a slight inroad into the cold mutton that adorned the tea-table, and confessed that he felt rather "done up" by the weather and the day's work.

"I have had a trying day, too," said Mary. "Alice has been very queer and troublesome all day, and I have had to speak to her quite seriously. You know I think her Sunday evenings out have a rather unsettling influence on the girl. But what is one to do?"

"Has she got a young man?"

"Of course: a grocer's assistant from the Goldhawk Road—Wilkin's, you know. I tried them when we settled here, but they were not very satisfactory."

"What do they do with themselves all the evening? They have from five to ten, haven't they?"

"Yes; five, or sometimes half-past, when the water won't boil. Well, I believe they go for walks usually. Once or twice he has taken her to the City Temple, and the Sunday before last they walked up and down Oxford Street, and then sat in the Park. But it seems that last Sunday they went to tea with his mother at Putney. I should like to tell the old woman what I really think of her."

"Why? What happened? Was she nasty to the girl?"

"No; that's just it. Before this, she has been very unpleasant on several occasions. When the young man first took Alice to see her—that was in March—the girl came away crying; she told me so herself. Indeed, she said she never wanted to see old Mrs. Murry again; and I told Alice that, if she had not exaggerated things, I could hardly blame her for feeling like that."

"Why? What did she cry for?"

"Well, it seems that the old lady—she lives in quite a small cottage in some Putney back street—was so stately that she would hardly speak. She had borrowed a little girl from some neighbour's family, and had managed to dress her up to imitate a servant, and Alice said nothing could be sillier than to see that mite opening the door, with her black dress and her white cap and apron, and she hardly able to turn the handle, as Alice said. George (that's the young man's name) had told Alice that it was a little bit of a house; but he said the kitchen was comfortable, though very plain and old-fashioned. But, instead of going straight to the back, and sitting by a big fire on the old settle that they had brought up from the country, that child asked for their names (did you ever hear such nonsense?) and showed them into a little poky parlour, where old Mrs. Murry was sitting "like a duchess," by a fire-place full of coloured paper, and the room as cold as ice. And she was so grand that she would hardly speak to Alice."

"That must have been very unpleasant."

"Oh, the poor girl had a dreadful time. She began with: 'Very pleased to make your acquaintance, Miss Dill. I know so very few persons in service.' Alice imitates her mincing way of talking, but I can't do it. And then she went on to talk about her family, how they had farmed their own land for five hundred years—such stuff! George had told Alice all about it: they had had an old cottage with a good strip of garden and two fields somewhere in Essex, and that old woman talked almost as if they had been country gentry, and boasted about the Rector, Dr. Somebody, coming to see them so often, and of Squire Somebody Else always looking them up, as if they didn't visit them out of kindness. Alice told me it was as much as she could do to keep from laughing in Mrs. Murry's face, her young man having told her all about the place, and how small it was, and how the Squire had been so kind about buying it when old Murry died and George was a little boy, and his mother not able to keep things going. However, that silly old woman 'laid it on thick,' as you say, and the young man got more and more uncomfortable, especially when she went on to speak about marrying in one's own class, and how unhappy she had known young men to be who had married beneath them, giving some very pointed looks at Alice as she talked. And then such an amusing thing happened: Alice had noticed George looking about him in a puzzled sort of way, as if he couldn't make out something or other, and at last he burst out and asked his mother if she had been buying up the neighbours' ornaments, as he remembered the two green cut-glass vases on the mantelpiece at Mrs. Ellis's, and the wax flowers at Miss Turvey's. He was going on, but his mother scowled at him, and upset some books, which he had to pick up; but Alice quite understood she had been borrowing things from her neighbours, just as she had borrowed the little girl, so as to look grander. And then they had tea—water bewitched, Alice calls it—and very thin bread and butter, and rubbishy foreign pastry from the Swiss shop in the High Street—all sour froth and rancid fat, Alice declares. And then Mrs. Murry began boasting again about her family, and snubbing Alice and talking at her, till the girl came away quite furious, and very unhappy, too. I don't wonder at it, do you?"

"It doesn't sound very enjoyable, certainly," said Darnell, looking dreamily at his wife. He had not been attending very carefully to the subject-matter of her story, but he loved to hear a voice that was incantation in his ears, tones that summoned before him the vision of a magic world.

"And has the young man's mother always been like this?" he said after a long pause, desiring that the music should continue.

"Always, till quite lately, till last Sunday in fact. Of course Alice spoke to George Murry at once, and said, like a sensible girl, that she didn't think it ever answered for a married couple to live with the man's mother, 'especially,' she went on, 'as I can see your mother hasn't taken much of a fancy to me.' He told her, in the usual style, it was only his mother's way, that she didn't really mean anything, and so on; but Alice kept away for a long time, and rather hinted, I think, that it might come to having to choose between her and his mother. And so affairs went on all through the spring and summer, and then, just before the August Bank Holiday, George spoke to Alice again about it, and told her how sorry the thought of any unpleasantness made him, and how he wanted his mother and her to get on with each other, and how she was only a bit old-fashioned and queer in her ways, and had spoken very nicely to him about her when there was nobody by. So the long and the short of it was that Alice said she might come with them on the Monday, when they had settled to go to Hampton Court—the girl was always talking about Hampton Court, and wanting to see it. You remember what a beautiful day it was, don't you?"

"Let me see," said Darnell dreamily. "Oh yes, of course—I sat out under the mulberry tree all day, and we had our meals there: it was quite a picnic. The caterpillars were a nuisance, but I enjoyed the day very much." His ears were charmed, ravished with the grave, supernal melody, as of antique song, rather of the first made world in which all speech was descant, and all words were sacraments of might, speaking not to the mind but to the soul. He lay back in his chair, and said—

"Well, what happened to them?"

"My dear, would you believe it; but that wretched old woman behaved worse than ever. They met as had been arranged, at Kew Bridge, and got places, with a good deal of difficulty, in one of those char-à-banc things, and Alice thought she was going to enjoy herself tremendously. Nothing of the kind. They had hardly said 'Good morning,' when old Mrs. Murry began to talk about Kew Gardens, and how beautiful it must be there, and how much more convenient it was than Hampton, and no expense at all; just the trouble of walking over the bridge. Then she went on to say, as they were waiting for the char-à-banc, that she had always heard there was nothing to see at Hampton, except a lot of nasty, grimy old pictures, and some of them not fit for any decent woman, let alone girl, to look at, and she wondered why the Queen allowed such things to be shown, putting all kinds of notions into girls' heads that were light enough already; and as she said that she looked at Alice so nastily—horrid old thing—that, as she told me afterwards, Alice would have slapped her face if she hadn't been an elderly woman, and George's mother. Then she talked about Kew again, saying how wonderful the hot-houses were, with palms and all sorts of wonderful things, and a lily as big as a parlour table, and the view over the river. George was very good, Alice told me. He was quite taken aback at first, as the old woman had promised faithfully to be as nice as ever she could be; but then he said, gently but firmly, 'Well, mother, we must go to Kew some other day, as Alice has set her heart on Hampton for to-day, and I want to see it myself!' All Mrs. Murry did was to snort, and look at the girl like vinegar, and just then the char-à-banc came up, and they had to scramble for their seats. Mrs. Murry grumbled to herself in an indistinct sort of voice all the way to Hampton Court. Alice couldn't very well make out what she said, but now and then she seemed to hear bits of sentences, like: *Pity to grow old, if sons grow bold;* and *Honour thy father and mother;* and *Lie on the shelf, said the housewife to the old shoe, and the wicked son to his mother;* and *I gave you milk and you give me the go-by.* Alice thought they must be proverbs (except the Commandment, of course), as George was always saying how old-fashioned his mother is; but she says there were so many of them, and all pointed at her and George, that she thinks now Mrs. Murry must have made them up as they drove along. She says it would be just like her to do it, being old-fashioned, and ill-natured too, and fuller of talk than a butcher on Saturday night. Well, they got to Hampton at last, and Alice thought the place would please her, perhaps, and they might have some enjoyment. But she did nothing but grumble, and out loud too, so that people looked at them, and a woman said, so that they could hear, 'Ah well, they'll be old themselves some day,' which made Alice very angry, for, as she said, they weren't doing anything. When they showed her the chestnut avenue in Bushey Park, she said it was so long and straight that it made her quite dull to look at it, and she thought the deer (you know how pretty they are, really) looked thin and miserable, as if they would be all the better for a good feed of hog-wash, with plenty of meal in it. She said she knew they weren't happy by the look in their eyes, which seemed to tell her that their keepers beat them. It was the same with everything; she said she remembered market-gardens in Hammersmith and Gunnersbury that had a better show of flowers, and when they took her to the place where the water is, under the trees, she burst out with its being rather hard to tramp her off her legs to show her a common canal, with not so much as a barge on it to liven it up a bit. She went on like that the whole day, and Alice told me she was only too thankful to get home and get rid of her. Wasn't it wretched for the girl?"

"It must have been, indeed. But what happened last Sunday?"

"That's the most extraordinary thing of all. I noticed that Alice was rather queer in her manner this morning; she was a longer time washing up the breakfast things, and she answered me quite sharply when I called to her to ask when she would be ready to help me with the wash; and when I went into the kitchen to see about something, I noticed that she was going about her work in a sulky sort of way. So I asked her what was the matter, and then it all came out. I could scarcely believe my own ears when she mumbled out something about Mrs. Murry thinking she could do very much better for herself; but I asked her one question after another till I had it all out of her. It just shows one how foolish and empty-headed these girls are. I told her she was no better than a weather-cock. If you will believe me, that horrid old woman was quite another person when Alice went to see her the other night. Why, I can't think, but so she was. She told the girl how pretty she was; what a neat figure she had; how well she walked; and how she'd known many a girl not half so clever or well-looking earning her twenty-five or thirty pounds a year, and with good families. She seems to have gone into all sorts of details, and made elaborate calculations as to what she would be able to save, 'with decent folks, who don't screw, and pinch, and lock up everything in the house,' and then she went off into a lot of hypocritical nonsense about how fond she was of Alice, and how she could go to her grave in peace, knowing how happy her dear George would be with such a good wife, and about her savings from good wages helping to set up a little home, ending up with 'And, if you take an old woman's advice, deary, it won't be long before you hear the marriage bells.'"

"I see," said Darnell; "and the upshot of it all is, I suppose, that the girl is thoroughly dissatisfied?"

"Yes, she is so young and silly. I talked to her, and reminded her of how nasty old Mrs. Murry had been, and told her that she might change her place and change for the worse. I think I have persuaded her to think it over quietly, at all events. Do you know what it is, Edward? I have an idea. I believe that wicked old woman is trying to get Alice to leave us, that she may tell her son how changeable she is; and I suppose she would make up some of her stupid old proverbs: 'A changeable wife, a troublesome life,' or some nonsense of the kind. Horrid old thing!"

"Well, well," said Darnell, "I hope she won't go, for your sake. It would be such a bother for you, hunting for a fresh servant."

He refilled his pipe and smoked placidly, refreshed somewhat after the emptiness and the burden of the day. The French window was wide open, and now at last there came a breath of quickening air, distilled by the night from such trees as still wore green in that arid valley. The song to which Darnell had listened in rapture, and now the breeze, which even in that dry, grim suburb still bore the word of the woodland, had summoned the dream to his eyes, and he meditated over matters that his lips could not express.

"She must, indeed, be a villainous old woman," he said at length.

"Old Mrs. Murry? Of course she is; the mischievous old thing! Trying to take the girl from a comfortable place where she is happy."

"Yes; and not to like Hampton Court! That shows how bad she must be, more than anything."

"It is beautiful, isn't it?"

"I shall never forget the first time I saw it. It was soon after I went into the City; the first year. I had my holidays in July, and I was getting such a small salary that I couldn't think of going away to the seaside, or anything like that. I remember one of the other men wanted me to come with him on a walking tour in Kent. I should have liked that, but the money wouldn't run to it. And do you know what I did? I lived in Great College Street then, and the first day I was off, I stayed in bed till past dinner-time, and lounged about in an arm-chair with a pipe all the afternoon. I had got a new kind of tobacco—one and four for the two-ounce packet—much dearer than I could afford to smoke, and I was enjoying it immensely. It was awfully hot, and when I shut the window and drew down the red blind it grew hotter; at five o'clock the room was like an oven. But I was so pleased at not having to go into the City, that I didn't mind anything, and now and again I read bits from a queer old book that had belonged to my poor dad. I couldn't make out what a lot of it meant, but it fitted in somehow, and I read and smoked till tea-time. Then I went out for a walk, thinking I should be better for a little fresh air before I went to bed; and I went wandering away, not much noticing where I was going, turning here and there as the fancy took me. I must have gone miles and miles, and a good many of them round and round, as they say they do in Australia if they lose their way in the bush; and I am sure I couldn't have gone exactly the same way all over again for any money. Anyhow, I was still in the streets when the twilight came on, and the lamplighters were trotting round from one lamp to another. It was a wonderful night: I wish you had been there, my dear."

"I was quite a little girl then."

"Yes, I suppose you were. Well, it was a wonderful night. I remember, I was walking in a little street of little grey houses all alike, with stucco copings and stucco door-posts; there were brass plates on a lot of the doors, and one had 'Maker of Shell Boxes' on it, and I was quite pleased, as I had often wondered where those boxes and things that you buy at the seaside came from. A few children were playing about in the road with some rubbish or other, and men were singing in a small public-house at the corner, and I happened to look up, and I noticed what a wonderful colour the sky had turned. I have seen it since, but I don't think it has ever been quite what it was that night, a dark blue, glowing like a violet, just as they say the sky looks in foreign countries. I don't know why, but the sky or something made me feel quite queer; everything seemed changed in a way I couldn't understand. I remember, I told an old gentleman I knew then—a friend of my poor father's, he's been dead for five years, if not more—about how I felt, and he looked at me and said something about fairyland; I don't know what he meant, and I dare say I didn't explain myself properly. But, do you know, for a moment or two I felt as if that little back street was beautiful, and the noise of the children and the men in the public-house seemed to fit in with the sky and become part of it. You know that old saying about 'treading on air' when one is glad! Well, I really felt like that as I walked, not exactly like air, you know, but as if the pavement was velvet or some very soft carpet. And then—I suppose it was all my fancy—the air seemed to smell sweet, like the incense in Catholic churches, and my breath came queer and catchy, as it does when one gets very excited about anything. I felt altogether stranger than I've ever felt before or since."

Darnell stopped suddenly and looked up at his wife. She was watching him with parted lips, with eager, wondering eyes.

"I hope I'm not tiring you, dear, with all this story about nothing. You have had a worrying day with that stupid girl; hadn't you better go to bed?"

"Oh, no, please, Edward. I'm not a bit tired now. I love to hear you talk like that. Please go on."

"Well, after I had walked a bit further, that queer sort of feeling seemed to fade away. I said a bit further, and I really thought I had been walking about five minutes, but I had looked at my watch just before I got into that little street, and when I looked at it again it was eleven o'clock. I must have done about eight miles. I could scarcely believe my own eyes, and I thought my watch must have gone mad; but I found out afterwards it was perfectly right. I couldn't make it out, and I can't now; I assure you the time passed as if I walked up one side of Edna Road and down the other. But there I was right in the open country, with a cool wind blowing on me from a wood, and the air full of soft rustling sounds, and notes of birds from the bushes, and the singing noise of a little brook that ran under the road. I was standing on the bridge when I took out my watch and struck a wax light to see the time; and it came upon me suddenly what a strange evening it had been. It was all so different, you see, to what I had been doing all my life, particularly for the year before, and it almost seemed as if I couldn't be the man who had been going into the City every day in the morning and coming back from it every evening, after writing a lot of uninteresting letters. It was like being pitched all of a sudden from one world into another. Well, I found my way back somehow or other, and as I went along I made up my mind how I'd spend my holiday. I said to myself, 'I'll have a walking tour as well as Ferrars, only mine is to be a tour of London and its environs,' and I had got it all settled when I let myself into the house about four o'clock in the morning, and the sun was shining, and the street almost as still as the wood at midnight!"

"I think that was a capital idea of yours. Did you have your tour? Did you buy a map of London?"

"I had the tour all right. I didn't buy a map; that would have spoilt it, somehow; to see everything plotted out, and named, and measured. What I wanted was to feel that I was going where nobody had been before. That's nonsense, isn't it? as if there could be any such places in London, or England either, for the matter of that."

"I know what you mean; you wanted to feel as if you were going on a sort of voyage of discovery. Isn't that it?"

"Exactly, that's what I was trying to tell you. Besides, I didn't want to buy a map. I made a map."

"How do you mean? Did you make a map out of your head?"

"I'll tell you about it afterwards. But do you really want to hear about my grand tour?"

"Of course I do; it must have been delightful. I call it a most original idea."

"Well, I was quite full of it, and what you said just now about a voyage of discovery reminds me of how I felt then. When I was a boy I was awfully fond of reading of great travellers—I suppose all boys are—and of sailors who were driven out of their course and found themselves in latitudes where no ship had ever sailed before, and of people who discovered wonderful cities in strange countries; and all the second day of my holidays I was feeling just as I used to when I read these books. I didn't get up till pretty late. I was tired to death after all those miles I had walked; but when I had finished my breakfast and filled my pipe, I had a grand time of it. It was such nonsense, you know; as if there could be anything strange or wonderful in London."

"Why shouldn't there be?"

"Well, I don't know; but I have thought afterwards what a silly lad I must have been. Anyhow, I had a great day of it, planning what I would do, half making-believe—just like a kid—that I didn't know where I might find myself, or what might happen to me. And I was enormously pleased to think it was all my secret, that nobody else knew anything about it, and that, whatever I might see, I would keep to myself. I had always felt like that about the books. Of course, I loved reading them, but it seemed to me that, if I had been a discoverer, I would have kept my discoveries a secret. If I had been Columbus, and, if it could possibly have been managed, I would have found America all by myself, and never have said a word about it to anybody. Fancy! how beautiful it would be to be walking about in one's own town, and talking to people, and all the while to have the thought that one knew of a great world beyond the seas, that nobody else dreamed of. I should have loved that!

"And that is exactly what I felt about the tour I was going to make. I made up my mind that nobody should know; and so, from that day to this, nobody has heard a word of it."

"But you are going to tell me?"

"You are different. But I don't think even you will hear everything; not because I won't, but because I can't tell many of the things I saw."

"Things you saw? Then you really did see wonderful, strange things in London?"

"Well, I did and I didn't. Everything, or pretty nearly everything, that I saw is standing still, and hundreds of thousands of people have looked at the same sights—there were many places that the fellows in the office knew quite well, I found out afterwards. And then I read a book called *London and its Surroundings.* But (I don't know how it is) neither the men at the office nor the writers of the book seem to have seen the things that I did. That's why I stopped reading the book; it seemed to take the life, the real heart, out of everything, making it as dry and stupid as the stuffed birds in a museum.

"I thought about what I was going to do all that day, and went to bed early, so as to be fresh. I knew wonderfully little about London, really; though, except for an odd week now and then, I had spent all my life in town. Of course I knew the main streets—the Strand, Regent Street, Oxford Street, and so on—and I knew the way to the school I used to go to when I was a boy, and the way into the City. But I had just kept to a few tracks, as they say the sheep do on the mountains; and that made it all the easier for me to imagine that I was going to discover a new world."

Darnell paused in the stream of his talk. He looked keenly at his wife to see if he were wearying her, but her eyes gazed at him with unabated interest—one would have almost said that they were the eyes of one who longed and half expected to be initiated into the mysteries, who knew not what great wonder was to be revealed. She sat with her back to the open window, framed in the sweet dusk of the night, as if a painter had made a curtain of heavy velvet behind her; and the work that she had been doing had fallen to the floor. She supported her head with her two hands placed on each side of her brow, and her eyes were as the wells in the wood of which Darnell dreamed in the night-time and in the day.

"And all the strange tales I had ever heard were in my head that morning," he went on, as if continuing the thoughts that had filled his mind while his lips were silent. "I had gone to bed early, as I told you, to get a thorough rest, and I had set my alarum clock to wake me at three, so that I might set out at an hour that was quite strange for the beginning of a journey. There was a hush in the world when I awoke, before the clock had rung to arouse me, and then a bird began to sing and twitter in the elm tree that grew in the next garden, and I looked out of the window, and everything was still, and the morning air breathed in pure and sweet, as I had never known it before. My room was at the back of the house, and most of the gardens had trees in them, and beyond these trees I could see the backs of the houses of the next street rising like the wall of an old city; and as I looked the sun rose, and the great light came in at my window, and the day began.

"And I found that when I was once out of the streets just about me that I knew, some of the queer feeling that had come to me two days before came back again. It was not nearly so strong, the streets no longer smelt of incense, but still there was enough of it to show me what a strange world I passed by. There were things that one may see again and again in many London streets: a vine or a fig tree on a wall, a lark singing in a cage, a curious shrub blossoming in a garden, an odd shape of a roof, or a balcony with an uncommon-looking trellis-work in iron. There's scarcely a street, perhaps, where you won't see one or other of such things as these; but that morning they rose to my eyes in a new light, as if I had on the magic spectacles in the fairy tale, and just like the man in the fairy tale, I went on and on in the new light. I remember going through wild land on a high place; there were pools of water shining in the sun, and great white houses in the middle of dark, rocking pines, and then on the turn of the height I came to a little lane that went aside from the main road, a lane that led to a wood, and in the lane was a little old shadowed house, with a bell turret in the roof, and a porch of trellis-work all dim and faded into the colour of the sea; and in the garden there were growing tall, white lilies, just as we saw them that day we went to look at the old pictures; they were shining like silver, and they filled the air with their sweet scent. It was from near that house I saw the valley and high places far away in the sun. So, as I say, I went 'on and on,' by woods and fields, till I came to a little town on the top of a hill, a town full of old houses bowing to the ground beneath their years, and the morning was so still that the blue smoke rose up straight into the sky from all the roof-tops, so still that I heard far down in the valley the song of a boy who was singing an old song through the streets as he went to school, and as I passed through the awakening town, beneath the old, grave houses, the church bells began to ring.

"It was soon after I had left this town behind me that I found the Strange Road. I saw it branching off from the dusty high road, and it looked so green that I turned aside into it, and soon I felt as if I had really come into a new country. I don't know whether it was one of the roads the old Romans made that my father used to tell me about; but it was covered with deep, soft turf, and the great tall hedges on each side looked as if they had not been touched for a hundred years; they had grown so broad and high and wild that they met overhead, and I could only get glimpses here and there of the country through which I was passing, as one passes in a dream. The

Strange Road led me on and on, up and down hill; sometimes the rose bushes had grown so thick that I could scarcely make my way between them, and sometimes the road broadened out into a green, and in one valley a brook, spanned by an old wooden bridge, ran across it. I was tired, and I found a soft and shady place beneath an ash tree, where I must have slept for many hours, for when I woke up it was late in the afternoon. So I went on again, and at last the green road came out into the highway, and I looked up and saw another town on a high place with a great church in the middle of it, and when I went up to it there was a great organ sounding from within, and the choir was singing."

There was a rapture in Darnell's voice as he spoke, that made his story well-nigh swell into a song, and he drew a long breath as the words ended, filled with the thought of that far-off summer day, when some enchantment had informed all common things, transmuting them into a great sacrament, causing earthly works to glow with the fire and the glory of the everlasting light.

And some splendour of that light shone on the face of Mary as she sat still against the sweet gloom of the night, her dark hair making her face more radiant. She was silent for a little while, and then she spoke—

"Oh, my dear, why have you waited so long to tell me these wonderful things? I think it is beautiful. Please go on."

"I have always been afraid it was all nonsense," said Darnell. "And I don't know how to explain what I feel. I didn't think I could say so much as I have tonight."

"And did you find it the same day after day?"

"All through the tour? Yes, I think every journey was a success. Of course, I didn't go so far afield every day; I was too tired. Often I rested all day long, and went out in the evening, after the lamps were lit, and then only for a mile or two. I would roam about old, dim squares, and hear the wind from the hills whispering in the trees; and when I knew I was within call of some great glittering street, I was sunk in the silence of ways where I was almost the only passenger, and the lamps were so few and faint that they seemed to give out shadows instead of light. And I would walk slowly, to and fro, perhaps for an hour at a time, in such dark streets, and all the time I felt what I told you about its being my secret—that the shadow, and the dim lights, and the cool of the evening, and trees that were like dark low clouds were all mine, and mine alone, that I was living in a world that nobody else knew of, into which no one could enter.

"I remembered one night I had gone farther. It was somewhere in the far west, where there are orchards and gardens, and great broad lawns that slope down to trees by the river. A great red moon rose that night through mists of sunset, and thin, filmy clouds, and I wandered by a road that passed through the orchards, till I came to a little hill, with the moon showing above it glowing like a great rose. Then I saw figures pass between me and the moon, one by one, in a long line, each bent double, with great packs upon their shoulders. One of them was singing, and then in the middle of the song I heard a horrible shrill laugh, in the thin cracked voice of a very old woman, and they disappeared into the shadow of the trees. I suppose they were people going to work, or coming from work in the gardens; but how like it was to a nightmare!

"I can't tell you about Hampton; I should never finish talking. I was there one evening, not long before they closed the gates, and there were very few people about. But the grey-red, silent, echoing courts, and the flowers falling into dreamland as the night came on, and the dark yews and shadowy-looking statues, and the far, still stretches of water beneath the avenues; and all melting into a blue mist, all being hidden from one's eyes, slowly, surely, as if veils were dropped, one by one, on a great ceremony! Oh! my dear, what could it mean? Far away, across the river, I heard a soft bell ring three times, and three times, and again three times, and I turned away, and my eyes were full of tears.

"I didn't know what it was when I came to it; I only found out afterwards that it must have been Hampton Court. One of the men in the office told me he had taken an A.B.C. girl there, and they had great fun. They got into the maze and couldn't get out again, and then they went on the river and were nearly drowned. He told me there were some spicy pictures in the galleries; his girl shrieked with laughter, so he said."

Mary quite disregarded this interlude.

"But you told me you had made a map. What was it like?"

"I'll show it you some day, if you want to see it. I marked down all the places I had gone to, and made signs—things like queer letters—

to remind me of what I had seen. Nobody but myself could understand it. I wanted to draw pictures, but I never learnt how to draw, so when I tried nothing was like what I wanted it to be. I tried to draw a picture of that town on the hill that I came to on the evening of the first day; I wanted to make a steep hill with houses on top, and in the middle, but high above them, the great church, all spires and pinnacles, and above it, in the air, a cup with rays coming from it. But it wasn't a success. I made a very strange sign for Hampton Court, and gave it a name that I made up out of my head."

The Darnells avoided one another's eyes as they sat at breakfast the next morning. The air had lightened in the night, for rain had fallen at dawn; and there was a bright blue sky, with vast white clouds rolling across it from the south-west, and a fresh and joyous wind blew in at the open window; the mists had vanished. And with the mists there seemed to have vanished also the sense of strange things that had possessed Mary and her husband the night before; and as they looked out into the clear light they could scarcely believe that the one had spoken and the other had listened a few hours before to histories very far removed from the usual current of their thoughts and of their lives. They glanced shyly at one another, and spoke of common things, of the question whether Alice would be corrupted by the insidious Mrs. Murry, or whether Mrs. Darnell would be able to persuade the girl that the old woman must be actuated by the worst motives.

"And I think, if I were you," said Darnell, as he went out, "I should step over to the stores and complain of their meat. That last piece of beef was very far from being up to the mark—full of sinew."

III

It might have been different in the evening, and Darnell had matured a plan by which he hoped to gain much. He intended to ask his wife if she would mind having only one gas, and that a good deal lowered, on the pretext that his eyes were tired with work; he thought many things might happen if the room were dimly lit, and the window opened, so that they could sit and watch the night, and listen to the rustling murmur of the tree on the lawn. But his plans were made in vain, for when he got to the garden gate his wife, in tears, came forth to meet him.

"Oh, Edward," she began, "such a dreadful thing has happened! I never liked him much, but I didn't think he would ever do such awful things."

"What do you mean? Who are you talking about? What has happened? Is it Alice's young man?"

"No, no. But come in, dear. I can see that woman opposite watching us: she's always on the look out."

"Now, what is it?" said Darnell, as they sat down to tea. "Tell me, quick! you've quite frightened me."

"I don't know how to begin, or where to start. Aunt Marian has thought that there was something queer for weeks. And then she found—oh, well, the long and short of it is that Uncle Robert has been carrying on dreadfully with some horrid girl, and aunt has found out everything!"

"Lord! you don't say so! The old rascal! Why, he must be nearer seventy than sixty!"

"He's just sixty-five; and the money he has given her—"

The first shock of surprise over, Darnell turned resolutely to his mince.

"We'll have it all out after tea," he said; "I am not going to have my meals spoilt by that old fool of a Nixon. Fill up my cup, will you, dear?"

"Excellent mince this," he went on, calmly. "A little lemon juice and a bit of ham in it? I thought there was something extra. Alice all right to-day? That's good. I expect she's getting over all that nonsense."

He went on calmly chattering in a manner that astonished Mrs. Darnell, who felt that by the fall of Uncle Robert the natural order had been inverted, and had scarcely touched food since the intelligence had arrived by the second post. She had started out to keep the appointment her aunt had made early in the morning, and had spent most of the day in a first-class waiting-room at Victoria Station, where she had heard all the story.

"Now," said Darnell, when the table had been cleared, "tell us all about it. How long has it been going on?"

"Aunt thinks now, from little things she remembers, that it must have been going on for a year at least. She says there has been a horrid kind of mystery about uncle's behaviour for a long time, and her nerves were quite shaken, as she thought he must be involved with Anarchists, or something dreadful of the sort."

"What on earth made her think that?"

"Well, you see, once or twice when she was out walking with her husband, she has been startled by whistles, which seemed to follow them everywhere. You know there are some nice country walks at Barnet, and one in particular, in the fields near Totteridge, that uncle and aunt rather made a point of going to on fine Sunday evenings. Of course, this was not the first thing she noticed, but, at the time, it made a great impression on her mind; she could hardly get a wink of sleep for weeks and weeks."

"Whistling?" said Darnell. "I don't quite understand. Why should she be frightened by whistling?"

"I'll tell you. The first time it happened was one Sunday in last May. Aunt had a fancy they were being followed a Sunday or two before, but she didn't see or hear anything, except a sort of crackling noise in the hedge. But this particular Sunday they had hardly got through the stile into the fields, when she heard a peculiar kind of low whistle. She took no notice, thinking it was no concern of hers or her husband's, but as they went on she heard it again, and then again, and it followed them the whole walk, and it made her so uncomfortable, because she didn't know where it was coming from or who was doing it, or why. Then, just as they got out of the fields into the lane, uncle said he felt quite faint, and he thought he would try a little brandy at the 'Turpin's Head,' a small public-house there is there. And she looked at him and saw his face was quite purple—more like apoplexy, as she says, than fainting fits which make people look a sort of greenish-white. But she said nothing, and thought perhaps uncle had a peculiar way of fainting of his own, as he always was a man to have his own way of doing everything. So she just waited in the road, and he went ahead and slipped into the public, and aunt says she thought she saw a little figure rise out of the dusk and slip in after him, but she couldn't be sure. And when uncle came out he looked red instead of purple, and said he felt much better; and so they went home quietly together, and nothing more was said. You see, uncle had said nothing about the whistling, and aunt had been so frightened that she didn't dare speak, for fear they might be both shot.

"She wasn't thinking anything more about it, when two Sundays afterwards the very same thing happened just as it had before. This time aunt plucked up a spirit, and asked uncle what it could be. And what do you think he said? 'Birds, my dear, birds.' Of course aunt said to him that no bird that ever flew with wings made a noise like that: sly, and low, with pauses in between; and then he said that many rare sorts of birds lived in North Middlesex and Hertfordshire. 'Nonsense, Robert,' said aunt, 'how can you talk so, considering it has followed us all the way, for a mile or more?' And then uncle told her that some birds were so attached to man that they would follow one about for miles sometimes; he said he had just been reading about a bird like that in a book of travels. And do you know that when they got home he actually showed her a piece in the *Hertfordshire Naturalist* which they took in to oblige a friend of theirs, all about rare birds found in the neighbourbood, all the most outlandish names, aunt says, that she had never heard or thought of, and uncle had the impudence to say that it must have been a purple sandpiper, which, the paper said, had 'a low shrill note, constantly repeated.' And then he took down a book of Siberian Travels from the bookcase and showed her a page which told how a man was followed by a bird all day long through a forest. And that's what Aunt Marian says vexes her more than anything almost; to think that he should be so artful and ready with those books, twisting them to his own wicked ends. But, at the time, when she was out walking, she simply couldn't make out what he meant by talking about birds in that random, silly sort of way, so unlike him, and they went on, that horrible whistling following them, she looking straight ahead and walking fast, really feeling more huffy and put out than frightened. And when they got to the next stile, she got over and turned round, and 'lo and behold,' as she says, there was no Uncle Robert to be seen! She felt herself go quite white with alarm, thinking of that whistle, and making sure he'd been spirited away or snatched in some way or another, and she had just screamed out 'Robert' like a mad woman, when he came quite slowly round the corner, as cool as a cucumber, holding something in his hand. He said there were some flowers he could never pass, and when aunt saw that he had got a dandelion torn up by the roots, she felt as if her head were going round."

Mary's story was suddenly interrupted. For ten minutes Darnell had been writhing in his chair, suffering tortures in his anxiety to avoid wounding his wife's feelings, but the episode of the dandelion was too much for him, and he burst into a long, wild shriek of laughter, aggravated by suppression into the semblance of a Red Indian's war-whoop. Alice, who was washing-up in the scullery, dropped some three shillings' worth of china, and the neighbours ran out into their gardens wondering if it were murder. Mary gazed reproachfully at her husband.

"How can you be so unfeeling, Edward?" she said, at length, when Darnell had passed into the feebleness of exhaustion. "If you had seen the tears rolling down poor Aunt Marian's cheeks as she told me, I don't think you would have laughed. I didn't think you were so hard-hearted."

"My dear Mary," said Darnell, faintly, through sobs and catching of the breath, "I am awfully sorry. I know it's very sad, really, and I'm not unfeeling; but it is such an odd tale, now, isn't it? The sandpiper, you know, and then the dandelion!"

His face twitched and he ground his teeth together. Mary looked gravely at him for a moment, and then she put her hands to her face, and Darnell could see that she also shook with merriment.

"I am as bad as you," she said, at last. "I never thought of it in that way. I'm glad I didn't, or I should have laughed in Aunt Marian's face, and I wouldn't have done that for the world. Poor old thing; she cried as if her heart would break. I met her at Victoria, as she asked me, and we had some soup at a confectioner's. I could scarcely touch it; her tears kept dropping into the plate all the time; and then we went to the waiting-room at the station, and she cried there terribly."

"Well," said Darnell, "what happened next? I won't laugh any more."

"No, we mustn't; it's much too horrible for a joke. Well, of course aunt went home and wondered and wondered what could be the matter, and tried to think it out, but, as she says, she could make nothing of it. She began to be afraid that uncle's brain was giving way through overwork, as he had stopped in the City (as he said) up to all hours lately, and he had to go to Yorkshire (wicked old story-teller!), about some very tiresome business connected with his leases. But then she reflected that however queer he might be getting, even his queerness couldn't make whistles in the air, though, as she said, he was always a wonderful man. So she had to give that up; and then she wondered if there were anything the matter with her, as she had read about people who heard noises when there was really nothing at all. But that wouldn't do either, because though it might account for the whistling, it wouldn't account for the dandelion or the sandpiper, or for fainting fits that turned purple, or any of uncle's queerness. So aunt said she could think of nothing but to read the Bible every day from the beginning, and by the time she got into Chronicles she felt rather better, especially as nothing had happened for three or four Sundays. She noticed uncle seemed absent-minded, and not as nice to her as he might be, but she put that down to too much work, as he never came home before the last train, and had a hansom twice all the way, getting there between three and four in the morning. Still, she felt it was no good bothering her head over what couldn't be made out or explained anyway, and she was just settling down, when one Sunday evening it began all over again, and worse things happened. The whistling followed them just as it did before, and poor aunt set her teeth and said nothing to uncle, as she knew he would only tell her stories, and they were walking on, not saying a word, when something made her look back, and there was a horrible boy with red hair, peeping through the hedge just behind, and grinning. She said it was a dreadful face, with something unnatural about it, as if it had been a dwarf, and before she had time to have a good look, it popped back like lightning, and aunt all but fainted away."

"A red-headed *boy?*" said Darnell. "I thought—What an extraordinary story this is. I've never heard of anything so queer. Who was the boy?"

"You will know in good time," said Mrs. Darnell. "It *is* very strange, isn't it?"

"Strange!" Darnell ruminated for a while.

"I know what I think, Mary," he said at length. "I don't believe a word of it. I believe your aunt is going mad, or has gone mad, and that she has delusions. The whole thing sounds to me like the invention of a lunatic."

"You are quite wrong. Every word is true, and if you will let me go on, you will understand how it all happened."

"Very good, go ahead."

"Let me see, where was I? Oh, I know, aunt saw the boy grinning in the hedge. Yes, well, she was dreadfully frightened for a minute or two; there was something so queer about the face, but then she plucked up a spirit and said to herself, 'After all, better a boy with red hair than a big man with a gun,' and she made up her mind to watch Uncle Robert closely, as she could see by his look he knew all about it; he seemed as if he were thinking hard and puzzling over something, as if he didn't know what to do next, and his mouth kept opening and shutting, like a fish's. So she kept her face straight, and didn't say a word, and when he said something to her about the fine sunset, she took no notice. 'Don't you hear what I say, Marian?' he said, speaking quite crossly, and bellowing as if it were to somebody in the next field. So aunt said she was very sorry, but her cold made her so deaf, she couldn't hear much. She noticed uncle looked quite pleased, and relieved too, and she knew he thought she hadn't heard the whistling. Suddenly uncle pretended to see a beautiful spray of honeysuckle high up in the hedge, and he said he must get it for aunt, only she must go on ahead, as it made him nervous to be watched. She said she would, but she just stepped aside behind a bush where there was a sort of cover in the hedge, and found she could see him quite well, though she scratched her face terribly with poking it into a rose bush. And in a minute or two out came the boy from behind the hedge, and she saw uncle and him talking, and she knew it was the same boy, as it wasn't dark enough to hide his flaming red head. And uncle put out his hand as if to catch him, but he just darted into the bushes and vanished. Aunt never said a word at the time, but that night when they got home she charged uncle with what she'd seen and asked him what it all meant. He was quite taken aback at first, and stammered and stuttered and said a spy wasn't his notion of a good wife, but at last he made her swear secrecy, and told her that he was a very high Freemason, and that the boy was an emissary of the order, who brought him messages of the greatest importance. But aunt didn't believe a word of it, as an uncle of hers was a mason, and he never behaved like that. It was then she began to be afraid that it was really Anarchists, or something of the kind, and every time the bell rang she thought that uncle had been found out, and the police had come for him."

"What nonsense! As if a man with house property would be an Anarchist."

"Well, she could see there must be some horrible secret, and she didn't know what else to think. And then she began to have the things through the post."

"Things through the post! What do you mean by that?"

"All sorts of things; bits of broken bottle-glass, packed carefully as if it were jewellery; parcels that unrolled and unrolled worse than Chinese boxes, and then had 'cat' in large letters when you came to the middle; old artificial teeth, a cake of red paint, and at last cockroaches."

"Cockroaches by post! Stuff and nonsense; your aunt's mad."

"Edward, she showed me the box; it was made to hold cigarettes, and there were three dead cockroaches inside. And when she found a box of exactly the same kind, half-full of cigarettes, in uncle's greatcoat pocket, then her head began to turn again."

Darnell groaned, and stirred uneasily in his chair, feeling that the tale of Aunt Marian's domestic troubles was putting on the semblance of an evil dream.

"Anything else?" he asked.

"My dear, I haven't repeated half the things poor aunt told me this afternoon. There was the night she thought she saw a ghost in the shrubbery. She was anxious about some chickens that were just due to hatch out, so she went out after dark with some egg and breadcrumbs, in case they might be out. And just before her she saw a figure gliding by the rhododendrons. It looked like a short, slim man dressed as they used to be hundreds of years ago; she saw the sword by his side, and the feather in his cap. She thought she should have died, she said, and though it was gone in a minute, and she tried to make out it was all her fancy, she fainted when she got into the house. Uncle was at home that night, and when she came to and told him he ran out, and stayed out for half-an-hour or more, and then came in and said he could find nothing; and the next minute aunt heard that low whistle just outside the window, and uncle ran out again."

"My dear Mary, do let us come to the point. What on earth does it all lead to?"

"Haven't you guessed? Why, of course it was that girl all the time."

"Girl? I thought you said it was a boy with a red head?"

"Don't you see? She's an actress, and she dressed up. She won't leave uncle alone. It wasn't enough that he was with her nearly every evening in the week, but she must be after him on Sundays too. Aunt found a letter the horrid thing had written, and so it has all come out. Enid Vivian she calls herself, though I don't suppose she has any right to one name or the other. And the question is, what is to be done?"

"Let us talk of that again. I'll have a pipe, and then we'll go to bed."

They were almost asleep when Mary said suddenly—

"Doesn't it seem queer, Edward? Last night you were telling me such beautiful things, and to-night I have been talking about that disgraceful old man and his goings on."

"I don't know," answered Darnell, dreamily. "On the walls of that great church upon the hill I saw all kinds of strange grinning monsters, carved in stone."

The misdemeanours of Mr. Robert Nixon brought in their train consequences strange beyond imagination. It was not that they continued to develop on the somewhat fantastic lines of these first adventures which Mrs. Darnell had related; indeed, when "Aunt Marian" came over to Shepherd's Bush, one Sunday afternoon, Darnell wondered how he had had the heart to laugh at the misfortunes of a broken-hearted woman.

He had never seen his wife's aunt before, and he was strangely surprised when Alice showed her into the garden where they were sitting on the warm and misty Sunday in September. To him, save during these latter days, she had always been associated with ideas of splendour and success: his wife had always mentioned the Nixons with a tinge of reverence; he had heard, many times, the epic of Mr. Nixon's struggles and of his slow but triumphant rise. Mary had told the story as she had received it from her parents, beginning with the flight to London from some small, dull, and unprosperous town in the flattest of the Midlands, long ago, when a young man from the country had great chances of fortune. Robert Nixon's father had been a grocer in the High Street, and in after days the successful coal merchant and builder loved to tell of that dull provincial life, and while he glorified his own victories, he gave his hearers to understand that he came of a race which had also known how to achieve. That had been long ago, he would explain: in the days when that rare citizen who desired to go to London or to York was forced to rise in the dead of night, and make his way, somehow or other, by ten miles of quagmirish, wandering lanes to the Great North Road, there to meet the "Lightning" coach, a vehicle which stood to all the countryside as the visible and tangible embodiment of tremendous speed—"and indeed," as Nixon would add, "it was always up to time, which is more than can be said of the Dunham Branch Line nowadays!" It was in this ancient Dunham that the Nixons had waged successful trade for perhaps a hundred years, in a shop with bulging bay windows looking on the market-place. There was no competition, and the townsfolk, and well-to-do farmers, the clergy and the country families, looked upon the house of Nixon as an institution fixed as the town hall (which stood on Roman pillars) and the parish church. But the change came: the railway crept nearer and nearer, the farmers and the country gentry became less well-to-do; the tanning, which was the local industry, suffered from a great business which had been established in a larger town, some twenty miles away, and the profits of the Nixons grew less and less. Hence the hegira of Robert, and he would dilate on the poorness of his beginnings, how he saved, by little and little, from his sorry wage of City clerk, and how he and a fellow clerk, "who had come into a hundred pounds," saw an opening in the coal trade—and filled it. It was at this stage of Robert's fortunes, still far from magnificent, that Miss Marian Reynolds had encountered him, she being on a visit to friends in Gunnersbury. Afterwards, victory followed victory; Nixon's wharf became a landmark to bargemen; his power stretched abroad, his dusky fleets went outwards to the sea, and inward by all the far reaches of canals. Lime, cement, and bricks were added to his merchandise, and at last he hit upon the great stroke—that extensive taking up of land in the north of London. Nixon himself ascribed this *coup* to native sagacity, and the possession of capital; and there were also obscure rumours to the effect that some one or other had been "done" in the course of the transaction. However that might be, the Nixons grew wealthy to excess, and Mary had often told her husband of the state in which they dwelt, of their liveried servants, of the glories of their drawing-room, of their broad lawn, shadowed by a splendid and ancient cedar. And so Darnell had somehow been led into conceiving the lady of this demesne as a personage of no small pomp. He saw her, tall, of dignified port and presence, inclining, it might be, to some measure of obesity, such a measure as was not unbefitting in an elderly lady of position, who lived well and lived at ease. He even imagined a slight ruddiness of complexion, which went very well with hair that was beginning to turn grey, and when he heard the door-bell ring, as he sat under the mulberry on the Sunday afternoon, he bent forward to catch sight of this stately figure, clad, of course, in the richest, blackest silk, girt about with heavy chains of gold.

He started with amazement when he saw the strange presence that followed the servant into the garden. Mrs. Nixon was a little, thin old woman, who bent as she feebly trotted after Alice; her eyes were on the ground, and she did not lift them when the Darnells rose to greet her. She glanced to the right, uneasily, as she shook hands with Darnell, to the left when Mary kissed her, and when she was placed on the garden seat with a cushion at her back, she looked away at the back of the houses in the next street. She was dressed in black, it was true, but even Darnell could see that her gown was old and shabby, that the fur trimming of her cape and the fur boa which was twisted about her neck were dingy and disconsolate, and had all the melancholy air which fur wears when it is seen in a second-hand clothes-shop in a back street. And her gloves—they were black kid, wrinkled with much wear, faded to a bluish hue at the finger-tips, which showed signs of painful mending. Her hair, plastered over her forehead, looked dull and colourless, though some greasy matter had evidently been used with a view of producing a becoming gloss, and on it perched an antique bonnet, adorned with black pendants that rattled paralytically one against the other.

And there was nothing in Mrs. Nixon's face to correspond with the imaginary picture that Darnell had made of her. She was sallow, wrinkled, pinched; her nose ran to a sharp point, and her red-rimmed eyes were a queer water-grey, that seemed to shrink alike from the light and from encounter with the eyes of others. As she sat beside his wife on the green garden-seat, Darnell, who occupied a wicker-chair brought out from the drawing-room, could not help feeling that this shadowy and evasive figure, muttering replies to

Mary's polite questions, was almost impossibly remote from his conceptions of the rich and powerful aunt, who could give away a hundred pounds as a mere birthday gift. She would say little at first; yes, she was feeling rather tired, it had been so hot all the way, and she had been afraid to put on lighter things as one never knew at this time of year what it might be like in the evenings; there were apt to be cold mists when the sun went down, and she didn't care to risk bronchitis.

"I thought I should never get here," she went on, raising her voice to an odd querulous pipe. "I'd no notion it was such an out-of-the-way place, it's so many years since I was in this neighbourhood."

She wiped her eyes, no doubt thinking of the early days at Turnham Green, when she married Nixon; and when the pocket-handkerchief had done its office she replaced it in a shabby black bag which she clutched rather than carried. Darnell noticed, as he watched her, that the bag seemed full, almost to bursting, and he speculated idly as to the nature of its contents: correspondence, perhaps, he thought, further proofs of Uncle Robert's treacherous and wicked dealings. He grew quite uncomfortable, as he sat and saw her glancing all the while furtively away from his wife and himself, and presently he got up and strolled away to the other end of the garden, where he lit his pipe and walked to and fro on the gravel walk, still astounded at the gulf between the real and the imagined woman.

Presently he heard a hissing whisper, and he saw Mrs. Nixon's head inclining to his wife's. Mary rose and came towards him.

"Would you mind sitting in the drawing-room, Edward?" she murmured. "Aunt says she can't bring herself to discuss such a delicate matter before you. I dare say it's quite natural."

"Very well, but I don't think I'll go into the drawing-room. I feel as if a walk would do me good."

"You mustn't be frightened if I am a little late," he said; "if I don't get back before your aunt goes, say good-bye to her for me."

He strolled into the main road, where the trams were humming to and fro. He was still confused and perplexed, and he tried to account for a certain relief he felt in removing himself from the presence of Mrs. Nixon. He told himself that her grief at her husband's ruffianly conduct was worthy of all pitiful respect, but at the same time, to his shame, he had felt a certain physical aversion from her as she sat in his garden in her dingy black, dabbing her red-rimmed eyes with a damp pocket-handkerchief. He had been to the Zoo when he was a lad, and he still remembered how he had shrunk with horror at the sight of certain reptiles slowly crawling over one another in their slimy pond. But he was enraged at the similarity between the two sensations, and he walked briskly on that level and monotonous road, looking about him at the unhandsome spectacle of suburban London keeping Sunday.

There was something in the tinge of antiquity which still exists in Acton that soothed his mind and drew it away from those unpleasant contemplations, and when at last he had penetrated rampart after rampart of brick, and heard no more the harsh shrieks and laughter of the people who were enjoying themselves, he found a way into a little sheltered field, and sat down in peace beneath a tree, whence he could look out on a pleasant valley. The sun sank down beneath the hills, the clouds changed into the likeness of blossoming rose-gardens; and he still sat there in the gathering darkness till a cool breeze blew upon him, and he rose with a sigh, and turned back to the brick ramparts and the glimmering streets, and the noisy idlers sauntering to and fro in the procession of their dismal festival. But he was murmuring to himself some words that seemed a magic song, and it was with uplifted heart that he let himself into his house.

Mrs. Nixon had gone an hour and a half before his return, Mary told him. Darnell sighed with relief, and he and his wife strolled out into the garden and sat down side by side.

They kept silence for a time, and at last Mary spoke, not without a nervous tremor in her voice.

"I must tell you, Edward," she began, "that aunt has made a proposal which you ought to hear. I think we should consider it."

"A proposal? But how about the whole affair? Is it still going on?"

"Oh, yes! She told me all about it. Uncle is quite unrepentant. It seems he has taken a flat somewhere in town for that woman, and furnished it in the most costly manner. He simply laughs at aunt's reproaches, and says he means to have some fun at last. You saw how broken she was?"

"Yes; very sad. But won't he give her any money? Wasn't she very badly dressed for a woman in her position?"

"Aunt has no end of beautiful things, but I fancy she likes to hoard them; she has a horror of spoiling her dresses. It isn't for want of money, I assure you, as uncle settled a very large sum on her two years ago, when he was everything that could be desired as a husband. And that brings me to what I want to say. Aunt would like to live with us. She would pay very liberally. What do you say?"

"Would like to live with us?" exclaimed Darnell, and his pipe dropped from his hand on to the grass. He was stupefied by the thought of Aunt Marian as a boarder, and sat staring vacantly before him, wondering what new monster the night would next produce.

"I knew you wouldn't much like the idea," his wife went on. "But I do think, dearest, that we ought not to refuse without very serious consideration. I am afraid you did not take to poor aunt very much."

Darnell shook his head dumbly.

"I thought you didn't; she was so upset, poor thing, and you didn't see her at her best. She is really so good. But listen to me, dear. Do you think we have the right to refuse her offer? I told you she has money of her own, and I am sure she would be dreadfully offended if we said we wouldn't have her. And what would become of me if anything happened to you? You know we have very little saved."

Darnell groaned.

"It seems to me," he said, "that it would spoil everything. We are so happy, Mary dear, by ourselves. Of course I am extremely sorry for your aunt. I think she is very much to be pitied. But when it comes to having her always here—"

"I know, dear. Don't think I am looking forward to the prospect; you know I don't want anybody but you. Still, we ought to think of the future, and besides we shall be able to live so very much better. I shall be able to give you all sorts of nice things that I know you ought to have after all that hard work in the City. Our income would be doubled."

"Do you mean she would pay us £150 a year?"

"Certainly. And she would pay for the spare room being furnished, and any extra she might want. She told me, specially, that if a friend or two came now and again to see her, she would gladly bear the cost of a fire in the drawing-room, and give something towards the gas bill, with a few shillings for the girl for any additional trouble.

We should certainly be more than twice as well off as we are now. You see, Edward, dear, it's not the sort of offer we are likely to have again. Besides, we must think of the future, as I said. Do you know aunt took a great fancy to you?"

He shuddered and said nothing, and his wife went on with her argument.

"And, you see, it isn't as if we should see so very much of her. She will have her breakfast in bed, and she told me she would often go up to her room in the evening directly after dinner. I thought that very nice and considerate. She quite understands that we shouldn't like to have a third person always with us. Don't you think, Edward, that, considering everything, we ought to say we will have her?"

"Oh, I suppose so," he groaned. "As you say, it's a very good offer, financially, and I am afraid it would be very imprudent to refuse. But I don't like the notion, I confess."

"I am so glad you agree with me, dear. Depend upon it, it won't be half so bad as you think. And putting our own advantage on one side, we shall really be doing poor aunt a very great kindness. Poor old dear, she cried bitterly after you were gone; she said she had made up her mind not to stay any longer in Uncle Robert's house, and she didn't know where to go, or what would become of her, if we refused to take her in. She quite broke down."

"Well, well; we will try it for a year, anyhow. It may be as you say; we shan't find it quite so bad as it seems now. Shall we go in?"

He stooped for his pipe, which lay as it had fallen, on the grass. He could not find it, and lit a wax match which showed him the pipe, and close beside it, under the seat, something that looked like a page torn from a book. He wondered what it could be, and picked it up.

The gas was lit in the drawing-room, and Mrs. Darnell, who was arranging some notepaper, wished to write at once to Mrs. Nixon, cordially accepting her proposal, when she was startled by an exclamation from her husband.

"What is the matter?" she said, startled by the tone of his voice. "You haven't hurt yourself?"

"Look at this," he replied, handing her a small leaflet. "I found it under the garden seat just now."

Mary glanced with bewilderment at her husband and read as follows:—

THE NEW AND CHOSEN SEED OF ABRAHAM

PROPHECIES TO BE FULFILLED IN THE PRESENT YEAR

1. The Sailing of a Fleet of One Hundred and Forty and Four Vessels for Tarshish and the Isles.

2. Destruction of the Power of the Dog, including all the instruments of anti-Abrahamic legislation.

3. Return of the Fleet from Tarshish, bearing with it the gold of Arabia, destined to be the Foundation of the New City of Abraham.

4. The Search for the Bride, and the bestowing of the Seals on the Seventy and Seven.

5. The Countenance of FATHER to become luminous, but with a greater glory than the face of Moses.

6. The Pope of Rome to be stoned with stones in the valley called Berek-Zittor.

7. FATHER to be acknowledged by Three Great Rulers. Two Great Rulers will deny FATHER, and will immediately perish in the Effluvia of FATHER'S Indignation.

8. Binding of the Beast with the Little Horn, and all judges cast down.

9. Finding of the Bride in the Land of Egypt, which has been revealed to FATHER as now existing in the western part of London.

10. Bestowal of the New Tongue on the Seventy and Seven, and on the One Hundred and Forty and Four. FATHER proceeds to the Bridal Chamber.

11. Destruction of London and rebuilding of the City called No, which is the New City of Abraham.

12. FATHER united to the Bride, and the present Earth removed to the Sun for the space of half an hour.

Mrs. Darnell's brow cleared as she read matter which seemed to her harmless if incoherent. From her husband's voice she had been led to fear something more tangibly unpleasant than a vague catena of prophecies.

"Well," she said, "what about it?"

"What about it? Don't you see that your aunt dropped it, and that she must be a raging lunatic?"

"Oh, Edward! don't say that. In the first place, how do you know that aunt dropped it at all? It might easily have blown over from any of the other gardens. And, if it were hers, I don't think you should call her a lunatic. I don't believe, myself, that there are any real prophets now; but there are many good people who think quite differently. I knew an old lady once who, I am sure, was very good, and she took in a paper every week that was full of prophecies and things very like this. Nobody called her mad, and I have heard father say that she had one of the sharpest heads for business he had ever come across."

"Very good; have it as you like. But I believe we shall both be sorry."

They sat in silence for some time. Alice came in after her "evening out," and they sat on, till Mrs. Darnell said she was tired and wanted to go to bed.

Her husband kissed her. "I don't think I will come up just yet," he said; "you go to sleep, dearest. I want to think things over. No, no; I am not going to change my mind: your aunt shall come, as I said. But there are one or two things I should like to get settled in my mind."

He meditated for a long while, pacing up and down the room. Light after light was extinguished in Edna Road, and the people of the suburb slept all around him, but still the gas was alight in Darnell's drawing-room, and he walked softly up and down the floor. He was thinking that about the life of Mary and himself, which had been so quiet, there seemed to be gathering on all sides grotesque and fantastic shapes, omens of confusion and disorder, threats of madness; a strange company from another world. It was as if into the quiet, sleeping streets of some little ancient town among the hills there had come from afar the sound of drum and pipe, snatches of wild song, and there had burst into the market-place the mad company of the players, strangely bedizened, dancing a furious measure to their hurrying music, drawing forth the citizens from their sheltered homes and peaceful lives, and alluring them to mingle in the significant figures of their dance.

Yet afar and near (for it was hidden in his heart) he beheld the glimmer of a sure and constant star. Beneath, darkness came on, and mists and shadows closed about the town. The red, flickering flame of torches was kindled in the midst of it. The song grew louder, with more insistent, magical tones, surging and falling in unearthly modulations, the very speech of incantation; and the drum beat madly, and the pipe shrilled to a scream, summoning all to issue forth, to leave their peaceful hearths; for a strange rite was preconized in their midst. The streets that were wont to be so still, so hushed with the cool and tranquil veils of darkness, asleep beneath the patronage of the evening star, now danced with glimmering lanterns, resounded with the cries of those who hurried forth, drawn as by a magistral spell; and the songs swelled and triumphed, the reverberant beating of the drum grew louder, and in the midst of the awakened town the players, fantastically arrayed, performed their interlude under the red blaze of torches. He knew not whether they were players, men that would vanish suddenly as they came, disappearing by the track that climbed the hill; or whether they were indeed magicians, workers of great and efficacious spells, who knew the secret word by which the earth may be transformed into the hall of Gehenna, so that they that gazed and listened, as at a passing spectacle, should be entrapped by the sound and the sight presented to them, should be drawn into the elaborated figures of that mystic dance, and so should be whirled away into those unending mazes on the wild hills that were abhorred, there to wander for evermore.

But Darnell was not afraid, because of the Daystar that had risen in his heart. It had dwelt there all his life, and had slowly shone forth with clearer and clearer light, and he began to see that though his earthly steps might be in the ways of the ancient town that was beset by the Enchanters, and resounded with their songs and their processions, yet he dwelt also in that serene and secure world of brightness, and from a great and unutterable height looked on the confusion of the mortal pageant, beholding mysteries in which he was no true actor, hearing magic songs that could by no means draw him down from the battlements of the high and holy city.

His heart was filled with a great joy and a great peace as he lay down beside his wife and fell asleep, and in the morning, when he woke up, he was glad.

IV

In a haze as of a dream Darnell's thoughts seemed to move through the opening days of the next week. Perhaps nature had not intended that he should be practical or much given to that which is usually called "sound common sense," but his training had made him desirous of good, plain qualities of the mind, and he uneasily strove to account to himself for his strange mood of the Sunday night, as he had often endeavoured to interpret the fancies of his boyhood and early manhood. At first he was annoyed by his want of success; the morning paper, which he always secured as the 'bus delayed at Uxbridge Road Station, fell from his hands unread, while he vainly reasoned, assuring himself that the threatened incursion of a whimsical old woman, though tiresome enough, was no rational excuse for those curious hours of meditation in which his thoughts seemed to have dressed themselves in unfamiliar, fantastic habits, and to parley with him in a strange speech, and yet a speech that he had understood.

With such arguments he perplexed his mind on the long, accustomed ride up the steep ascent of Holland Park, past the incongruous hustle of Notting Hill Gate, where in one direction a road shows the way to the snug, somewhat faded bowers and retreats of Bayswater, and in another one sees the portal of the murky region of the slums. The customary companions of his morning's journey were in the seats about him; he heard the hum of their talk, as they disputed concerning politics, and the man next to him, who came from Acton, asked him what he thought of the Government now. There was a discussion, and a loud and excited one, just in front, as to whether rhubarb was a fruit or vegetable, and in his ear he heard Redman, who was a near neighbour, praising the economy of "the wife."

"I don't know how she does it. Look here; what do you think we had yesterday? Breakfast: fish-cakes, beautifully fried—rich, you know, lots of herbs, it's a receipt of her aunt's; you should just taste 'em. Coffee, bread, butter, marmalade, and, of course, all the usual etceteras. Dinner: roast beef, Yorkshire, potatoes, greens, and horse-radish sauce, plum tart, cheese. And where will you get a better dinner than that? Well, I call it wonderful, I really do."

But in spite of these distractions he fell into a dream as the 'bus rolled and tossed on its way Citywards, and still he strove to solve the enigma of his vigil of the night before, and as the shapes of trees and green lawns and houses passed before his eyes, and as he saw the procession moving on the pavement, and while the murmur of the streets sounded in his ears, all was to him strange and unaccustomed, as if he moved through the avenues of some city in a foreign land. It was, perhaps, on these mornings, as he rode to his mechanical work, that vague and floating fancies that must have long haunted his brain began to shape themselves, and to put on the form of definite conclusions, from which he could no longer escape, even if he had wished it. Darnell had received what is called a sound commercial education, and would therefore have found very great difficulty in putting into articulate speech any thought that was worth thinking; but he grew certain on these mornings that the "common sense" which he had always heard exalted as man's supremest faculty was, in all probability, the smallest and least-considered item in the equipment of an ant of average intelligence. And with this, as an almost necessary corollary, came a firm belief that the whole fabric of life in which he moved was sunken, past all thinking, in the grossest absurdity; that he and all his friends and acquaintances and fellow-workers were interested in matters in which men were never meant to be interested, were pursuing aims which they were never meant to pursue, were, indeed, much like fair stones of an altar serving as a pigsty wall. Life, it seemed to him, was a great search for—he knew not what; and in the process of the ages one by one the true marks upon the ways had been shattered, or buried, or the meaning of the words had been slowly forgotten; one by one the signs had been turned awry, the true entrances had been thickly overgrown, the very way itself had been diverted from the heights to the depths, till at last the race of pilgrims had become hereditary stone-breakers and ditch-scourers on a track that led to destruction—if it led anywhere at all. Darnell's heart thrilled with a strange and trembling joy, with a sense that was all new, when it came to his mind that this great loss might not be a hopeless one, that perhaps the difficulties were by no means insuperable. It might be, he considered, that the stone-breaker had merely to throw down his hammer and set out, and the way would be plain before him; and a single step would free the delver in rubbish from the foul slime of the ditch.

It was, of course, with difficulty and slowly that these things became clear to him. He was an English City clerk, "flourishing" towards the end of the nineteenth century, and the rubbish heap that had been accumulating for some centuries could not be cleared away in an instant. Again and again the spirit of nonsense that had been implanted in him as in his fellows assured him that the true world was the visible and tangible world, the world in which good and faithful letter-copying was exchangeable for a certain quantum of bread, beef, and house-room, and that the man who copied letters well, did not beat his wife, nor lose money foolishly, was a good man, fulfilling the end for which he had been made. But in spite of these arguments, in spite of their acceptance by all who were about him, he had the grace to perceive the utter falsity and absurdity of the whole position. He was fortunate in his entire ignorance of sixpenny "science," but if the whole library had been projected into his brain it would not have moved him to "deny in the darkness that which he had known in the light." Darnell knew by experience that man is made a mystery for mysteries and visions, for the realization in his consciousness of ineffable bliss, for a great joy that transmutes the whole world, for a joy that surpasses all joys and overcomes all sorrows. He knew this certainly, though he knew it dimly; and he was apart from other men, preparing himself for a great experiment.

With such thoughts as these for his secret and concealed treasure, he was able to bear the threatened invasion of Mrs. Nixon with something approaching indifference. He knew, indeed, that her presence between his wife and himself would be unwelcome to him, and he was not without grave doubts as to the woman's sanity; but after all, what did it matter? Besides, already a faint glimmering light had risen within him that showed the profit of self-negation, and in this matter he had preferred his wife's will to his own. *Et non sua poma;* to his astonishment he found a delight in denying himself his own wish, a process that he had always regarded as thoroughly detestable. This was a state of things which he could not in the least understand; but, again, though a member of a most hopeless class, living in the most hopeless surroundings that the world has ever seen, though he knew as much of the *askesis* as of Chinese metaphysics; again, he had the grace not to deny the light that had begun to glimmer in his soul.

And he found a present reward in the eyes of Mary, when she welcomed him home after his foolish labours in the cool of the evening. They sat together, hand in hand, under the mulberry tree, at the coming of the dusk, and as the ugly walls about them became obscure and vanished into the formless world of shadows, they seemed to be freed from the bondage of Shepherd's Bush, freed to wander in that undisfigured, undefiled world that lies beyond the walls. Of this region Mary knew little or nothing by experience, since her relations had always been of one mind with the modern world, which has for the true country an instinctive and most significant horror and dread. Mr. Reynolds had also shared in another odd superstition of these later days—that it is necessary to leave London at least once a year; consequently Mary had some knowledge of various seaside resorts on the south and east coasts, where Londoners gather in hordes, turn the sands into one vast, bad music-hall, and derive, as they say, enormous benefit from the change. But experiences such as these give but little knowledge of the country in its true and occult sense; and yet Mary, as she sat in the dusk beneath the whispering tree, knew something of the secret of the wood, of the valley shut in by high hills, where the sound of pouring water always echoes from the clear brook. And to Darnell these were nights of great dreams; for it was the hour of the work, the time of transmutation, and he who could not understand the miracle, who could scarcely believe in it, yet knew, secretly and half consciously, that the water was being changed into the wine of a new life. This was ever the inner music of his dreams, and to it he added on these still and sacred nights the far-off memory of that time long ago when, a child, before the world had overwhelmed him, he journeyed down to the old grey house in the west, and for a whole month heard the murmur of the forest through his bedroom window, and when the wind was hushed, the washing of the tides about the reeds; and sometimes awaking very early he had heard the strange cry of a bird as it rose from its nest among the reeds, and had looked out and had seen the valley whiten to the dawn, and the winding river whiten as it swam down to the sea. The memory of all this had faded and become shadowy as he grew older and the chains of common life were riveted firmly about his soul; all the atmosphere by which he was surrounded was well-nigh fatal to such thoughts, and only now and again in half-conscious moments or in sleep he had revisited that valley in the far-off west, where the breath of the wind was an incantation, and every leaf and stream and hill spoke of great and ineffable mysteries. But now the broken vision was in great part restored to him, and looking with love in his wife's eyes he saw the gleam of water-pools in the still forest, saw the mists rising in the evening, and heard the music of the winding river.

They were sitting thus together on the Friday evening of the week that had begun with that odd and half-forgotten visit of Mrs. Nixon, when, to Darnell's annoyance, the door-bell gave a discordant peal, and Alice with some disturbance of manner came out and announced that a gentleman wished to see the master. Darnell went into the drawing-room, where Alice had lit one gas so that it flared and burnt with a rushing sound, and in this distorting light there waited a stout, elderly gentleman, whose countenance was altogether unknown to him. He stared blankly, and hesitated, about to speak, but the visitor began.

"You don't know who I am, but I expect you'll know my name. It's Nixon."

He did not wait to be interrupted. He sat down and plunged into narrative, and after the first few words, Darnell, whose mind was not altogether unprepared, listened without much astonishment.

"And the long and the short of it is," Mr. Nixon said at last, "she's gone stark, staring mad, and we had to put her away to-day—poor thing."

His voice broke a little, and he wiped his eyes hastily, for though stout and successful he was not unfeeling, and he was fond of his wife. He had spoken quickly, and had gone lightly over many details which might have interested specialists in certain kinds of mania, and Darnell was sorry for his evident distress.

"I came here," he went on after a brief pause, "because I found out she had been to see you last Sunday, and I knew the sort of story she must have told."

Darnell showed him the prophetic leaflet which Mrs. Nixon had dropped in the garden. "Did you know about this?" he said.

"Oh, *him,*" said the old man, with some approach to cheerfulness; "oh yes, I thrashed *him* black and blue the day before yesterday."

"Isn't he mad? Who is the man?"

"He's not mad, he's bad. He's a little Welsh skunk named Richards. He's been running some sort of chapel over at New Barnet for the last few years, and my poor wife—she never could find the parish church good enough for her—had been going to his damned schism shop for the last twelve-month. It was all that finished her off. Yes; I thrashed *him* the day before yesterday, and I'm not afraid of a summons either. I know him, and he knows I know him."

Old Nixon whispered something in Darnell's ear, and chuckled faintly as he repeated for the third time his formula—

"I thrashed *him* black and blue the day before yesterday."

Darnell could only murmur condolences and express his hope that Mrs. Nixon might recover.

The old man shook his head.

"I'm afraid there's no hope of that," he said. "I've had the best advice, but they couldn't do anything, and told me so."

Presently he asked to see his niece, and Darnell went out and prepared Mary as well as he could. She could scarcely take in the news that her aunt was a hopeless maniac, for Mrs. Nixon, having been extremely stupid all her days, had naturally succeeded in passing with her relations as typically sensible. With the Reynolds family, as with the great majority of us, want of imagination is always equated with sanity, and, though many of us have never heard of Lombroso we are his ready-made converts. We have always believed that poets are mad, and if statistics unfortunately show that few poets have really been inhabitants of lunatic asylums, it is soothing to learn that nearly all poets have had whooping-cough, which is doubtless, like intoxication, a minor madness.

"But is it really true?" she asked at length. "Are you certain uncle is not deceiving you? Aunt seemed so sensible always."

She was helped at last by recollecting that Aunt Marian used to get up very early of mornings, and then they went into the drawing-room and talked to the old man. His evident kindliness and honesty grew upon Mary, in spite of a lingering belief in her aunt's fables, and when he left, it was with a promise to come to see them again.

Mrs. Darnell said she felt tired, and went to bed; and Darnell returned to the garden and began to pace to and fro, collecting his thoughts. His immeasurable relief at the intelligence that, after all, Mrs. Nixon was not coming to live with them taught him that, despite his submission, his dread of the event had been very great. The weight was removed, and now he was free to consider his life without reference to the grotesque intrusion that he had feared. He sighed for joy, and as he paced to and fro he savoured the scent of the night, which, though it came faintly to him in that brick-bound suburb, summoned to his mind across many years the odour of the world at night as he had known it in that short sojourn of his boyhood; the odour that rose from the earth when the flame of the sun had gone down beyond the mountain, and the afterglow had paled in the sky and on the fields. And as he recovered as best he could these lost dreams of an enchanted land, there came to him other images of his childhood, forgotten and yet not forgotten, dwelling unheeded in dark places of the memory, but ready to be summoned forth. He remembered one fantasy that had long haunted him. As he lay half asleep in the forest on one hot afternoon of that memorable visit to the country, he had "made believe" that a little companion had come to him out of the blue mists and the green light beneath the leaves—a white girl with long black hair, who had played with him and whispered her secrets in his ear, as his father lay sleeping under a tree; and from that summer afternoon, day by day, she had been beside him; she had visited him in the wilderness of London, and even in recent years there had come to him now and again the sense of her presence, in the midst of the heat and turmoil of the City. The last visit he remembered well; it was a few weeks before he married, and from the depths of some futile task he had looked up with puzzled eyes, wondering why the close air suddenly grew scented with green leaves, why the murmur of the trees and the wash of the river on the reeds came to his ears; and then that sudden rapture to which he had given a name and an individuality possessed him utterly. He knew then how the dull flesh of man can be like fire; and now, looking back from a new standpoint on this and other experiences, he realized how all that was real in his life had been unwelcomed, uncherished by him, had come to him, perhaps, in virtue of merely negative qualities on his part. And yet, as he reflected, he saw that there had been a chain of witnesses all through his life: again and again voices had whispered in his ear words in a strange language that he now recognized as his native tongue; the common street had not been lacking in visions of the true land of his birth; and in all the passing and repassing of the world he saw that there had been emissaries ready to guide his feet on the way of the great journey.

A week or two after the visit of Mr. Nixon, Darnell took his annual holiday.

There was no question of Walton-on-the-Naze, or of anything of the kind, as he quite agreed with his wife's longing for some substantial sum put by against the evil day. But the weather was still fine, and he lounged away the time in his garden beneath the tree, or he sauntered out on long aimless walks in the western purlieus of London, not unvisited by that old sense of some great ineffable beauty, concealed by the dim and dingy veils of grey interminable streets. Once, on a day of heavy rain he went to the "box-room," and began to turn over the papers in the old hair trunk—scraps and odds and ends of family history, some of them in his father's handwriting, others in faded ink, and there were a few ancient pocket-books, filled with manuscript of a still earlier time, and in these the ink was glossier and blacker than any writing fluids supplied by stationers of later days. Darnell had hung up the portrait of the ancestor in this room, and had bought a solid kitchen table and a chair; so that Mrs. Darnell, seeing him looking over his old documents, half thought of naming the room "Mr. Darnell's study." He had not glanced at these relics of his family for many years, but from the hour when the rainy morning sent him to them, he remained constant to research till the end of the holidays. It was a new interest, and he began to fashion in his mind a faint picture of his forefathers, and of their life in that grey old house in the river valley, in the western land of wells and streams and dark and ancient woods. And there were stranger things than mere notes on family history amongst that odd litter of old disregarded papers, and when he went back to his work in the City some of the men fancied that he was in some vague manner changed in appearance; but he only laughed when they asked him where he had been, and what he had been doing with himself. But Mary noticed that every evening he spent at least an hour in the box-room; she was rather sorry at the waste of time involved in reading old papers about dead people. And one afternoon, as they were out together on a somewhat dreary walk towards Acton, Darnell stopped at a hopeless second-hand bookshop, and after scanning the rows of shabby books in the window, went in and purchased two volumes. They proved to be a Latin dictionary and grammar, and she was surprised to hear her husband declare his intention of acquiring the Latin language.

But, indeed, all his conduct impressed her as indefinably altered; and she began to be a little alarmed, though she could scarcely have formed her fears in words. But she knew that in some way that was all indefined and beyond the grasp of her thought their lives had altered since the summer, and no single thing wore quite the same aspect as before. If she looked out into the dull street with its rare loiterers, it was the same and yet it had altered, and if she opened the window in the early morning the wind that entered came with a changed breath that spoke some message that she could not understand. And day by day passed by in the old course, and not even the four walls were altogether familiar, and the voices of men and women sounded with strange notes, with the echo, rather of a music that came over unknown hills. And day by day as she went about her household work, passing from shop to shop in those dull streets that were a network, a fatal labyrinth of grey desolation on every side, there came to her sense half-seen images of some other world, as if she walked in a dream, and every moment must bring her to light and to awakening, when the grey should fade, and regions long desired should appear in glory. Again and again it seemed as if that which was hidden would be shown even to the sluggish testimony of sense; and as she went to and fro from street to street of that dim and weary suburb, and looked on those grey material walls, they seemed as if a light glowed behind them, and again and again the mystic fragrance of incense was blown to her nostrils from across the verge of that world which is not so much the impenetrable as ineffable, and to her ears came the dream of a chant that spoke of hidden choirs about all her ways. She struggled against these impressions, refusing her assent to the testimony of them, since all the pressure of credited opinion for three hundred years has been directed towards stamping out real knowledge, and so effectually has this been accomplished that we can only recover the truth through much anguish. And so Mary passed the days in a strange perturbation, clinging to common things and common thoughts, as if she feared that one morning she would wake up in an unknown world to a changed life. And Edward Darnell went day by day to his labor and returned, in the evening, always with that shining of light within his eyes and upon his face, with the gaze of wonder that was greater day by day, as if for him the veil grew thin and soon would disappear.

From these great matters both in herself and in her husband Mary shrank back, afraid, perhaps, that if she began the question the answer might be too wonderful. She rather taught herself to be troubled over little things; she asked herself what attraction there could be in the old records over which she supposed Edward to be poring night after night in the cold room upstairs. She had glanced over the papers at Darnell's invitation, and could see but little interest in them; there were one or two sketches, roughly done in pen and ink, of the old house in the west: it looked a shapeless and fantastic place, furnished with strange pillars and stranger ornaments on the projecting porch; and on one side a roof dipped down almost to the earth, and in the centre there was something that might almost be a tower rising above the rest of the building. Then there were documents that seemed all names and dates, with here and there a coat of arms done in the margin, and she came upon a string of uncouth Welsh names linked together by the word "ap" in a chain that looked endless. There was a paper covered with signs and figures that meant nothing to her, and then there were the pocket-books, full of old-fashioned writing, and much of it in Latin, as her husband told her—it was a collection as void of significance as a treatise on conic sections, so far as Mary was concerned. But night after night Darnell shut himself up with the musty rolls, and more than ever when he rejoined her he bore upon his face the blazonry of some great adventure. And one night she asked him what interested him so much in the papers he had shown her.

He was delighted with the question. Somehow they had not talked much together for the last few weeks, and he began to tell her of the records of the old race from which he came, of the old strange house of grey stone between the forest and the river. The family went back and back, he said, far into the dim past, beyond the Normans, beyond the Saxons, far into the Roman days, and for many hundred years they had been petty kings, with a strong fortress high up on the hill, in the heart of the forest; and even now the great mounds remained, whence one could look through the trees towards the mountain on one side and across the yellow sea on the other. The real name of the family was not Darnell; that was assumed by one Iolo ap Taliesin ap Iorwerth in the sixteenth century—why, Darnell did not seem to understand. And then he told her how the race had dwindled in prosperity, century by century, till at last there was nothing left but the grey house and a few acres of land bordering the river.

"And do you know, Mary," he said, "I suppose we shall go and live there some day or other. My great-uncle, who has the place now, made money in business when he was a young man, and I believe he will leave it all to me. I know I am the only relation he has. How strange it would be. What a change from the life here."

"You never told me that. Don't you think your great-uncle might leave his house and his money to somebody he knows really well? You haven't seen him since you were a little boy, have you?"

"No; but we write once a year. And from what I have heard my father say, I am sure the old man would never leave the house out of the family. Do you think you would like it?"

"I don't know. Isn't it very lonely?"

"I suppose it is. I forget whether there are any other houses in sight, but I don't think there are any at all near. But what a change! No City, no streets, no people passing to and fro; only the sound of the wind and the sight of the green leaves and the green hills, and the song of the voices of the earth." . . . He checked himself suddenly, as if he feared that he was about to tell some secret that must not yet be uttered; and indeed, as he spoke of the change from the little street in Shepherd's Bush to that ancient house in the woods of the far west, a change seemed already to possess himself, and his voice put on the modulation of an antique chant. Mary looked at him steadily and touched his arm, and he drew a long breath before he spoke again.

"It is the old blood calling to the old land," he said. "I was forgetting that I am a clerk in the City."

It was, doubtless, the old blood that had suddenly stirred in him; the resurrection of the old spirit that for many centuries had been faithful to secrets that are now disregarded by most of us, that now day by day was quickened more and more in his heart, and grew so strong that it was hard to conceal. He was indeed almost in the position of the man in the tale, who, by a sudden electric shock, lost the vision of the things about him in the London streets, and gazed instead upon the sea and shore of an island in the Antipodes; for Darnell only clung with an effort to the interests and the atmosphere which, till lately, had seemed all the world to him; and the grey house and the wood and the river, symbols of the other sphere, intruded as it were into the landscape of the London suburb.

But he went on, with more restraint, telling his stories of far-off ancestors, how one of them, the most remote of all, was called a saint, and was supposed to possess certain mysterious secrets often alluded to in the papers as the "Hidden Songs of Iolo Sant." And then with an abrupt transition he recalled memories of his father and of the strange, shiftless life in dingy lodgings in the backwaters of London, of the dim stucco streets that were his first recollections, of forgotten squares in North London, and of the figure of his father, a grave bearded man who seemed always in a dream, as if he too sought for the vision of a land beyond the strong walls, a land where there were deep orchards and many shining hills, and fountains and water-pools gleaming under the leaves of the wood.

"I believe my father earned his living," he went on, "such a living as he did earn, at the Record Office and the British Museum. He used to hunt up things for lawyers and country parsons who wanted old deeds inspected. He never made much, and we were always moving from one lodging to another—always to out-of-the-way places where everything seemed to have run to seed. We never knew our neighbours—we moved too often for that—but my father had about half a dozen friends, elderly men like himself, who used to come to see us pretty often; and then, if there was any money, the lodging-house servant would go out for beer, and they would sit and smoke far into the night.

"I never knew much about these friends of his, but they all had the same look, the look of longing for something hidden. They talked of mysteries that I never understood, very little of their own lives, and when they did speak of ordinary affairs one could tell that they thought such matters as money and the want of it were unimportant trifles. When I grew up and went into the City, and met other young fellows and heard their way of talking, I wondered whether my father and his friends were not a little queer in their heads; but I know better now."

So night after night Darnell talked to his wife, seeming to wander aimlessly from the dingy lodging-houses, where he had spent his boyhood in the company of his father and the other seekers, to the old house hidden in that far western valley, and the old race that had so long looked at the setting of the sun over the mountain. But in truth there was one end in all that he spoke, and Mary felt that beneath his words, however indifferent they might seem, there was hidden a purpose, that they were to embark on a great and marvellous adventure.

So day by day the world became more magical; day by day the work of separation was being performed, the gross accidents were being refined away. Darnell neglected no instruments that might be useful in the work; and now he neither lounged at home on Sunday mornings, nor did he accompany his wife to the Gothic blasphemy which pretended to be a church. They had discovered a little church of another fashion in a back street, and Darnell, who had found in one of the old notebooks the maxim *Incredibilia sola Credenda,* soon perceived how high and glorious a thing was that service at which he assisted. Our stupid ancestors taught us that we could become wise by studying books on "science," by meddling with test-tubes, geological specimens, microscopic preparations, and the like; but they who have cast off these follies know that they must read not "science" books, but mass-books, and that the soul is made wise by the contemplation of mystic ceremonies and elaborate and curious rites. In such things Darnell found a wonderful mystery language, which spoke at once more secretly and more directly than the formal creeds; and he saw that, in a sense, the whole world is but a great ceremony or sacrament, which teaches under visible forms a hidden and transcendent doctrine. It was thus that he found in the ritual of the church a perfect image of the world; an image purged, exalted, and illuminate, a holy house built up of shining and translucent stones, in which the burning torches were more significant than the wheeling stars, and the fuming incense was a more certain token than the rising of the mist. His soul went forth with the albed procession in its white and solemn order, the mystic dance that signifies rapture and a joy above all joys, and when he beheld Love slain and rise again victorious he knew that he witnessed, in a figure, the consummation of all things, the Bridal of all Bridals, the mystery that is beyond all mysteries, accomplished from the foundation of the world. So day by day the house of his life became more magical.

And at the same time he began to guess that if in the New Life there are new and unheard-of joys, there are also new and unheard-of dangers. In his manuscript books which professed to deliver the outer sense of those mysterious "Hidden Songs of Iolo Sant" there was a little chapter that bore the heading: *Fons Sacer non in communem Vsum convertendus est,* and by diligence, with much use of the grammar and dictionary, Darnell was able to construe the by no means complex Latin of his ancestor. The special book which contained the chapter in question was one of the most singular in the collection, since it bore the title *Terra de Iolo,* and on the surface, with an ingenious concealment of its real symbolism, it affected to give an account of the orchards, fields, woods, roads, tenements, and waterways in the possession of Darnell's ancestors. Here, then, he read of the Holy Well, hidden in the Wistman's Wood—*Sylva Sapientum*—"a fountain of abundant water, which no heats of summer can ever dry, which no flood can ever defile, which is as a water of life, to them that thirst for life, a stream of cleansing to them that would be pure, and a medicine of such healing virtue that by it, through the might of God and the intercession of His saints, the most grievous wounds are made whole." But the water of this well was to be kept sacred perpetually, it was not to be used for any common purpose, nor to satisfy any bodily thirst; but ever to be esteemed as holy, "even as the water which the priest hath hallowed." And in the margin a comment in a later hand taught Darnell something of the meaning of these prohibitions. He was warned not to use the Well of Life as a mere luxury of mortal life, as a new sensation, as a means of making the insipid cup of everyday existence more palatable. "For," said the commentator, "we are not called to sit as the spectators in a theatre, there to watch the play performed before us, but we are rather summoned to stand in the very scene itself, and there fervently to enact our parts in a great and wonderful mystery."

Darnell could quite understand the temptation that was thus indicated. Though he had gone but a little way on the path, and had barely tested the overrunnings of that mystic well, he was already aware of the enchantment that was transmuting all the world about him, informing his life with a strange significance and romance. London seemed a city of the Arabian Nights, and its labyrinths of streets an enchanted maze; its long avenues of lighted lamps were as starry systems, and its immensity became for him an image of the endless universe. He could well imagine how pleasant it might be to linger in such a world as this, to sit apart, and dream, beholding the strange pageant played before him; but the Sacred Well was not for common use, it was for the cleansing of the soul, and the healing of the grievous wounds of the spirit. There must be yet another transformation: London had become Bagdad; it must at last be transmuted to Syon, or in the phrase of one of his old documents, the City of the Cup.

And there were yet darker perils which the Iolo mss. (as his father had named the collection) hinted at more or less obscurely. There were suggestions of an awful region which the soul might enter, of a transmutation that was unto death, of evocations which could summon the utmost forces of evil from their dark places—in a word, of that sphere which is represented to most of us under the crude and somewhat childish symbolism of Black Magic. And here again he was not altogether without a dim comprehension of what was meant. He found himself recalling an odd incident that had happened long ago, which had remained all the years in his mind unheeded, amongst the many insignificant recollections of his childhood, and now rose before him, clear and distinct and full of meaning. It was on that memorable visit to the old house in the west, and the whole scene returned, with its smallest events, and the voices seemed to sound in his ears. It was a grey, still day of heavy heat that he remembered: he had stood on the lawn after breakfast, and wondered at the great peace and silence of the world. Not a leaf stirred in the trees on the lawn, not a whisper came from the myriad leaves of the wood; the flowers gave out sweet and heavy odours as if they breathed the dreams of the summer night; and far down the valley, the winding river was like dim silver under that dim and silvery sky, and the far hills and woods and fields vanished in the mist. The stillness of the air held him as with a charm; he leant all the morning against the rails that parted the lawn from the meadow, breathing the mystic breath of summer, and watching the fields brighten as with a sudden blossoming of shining flowers as the high mist grew thin for a moment before the hidden sun. As he watched thus, a man weary with heat, with some glance of horror in his eyes, passed him on his way to the house; but he stayed at his post till the old bell in the turret rang, and they dined all together, masters and servants, in the dark cool room that looked towards the still leaves of the wood. He could see that his uncle was upset about something, and when they had finished dinner he heard him tell his father that there was trouble at a farm; and it was settled that they should all drive over in the afternoon to some place with a strange name. But when the time came Mr. Darnell was too deep in old books and tobacco smoke to be stirred from his corner, and Edward and his uncle went alone in the dog-cart. They drove swiftly down the narrow lane, into the road that followed the winding river, and crossed the bridge at Caermaen by the mouldering Roman walls, and then, skirting the deserted, echoing village, they came out on a broad white turnpike road, and the limestone dust followed them like a cloud. Then, suddenly, they turned to the north by such a road as Edward had never seen before. It was so narrow that there was barely room for the cart to pass, and the footway was of rock, and the banks rose high above them as they slowly climbed the long, steep way, and the untrimmed hedges on either side shut out the light. And the ferns grew thick and green upon the banks, and hidden wells dripped down upon them; and the old man told him how the lane in winter was a torrent of swirling water, so that no one could pass by it. On they went, ascending and then again descending, always in that deep hollow under the wild woven boughs, and the boy wondered vainly what the country was like on either side. And now the air grew darker, and the hedge on one bank was but the verge of a dark and rustling wood, and the grey limestone rocks had changed to dark-red earth flecked with green patches and veins of marl, and suddenly in the stillness from the depth of the wood a bird began to sing a melody that charmed the heart into another world, that sang to the child's soul of the blessed faery realm beyond the woods of the earth, where the wounds of man are healed. And so at last, after many turnings and windings, they came to a high bare land where the lane broadened out into a kind of common, and along the edge of this place there were scattered three or four old cottages, and one of them was a little tavern. Here they stopped, and a man came out and tethered the tired horse to a post and gave him water; and old Mr. Darnell took the child's hand and led him by a path across the fields. The boy could see the country now, but it was all a strange, undiscovered land; they were in the heart of a wilderness of hills and valleys that he had never looked upon, and they were going down a wild, steep hillside, where the narrow path wound in and out amidst gorse and towering bracken, and the sun gleaming out for a moment, there was a gleam of white water far below in a narrow valley, where a little brook poured and rippled from stone to stone. They went down the hill, and through a brake, and then, hidden in dark-green orchards, they came upon a long, low whitewashed house, with a stone roof strangely coloured by the growth of moss and lichens. Mr. Darnell knocked at a heavy oaken door, and they came into a dim room where but little light entered through the thick glass in the deep-set window. There were heavy beams in the ceiling, and a great fire-place sent out an odour of burning wood that Darnell never forgot, and the room seemed to him full of women who talked all together in frightened tones. Mr. Darnell beckoned to a tall, grey old man, who wore corduroy knee-breeches, and the boy, sitting on a high straight-backed chair, could see the old man and his uncle passing to and fro across the window-panes, as they walked together on the garden path. The women stopped their talk for a moment, and one of them brought him a glass of milk and an apple from some cold inner chamber; and then, suddenly, from a room above there rang out a shrill and terrible shriek, and then, in a young girl's voice, a more terrible song. It was not like anything the child had ever heard, but as the man recalled it to his memory, he knew to what song it might be compared—to a certain chant indeed that summons the angels and archangels to assist in the great Sacrifice. But as this song chants of the heavenly army, so did that seem to summon all the hierarchy of evil, the hosts of Lilith and Samael; and the words that rang out with such awful modulations—*neumata inferorum*—were in some unknown tongue that few men have ever heard on earth.

The women glared at one another with horror in their eyes, and he saw one or two of the oldest of them clumsily making an old sign upon their breasts. Then they began to speak again, and he remembered fragments of their talk.

"She has been up there," said one, pointing vaguely over her shoulder.

"She'd never know the way," answered another. "They be all gone that went there."

"There be nought there in these days."

"How can you tell that, Gwenllian? 'Tis not for us to say that."

"My great-grandmother did know some that had been there," said a very old woman. "She told me how they was taken afterwards."

And then his uncle appeared at the door, and they went their way as they had come. Edward Darnell never heard any more of it, nor whether the girl died or recovered from her strange attack; but the scene had haunted his mind in boyhood, and now the recollection of it came to him with a certain note of warning, as a symbol of dangers that might be in the way.

* * *

It would be impossible to carry on the history of Edward Darnell and of Mary his wife to a greater length, since from this point their legend is full of impossible events, and seems to put on the semblance of the stories of the Graal. It is certain, indeed, that in this world they changed their lives, like King Arthur, but this is a work which no chronicler has cared to describe with any amplitude of detail. Darnell, it is true, made a little book, partly consisting of queer verse which might have been written by an inspired infant, and partly made up of "notes and exclamations" in an odd dog-Latin which he had picked up from the Iolo mss., but it is to be feared that this work, even if published in its entirety, would cast but little light on a perplexing story. He called this piece of literature *In Exitu Israel,* and wrote on the title page the motto, doubtless of his own composition, *"Nunc certe scio quod omnia legenda; omnes historiæ, omnes fabulæ, omnis Scriptura sint de ME narrata."* It is only too evident that his Latin was not learnt at the feet of Cicero; but in this dialect he relates the great history of the "New Life" as it was manifested to him. The "poems" are even stranger. One, headed (with an odd reminiscence of old-fashioned books) "Lines written on looking down from a Height in London on a Board School suddenly lit up by the Sun" begins thus:—

One day when I was all alone
I found a wondrous little stone,
It lay forgotten on the road
Far from the ways of man's abode.
When on this stone mine eyes I cast
I saw my Treasure found at last.
I pressed it hard against my face,
I covered it with my embrace,
I hid it in a secret place.
And every day I went to see
This stone that was my ecstasy;
And worshipped it with flowers rare,
And secret words and sayings fair.
O stone, so rare and red and wise
O fragment of far Paradise,
O Star, whose light is life! O Sea,
Whose ocean is infinity!
Thou art a fire that ever burns,
And all the world to wonder turns;
And all the dust of the dull day
By thee is changed and purged away,
So that, where'er I look, I see
A world of a Great Majesty.
The sullen river rolls all gold,
The desert park's a faery wold,
When on the trees the wind is borne
I hear the sound of Arthur's horn
I see no town of grim grey ways,
But a great city all ablaze
With burning torches, to light up
The pinnacles that shrine the Cup.
Ever the magic wine is poured,
Ever the Feast shines on the board,
Ever the Song is borne on high
That chants the holy Magistry—
    Etc. etc. etc.

From such documents as these it is clearly impossible to gather any very definite information. But on the last page Darnell has written—

"So I awoke from a dream of a London suburb, of daily labor, of weary, useless little things; and as my eyes were opened I saw that I was in an ancient wood, where a clear well rose into grey film and vapour beneath a misty, glimmering heat. And a form came towards me from the hidden places of the wood, and my love and I were united by the well." ❋

The Angels of Mons

Introduction

I HAVE been asked to write an introduction to the story of "The Bowmen," on its publication in book form together with three other tales of similar fashion. And I hesitate. This affair of "The Bowmen" has been such an odd one from first to last, so many queer complications have entered into it, there have been so many and so divers currents and cross-currents of rumour and speculation concerning it, that I honestly do not know where to begin. I propose, then, to solve the difficulty by apologising for beginning at all.

For, usually and fitly, the presence of an introduction is held to imply that there is something of consequence and importance to be introduced. If, for example, a man has made an anthology of great poetry, he may well write an introduction justifying his principle of selection, pointing out here and there, as the spirit moves him, high beauties and supreme excellencies, discoursing of the magnates and lords and princes of literature, whom he is merely serving as groom of the chamber. Introductions, that is, belong to the masterpieces and classics of the world, to the great and ancient and accepted things; and I am here introducing a short, small story of my own which appeared in *The Evening News* about ten months ago.

I appreciate the absurdity, nay, the enormity of the position in all its grossness. And my excuse for these pages must be this: that though the story itself is nothing, it has yet had such odd and unforeseen consequences and adventures that the tale of them may possess some interest. And then, again, there are certain psychological morals to be drawn from the whole matter of the tale and its sequel of rumours and discussions that are not, I think, devoid of consequence; and so to begin at the beginning.

* * *

This was in last August; to be more precise, on the last Sunday of last August. There were terrible things to be read on that hot Sunday morning between meat and mass. It was in *The Weekly Dispatch* that I saw the awful account of the retreat from Mons. I no longer recollect the details; but I have not forgotten the impression that was then made on my mind. I seemed to see a furnace of torment and death and agony and terror seven times heated, and in the midst of the burning was the British Army. In the midst of the flame, consumed by it and yet aureoled in it, scattered like ashes and yet triumphant, martyred and for ever glorious. So I saw our men with a shining about them, so I took these thoughts with me to church, and, I am sorry to say, was making up a story in my head while the deacon was singing the Gospel.

This was not the tale of "The Bowmen." It was the first sketch, as it were, of "The Soldiers' Rest," which is reprinted in this volume. I only wish I had been able to write it as I conceived it. The tale as it stands is, I think, a far better piece of craft than "The Bowmen," but the tale that came to me as the blue incense floated above the Gospel Book on the desk between the tapers: that indeed was a noble story—like all the stories that never get written. I conceived the dead men coming up through the flames and in the flames, and being welcomed in the Eternal Tavern with songs and flowing cups and everlasting mirth. But every man is the child of his age, however much he may hate it; and our popular religion has long determined that jollity is wicked. As far as I can make out modern Protestantism believes that Heaven is something like Evensong in an English cathedral, the service by Stainer and the Dean preaching. For those opposed to dogma of any kind—even the mildest—I suppose it is held that a Course of Ethical Lectures will be arranged.

Well, I have long maintained that on the whole the average church, considered as a house of preaching, is a much more poisonous place than the average tavern; still, as I say, one's age masters one, and clouds and bewilders the intelligence, and the real story of "The Soldiers' Rest," with its "sonus epulantium in æterno convivio," was ruined at the moment of its birth, and it was some time later that the actual story, as here printed, got written. And in the meantime the plot of "The Bowmen" occurred to me. Now it has been murmured and hinted and suggested and whispered in all sorts of quarters that before I wrote the tale I had heard something. The most decorative of these legends is also the most precise: "I know for a fact that the whole thing was given him in typescript by a lady-in-waiting." This was not the case; and all vaguer reports to the effect that I had heard some rumours or hints of rumours are equally void of any trace of truth.

Again I apologise for entering so pompously into the minutiæ of my bit of a story, as if it were the lost poems of Sappho; but it appears that the subject interests the public, and I comply with my instructions. I take it, then, that the origins of "The Bowmen" were composite. First of all, all ages and nations have cherished the thought that spiritual hosts may come to the help of earthly arms, that gods and heroes and saints have descended from their high immortal places to fight for their worshippers and clients. Then Kipling's story of the ghostly Indian regiment got in my head and got mixed with the mediævalism that is always there; and so "The Bowmen" was written. I was heartily disappointed with it, I remember, and thought it—as I still think it—an indifferent piece of work. However, I have tried to write for these thirty-five long years, and if I have not become practised in letters, I am at least a past master in the Lodge of Disappointment. Such as it was, "The Bowmen" appeared in *The Evening News* of September 29th, 1914.

Now the journalist does not, as a rule, dwell much on the prospect of fame; and if he be an evening journalist, his anticipations of immortality are bounded by twelve o'clock at night at the latest; and it may well be that those insects which begin to live in the morning and are dead by sunset deem themselves immortal. Having written my story, having groaned and growled over it and printed it, I certainly never thought to hear another word of it. My colleague "The Londoner" praised it warmly to my face, as his kindly fashion is; entering, very properly, a technical caveat as to the language of the battle-cries of the bowmen. "Why should English archers use French terms?" he said. I replied that the only reason was this—that a "Monseigneur" here and there struck me as picturesque; and I reminded him that, as a matter of cold historical fact, most of the archers of Agincourt were mercenaries from Gwent, my native country, who would appeal to Mihangel and to saints not known to the Saxons—Teilo, Iltyd, Dewi, Cadwaladyr Vendigeid. And I thought that that was the first and last discussion of "The Bowmen." But in a few days from its publication the editor of *The Occult Review* wrote to me. He wanted to know whether the story had any foundation in fact. I told him that it had no foundation in fact of any kind or sort;

I forget whether I added that it had no foundation in rumour, but I should think not, since to the best of my belief there were no rumours of heavenly interposition in existence at that time. Certainly I had heard of none. Soon afterwards the editor of *Light* wrote asking a like question, and I made him a like reply. It seemed to me that I had stifled any "Bowmen" mythos in the hour of its birth.

A month or two later, I received several requests from editors of parish magazines to reprint the story. I—or, rather, my editor—readily gave permission; and then, after another month or two, the conductor of one of these magazines wrote to me, saying that the February issue containing the story had been sold out, while there was still a great demand for it. Would I allow them to reprint "The Bowmen" as a pamphlet, and would I write a short preface giving the exact authorities for the story? I replied that they might reprint in pamphlet form with all my heart, but that I could not give my authorities, since I had none, the tale being pure invention. The priest wrote again, suggesting—to my amazement—that I must be mistaken, that the main "facts" of "The Bowmen" must be true, that my share in the matter must surely have been confined to the elaboration and decoration of a veridical history. It seemed that my light fiction had been accepted by the congregation of this particular church as the solidest of facts; and it was then that it began to dawn on me that if I had failed in the art of letters, I had succeeded, unwittingly, in the art of deceit. This happened, I should think, some time in April, and the snowball of rumour that was then set rolling has been rolling ever since, growing bigger and bigger, till it is now swollen to a monstrous size.

It was at about this period that variants of my tale began to be told as authentic histories. At first, these tales betrayed their relation to their original. In several of them the vegetarian restaurant appeared, and St. George was the chief character. In one case an officer—name and address missing—said that there was a portrait of St. George in a certain London restaurant, and that a figure, just like the portrait, appeared to him on the battlefield, and was invoked by him, with the happiest results. Another variant—this, I think, never got into print—told how dead Prussians had been found on the battlefield with arrow wounds in their bodies. This notion amused me, as I had imagined a scene, when I was thinking out the story, in which a German general was to appear before the Kaiser to explain his failure to annihilate the English.

"All-Highest," the general was to say, "it it is true, it is impossible to deny it. The men were killed by arrows; the shafts were found in their bodies by the burying parties."

I rejected the idea as over-precipitous even for a mere fantasy. I was therefore entertained when I found that what I had refused as too fantastical for fantasy was accepted in certain occult circles as hard fact.

Other versions of the story appeared in which a cloud interposed between the attacking Germans and the defending British. In some examples the cloud served to conceal our men from the advancing enemy; in others, it disclosed shining shapes which frightened the horses of the pursuing German cavalry. St. George, it will be noted, has disappeared—he persisted some time longer in certain Roman Catholic variants—and there are no more bowmen, no more arrows. But so far angels are not mentioned; yet they are ready to appear, and I think that I have detected the machine which brought them into the story.

In "The Bowmen" my imagined soldier saw "a long line of shapes, with a shining about them." And Mr. A. P. Sinnett, writing in the May issue of *The Occult Review,* reporting what he had heard, states that "those who could see said they saw 'a row of shining beings' between the two armies." Now I conjecture that the word "shining" is the link between my tale and the derivative from it. In the popular view shining and benevolent supernatural beings are angels and nothing else, and must be angels, and so, I believe, the Bowmen of my story have become "the Angels of Mons." In this shape they have been received with respect and credence everywhere, or almost everywhere.

And here, I conjecture, we have the key to the large popularity of the delusion—as I think it. We have long ceased in England to take much interest in saints, and in the recent revival of the cultus of St. George, the saint is little more than a patriotic figurehead. And the appeal to the saints to succour us is certainly not a common English practice; it is held Popish by most of our countrymen. But angels, with certain reservations, have retained their popularity, and so, when it was settled that the English army in its dire peril was delivered by angelic aid, the way was clear for general belief, and for the enthusiasms of the religion of the man in the street. And so soon as the legend got the title "The Angels of Mons" it became impossible to avoid it. It permeated the Press: it would not be neglected; it appeared in the most unlikely quarters—in *Truth* and *Town Topics, The New Church Weekly* (Swedenborgian) and *John Bull.* The editor of *The Church Times* has exercised a wise reserve: he awaits that evidence which so far is lacking; but in one issue of the paper I noted that the story furnished a text for a sermon, the subject of a letter, and the matter for an article. People send me cuttings from provincial papers containing hot controversy as to the exact nature of the appearances; the "Office Window" of *The Daily Chronicle* suggests scientific explanations of the hallucination; the *Pall Mall* in a note about St. James says he is of the brotherhood of the Bowmen of Mons—this reversion to the bowmen from the angels being possibly due to the strong statements that I have made on the matter. The pulpits both of the Church and of Nonconformity have been busy: Bishop Welldon, Dean Hensley Henson (a disbeliever), Bishop Taylor Smith (the Chaplain-General), and many other clergy have occupied themselves with the matter. Dr. Horton preached about the "angels" at Manchester; Sir Joseph Compton Rickett (President of the National Federation of Free Church Councils) stated that the soldiers at the front had seen visions and dreamed dreams, and had given testimony of powers and principalities fighting for them or against them. Letters come from all the ends of the earth to the Editor of *The Evening News* with theories, beliefs, explanations, suggestions. It is all somewhat wonderful; one can say that the whole affair is a psychological phenomenon of considerable interest, fairly comparable with the great Russian delusion of last August and September.

* * *

Now it is possible that some persons, judging by the tone of these remarks of mine, may gather the impression that I am a profound disbeliever in the possibility of any intervention of the superphysical order in the affairs of the physical order. They will be mistaken if they make this inference; they will be mistaken if they suppose that I think miracles in Judæa credible but miracles in France or Flanders incredible. I hold no such absurdities. But I confess, very frankly, that

I credit none of the "Angels of Mons" legends, partly because I see, or think I see, their derivation from my own idle fiction, but chiefly because I have, so far, not received one jot or tittle of evidence that should dispose me to belief. It is idle, indeed, and foolish enough for a man to say: "I am sure that story is a lie, because the supernatural element enters into it"; here, indeed, we have the maggot writhing in the midst of corrupted offal denying the existence of the sun. But if this fellow be a fool—as he is—equally foolish is he who says, "If the tale has anything of the supernatural it is true, and the less evidence the better"; and I am afraid this tends to be the attitude of many who call themselves occultists. I hope that I shall never get to that frame of mind. So I say, not that super-normal interventions are impossible, not that they have not happened during this war—I know nothing as to that point, one way or the other—but that there is not one atom of evidence (so far) to support the current stories of the angels of Mons. For, be it remarked, these stories are specific stories. They rest on the second, third, fourth, fifth hand stories told by "a soldier," by "an officer," by "a Catholic correspondent," by "a nurse," by any number of anonymous people. Indeed, names have been mentioned. A lady's name has been drawn, most unwarrantably as it appears to me, into the discussion, and I have no doubt that this lady has been subject to a good deal of pestering and annoyance. She has written to the Editor of *The Evening News* denying all knowledge of the supposed miracle. The Psychical Research Society's expert confesses that no real evidence has been proffered to her Society on the matter. And then, to my amazement, she accepts as fact the proposition that some men on the battlefield have been "hallucinated," and proceeds to give the theory of sensory hallucination. She forgets that, by her own showing, there is no reason to suppose that anybody has been hallucinated at all. Someone (unknown) has met a nurse (unnamed) who has talked to a soldier (anonymous) who has seen angels. But *that* is not evidence; and not even Sam Weller at his gayest would have dared to offer it as such in the Court of Common Pleas. So far, then, nothing remotely approaching proof has been offered as to any supernatural intervention during the Retreat from Mons. Proof may come; if so, it will be interesting and more than interesting.

* * *

But, taking the affair as it stands at present, how is it that a nation plunged in materialism of the grossest kind has accepted idle rumours and gossip of the supernatural as certain truth? The answer is contained in the question: it is precisely because our whole atmosphere is materialist that we are ready to credit anything—save the truth. Separate a man from good drink, he will swallow methylated spirit with joy. Man is created to be inebriated; to be "nobly wild, not mad." Suffer the Cocoa Prophets and their company to seduce him in body and spirit, and he will get himself stuff that will make him ignobly wild and mad indeed. It took hard, practical men of affairs, business men, advanced thinkers, Freethinkers, to believe in Madame Blavatsky and Mahatmas and the famous message from the Golden Shore: "Judge's plan is right; follow him and *stick.*"

And the main responsibility for this dismal state of affairs undoubtedly lies on the shoulders of the majority of the clergy of the Church of England. Christianity, as Mr. W. L. Courtney has so admirably pointed out, is a great Mystery Religion; it is *the* Mystery Religion. Its priests are called to an awful and tremendous hierurgy; its pontiffs are to be the pathfinders, the bridge-makers between the world of sense and the world of spirit. And, in fact, they pass their time in preaching, not the eternal mysteries, but a twopenny morality, in changing the Wine of Angels and the Bread of Heaven into gingerbeer and mixed biscuits: a sorry transubstantiation, a sad alchemy, as it seems to me. ❋

The Bowmen

IT was during the Retreat of the Eighty Thousand, and the authority of the Censorship is sufficient excuse for not being more explicit. But it was on the most awful day of that awful time, on the day when ruin and disaster came so near that their shadow fell over London far away; and, without any certain news, the hearts of men failed within them and grew faint; as if the agony of the army in the battlefield had entered into their souls.

On this dreadful day, then, when three hundred thousand men in arms with all their artillery swelled like a flood against the little English company, there was one point above all other points in our battle line that was for a time in awful danger, not merely of defeat, but of utter annihilation. With the permission of the Censorship and of the military expert, this corner may, perhaps, be described as a salient, and if this angle were crushed and broken, then the English force as a whole would be shattered, the Allied left would be turned, and Sedan would inevitably follow.

All the morning the German guns had thundered and shrieked against this corner, and against the thousand or so of men who held it. The men joked at the shells, and found funny names for them, and had bets about them, and greeted them with scraps of music-hall songs. But the shells came on and burst, and tore good Englishmen limb from limb, and tore brother from brother, and as the heat of the day increased so did the fury of that terrific cannonade. There was no help, it seemed. The English artillery was good, but there was not nearly enough of it; it was being steadily battered into scrap iron.

There comes a moment in a storm at sea when people say to one another, "It is at its worst; it can blow no harder," and then there is a blast ten times more fierce than any before it. So it was in these British trenches.

There were no stouter hearts in the whole world than the hearts of these men; but even they were appalled as this seven-times-heated hell of the German cannonade fell upon them and overwhelmed them and destroyed them. And at this very moment they saw from their trenches that a tremendous host was moving against their lines. Five hundred of the thousand remained, and as far as they could see the German infantry was pressing on against them, column upon column, a grey world of men, ten thousand of them, as it appeared afterwards.

There was no hope at all. They shook hands, some of them. One man improvised a new version of the battle-song, "Good-bye, good-bye to Tipperary," ending with "And we shan't get there." And they all went on firing steadily. The officers pointed out that such an opportunity for high-class, fancy shooting might never occur again; the Germans dropped line after line; the Tipperary humorist asked, "What price Sidney Street?" And the few machine guns did their best. But everybody knew it was of no use. The dead grey bodies lay in companies and battalions, as others came on and on and on, and they swarmed and stirred and advanced from beyond and beyond.

"World without end. Amen," said one of the British soldiers with some irrelevance as he took aim and fired. And then he remembered—he says he cannot think why or wherefore—a queer vegetarian restaurant in London where he had once or twice eaten eccentric dishes of cutlets made of lentils and nuts that pretended to be steak. On all the plates in this restaurant there was printed a figure of St. George in blue, with the motto, *Adsit Anglis Sanctus Georgius*—May St. George be a present help to the English. This soldier happened to know Latin and other useless things, and now, as he fired at his man in the grey advancing mass—300 yards away—he uttered the pious vegetarian motto. He went on firing to the end, and at last Bill on his right had to clout him cheerfully over the head to make him stop, pointing out as he did so that the King's ammunition cost money and was not lightly to be wasted in drilling funny patterns into dead Germans.

For as the Latin scholar uttered his invocation he felt something between a shudder and an electric shock pass through his body. The roar of the battle died down in his ears to a gentle murmur; instead of it, he says, he heard a great voice and a shout louder than a thunder-peal crying, "Array, array, array!"

His heart grew hot as a burning coal, it grew cold as ice within him, as it seemed to him that a tumult of voices answered to his summons. He heard, or seemed to hear, thousands shouting: "St. George! St. George!"

"Ha! messire; ha! sweet Saint, grant us good deliverance!"

"St. George for merry England!"

"Harow! Harow! Monseigneur St. George, succour us."

"Ha! St. George! Ha! St. George! a long bow and a strong bow."

"Heaven's Knight, aid us!"

And as the soldier heard these voices he saw before him, beyond the trench, a long line of shapes, with a shining about them. They were like men who drew the bow, and with another shout, their cloud of arrows flew singing and tingling through the air towards the German hosts.

* * *

The other men in the trench were firing all the while. They had no hope; but they aimed just as if they had been shooting at Bisley.

Suddenly one of them lifted up his voice in the plainest English.

"Gawd help us!" he bellowed to the man next to him, "but we're blooming marvels! Look at those grey . . . gentlemen, look at them! D'ye see them? They're not going down in dozens, nor in 'undreds; it's thousands, it is. Look! look! there's a regiment gone while I'm talking to ye."

"Shut it!" the other soldier bellowed, taking aim, "what are ye gassing about?"

But he gulped with astonishment even as he spoke, for, indeed, the grey men were falling by the thousands. The English could hear the guttural scream of the German officers, the crackle of their revolvers as they shot the reluctant; and still line after line crashed to the earth.

* * *

All the while the Latin-bred soldier heard the cry:

"Harow! Harow! Monseigneur, dear saint, quick to our aid! St. George help us!"

"High Chevalier, defend us!"

The singing arrows fled so swift and thick that they darkened the air; the heathen horde melted from before them.

* * *

"More machine guns!" Bill yelled to Tom.

"Don't hear them," Tom yelled back. "But, thank God, anyway; they've got it in the neck."

In fact, there were ten thousand dead German soldiers left before that salient of the English army, and consequently there was no Sedan. In Germany, a country ruled by scientific principles, the Great General Staff decided that the contemptible English must have employed shells containing an unknown gas of a poisonous nature, as no wounds were discernible on the bodies of the dead German soldiers. But the man who knew what nuts tasted like when they called themselves steak knew also that St. George had brought his Agincourt Bowmen to help the English. ❋

The Soldiers' Rest

THE soldier with the ugly wound in the head opened his eyes at last, and looked about him with an air of pleasant satisfaction.

He still felt drowsy and dazed with some fierce experience through which he had passed, but so far he could not recollect much about it. But an agreeable glow began to steal about his heart—such a glow as comes to people who have been in a tight place and have come through it better than they had expected. In its mildest form this set of emotions may be observed in passengers who have crossed the Channel on a windy day without being sick. They triumph a little internally, and are suffused with vague, kindly feelings.

The wounded soldier was somewhat of this disposition as he opened his eyes, pulled himself together, and looked about him. He felt a sense of delicious ease and repose in bones that had been racked and weary, and deep in the heart that had so lately been tormented there was an assurance of comfort—of the battle won. The thundering, roaring waves were passed; he had entered into the haven of calm waters. After fatigues and terrors that as yet he could not recollect he seemed now to be resting in the easiest of all easy chairs in a dim, low room.

In the hearth there was a glint of fire and a blue, sweet-scented puff of wood smoke; a great black oak beam roughly hewn crossed the ceiling. Through the leaded panes of the windows he saw a rich glow of sunlight, green lawns, and against the deepest and most radiant of all blue skies the wonderful far-lifted towers of a vast Gothic cathedral—mystic, rich with imagery.

"Good Lord!" he murmured to himself. "I didn't know they had such places in France. It's just like Wells. And it might be the other day when I was going past the Swan, just as it might be past that window, and asked the ostler what time it was, and he says, 'What time? Why, summer-time'; and there outside it looks like summer that would last for ever. If this was an inn they ought to call it 'The Soldiers' Rest.'"

He dozed off again, and when he opened his eyes once more a kindly looking man in some sort of black robe was standing by him.

"It's all right now, isn't it?" he said, speaking in good English.

"Yes, thank you, sir, as right as can be. I hope to be back again soon."

"Well, well; but how did you come here? Where did you get that?" He pointed to the wound on the soldier's forehead.

The soldier put his hand up to his brow and looked dazed and puzzled.

"Well, sir," he said at last, "it was like this, to begin at the beginning. You know how we came over in August, and there we were in the thick of it, as you might say, in a day or two. An awful time it was, and I don't know how I got through it alive. My best friend was killed dead beside me as we lay in the trenches. By Cambrai, I think it was.

"Then things got a little quieter for a bit, and I was quartered in a village for the best part of a week. She was a very nice lady where I was, and she treated me proper with the best of everything. Her husband he was fighting; but she had the nicest little boy I ever knew, a little fellow of five, or six it might be, and we got on splendid. The amount of their lingo that kid taught me—'We, we' and 'Bong swor' and 'Commong voo porty voo,' and all—and I taught him English. You should have heard that nipper say ''Arf a mo', old un'!' It was a treat.

"Then one day we got surprised. There was about a dozen of us in the village, and two or three hundred Germans came down on us early one morning. They got us; no help for it. Before we could shoot.

* * *

"Well, there we were. They tied our hands behind our backs, and smacked our faces and kicked us a bit, and we were lined up opposite the house where I'd been staying.

"And then that poor little chap broke away from his mother, and he run out and saw one of the Boshes, as we call them, fetch me one over the jaw with his clenched fist. Oh dear! oh dear! he might have done it a dozen times if only that little child hadn't seen him.

"He had a poor bit of a toy I'd bought him at the village shop; a toy gun it was. And out he came running, as I say, crying out something in French like 'Bad man! bad man! don't hurt my Anglish or I shoot you'; and he pointed that gun at the German soldier. The

German, he took his bayonet, and he drove it right through the poor little chap's throat."

The soldier's face worked and twitched and twisted itself into a sort of grin, and he sat grinding his teeth and staring at the man in the black robe. He was silent for a little. And then he found his voice, and the oaths rolled terrible, thundering from him, as he cursed that murderous wretch, and bade him go down and burn for ever in hell. And the tears were raining down his face, and they choked him at last.

"I beg your pardon, sir, I'm sure," he said, "especially you being a minister of some kind, I suppose; but I can't help it. He was such a dear little man."

The man in black murmured something to himself: *"Pretiosa in conspectu Domini mors innocentium ejus"*—Dear in the sight of the Lord is the death of His innocents. Then he put a kind hand very gently on the soldier's shoulder.

"Never mind," said he; "I've seen some service in my time, myself. But what about that wound?"

"Oh, that; that's nothing. But I'll tell you how I got it. It was just like this. The Germans had us fair, as I tell you, and they shut us up in a barn in the village; just flung us on the ground and left us to starve seemingly. They barred up the big door of the barn, and put a sentry there, and thought we were all right.

"There were sort of slits like very narrow windows in one of the walls, and on the second day it was, I was looking out of these slits down the street, and I could see those German devils were up to mischief. They were planting their machine guns everywhere handy where an ordinary man coming up the street would never see them, but I see them, and I see the infantry lining up behind the garden walls. Then I had a sort of a notion of what was coming; and presently, sure enough, I could hear some of our chaps singing 'Hullo, hullo, hullo!' in the distance; and I says to myself, 'Not this time.'

"So I looked about me, and I found a hole under the wall; a kind of a drain I should think it was, and I found I could just squeeze through. And I got out and crept round, and away I goes running down the street, yelling for all I was worth, just as our chaps were getting round the corner at the bottom. 'Bang, bang!' went the guns, behind me and in front of me, and on each side of me, and then—bash! something hit me on the head and over I went; and I don't remember anything more till I woke up here just now."

The soldier lay back in his chair and closed his eyes for a moment. When he opened them he saw that there were other people in the room besides the minister in the black robes. One was a man in a big black cloak. He had a grim old face and a great beaky nose. He shook the soldier by the hand.

"By God! sir," he said, "you're a credit to the British Army; you're a damned fine soldier and a good man, and, by God! I'm proud to shake hands with you."

And then someone came out of the shadow, someone in queer clothes such as the soldier had seen worn by the heralds when he had been on duty at the opening of Parliament by the King.

"Now, by Corpus Domini," this man said, "of all knights ye be noblest and gentlest, and ye be of fairest report, and now ye be a brother of the noblest brotherhood that ever was since this world's beginning, since ye have yielded dear life for your friends' sake."

The soldier did not understand what the man was saying to him. There were others, too, in strange dresses, who came and spoke to him. Some spoke in what sounded like French. He could not make it out; but he knew that they all spoke kindly and praised him.

"What does it all mean?" he said to the minister. "What are they talking about? They don't think I'd let down my pals?"

"Drink this," said the minister, and he handed the soldier a great silver cup, brimming with wine.

The soldier took a deep draught, and in that moment all his sorrows passed from him.

"What is it?" he asked.

"Vin nouveau du Royaume," said the minister. "New Wine of the Kingdom, you call it." And then he bent down and murmured in the soldier's ear.

"What," said the wounded man, "the place they used to tell us about in Sunday School? With such drink and such joy—"

His voice was hushed. For as he looked at the minister the fashion of his vesture was changed. The black robe seemed to melt away from him. He was all in armour, if armour be made of starlight, of the rose of dawn, and of sunset fires; and he lifted up a great sword of flame.

Full in the midst, his Cross of Red
Triumphant Michael brandished,
And trampled the Apostate's pride. ❋

The Monstrance

Then it fell out in the sacring of the Mass that right as the priest heaved up the Host there came a beam redder than any rose and smote upon it, and then it was changed bodily into the shape and fashion of a Child having his arms stretched forth, as he had been nailed upon the Tree.—Old Romance.

So far things were going very well indeed. The night was thick and black and cloudy, and the German force had come three-quarters of their way or more without an alarm. There was no challenge from the English lines; and indeed the English were being kept busy by a high shell-fire on their front. This had been the German plan; and it was coming off admirably. Nobody thought that there was any danger on the left; and so the Prussians, writhing on their stomachs over the ploughed field, were drawing nearer and nearer to the wood. Once there they could establish themselves comfortably and securely during what remained of the night; and at dawn the English left would be hopelessly enfiladed—and there would be another of those movements which people who really understand military matters call "readjustments of our line."

The noise made by the men creeping and crawling over the fields was drowned by the cannonade, from the English side as well as the German. On the English centre and right things were indeed very brisk; the big guns were thundering and shrieking and roaring, the machine guns were keeping up the very devil's racket; the flares and illuminating shells were as good as the Crystal Palace in the old days, as the soldiers said to one another. All this had been thought of and thought out on the other side. The German force was beautifully organised. The men who crept nearer and nearer to the wood carried quite a number of machine guns in bits on their backs; others of them had small bags full of sand; yet others big bags that were empty. When the wood was reached the sand from the small bags was to be emptied into the big bags; the machine-gun parts were to be put together, the guns mounted behind the sandbag redoubt, and then, as Major Von und Zu pleasantly observed, "the English pigs shall to gehenna-fire quickly come."

The major was so well pleased with the way things had gone that he permitted himself a very low and guttural chuckle; in another ten minutes success would be assured. He half turned his head round to whisper a caution about some detail of the sandbag business to the big sergeant-major, Karl Heinz, who was crawling just behind him. At that instant Karl Heinz leapt into the air with a scream that rent through the night and through all the roaring of the artillery. He cried in a terrible voice, "The Glory of the Lord!" and plunged and pitched forward, stone dead. They said that his face as he stood up there and cried aloud was as if it had been seen through a sheet of flame.

"They" were one or two out of the few who got back to the German lines. Most of the Prussians stayed in the ploughed field. Karl Heinz's scream had frozen the blood of the English soldiers, but it had also ruined the major's plans. He and his men, caught all unready, clumsy with the burdens that they carried, were shot to pieces; hardly a score of them returned. The rest of the force were attended to by an English burying party. According to custom the dead men were searched before they were buried, and some singular relics of the campaign were found upon them, but nothing so singular as Karl Heinz's diary.

He had been keeping it for some time. It began with entries about bread and sausage and the ordinary incidents of the trenches; here and there Karl wrote about an old grandfather, and a big china pipe, and pinewoods and roast goose. Then the diarist seemed to get fidgety about his health. Thus:

> *April 17.*—Annoyed for some days by murmuring sounds in my head. I trust I shall not become deaf, like my departed uncle Christopher.
>
> *April 20.*—The noise in my head grows worse; it is a humming sound. It distracts me; twice I have failed to hear the captain and have been reprimanded.
>
> *April 22.*—So bad is my head that I go to see the doctor. He speaks of *tinnitus,* and gives me an inhaling apparatus that shall reach, he says, the middle ear.
>
> *April 25.*—The apparatus is of no use. The sound is now become like the booming of a great church bell. It reminds me of the bell at St. Lambart on that terrible day of last August.

> *April 26.*—I could swear that it is the bell of St. Lambart that I hear all the time. They rang it as the procession came out of the church.

The man's writing, at first firm enough, begins to straggle unevenly over the page at this point. The entries show that he became convinced that he heard the bell of St. Lambart's Church ringing, though (as he knew better than most men) there had been no bell and no church at St. Lambart's since the summer of 1914. There was no village either—the whole place was a rubbish-heap.

Then the unfortunate Karl Heinz was beset with other troubles.

> *May 2.*—I fear I am becoming ill. To-day Joseph Kleist, who is next to me in the trench, asked me why I jerked my head to the right so constantly. I told him to hold his tongue; but this shows that I am noticed. I keep fancying that there is something white just beyond the range of my sight on the right hand.

> *May 3.*—This whiteness is now quite clear, and in front of me. All this day it has slowly passed before me. I asked Joseph Kleist if he saw a piece of newspaper just beyond the trench. He stared at me solemnly—he is a stupid fool—and said, "There is no paper."

> *May 4.*—It looks like a white robe. There was a strong smell of incense to-day in the trench. No one seemed to notice it. There is decidedly a white robe, and I think I can see feet, passing very slowly before me at this moment while I write.

There is no space here for continuous extracts from Karl Heinz's diary. But to condense with severity, it would seem that he slowly gathered about himself a complete set of sensory hallucinations. First the auditory hallucination of the sound of a bell, which the doctor called *tinnitus.* Then a patch of white growing into a white robe, then the smell of incense. At last he lived in two worlds. He saw his trench, and the level before it, and the English lines; he talked with his comrades and obeyed orders, though with a certain difficulty; but he also heard the deep boom of St. Lambart's bell, and saw continually advancing towards him a white procession of little children, led by a boy who was swinging a censer. There is one extraordinary entry: "But in August those children carried no lilies; now they have lilies in their hands. Why should they have lilies?"

It is interesting to note the transition over the border line. After May 2 there is no reference in the diary to bodily illness, with two notable exceptions. Up to and including that date the sergeant knows that he is suffering from illusions; after that he accepts his hallucinations as actualities. The man who cannot see what he sees and hear what he hears is a fool. So he writes: "I ask who is singing 'Ave Maria Stella.' That blockhead Friedrich Schumacher raises his crest and answers insolently that no one sings, since singing is strictly forbidden for the present."

A few days before the disastrous night expedition the last figure in the procession appeared to those sick eyes.

> The old priest now comes in his golden robe, the two boys holding each side of it. He is looking just as he did when he died, save that when he walked in St. Lambart there was no shining round his head. But this is illusion and contrary to reason, since no one has a shining about his head. I must take some medicine.

Note here that Karl Heinz absolutely accepts the appearance of the martyred priest of St. Lambart as actual, while he thinks that the halo must be an illusion; and so he reverts again to his physical condition.

The priest held up both his hands, the diary states, "as if there were something between them. But there is a sort of cloud or dimness over this object, whatever it may be. My poor Aunt Kathie suffered much from her eyes in her old age."

* * *

One can guess what the priest of St. Lambart carried in his hands when he and the little children went out into the hot sunlight to implore mercy, while the great resounding bell of St. Lambart boomed over the plain. Karl Heinz knew what happened then; they said that it was he who killed the old priest and helped to crucify the little child against the church door. The baby was only three years old. He died calling piteously for "mummy" and "daddy."

* * *

And those who will may guess what Karl Heinz saw when the mist cleared from before the monstrance in the priest's hands. Then he shrieked and died. ❋

The Dazzling Light

The new head-covering is made of heavy steel, which has been specially treated to increase its resisting power. The walls protecting the skull are particularly thick, and the weight of the helmet renders its use in open warfare out of the question. The rim is large, like that of the headpiece of Mambrino, and the soldier can at will either bring the helmet forward and protect his eyes or wear it so as to protect the base of the skull. . . . Military experts admit that a continuance of the present trench warfare may lead to those engaged in it, especially bombing parties and barbed wire cutters, being more heavily armoured than the knights who fought at Bouvines and and at Agincourt.—The Times, July 22, 1915.

THE war is already a fruitful mother of legends. Some people think that there are too many war legends, and a Croydon gentleman—or lady, I am not sure which—wrote to me quite recently telling me that a certain particular legend, which I will not specify, had become the "chief horror of the war." There may be something to be said for this point of view, but it strikes me as interesting that the old myth-making faculty has survived into these days, a relic of noble, far-off Homeric battles. And after all, what do we know? It does not do to be too sure that this, that, or the other hasn't happened and couldn't have happened.

What follows, at any rate, has no claim to be considered either as legend or as myth. It is merely one of the odd circumstances of these times, and I have no doubt it can easily be "explained away." In fact, the rationalistic explanation of the whole thing is patent and on the surface. There is only one little difficulty, and that, I fancy, is by no means insuperable. In any case this one knot or tangle may be put down as a queer coincidence and nothing more.

Here, then, is the curiosity or oddity in question. A young fellow, whom we will call for avoidance of all identification Delamere Smith—he is now Lieutenant Delamere Smith—was spending his holidays on the coast of west South Wales at the beginning of the war. He was something or other not very important in the City, and in his leisure hours he smattered lightly and agreeably a little literature, a little art, a little antiquarianism. He liked the Italian primitives, he knew the difference between first, second, and third pointed, he had looked through Boutell's "Engraved Brasses." He had been heard indeed to speak with enthusiasm of the brasses of Sir Robert de Septvans and Sir Roger de Trumpington.

One morning—he thinks it must have been the morning of August 16, 1914—the sun shone so brightly into his room that he woke early, and the fancy took him that it would be fine to sit on the cliffs in the pure sunlight. So he dressed and went out, and climbed up Giltar Point, and sat there enjoying the sweet air and the radiance of the sea, and the sight of the fringe of creaming foam about the grey foundations of St. Margaret's Island. Then he looked beyond and gazed at the new white monastery on Caldy, and wondered who the architect was, and how he had contrived to make the group of buildings look exactly like the background of a mediæval picture.

After about an hour of this and a couple of pipes, Smith confesses that he began to feel extremely drowsy. He was just wondering whether it would not be pleasant to stretch himself out on the wild thyme that scented the high place and go to sleep till breakfast, when the mounting sun caught one of the monastery windows, and Smith stared sleepily at the darting flashing light till it dazzled him. Then he felt "queer." There was an odd sensation as if the top of his head were dilating and contracting, and then he says he had a sort of shock, something between a mild current of electricity and the sensation of putting one's hand into the ripple of a swift brook.

Now, what happened next Smith cannot describe at all clearly. He knew he was on Giltar, looking across the waves to Caldy; he heard all the while the hollow, booming tide in the caverns of the rocks far below him. And yet he saw, as if in a glass, a very different country—a level fenland cut by slow streams, by long avenues of trimmed trees.

"It looked," he says, "as if it ought to have been a lonely country, but it was swarming with men; they were thick as ants in an anthill. And they were all dressed in armour; that was the strange thing about it.

"I thought I was standing by what looked as if it had been a farmhouse; but it was all battered to bits, just a heap of ruins and rubbish. All that was left was one tall round chimney, shaped very much like the fifteenth-century chimneys in Pembrokeshire. And thousands and tens of thousands went marching by.

"They were all in armour, and in all sorts of armour. Some of them had overlapping tongues of bright metal fastened on their clothes, others were in chain mail from head to foot, others were in heavy plate armour.

"They wore helmets of all shapes and sorts and sizes. One regiment had steel caps with wide brims, something like the old barbers' basins. Another lot had knights' tilting helmets on, closed up so that you couldn't see their faces. Most of them wore metal gauntlets, either of steel rings or plates, and they had steel over their boots. A great many had things like battle-maces swinging by their sides, and all these fellows carried a sort of string of big metal balls round their waist. Then a dozen regiments went by, every man with a steel shield slung over his shoulder. The last to go by were cross-bowmen."

In fact, it appeared to Delamere Smith that he watched the passing of a host of men in mediæval armour before him, and yet he knew—by the position of the sun and of a rosy cloud that was passing over the Worm's Head—that this vision, or whatever it was, only lasted a second or two. Then that slight sense of shock returned, and Smith returned to the contemplation of the physical phenomena of the Pembrokeshire coast—blue waves, grey St. Margaret's, and Caldy Abbey white in the sunlight.

It will be said, no doubt, and very likely with truth, that Smith fell asleep on Giltar, and mingled in a dream the thought of the great war just begun with his smatterings of mediæval battle and arms and armour. The explanation seems tolerable enough.

But there is the one little difficulty. It has been said that Smith is now Lieutenant Smith. He got his commission last autumn, and went out in May. He happens to speak French rather well, and so he has become what is called, I believe, an officer of liaison, or some such term. Anyhow, he is often behind the French lines.

He was home on short leave last week, and said:

"Ten days ago I was ordered to ——. I got there early in the morning, and had to wait a bit before I could see the General. I looked about me, and there on the left of us was a farm shelled into a heap of ruins, with one round chimney standing, shaped like the 'Flemish' chimneys in Pembrokeshire. And then the men in armour marched by, just as I had seen them—French regiments. The things like battle-maces were bomb-throwers, and the metal balls round the men's waists were the bombs. They told me that the crossbows were used for bomb-shooting.

"The march I saw was part of a big movement; you will hear more of it before long." ❋

The Great Return

I. The Rumour of the Marvellous

THERE are strange things lost and forgotten in obscure corners of the newspaper. I often think that the most extraordinary item of intelligence that I have read in print appeared a few years ago in the London press. It came from a well-known and most respected news agency; I imagine it was in all the papers. It was astounding.

The circumstances necessary—not to the understanding of this paragraph, for that is out of the question—but, we will say, to the understanding of the events which made it possible, are these. We had invaded Tibet, and there had been trouble in the hierarchy of that country, and a personage known as the Tashi Lama had taken refuge with us in India. He went on pilgrimage from one Buddhist shrine to another, and came at last to a holy mountain of Buddhism, the name of which I have forgotten. And thus the morning paper:

> His Holiness the Tashi Lama then ascended the Mountain and was transfigured—Reuter.

That was all. And from that day to this I have never heard a word of explanation or comment on this amazing statement.

There was no more, it seemed, to be said. "Reuter," apparently, thought he had made his simple statement of the facts of the case, had thereby done his duty, and so it all ended. Nobody, so far as I know, ever wrote to any paper asking what Reuter meant by it, or what the Tashi Lama meant by it. I suppose the fact was that nobody cared twopence about the matter; and so this strange event—if there were any such event—was exhibited to us for a moment, and the lantern show revolved to other spectacles.

This is an extreme instance of the manner in which the marvellous is flashed out to us and then withdrawn behind its black veils and concealments; but I have known of other cases. Now and again, at intervals of a few years, there appear in the newspapers strange stories of the strange doings of what are technically called "poltergeists." Some house, often a lonely farm, is suddenly subjected to an infernal bombardment. Great stones crash through the windows, thunder down the chimneys, impelled by no visible hand. The plates and cups and saucers are whirled from the dresser into the middle of the kitchen, no one can say how or by what agency. Upstairs the big bedstead and an old chest or two are heard bounding on the floor as if in a mad ballet. Now and then such doings as these excite a whole neighbourhood; sometimes a London paper sends a man down to make an investigation. He writes half a column of description on the Monday, a couple of paragraphs on the Tuesday, and then returns to town. Nothing has been explained, the matter vanishes away; and nobody cares. The tale trickles for a day or two through the press, and then instantly disappears, like an Australian stream, into the bowels of darkness. It is possible, I suppose, that this singular incuriousness as to marvellous events and reports is not wholly unaccountable. It may be that the events in question are, as it were, psychic accidents and misadventures. They are not meant to happen, or, rather, to be manifested. They belong to the world on the other side of the dark curtain; and it is only by some queer mischance that a corner of that curtain is twitched aside for an instant. Then—for an instant—we see; but the personages whom Mr. Kipling calls the Lords of Life and Death take care that we do not see too much. Our business is with things higher and things lower, with things different, anyhow; and on the whole we are not suffered to distract ourselves with that which does not really concern us. The transfiguration of the Lama and the tricks of the poltergeist are evidently no affairs of ours; we raise an uninterested eyebrow and pass on—to poetry or to statistics.

* * *

Be it noted; I am not professing any fervent personal belief in the reports to which I have alluded. For all I know, the Lama, in spite of Reuter, was not transfigured, and the poltergeist, in spite of the late Mr. Andrew Lang, may in reality be only mischievous Polly, the servant girl at the farm. And to go farther: I do not know that I should be justified in putting either of these cases of the marvellous in line with a chance paragraph that caught my eye last summer; for this had not, on the face of it at all events, anything wildly out of the common. Indeed, I dare say that I should not have read it, should not have seen it, if it had not contained the name of a place which I had once visited, which had then moved me in an odd manner that I could not understand. Indeed, I am sure that this particular paragraph deserves to stand alone, for even if the poltergeist be a real poltergeist, it merely reveals the psychic whimsicality of some region that is not our region. There were better things and more relevant things behind the few lines dealing with Llantrisant, the little town by the sea in Arfonshire.

Not on the surface, I must say, for the cutting—I have preserved it—reads as follows:

> LLANTRISANT.—The season promises very favourably: temperature of the sea yesterday at noon, 65 deg. Remarkable occurrences are supposed to have taken place during the recent Revival. The lights have not been observed lately. The Crown. The Fisherman's Rest.

The style was odd certainly; knowing a little of newspapers, I could see that the figure called, I think, "tmesis," or "cutting," had been generously employed; the exuberances of the local correspondent had been pruned by a Fleet Street expert. And these poor men are often hurried; but what did those "lights" mean? What strange matters had the vehement blue pencil blotted out and brought to naught?

That was my first thought, and then, thinking still of Llantrisant and how I had first discovered it and found it strange, I read the paragraph again, and was saddened almost to see, as I thought, the obvious explanation. I had forgotten for the moment that it was wartime, that scares and rumours and terrors about traitorous signals and flashing lights were current everywhere by land and sea; someone, no doubt, had been watching innocent farmhouse windows and thoughtless fanlights of lodging-houses; these were the "lights" that had not been observed lately.

I found out afterwards that the Llantrisant correspondent had no such treasonous lights in his mind, but something very different. Still; what do we know? He may have been mistaken, "the great rose of fire" that came over the deep may have been the port light of a coasting-ship. Did it shine at last from the old chapel on the headland? Possibly; or possibly it was the doctor's lamp at Sarnau, some miles away. I have had wonderful opportunities lately of analysing the marvels of lying, conscious and unconscious; and indeed almost incredible feats in this way can be performed. If I incline to the less likely explanation of the "lights" at Llantrisant, it is merely because this explanation seems to me to be altogether congruous with the "remarkable occurrences" of the newspaper paragraph.

After all, if rumour and gossip and hearsay are crazy things to be utterly neglected and laid aside: on the other hand, evidence is evidence, and when a couple of reputable surgeons assert, as they do assert in the case of Olwen Phillips, Croeswen, Llantrisant, that there has been a "kind of resurrection of the body," it is merely foolish to say that these things don't happen. The girl was a mass of tuberculosis, she was within a few hours of death; she is now full of life. And so, I do not believe that the rose of fire was merely a ship's light, magnified and transformed by dreaming Welsh sailors.

* * *

But now I am going forward too fast. I have not dated the paragraph, so I cannot give the exact day of its appearance, but I think it was somewhere between the second and third week of June. I cut it out partly because it was about Llantrisant, partly because of the "remarkable occurrences." I have an appetite for these matters, though I also have this misfortune, that I require evidence before I am ready to credit them, and I have a sort of lingering hope that some day I shall be able to elaborate some scheme or theory of such things.

But in the meantime, as a temporary measure, I hold what I call the doctrine of the jig-saw puzzle. That is: this remarkable occurrence, and that, and the other may be, and usually are, of no significance. Coincidence and chance and unsearchable causes will now and again make clouds that are undeniable fiery dragons, and potatoes that resemble eminent statesmen exactly and minutely in every feature, and rocks that are like eagles and lions. All this is nothing; it is when you get your set of odd shapes and find that they fit into one another, and at last that they are but parts of a large design; it is then that research grows interesting and indeed amazing, it is then that one queer form confirms the other, that the whole plan displayed justifies, corroborates, explains each separate piece.

So; it was within a week or ten days after I had read the paragraph about Llantrisant and had cut it out that I got a letter from a friend who was taking an early holiday in those regions.

"You will be interested," he wrote, "to hear that they have taken to ritualistic practices at Llantrisant. I went into the church the other day, and instead of smelling like a damp vault as usual, it was positively reeking with incense."

I knew better than that. The old parson was a firm Evangelical; he would rather have burnt sulphur in his church than incense any day. So I could not make out this report at all; and went down to Arfon a few weeks later determined to investigate this and any other remarkable occurrence at Llantrisant.

II. Odours of Paradise

I went down to Arfon in the very heat and bloom and fragrance of the wonderful summer that they were enjoying there. In London there was no such weather; it rather seemed as if the horror and fury of the war had mounted to the very skies and were there reigning. In the mornings the sun burnt down upon the city with a heat that scorched and consumed; but then clouds heavy and horrible would roll together from all quarters of the heavens, and early in the afternoon the air would darken, and a storm of thunder and lightning, and furious, hissing rain would fall upon the streets. Indeed, the torment of the world was in the London weather. The city wore a terrible vesture; within our hearts was dread; without we were clothed in black clouds and angry fire.

It is certain that I cannot show in any words the utter peace of that Welsh coast to which I came; one sees, I think, in such a change a figure of the passage from the disquiets and the fears of earth to the peace of paradise. A land that seemed to be in a holy, happy dream, a sea that changed all the while from olivine to emerald, from emerald to sapphire, from sapphire to amethyst, that washed in white foam at the bases of the firm, grey rocks, and about the huge crimson bastions that hid the western bays and inlets of the waters; to this land I came, and to hollows that were purple and odorous with wild thyme, wonderful with many tiny, exquisite flowers. There was benediction in centaury, pardon in eyebright, joy in lady's slipper; and so the weary eyes were refreshed, looking now at the little flowers and the happy bees about them, now on the magic mirror of the deep, changing from marvel to marvel with the passing of the great white clouds, with the brightening of the sun. And the ears, torn with jangle and racket and idle, empty noise, were soothed and comforted by the ineffable, unutterable, unceasing murmur, as the tides swam to and fro, uttering mighty, hollow voices in the caverns of the rocks.

* * *

For three or four days I rested in the sun and smelt the savour of the blossoms and of the salt water, and then, refreshed, I remembered that there was something queer about Llantrisant that I might as well investigate. It was no great thing that I thought to find, for, it will be remembered, I had ruled out the apparent oddity of the reporter's—or commissioner's?—reference to lights, on the ground that he must have been referring to some local panic about signalling to the enemy; who had certainly torpedoed a ship or two off Lundy in the Bristol Channel. All that I had to go upon was the reference to the "remarkable occurrences" at some revival, and then that letter of Jackson's, which spoke of Llantrisant church as "reeking" with incense, a wholly incredible and impossible state of things. Why, old Mr. Evans, the rector, looked upon coloured stoles as the very robe of Satan and his angels, as things dear to the heart of the Pope of Rome. But as to incense! As I have already familiarly observed, I knew better.

But as a hard matter of fact, this may be worth noting: when I went over to Llantrisant on Monday, August 9th, I visited the church, and it was still fragrant and exquisite with the odour of rare gums that had fumed there.

* * *

Now I happened to have a slight acquaintance with the rector. He was a most courteous and delightful old man, and on my last visit he had come across me in the churchyard, as I was admiring the very fine Celtic cross that stands there. Besides the beauty of the interlaced ornament there is an inscription in Ogham on one of the edges, concerning which the learned dispute; it is altogether one of the more famous crosses of Celtdom. Mr. Evans, I say, seeing me looking at the cross, came up and began to give me, the stranger, a résumé—somewhat of a shaky and uncertain résumé, I found afterwards—of the various debates and questions that had arisen as to the exact meaning of the inscription, and I was amused to detect an evident but underlying belief of his own: that the supposed Ogham characters were, in fact, due to boys' mischief and weather and the passing of the ages. But then I happened to put a question as to the sort of stone of which the cross was made, and the rector brightened amazingly. He began to talk geology, and, I think, demonstrated that the cross or the material for it must have been brought to Llantrisant from the southwest coast of Ireland. This struck me as interesting, because it was curious evidence of the migrations of the Celtic saints, whom the rector, I was delighted to find, looked upon as good Protestants, though shaky on the subject of crosses; and so, with concessions on my part, we got on very well. Thus, with all this to the good, I was emboldened to call upon him.

I found him altered. Not that he was aged; indeed, he was rather made young, with a singular brightening upon his face, and something of joy upon it that I had not seen before, that I have seen on very few faces of men. We talked of the war, of course, since that is not to be avoided; of the farming prospects of the county; of general things, till I ventured to remark that I had been in the church, and had been surprised to find it perfumed with incense.

"You have made some alterations in the service since I was here last? You use incense now?"

The old man looked at me strangely, and hesitated.

"No," he said, "there has been no change. I use no incense in the church. I should not venture to do so."

"But," I was beginning, "the whole church is as if High Mass had just been sung there, and—"

He cut me short, and there was a certain grave solemnity in his manner that struck me almost with awe.

"I know you are a railer," he said, and the phrase coming from this mild old gentleman astonished me unutterably. "You are a railer and a bitter railer; I have read articles that you have written, and I know your contempt and your hatred for those you call Protestants in your derision; though your grandfather, the vicar of Caerleon-on-Usk, called himself Protestant and was proud of it, and your great-grand-uncle Hezekiah, *ffeiriad coch yr Castletown*—the Red Priest of Castletown—was a great man with the Methodists in his day, and the people flocked by their thousands when he administered the Sacrament. I was born and brought up in Glamorganshire, and old men have wept as they told me of the weeping and contrition that there was when the Red Priest broke the Bread and raised the Cup. But you are a railer, and see nothing but the outside and the show. You are not worthy of this mystery that has been done here."

I went out from his presence rebuked indeed, and justly rebuked; but rather amazed. It is curiously true that the Welsh are still one people, one family almost, in a manner that the English cannot understand, but I had never thought that this old clergyman would have known anything of my ancestry or their doings. And as for my articles and suchlike, I knew that the country clergy sometimes read, but I had fancied my pronouncements sufficiently obscure, even in London, much more in Arfon.

But so it happened, and so I had no explanation from the rector of Llantrisant of the strange circumstance, that his church was full of incense and odours of paradise.

* * *

I went up and down the ways of Llantrisant wondering, and came to the harbour, which is a little place, with little quays where some small coasting trade still lingers. A brigantine was at anchor here, and very lazily in the sunshine they were loading it with anthracite; for it is one of the oddities of Llantrisant that there is a small colliery in the heart of the wood on the hillside. I crossed a causeway which parts the outer harbour from the inner harbour, and settled down on a rocky beach hidden under a leafy hill. The tide was going out, and some children were playing on the wet sand, while two ladies—their mothers, I suppose—talked together as they sat comfortably on their rugs at a little distance from me.

At first they talked of the war, and I made myself deaf, for of that talk one gets enough, and more than enough, in London. Then there was a period of silence, and the conversation had passed to quite a different topic when I caught the thread of it again. I was sitting on the further side of a big rock, and I do not think that the two ladies had noticed my approach. However, though they spoke of strange things, they spoke of nothing which made it necessary for me to announce my presence.

"And, after all," one of them was saying, "what is it all about? I can't make out what is come to the people."

This speaker was a Welshwoman; I recognized the clear, overemphasized consonants, and a faint suggestion of an accent. Her friend came from the Midlands, and it turned out that they had only known each other for a few days. Theirs was a friendship of the beach and of bathing; such friendships are common at small seaside places.

"There is certainly something odd about the people here. I have never been to Llantrisant before, you know; indeed, this is the first time we've been in Wales for our holidays, and knowing nothing about the ways of the people and not being accustomed to hear Welsh spoken, I thought, perhaps, it must be my imagination. But you think there really is something a little queer?"

"I can tell you this: that I have been in two minds whether I should not write to my husband and ask him to take me and the children away. You know where I am at Mrs. Morgan's, and the Morgans' sitting-room is just the other side of the passage, and sometimes they leave the door open, so that I can hear what they say quite plainly. And you see I understand the Welsh, though they don't know it. And I hear them saying the most alarming things!"

"What sort of things?"

"Well, indeed, it sounds like some kind of a religious service, but it's not Church of England, I know that. Old Morgan begins it, and the wife and children answer. Something like: 'Blessed be God for the messengers of Paradise.' 'Blessed be His Name for Paradise in the meat and in the drink.' 'Thanksgiving for the old offering.' 'Thanksgiving for the appearance of the old altar.' 'Praise for the joy of the ancient garden.' 'Praise for the return of those that have been long absent.' And all that sort of thing. It is nothing but madness."

"Depend upon it," said the lady from the Midlands, "there's no real harm in it. They're Dissenters; some new sect, I dare say. You know some Dissenters are very queer in their ways."

"All that is like no Dissenters that I have ever known in all my life whatever," replied the Welsh lady somewhat vehemently, with a very distinct intonation of the land. "And have you heard them speak of the bright light that shone at midnight from the church?"

III. A Secret in a Secret Place

Now here was I altogether at a loss and quite bewildered. The children broke into the conversation of the two ladies and cut it short, just as the midnight lights from the church came on the field, and when the little girls and boys went back again to the sands whooping, the tide of talk had turned, and Mrs. Harland and Mrs. Williams were quite safe and at home with Janey's measles, and a wonderful treatment for infantile ear-ache, as exemplified in the case of Trevor. There was no more to be got out of them, evidently, so I left the beach, crossed the harbour causeway, and drank beer at the Fisherman's Rest till it was time to climb up two miles of deep lane and catch the train for Penvro, where I was staying. And I went up the lane, as I say, in a kind of amazement; and not so much, I think, because of evidences and hints of things strange to the senses, such as the savour of incense where no incense had smoked for three hundred and fifty years and more, or the story of bright light shining from the dark, closed church at dead of night, as because of that sentence of thanksgiving "for paradise in meat and in drink."

For the sun went down and the evening fell as I climbed the long hill through the deep woods and the high meadows, and the scent of all the green things rose from the earth and from the heart of the wood, and at a turn of the lane far below was the misty glimmer of the still sea, and from far below its deep murmur sounded as it washed on the little hidden, enclosed bay where Llantrisant stands. And I thought, if there be paradise in meat and in drink, so much the more is there paradise in the scent of the green leaves at evening and in the appearance of the sea and in the redness of the sky; and there came to me a certain vision of a real world about us all the while, of a language that was only secret because we would not take the trouble to listen to it and discern it.

It was almost dark when I got to the station, and here were the few feeble oil lamps lit, glimmering in that lonely land, where the way is long from farm to farm. The train came on its way, and I got into it; and just as we moved from the station I noticed a group under one of those dim lamps. A woman and her child had got out, and they were being welcomed by a man who had been waiting for them. I had not noticed his face as I stood on the platform, but now I saw it as he pointed down the hill towards Llantrisant, and I think I was almost frightened.

He was a young man, a farmer's son, I would say, dressed in rough brown clothes, and as different from old Mr. Evans, the rector, as one man might be from another. But on his face, as I saw it in the lamp-light, there was the like brightening that I had seen on the face of the rector. It was an illuminated face, glowing with an ineffable joy, and I thought it rather gave light to the platform lamp than received light from it. The woman and her child, I inferred, were strangers to the place, and had come to pay a visit to the young man's family. They had looked about them in bewilderment, half alarmed, before they saw him; and then his face was radiant in their sight, and it was easy to see that all their troubles were ended and over. A wayside station and a darkening country; and it was as if they were welcomed by shining, immortal gladness—even into paradise.

* * *

But though there seemed in a sense light all about my ways, I was myself still quite bewildered. I could see, indeed, that something strange had happened or was happening in the little town hidden under the hill, but there was so far no clue to the mystery, or rather, the clue had been offered to me, and I had not taken it, I had not even known that it was there; since we do not so much as see what we have determined, without judging, to be incredible, even though it be held up before our eyes. The dialogue that the Welsh Mrs. Williams had reported to her English friend might have set me on the right way; but the right way was outside all my limits of possibility, outside the circle of my thought. The palæontologist might see monstrous, significant marks in the slime of a river bank, but he would never draw the conclusions that his own peculiar science would seem to suggest to him; he would choose any explanation rather than the obvious, since the obvious would also be the outrageous—according to our established habit of thought, which we deem final.

* * *

The next day I took all these strange things with me for consideration to a certain place that I knew of not far from Penvro. I was now in the early stages of the jig-saw process, or rather I had only a few pieces before me, and—to continue the figure—my difficulty was this: that though the markings on each piece seemed to have design and significance, yet I could not make the wildest guess as to the nature of the whole picture, of which these were the parts. I had clearly seen that there was a great secret; I had seen that on the face of the young farmer on the platform of Llantrisant station; and in my mind there was all the while the picture of him going down the dark, steep, winding lane that led to the town and the sea, going down through the heart of the wood, with light about him.

But there was bewilderment in the thought of this, and in the endeavour to match it with the perfumed church and the scraps of talk that I had heard and the rumour of midnight brightness; and though Penvro is by no means populous, I thought I would go to a certain solitary place called the Old Camp Head, which looks towards Cornwall and to the great deeps that roll beyond Cornwall to the far ends of the world; a place where fragments of dreams—they seemed such then—might, perhaps, be gathered into the clearness of vision.

It was some years since I had been to the Head, and I had gone on that last time and on a former visit by the cliffs, a rough and difficult path. Now I chose a landward way, which the county map seemed to justify, though doubtfully, as regarded the last part of the journey. So, I went inland and climbed the hot summer by-roads, till I came at last to a lane which gradually turned turfy and grass-grown, and then on high ground, ceased to be. It left me at a gate in a hedge of old thorns; and across the field beyond there seemed to be some faint indications of a track. One would judge that sometimes men did pass by that way, but not often.

It was high ground but not within sight of the sea. But the breath of the sea blew about the hedge of thorns, and came with a keen savour to the nostrils. The ground sloped gently from the gate and then rose again to a ridge, where a white farmhouse stood all alone. I passed by this farmhouse, threading an uncertain way, followed a hedgerow doubtfully; and saw suddenly before me the Old Camp, and beyond it the sapphire plain of waters and the mist where sea and sky met. Steep from my feet the hill fell away, a land of gorse-blossom, red-gold and mellow, of glorious purple heather. It fell into a hollow that went down, shining with rich green bracken, to the glimmering sea; and before me and beyond the hollow rose a height of turf, bastioned at the summit with the awful, age-old walls of the Old Camp; green, rounded circumvallations, wall within wall, tremendous, with their myriad years upon them.

Within these smoothed, green mounds, looking across the shining and changing of the waters in the happy sunlight, I took out the bread and cheese and beer that I had carried in a bag, and ate and drank, and lit my pipe, and set myself to think over the enigmas of Llantrisant. And I had scarcely done so when, a good deal to my annoyance, a man came climbing up over the green ridges, and took up his stand close by, and stared out to sea. He nodded to me, and began with "Fine weather for the harvest" in the approved manner, and so sat down and engaged me in a net of talk. He was of Wales, it seemed, but from a different part of the country, and was staying for a few days with relations—at the white farmhouse which I had passed on my way. His tale of nothing flowed on to his pleasure and my pain, till he fell suddenly on Llantrisant and its doings. I listened then with wonder, and here is his tale condensed. Though it must be clearly understood that the man's evidence was only second-hand; he had heard it from his cousin, the farmer.

So, to be brief, it appeared that there had been a long feud at Llantrisant between a local solicitor, Lewis Prothero (we will say), and a farmer named James. There had been a quarrel about some trifle, which had grown more and more bitter as the two parties forgot the merits of the original dispute, and by some means or other, which I could not well understand, the lawyer had got the small freeholder "under his thumb." James, I think, had given a bill of sale in a bad season, and Prothero had bought it up; and the end was that the farmer was turned out of the old house, and was lodging in a cottage. People said he would have to take a place on his own farm as a labourer; he went about in dreadful misery, piteous to see. It was thought by some that he might very well murder the lawyer, if he met him.

They did meet, in the middle of the market-place at Llantrisant one Saturday in June. The farmer was a little black man, and he gave a shout of rage, and the people were rushing at him to keep him off Prothero.

"And then," said my informant, "I will tell you what happened. This lawyer, as they tell me, he is a great big brawny fellow, with a big jaw and a wide mouth, and a red face and red whiskers. And there he was in his black coat and his high hard hat, and all his money at his back, as you may say. And, indeed, he did fall down on his knees in the dust there in the street in front of Philip James, and every one could see that terror was upon him. And he did beg Philip James's pardon, and beg of him to have mercy, and he did implore him by God and man and the saints of paradise. And my cousin, John Jenkins, Penmawr, he do tell me that the tears were falling from Lewis Prothero's eyes like the rain. And he put his hand into his pocket and drew out the deed of Pantyreos, Philip James's old farm that was, and did give him the farm back and a hundred pounds for the stock that was on it, and two hundred pounds, all in notes of the bank, for amendment and consolation.

"And then, from what they do tell me, all the people did go mad, crying and weeping and calling out all manner of things at the top of their voices. And at last nothing would do but they must all go up to the churchyard, and there Philip James and Lewis Prothero they swear friendship to one another for a long age before the old cross, and everyone sings praises. And my cousin he do declare to me that there were men standing in that crowd that he did never see before in Llantrisant in all his life, and his heart was shaken within him as if it had been in a whirlwind."

I had listened to all this in silence. I said then:

"What does your cousin mean by that? Men that he had never seen in Llantrisant? What men?"

"The people," he said very slowly, "call them the Fishermen."

And suddenly there came into my mind the Rich Fisherman who in the old legend guards the holy mystery of the Graal.

IV. The Ringing of the Bell

So far I have not told the story of the things of Llantrisant, but rather the story of how I stumbled upon them and among them, perplexed and wholly astray, seeking, but yet not knowing at all what I sought; bewildered now and again by circumstances which seemed to me wholly inexplicable; devoid, not so much of the key to the enigma, but of the key to the nature of the enigma. You cannot begin to solve a puzzle till you know what the puzzle is about. "Yards divided by minutes," said the mathematical master to me long ago, "will give neither pigs, sheep, nor oxen." He was right; though his manner on this and on all other occasions was highly offensive. This is enough of the personal process, as I may call it; and here follows the story of what happened at Llantrisant last summer, the story as I pieced it together at last.

It all began, it appears, on a hot day, early in last June; so far as I can make out, on the first Saturday in the month. There was a deaf old woman, a Mrs. Parry, who lived by herself in a lonely cottage a mile or so from the town. She came into the marketplace early on the Saturday morning in a state of some excitement, and as soon as she had taken up her usual place on the pavement by the churchyard, with her ducks and eggs and a few very early potatoes, she began to tell her neighbours about her having heard the sound of a great bell. The good women on each side smiled at one another behind Mrs. Parry's back, for one had to bawl into her ear before she could make out what one meant; and Mrs. Williams, Penycoed, bent over and yelled: "What bell should that be, Mrs. Parry? There's no church near you up at Penrhiw. Do you hear what nonsense she talks?" said Mrs. Williams in a low voice to Mrs. Morgan. "As if she could hear any bell, whatever."

"What makes you talk nonsense yourself?" said Mrs. Parry, to the amazement of the two women. "I can hear a bell as well as you, Mrs. Williams, and as well as your whispers either."

And there is the fact, which is not to be disputed; though the deductions from it may be open to endless disputations; this old woman who had been all but stone deaf for twenty years—the defect had always been in her family—could suddenly hear on this June morning as well as anybody else. And her two old friends stared at her, and it was some time before they had appeased her indignation, and induced her to talk about the bell.

It had happened in the early morning, which was very misty. She had been gathering sage in her garden, high on a round hill looking over the sea. And there came in her ears a sort of throbbing and singing and trembling, "as if there were music coming out of the earth," and then something seemed to break in her head, and all the birds began to sing and make melody together, and the leaves of the poplars round the garden fluttered in the breeze that rose from the sea, and the cock crowed far off at Twyn, and the dog barked down in Kemeys Valley. But above all these sounds, unheard for so many years, there thrilled the deep and chanting note of the bell, "like a bell and a man's voice singing at once."

They stared again at her and at one another. "Where did it sound from?" asked one. "It came sailing across the sea," answered Mrs. Parry quite composedly, "and I did hear it coming nearer and nearer to the land."

"Well, indeed," said Mrs. Morgan, "it was a ship's bell then, though I can't make out why they would be ringing like that."

"It was not ringing on any ship, Mrs. Morgan," said Mrs. Parry.

"Then where do you think it was ringing?"

"Ym mharadwys," replied Mrs. Parry. Now that means "in paradise," and the two others changed the conversation quickly. They thought that Mrs. Parry had got back her hearing suddenly—such things did happen now and then—and that the shock had made her "a bit queer." And this explanation would no doubt have stood its ground, if it had not been for other experiences. Indeed, the local doctor (who had treated Mrs. Parry for a dozen years, not for her deafness, which he took to be hopeless and beyond cure, but for a tiresome and recurrent winter cough), sent an account of the case to a colleague at Bristol, suppressing, naturally enough, the reference to paradise. The Bristol physician gave it as his opinion that the symptoms were absolutely what might have been expected. "You have here, in all probability," he wrote, "the sudden breaking down of an old obstruction in the aural passage, and I should quite expect this process to be accompanied by tinnitus of a pronounced and even violent character."

* * *

But for the other experiences? As the morning wore on and drew to noon, high market, and to the utmost brightness of that summer day, all the stalls and the streets were full of rumours and of awed faces. Now from one lonely farm, now from another, men and women came and told the story of how they had listened in the early morning with thrilling hearts to the thrilling music of a bell that was like no bell ever heard before. And it seemed that many people in the town had been roused, they knew not how, from sleep; waking up, as one of them said, as if bells were ringing and the organ playing, and a choir of sweet voices singing all together: "There were such melodies and songs that my heart was full of joy."

And a little past noon some fishermen who had been out all night returned, and brought a wonderful story into the town of what they had heard in the mist; and one of them said he had seen something go by at a little distance from his boat. "It was all golden and bright," he said, "and there was glory about it." Another fisherman declared: "There was a song upon the water that was like heaven."

And here I would say in parenthesis that on returning to town I sought out a very old friend of mine, a man who has devoted a lifetime to strange and esoteric studies. I thought that I had a tale that would interest him profoundly, but I found that he heard me with a good deal of indifference. And at this very point of the sailors' stories I remember saying: "Now what do you make of that? Don't you think it's extremely curious?" He replied: "I hardly think so. Possibly the sailors were lying; possibly it happened as they say. Well; that sort of thing has always been happening." I give my friend's opinion; I make no comment on it.

Let it be noted that there was something remarkable as to the manner in which the sound of the bell was heard—or supposed to be heard. There are, no doubt, mysteries in sounds as in all else; indeed, I am informed that during one of the horrible outrages that have been perpetrated on London during this autumn there was an instance of a great block of workmen's dwellings in which the only person who heard the crash of a particular bomb falling was an old deaf woman, who had been fast asleep till the moment of the explosion. This is strange enough of a sound that was entirely in the natural (and horrible) order; and so it was at Llantrisant, where the sound was either a collective auditory hallucination or a manifestation of what is conveniently, if inaccurately, called the supernatural order.

For the thrill of the bell did not reach to all ears—or hearts. Deaf Mrs. Parry heard it in her lonely cottage garden, high above the misty sea; but then, in a farm on the other or western side of Llantrisant, a little child, scarcely three years old, was the only one out of a household of ten people who heard anything. He called out in stammering baby Welsh something that sounded like *"Clychau fawr, clychau fawr"*—the great bells, the great bells—and his mother wondered what he was talking about. Of the crews of half a dozen trawlers that were swinging from side to side in the mist, not more than four men had any tale to tell. And so it was that for an hour or two the man who had heard nothing suspected his neighbour, who had heard marvels, of lying; and it was some time before the mass of evidence coming from all manners of diverse and remote quarters convinced the people that there was a true story here. A might suspect B, his neighbour, of making up a tale; but when C, from some place on the hills five miles away, and D, the fisherman on the waters, each had a like report, then it was clear that something had happened.

* * *

And even then, as they told me, the signs to be seen upon the people were stranger than the tales told by them and among them. It has struck me that many people in reading some of the phrases that I have reported will dismiss them with laughter as very poor and fantastic inventions; fishermen, they will say, do not speak of "a song like heaven" or of "a glory about it." And I dare say this would be a just enough criticism if I were reporting English fishermen; but, odd though it may be, Wales has not yet lost the last shreds of the grand manner. And let it be remembered also that in most cases such phrases are translated from another language, that is, from the Welsh.

So, they come trailing, let us say, fragments of the cloud of glory in their common speech; and so, on this Saturday, they began to display, uneasily enough in many cases, their consciousness that the things that were reported were of their ancient right and former custom. The comparison is not quite fair; but conceive Hardy's old Durbeyfield suddenly waking from long slumber to find himself in a noble thirteenth-century hall, waited on by kneeling pages, smiled on by sweet ladies in silken cotehardies.

So by evening time there had come to the old people the recollection of stories that their fathers had told them as they sat round the hearth of winter nights, fifty, sixty, seventy years ago; stories of the wonderful bell of Teilo Sant, that had sailed across the glassy seas from Syon, that was called a portion of paradise, "and the sound of its ringing was like the perpetual choir of the angels."

Such things were remembered by the old and told to the young that evening, in the streets of the town and in the deep lanes that climbed far hills. The sun went down to the mountain red with fire like a burnt offering, the sky turned violet, the sea was purple, as one told another of the wonder that had returned to the land after long ages.

V. The Rose of Fire

It was during the next nine days, counting from that Saturday early in June—the first Saturday in June, as I believe—that Llantrisant and all the regions about became possessed either by an extraordinary set of hallucinations or by a visitation of great marvels.

This is not the place to strike the balance between the two possibilities. The evidence is, no doubt, readily available; the matter is open to systematic investigation.

But this may be said: The ordinary man, in the ordinary passages of his life, accepts in the main the evidence of his senses, and is entirely right in doing so. He says that he sees a cow, that he sees a stone wall, and that the cow and the stone wall are "there." This is very well for all the practical purposes of life, but I believe that the metaphysicians are by no means so easily satisfied as to the reality of the stone wall and the cow. Perhaps they might allow that both objects are "there" in the sense that one's reflection is in a glass; there is an actuality, but is there a reality external to oneself? In any event, it is solidly agreed that, supposing a real existence, this much is certain—it is not in the least like our conception of it. The ant and the microscope will quickly convince us that we do not see things as they really are, even supposing that we see them at all. If we could "see" the real cow she would appear utterly incredible, as incredible as the things I am to relate.

Now, there is nothing that I know much more unconvincing than the stories of the red light on the sea. Several sailors, men on small coasting ships, who were working up or down the Channel on that Saturday night, spoke of "seeing" the red light, and it must be said that there is a very tolerable agreement in their tales. All make the time as between midnight of the Saturday and one o'clock on the Sunday morning. Two of those sailormen are precise as to the time of the apparition; they fix it by elaborate calculations of their own as occurring at 12.20 a.m. And the story?

A red light, a burning spark seen far away in the darkness, taken at the first moment of seeing for a signal, and probably an enemy signal. Then it approached at a tremendous speed, and one man said he took it be the port light of some new kind of navy motor boat which was developing a rate hitherto unheard of, a hundred or a hundred and fifty knots an hour. And then, in the third instant of the sight, it was clear that this was no earthly speed. At first a red spark in the farthest distance; then a rushing lamp; and then, as if in an incredible point of time, it swelled into a vast rose of fire that filled all the sea and all the sky and hid the stars and possessed the land. "I thought the end of the world had come," one of the sailors said.

And then, an instant more, and it was gone from them, and four of them say that there was a red spark on Chapel Head, where the old grey chapel of St. Teilo stands, high above the water, in a cleft of the limestone rocks.

And thus the sailors; and thus their tales are incredible; but *they* are not incredible. I believe that men of the highest eminence in physical science have testified to the occurrence of phenomena every whit as marvellous, to things as absolutely opposed to all natural order, as we conceive it; and it may be said that nobody minds them. "That sort of thing has always been happening," as my friend remarked to me. But the men, whether or no the fire had ever been without them, there was no doubt that it was now within them, for it burned in their eyes. They were purged as if they had passed through the Furnace of the Sages governed with Wisdom that the alchemists know. They spoke without much difficulty of what they had seen, or had seemed to see, with their eyes, but hardly at all of what their hearts had known when for a moment the glory of the fiery rose had been about them.

For some weeks afterwards they were still, as it were, amazed; almost, I would say, incredulous. If there had been nothing more than the splendid and fiery appearance, showing and vanishing, I do believe that they themselves would have discredited their own senses and denied the truth of their own tales. And one does not dare to say whether they would not have been right. Men like Sir William Crookes and Sir Oliver Lodge are certainly to be heard with respect, and they bear witness to all manner of apparent eversions of laws which we, or most of us, consider far more deeply founded than the ancient hills. They may be justified; but in our hearts we doubt. We cannot wholly believe in inner sincerity that the solid table did rise, without mechanical reason or cause, into the air, and so defy that which we name the "law of gravitation." I know what may be said on the other side; I know that there is no true question of "law" in the case; that the law of gravitation really means just this: that I have never seen a table rising without mechanical aid, or an apple, detached from the bough, soaring to the skies instead of falling to the ground. The so-called law is just the sum of common observation and nothing more; yet I say, in our hearts we do not believe that the tables rise; much less do we believe in the rose of fire that for a moment swallowed up the skies and seas and shores of the Welsh coast last June.

And the men who saw it would have invented fairy tales to account for it, I say again, if it had not been for that which was within them.

They said, all of them and it was certain now that they spoke the truth, that in the moment of the vision, every pain and ache and malady in their bodies had passed away. One man had been vilely drunk on venomous spirit, procured at Jobson's Hole down by the Cardiff Docks. He was horribly ill; he had crawled up from his bunk for a little fresh air; and in an instant his horrors and his deadly nausea had left him. Another man was almost desperate with the raging hammering pain of an abscess on a tooth; he says that when the red flame came near he felt as if a dull, heavy blow had fallen on his jaw, and then the pain was quite gone; he could scarcely believe that there had been any pain there.

And they all bear witness to an extraordinary exaltation of the senses. It is indescribable, this; for they cannot describe it. They are amazed, again; they do not in the least profess to know what happened; but there is no more possibility of shaking their evidence than there is a possibility of shaking the evidence of a man who says that water is wet and fire hot.

"I felt a bit queer afterwards," said one of them, "and I steadied myself by the mast, and I can't tell how I felt as I touched it. I didn't know that touching a thing like a mast could be better than a big drink when you're thirsty, or a soft pillow when you're sleepy."

I heard other instances of this state of things, as I must vaguely call it, since I do not know what else to call it. But I suppose we can all agree that to the man in average health, the average impact of the external world on his senses is a matter of indifference. The average impact; a harsh scream, the bursting of a motor tire, any violent assault on the aural nerves will annoy him, and he may say "damn." Then, on the other hand, the man who is not "fit" will easily be annoyed and irritated by someone pushing past him in a crowd, by the ringing of a bell, by the sharp closing of a book.

But so far as I could judge from the talk of these sailors, the average impact of the external world had become to them a fountain of pleasure. Their nerves were on edge, but an edge to receive exquisite sensuous impressions. The touch of the rough mast, for example; that was a joy far greater than is the joy of fine silk to some luxurious skins; they drank water and stared as if they had been *fins gourmets* tasting an amazing wine; the creak and whine of their ship on its slow way were as exquisite as the rhythm and song of a Bach fugue to an amateur of music.

And then, within; these rough fellows have their quarrels and strifes and variances and envyings like the rest of us; but that was all over between them that had seen the rosy light; old enemies shook hands heartily, and roared with laughter as they confessed one to another what fools they had been.

"I can't exactly say how it has happened or what has happened at all," said one, "but if you have all the world and the glory of it, how can you fight for fivepence?"

* * *

The church of Llantrisant is a typical example of a Welsh parish church, before the evil and horrible period of "restoration."

This lower world is a palace of lies, and of all foolish lies there is none more insane than a certain vague fable about the mediæval freemasons, a fable which somehow imposed itself upon the cold intellect of Hallam the historian. The story is, in brief, that throughout the Gothic period, at any rate, the art and craft of church building were executed by wandering guilds of "freemasons," possessed of various secrets of building and adornment, which they employed wherever they went. If this nonsense were true, the Gothic of Cologne would be as the Gothic of Colne, and the Gothic of Arles like to the Gothic of Abingdon. It is so grotesquely untrue that almost every county, let alone every country, has its distinctive style in Gothic architecture. Arfon is in the west of Wales; its churches have marks and features which distinguish them from the churches in the east of Wales.

The Llantrisant church has that primitive division between nave and chancel which only very foolish people decline to recognize as equivalent to the Oriental iconostasis and as the origin of the Western rood-screen. A solid wall divided the church into two portions; in the centre was a narrow opening with a rounded arch, through which those who sat towards the middle of the church could see the small, red-carpeted altar and the three roughly shaped lancet windows above it.

The "reading pew" was on the outer side of this wall of partition, and here the rector did his service, the choir being grouped in seats about him. On the inner side were the pews of certain privileged houses of the town and district.

On the Sunday morning the people were all in their accustomed places, not without a certain exultation in their eyes, not without a certain expectation of they knew not what. The bells stopped ringing, the rector, in his old-fashioned, ample surplice, entered the reading-desk, and gave out the hymn: "My God, and is Thy table spread."

And, as the singing began, all the people who were in the pews within the wall came out of them and streamed through the archway into the nave. They took what places they could find up and down the church, and the rest of the congregation looked at them in amazement.

Nobody knew what had happened. Those whose seats were next to the aisle tried to peer into the chancel, to see what had happened or what was going on there. But somehow the light flamed so brightly from the windows above the altar, those being the only windows in the chancel, one small lancet in the south wall excepted, that no one could see anything at all.

"It was as if a veil of gold adorned with jewels was hanging there," one man said; and indeed there are a few odds and scraps of old painted glass left in the eastern lancets.

But there were few in the church who did not hear now and again voices speaking beyond the veil.

VI. Olwen's Dream

The well-to-do and dignified personages who left their pews in the chancel of Llantrisant church and came hurrying into the nave could give no explanation of what they had done. They felt, they said, that they "had to go," and to go quickly; they were driven out, as it were, by a secret, irresistible command. But all who were present in the church that morning were amazed, though all exulted in their hearts; for they, like the sailors who saw the rose of fire on the waters, were filled with a joy that was literally ineffable, since they could not utter it or interpret it to themselves.

And they too, like the sailors, were transmuted, or the world was transmuted for them. They experienced what the doctors call a sense of *bien être,* but a *bien être* raised to the highest power. Old men felt young again, eyes that had been growing dim now saw clearly, and saw a world that was like paradise, the same world, it is true, but a world rectified and glowing, as if an inner flame shone in all things, and behind all things.

And the difficulty in recording this state is this, that it is so rare an experience that no set language to express it is in existence. A shadow of its raptures and ecstasies is found in the highest poetry; there are phrases in ancient books telling of the Celtic saints that dimly hint at it; some of the old Italian masters of painting had known it, for the light of it shines in their skies and about the battlements of their cities that are founded on magic hills. But these are but broken hints.

It is not poetic to go to Apothecaries' Hall for similes. But for many years I kept by me an article from the *Lancet* or the *British Medical Journal*—I forget which—in which a doctor gave an account of certain experiments he had conducted with a drug called the mescal button, or *Anhelonium lewinii.* He said that while under the influence of the drug he had but to shut his eyes, and immediately before him there would rise incredible Gothic cathedrals, of such majesty and splendour and glory that no heart had ever conceived. They seemed to surge from the depths to the very heights of heaven, their spires swayed amongst the clouds and the stars, they were fretted with admirable imagery. And as he gazed, he would presently become aware that all the stones were living stones, that they were quickening and palpitating, and then that they were glowing jewels, say, emeralds, sapphires, rubies, opals, but of hues that the mortal eye had never seen.

That description gives, I think, some faint notion of the nature of the transmuted world into which these people by the sea had entered, a world quickened and glorified and full of pleasures. Joy and wonder were on all faces; but the deepest joy and the greatest wonder were on the face of the rector. For he had heard through the veil the Greek word for "holy," three times repeated. And he, who had once been a horrified assistant at High Mass in a foreign church, recognized the perfume of incense that filled the place from end to end.

* * *

It was on that Sunday night that Olwen Phillips of Croeswen dreamed her wonderful dream. She was a girl of sixteen, the daughter of small farming people, and for many months she had been doomed to certain death. Consumption, which flourishes in that damp, warm climate, had laid hold of her; not only her lungs but her whole system was a mass of tuberculosis. As is common enough, she had enjoyed many fallacious brief recoveries in the early stages of the disease, but all hope had long been over, and now for the last few weeks she had seemed to rush vehemently to death. The doctor had come on the Saturday morning, bringing with him a colleague. They had both agreed that the girl's case was in its last stages. "She cannot possibly last more than a day or two," said the local doctor to her mother. He came again on the Sunday morning and found his patient perceptibly worse, and soon afterwards she sank into a heavy sleep, and her mother thought that she would never wake from it.

The girl slept in an inner room communicating with the room occupied by her father and mother. The door between was kept open, so that Mrs. Phillips could hear her daughter if she called to her in the night. And Olwen called to her mother that night, just as the dawn was breaking. It was no faint summons from a dying bed that came to the mother's ears, but a loud cry that rang through the house, a cry of great gladness. Mrs. Phillips started up from sleep in wild amazement, wondering what could have happened. And then she saw Olwen, who had not been able to rise from her bed for many weeks past, standing in the doorway in the faint light of the growing day. The girl called to her mother: "Mam! mam! It is all over. I am quite well again."

Mrs. Phillips roused her husband, and they sat up in bed staring, not knowing on earth, as they said afterwards, what had been done with the world. Here was their poor girl wasted to a shadow, lying on her death-bed, and the life sighing from her with every breath, and her voice, when she last uttered it, so weak that one had to put one's ear to her mouth. And here in a few hours she stood up before them; and even in that faint light they could see that she was changed almost beyond knowing. And, indeed, Mrs. Phillips said that for a moment or two she fancied that the Germans must have come and killed them in their sleep, and so they were all dead together. But Olwen called out again, so the mother lit a candle and got up and went tottering across the room, and there was Olwen all gay and plump again, smiling with shining eyes. Her mother led her into her own room, and set down the candle there, and felt her daughter's flesh, and burst into prayers and tears of wonder and delight, and thanksgivings, and held the girl again to be sure that she was not deceived. And then Olwen told her dream, though she thought it was not a dream.

She said she woke up in the deep darkness, and she knew the life was fast going from her. She could not move so much as a finger, she tried to cry out, but no sound came from her lips. She felt that in another instant the whole world would fall from her—her heart was full of agony. And as the last breath was passing her lips, she heard a very faint, sweet sound, like the tinkling of a silver bell. It came from far away, from over by Ty-newydd. She forgot her agony and listened, and even then, she says, she felt the swirl of the world as it came back to her. And the sound of the bell swelled and grew louder, and it thrilled all through her body, and the life was in it. And as the bell rang and trembled in her ears, a faint light touched the wall of her room and reddened, till the whole room was full of rosy fire. And then she saw standing before her bed three men in blood-coloured robes with shining faces. And one man held a golden bell in his hand. And the second man held up something shaped like the top of a table. It was like a great jewel, and it was of a blue colour, and there were rivers of silver and of gold running through it and flowing as quick streams flow, and there were pools in it as if violets had been poured out into water, and then it was green as the sea near the shore, and then it was the sky at night with all the stars shining, and then the sun and the moon came down and washed in it. And the third man held up high above this a cup that was like a rose on fire; "there was a great burning in it, and a dropping of blood in it, and a red cloud above it, and I saw a great secret. And I heard a voice that sang nine times: 'Glory and praise to the Conqueror of Death, to the Fountain of Life immortal.' Then the red light went from the wall, and it was all darkness, and the bell rang faint again by Capel Teilo, and then I got up and called to you."

The doctor came on the Monday morning with the death certificate in his pocket-book, and Olwen ran out to meet him. I have quoted his phrase in the first chapter of this record: "A kind of resurrection of the body." He made a most careful examination of the girl; he has stated that he found that every trace of disease had disappeared. He left on the Sunday morning a patient entering into the coma that precedes death, a body condemned utterly and ready for the grave. He met at the garden gate on the Monday morning a young woman in whom life sprang up like a fountain, in whose body life laughed and rejoiced as if it had been a river flowing from an unending well.

* * *

Now this is the place to ask one of those questions—there are many such—which cannot be answered. The question is as to the continuance of tradition; more especially as to the continuance of tradition among the Welsh Celts of to-day. On the one hand, such waves and storms have gone over them. The wave of the heathen Saxons went over them, then the wave of Latin mediævalism, then the waters of Anglicanism; last of all the flood of their queer Calvinistic Methodism, half Puritan, half pagan. It may well be asked whether any memory can possibly have survived such a series of deluges. I have said that the old people of Llantrisant had their tales of the bell of Teilo Sant; but these were but vague and broken recollections. And then there is the name by which the "strangers" who were seen in the market-place were known; that is more precise. Students of the Graal legend know that the keeper of the Graal in the romances is the King Fisherman, or the Rich Fisherman; students of Celtic hagiology know that it was prophesied before the birth of Dewi (or David) that he should be "a man of aquatic life," that another legend tells how a little child, destined to be a saint, was discovered on a stone in the river, how through his childhood a fish for his nourishment was found on that stone every day, while another saint, Ilar, if I remember, was expressly known as the Fisherman. But has the memory of all this persisted in the church-going and chapel-going people of Wales at the present day? It is difficult to say. There is the affair of the Healing Cup of Nant Eos, or Tregaron Healing Cup, as it is also called. It is only a few years ago since it was shown to a wandering harper, who treated it lightly, and then spent a wretched night, as he said, and came back penitently and was left alone with the sacred vessel to pray over it, till "his mind was at rest." That was in 1887.

Then for my part—I only know modern Wales on the surface, I am sorry to say—I remember three or four years ago speaking to my temporary landlord of certain relics of Saint Teilo, which are supposed to be in the keeping of a particular family in that country. The landlord is a very jovial merry fellow, and I observed with some astonishment that his ordinary, easy manner was completely altered as he said, gravely, "That will be over there, up by the mountain," pointing vaguely to the north. And he changed the subject, as a freemason changes the subject.

There the matter lies, and its appositeness to the story of Llantrisant is this: that the dream of Olwen Phillips was, in fact, the vision of the Holy Graal.

VII. The Mass of the Sangraal

"*Ffeiriadwyr Melcisidec! Ffeiriadwyr Melcisidec!*" shouted the old Calvinistic Methodist deacon with the grey beard, "Priesthood of Melchizedek! Priesthood of Melchizedek!"

And he went on:

"The Bell that is like *y glwys yr angel ym mharadwys*—the joy of the angels in paradise—is returned; the Altar that is of a colour that no men can discern is returned, the Cup that came from Syon is returned, the ancient Offering is restored, the Three Saints have come back to the church of the *tri sant,* the Three Holy Fishermen are amongst us, and their net is full. *Gogoniant, gogoniant*—glory, glory!"

Then another Methodist began to recite in Welsh a verse from Wesley's hymn.

> God still respects Thy sacrifice,
> Its savour sweet doth always please;
> The Offering smokes through earth and skies,
> Diffusing life and joy and peace;
> To these Thy lower courts it comes
> And fills them with Divine perfumes.

The whole church was full, as the old books tell, of the odour of the rarest spiceries. There were lights shining within the sanctuary, through the narrow archway.

This was the beginning of the end of what befell at Llantrisant. For it was the Sunday after that night on which Olwen Phillips had been restored from death to life. There was not a single chapel of the Dissenters open in the town that day. The Methodists with their minister and their deacons and all the Nonconformists had returned on this Sunday morning to "the old hive." One would have said, a church of the Middle Ages, a church in Ireland to-day. Every seat—save those in the chancel—was full, all the aisles were full, the churchyard was full; everyone on his knees, and the old rector kneeling before the door into the holy place.

Yet they can say but very little of what was done beyond the veil. There was no attempt to perform the usual service; when the bells had stopped the old deacon raised his cry, and priest and people fell down on their knees as they thought they heard a choir within singing "Alleluya, alleluya, alleluya." And as the bells in the tower ceased ringing, there sounded the thrill of the bell from Syon, and the golden veil of sunlight fell across the door into the altar, and the heavenly voices began their melodies.

A voice like a trumpet cried from within the brightness:

Agyos, Agyos, Agyos.

And the people, as if an age-old memory stirred in them, replied:

Agyos yr Tâd, agyos yr Mab, agyos yr Ysbryd Glan. Sant, sant, sant, Drindod sant vendigeid. Sanctus Arglwydd Dduw Sabaoth, Dominus Deus.

There was a voice that cried and sang from within the altar; most of the people had heard some faint echo of it in the chapels; a voice rising and falling and soaring in awful modulations that rang like the trumpet of the Last Angel. The people beat upon their breasts, the tears were like rain of the mountains on their cheeks; those that were able fell down on their faces before the glory of the veil. They said afterwards that men of the hills, twenty miles away, heard that cry and that singing, rushing upon them on the wind, and they fell down on their faces, and cried: "The offering is accomplished," knowing nothing of what they said.

There were a few who saw three come out of the door of the sanctuary, and stand for a moment on the pace before the door. These three were in dyed vesture, red as blood. One stood before two, looking to the west, and he rang the bell. And they say that all the birds of the wood, and all the waters of the sea, and all the leaves of the trees, and all the winds of the high rocks uttered their voices with the ringing of the bell. And the second and the third; they turned their faces one to another. The second held up the lost altar that they once called "Sapphirus," which was like the changing of the sea and of the sky, and like the immixture of gold and silver. And the third heaved up high over the altar a cup that was red with burning and the blood of the offering.

And the old rector cried aloud then before the entrance:

Bendigeid yr Offeren yn oes oesoedd—blessed be the Offering unto the age of ages.

And then the Mass of the Sangraal was ended, and then began the passing out of that land of the holy persons and holy things that had returned to it after the long years. It seemed, indeed, to many that the thrilling sound of the bell was in their ears for days, even for weeks after that Sunday morning. But thenceforth neither bell nor altar nor cup was seen by anyone; not openly, that is, but only in dreams by day and by night. Nor did the people see strangers again in the market of Llantrisant, nor in the lonely places where certain persons oppressed by great affliction and sorrow had once or twice encountered them.

But that time of visitation will never be forgotten by the people. Many things happened in the nine days that have not been set down in this record—or legend. Some of them were trifling matters, though strange enough in other times. Thus a man in the town who had a fierce dog that was always kept chained up found one day that the beast had become mild and gentle.

And this is stranger: Edward Davies, of Lanafon, a farmer, was roused from sleep one night by a queer yelping and barking in his yard. He looked out of the window and saw his sheep-dog playing with a big fox; they were chasing each other by turns, rolling over and over one another, "cutting such capers as I did never see the like," as the astonished farmer put it. And some of the people said that during this season of wonder the corn shot up, and the grass thickened, and the fruit was multiplied on the trees in a very marvellous manner.

More important, it seemed, was the case of Williams, the grocer; though this may have been a purely natural deliverance. Mr. Williams was to marry his daughter Mary to a smart young fellow from Carmarthen, and he was in great distress over it. Not over the marriage itself, but because things had been going very badly with him for some time, and he could not see his way to giving anything like the wedding entertainment that would be expected of him. The wedding was to be on the Saturday—that was the day on which the lawyer, Lewis Prothero, and the farmer, Philip James, were reconciled—and this John Williams, without money or credit, could not think how shame would not be on him for the meagreness and poverty of the wedding feast. And then on the Tuesday came a letter from his brother, David Williams, Australia, from whom he had not heard for fifteen years. And David, it seemed, had been making a great deal of money, and was a bachelor, and here was with his letter a paper good for a thousand pounds: "You may as well enjoy it now as wait till I am dead." This was enough, indeed, one might say; but hardly an hour after the letter had come the lady from the big house (Plas Mawr) drove up in all her grandeur, and went into the shop and said: "Mr. Williams, your daughter Mary has always been a very good girl, and my husband and I feel that we must give her some little thing on her wedding, and we hope she'll be very happy." It was a gold watch worth fifteen pounds. And after Lady Watcyn, advances the old doctor with a dozen of port, forty years upon it, and a long sermon on how to decant it. And the old rector's old wife brings to the beautiful dark girl two yards of creamy lace, like an enchantment, for her wedding veil, and tells Mary how she wore it for her own wedding fifty years ago; and the squire, Sir Watcyn, as if his wife had not been already with a fine gift, calls from his horse, and brings out Williams and barks like a dog at him: "Goin' to have a weddin', eh, Williams? Can't have a weddin' without champagne, y' know; wouldn't be legal, don't y' know. So look out for a couple of cases." So Williams tells the story of the gifts; and certainly there was never so famous a wedding in Llantrisant before.

All this, of course, may have been altogether in the natural order; the "glow," as they call it, seems more difficult to explain. For they say that all through the nine days, and indeed after the time had ended, there never was a man weary or sick at heart in Llantrisant, or in the country round it. For if a man felt that his work of the body or the mind was going to be too much for his strength, then there would come to him of a sudden a warm glow and a thrilling all over him, and he felt as strong as a giant, and happier than he had ever been in his life before, so that lawyer and hedger each rejoiced in the task that was before him, as if it were sport and play.

And much more wonderful than this or any other wonders was forgiveness, with love to follow it. There were meetings of old enemies in the market-place and in the street that made the people lift up their hands and declare that it was as if one walked the miraculous streets of Syon.

* * *

But as to the "phenomena," the occurrences for which, in ordinary talk, we should reserve the word "miraculous"? Well, what do we know? The question that I have already stated comes up again, as to the possible survival of old tradition in a kind of dormant, or torpid, semi-conscious state. In other words, did the people "see" and "hear" what they expected to see and hear? This point, or one similar to it, occurred in a debate between Andrew Lang and Anatole France as to the visions of Joan of Arc. M. France stated that when Joan saw St. Michael, she saw the traditional archangel of the religious art of her day, but to the best of my belief Andrew Lang proved that the visionary figure Joan described was not in the least like the fifteenth-century conception of St. Michael. So, in the case of Llantrisant, I have stated that there was a sort of tradition about the holy bell of Teilo Sant; and it is, of course, barely possible that some vague notion of the Graal cup may have reached even Welsh country folks through Tennyson's *Idylls.* But so far I see no reason to suppose that these people had ever heard of the portable altar (called "Sapphirus" in William of Malmesbury) or of its changing colours "that no man could discern."

And then there are the other questions of the distinction between hallucination and vision, of the average duration of one and the other, and of the possibility of collective hallucination. If a number of people all see (or think they see) the same appearances, can this be merely hallucination? I believe there is a leading case on the matter, which concerns a number of people seeing the same appearance on a church wall in Ireland; but there is, of course, this difficulty, that one may be hallucinated and communicate his impression to the others, telepathically.

But at the last, what do we know? ❋

Out of the Earth

THERE was some sort of confused complaint during last August of the ill-behaviour of the children at certain Welsh watering-places. Such reports and vague rumours are most difficult to trace to their heads and fountains; none has better reason to know that than myself. I need not go over the old ground here, but I am afraid that many people are wishing by this time that they had never heard my name; again, a considerable number of estimable persons are concerning themselves gloomily enough, from my point of view, with my everlasting welfare. They write me letters, some in kindly remonstrance, begging me not to deprive poor, sick-hearted souls of what little comfort they possess amidst their sorrows. Others send me tracts and pink leaflets with allusions to "the daughter of a well-known canon"; others again are violently and anonymously abusive. And then in open print, in fair book-form, Mr. Begbie has dealt with me righteously but harshly, as I cannot but think.

Yet, it was all so entirely innocent, nay casual, on my part. A poor linnet of prose, I did but perform my indifferent piping in the *Evening News* because I wanted to do so, because I felt that the story of "The Bowmen" ought to be told. An inventor of fantasies is a poor creature, heaven knows, when all the world is at war; but I thought that no harm would be done, at any rate, if I bore witness, after the fashion of the fantastic craft, to my belief in the heroic glory of the English host who went back from Mons fighting and triumphing.

And then, somehow or other, it was as if I had touched a button and set in action a terrific, complicated mechanism of rumours that pretended to be sworn truth, of gossip that posed as evidence, of wild tarradiddles that good men most firmly believed. The supposed testimony of that "daughter of a well-known canon" took parish magazines by storm, and equally enjoyed the faith of dissenting divines. The "daughter" denied all knowledge of the matter, but people still quoted her supposed sure word; and the issues were confused with tales, probably true, of painful hallucinations and deliriums of our retreating soldiers, men fatigued and shattered to the very verge of death. It all became worse than the Russian myths, and as in the fable of the Russians, it seemed impossible to follow the streams of delusion to their fountain-head—or heads. Who was it who said that "Miss M. knew two officers who, etc., etc."? I suppose we shall never know his lying, deluding name.

And so, I dare say, it will be with this strange affair of the troublesome children of the Welsh seaside town, or rather of a group of small towns and villages lying within a certain section or zone, which I am not going to indicate more precisely than I can help, since I love that country, and my recent experiences with "The Bowmen" have taught me that no tale is too idle to be believed. And, of course, to begin with, nobody knew how this odd and malicious piece of gossip originated. So far as I know, it was more akin to the Russian myth than to the tale of "The Angels of Mons." That is, rumour preceded print; the thing was talked of here and there and passed from letter to letter long before the papers were aware of its existence. And—here it resembles rather the Mons affair—London and Manchester, Leeds and Birmingham were muttering vague unpleasant things while the little villages concerned basked innocently in the sunshine of an unusual prosperity.

In this last circumstance, as some believe, is to be sought the root of the whole matter. It is well known that certain East Coast towns suffered from the dread of air-raids, and that a good many of their usual visitors went westward for the first time. So there is a theory that the East Coast was mean enough to circulate reports against the West Coast out of pure malice and envy. It may be so; I do not pretend to know. But here is a personal experience, such as it is, which illustrated the way in which the rumour was circulated. I was lunching one day at my Fleet Street tavern—this was early in July—and a friend of mine, a solicitor, of Serjeants' Inn, came in and sat at the same table. We began to talk of holidays and my friend Eddis asked me where I was going. "To the same old place," I said. "Manavon. You know we always go there." "Are you really?" said the lawyer. "I thought that coast had gone off a lot. My wife has a friend who's heard that it's not at all that it was."

I was astonished to hear this, not seeing how a little village like Manavon could have "gone off." I had known it for ten years as having accommodation for about twenty visitors, and I could not believe that rows of lodging houses had sprung up since the August of 1914. Still I put the question to Eddis: "Trippers?" I asked, knowing firstly that trippers hate the solitudes of the country and the sea; secondly, that there are no industrial towns within cheap and easy distance, and thirdly, that the railways were issuing no excursion tickets during the war.

"No, not exactly trippers," the lawyer replied. "But my wife's friend knows a clergyman who says that the beach at Tremaen is not at all pleasant now, and Tremaen's only a few miles from Manavon, isn't it?"

"In what way not pleasant?" I carried on my examination. "Pierrots and shows, and that sort of thing?" I felt that it could not be so, for the solemn rocks of Tremaen would have turned the liveliest Pierrot to stone. He would have frozen into a crag on the beach, and the seagulls would carry away his song and make it a lament by lonely, booming caverns that look on Avalon. Eddis said he had heard nothing about showmen; but he understood that since the war the children of the whole district had got quite out of hand.

"Bad language, you know," he said, "and all that sort of thing, worse than London slum children. One doesn't want one's wife and children to hear foul talk at any time, much less on their holiday. And they say that Castell Coch is quite impossible; no decent woman would be seen there!"

I said: "Really, that's a great pity," and changed the subject. But I could not make it out at all. I knew Castell Coch well—a little bay bastioned by dunes and red sandstone cliffs, rich with greenery. A stream of cold water runs down there to the sea; there is the ruined Norman Castle, the ancient church and the scattered village; it is altogether a place of peace and quiet and great beauty. The people there, children and grown-ups alike, were not merely decent but courteous folk: if one thanked a child for opening a gate, there would come the inevitable response: "And welcome kindly, sir." I could not make it out at all. I didn't believe the lawyer's tales; for the life of me I could not see what he could be driving at. And, for the avoidance of all unnecessary mystery, I may as well say that my wife and child and myself went down to Manavon last August and had a most delightful holiday. At the time we were certainly conscious of no annoyance or unpleasantness of any kind. Afterwards, I confess, I heard a story that puzzled and still puzzles me, and this story, if it be received, might give its own interpretation to one or two circumstances which seemed in themselves quite insignificant.

But all through July I came upon traces of evil rumours affecting this most gracious corner of the earth. Some of these rumours were repetitions of Eddis's gossip; others amplified his vague story and made it more definite. Of course, no first-hand evidence was available. There never is any first-hand evidence in these cases. But A knew B who had heard from C that her second-cousin's little girl had been set upon and beaten by a pack of young Welsh savages. Then people quoted "a doctor in large practice in a well-known town in the Midlands," to the effect that Tremaen was a sink of juvenile depravity. They said that a responsible medical man's evidence was final and convincing; but they didn't bother to find out who the doctor was, or whether there was any doctor at all—or any doctor relevant to the issue. Then the thing began to get into the papers in a sort of oblique, by-the-way sort of manner. People cited the case of these imaginary bad children in support of their educational views. One side said that "these unfortunate little ones" would have been quite well-behaved if they had had no education at all; the opposition declared that continuation schools would speedily reform them and make them into admirable citizens. Then the poor Arfonshire children seemed to become involved in quarrels about Welsh Disestablishment and in the question of the miners; and all the while they were going about behaving politely and admirably as they always do behave. I knew all the time that it was all nonsense, but I couldn't understand in the least what it meant, or who was pulling the wires of rumour, or their purpose in so pulling. I began to wonder whether the pressure and anxiety and suspense of a terrible war had unhinged the public mind, so that it was ready to believe any fable, to debate the reasons for happenings which had never happened. At last, quite incredible things began to be whispered: visitors' children had not only been beaten, they had been tortured; a little boy had been found impaled on a stake in a lonely field near Manavon; another child had been lured to destruction over the cliffs at Castell Coch. A London paper sent a good man down quietly to Arfon to investigate. He was away for a week, and at the end of that period returned to his office and in his own phrase, "threw the whole story down." There was not a word of truth, he said, in any of these rumours; no vestige of a foundation for the mildest forms of all this gossip. He had never seen such a beautiful country; he had never met pleasanter men, women or children; there was not a single case of anyone having been annoyed or troubled in any sort or fashion.

Yet all the while the story grew, and grew more monstrous and incredible. I was too much occupied in watching the progress of my own mythological monster to pay much attention. The Town Clerk of Tremaen, to which the legend had at length penetrated, wrote a brief letter to the Press indignantly denying that there was the slightest foundation for "the unsavoury rumours" which, he understood, were being circulated; and about this time we went down to Manavon and, as I say, enjoyed ourselves extremely. The weather was perfect: blues of paradise in the skies, the seas all a shimmering wonder, olive greens and emeralds, rich purples, glassy sapphires changing by the rocks; far away a haze of magic lights and colours at the meeting of sea and sky. Work and anxiety had harried me; I found nothing better than to rest on the thymy banks by the shore, finding an infinite balm and refreshment in the great sea before me, in the tiny flowers beside me. Or we would rest all the summer afternoon on a "shelf" high on the grey cliffs and watch the tide creaming and surging about the rocks, and listen to it booming in the hollows and caverns below. Afterwards, as I say, there were one or two things that struck cold. But at the time those were nothing. You see a man in an odd white hat pass by and think little or nothing about it. Afterwards, when you hear that a man wearing just such a hat had committed murder in the next street five minutes before, then you find in that hat a certain interest and significance. "Funny children," was the phrase my little boy used; and I began to think they were "funny" indeed.

If there be a key at all to this queer business, I think it is to be found in a talk I had not long ago with a friend of mine named Morgan. He is a Welshman and a dreamer, and some people say he is like a child who has grown up and yet has not grown up like other children of men. Though I did not know it, while I was at Manavon, he was spending his holiday time at Castell Coch. He was a lonely man and he liked lonely places, and when we met in the autumn he told me how, day after day, he would carry his bread and cheese and beer in a basket to a remote headland on that coast known as the Old

Camp. Here, far above the waters, are solemn, mighty walls, turf-grown; circumvallations rounded and smooth with the passing of many thousand years. At one end of this most ancient place there is a tumulus, a tower of observation, perhaps, and underneath it slinks the green, deceiving ditch that seems to wind into the heart of the camp, but in reality rushes down to sheer rock and a precipice over the waters.

Here came Morgan daily, as he said, to dream of Avalon, to purge himself from the fuming corruption of the streets.

And so, as he told me, it was with singular horror that one afternoon as he dozed and dreamed and opened his eyes now and again to watch the miracle and magic of the sea, as he listened to the myriad murmurs of the waves, his meditation was broken by a sudden burst of horrible raucous cries—and the cries of children, too, but children of the lowest type. Morgan says that the very tones made him shudder—"They were to the ear what slime is to the touch," and then the words: every foulness, every filthy abomination of speech; blasphemies that struck like blows at the sky, that sank down into the pure, shining depths, defiling them! He was amazed. He peered over the green wall of the fort, and there in the ditch he saw a swarm of noisome children, horrible little stunted creatures with old men's faces, with bloated faces, with little sunken eyes, with leering eyes. It was worse than uncovering a brood of snakes or a nest of worms.

No; he would not describe what they were about. "Read about Belgium," said Morgan, "and think they couldn't have been more than five or six years old." There was no infamy, he said, that they did not perpetrate; they spared no horror of cruelty. "I saw blood running in streams, as they shrieked with laughter, but I could not find the mark of it on the grass afterwards."

Morgan said he watched them and could not utter a word; it was as if a hand held his mouth tight. But at last he found his voice and shrieked at them, and they burst into a yell of obscene laughter and shrieked back at him, and scattered out of sight. He could not trace them; he supposes that they hid in the deep bracken behind the Old Camp.

"Sometimes I can't understand my landlord at Castell Coch," Morgan went on. "He's the village postmaster and has a little farm of his own—a decent, pleasant, ordinary sort of chap. But now and again he will talk oddly. I was telling him about these beastly children and wondering who they could be when he broke into Welsh, something like 'the battle that is for age unto ages; and the People take delight in it.'"

So far Morgan, and it was evident that he did not understand at all. But this strange tale of his brought back an odd circumstance or two that I recollected: a matter of our little boy straying away more than once, and getting lost among the sand dunes and coming back screaming, evidently frightened horribly, and babbling about "funny children." We took no notice; did not trouble, I think, to look whether there were any children wandering about the dunes or not. We were accustomed to his small imaginations.

But after hearing Morgan's story I was interested and I wrote an account of the matter to my friend, old Doctor Duthoit, of Hereford. And he:

"They were only visible, only audible to children and the childlike. Hence the explanation of what puzzled you at first; the rumours, how did they arise? They arose from nursery gossip, from scraps and odds and ends of half-articulate children's talk of horrors that they didn't understand, of words that shamed their nurses and their mothers.

"These little people of the earth rise up and rejoice in these times of ours. For they are glad, as the Welshman said, when they know that men follow their ways." ❋

The Coming of the Terror

After two years we are turning once more to the morning's news with a sense of appetite and glad expectation. There were thrills at the beginning of the war, the thrill of horror and of a doom that seemed at once incredible and certain. This was when Namur fell, and the German host swelled like a flood over the French fields, and drew very near to the walls of Paris. Then we felt the thrill of exultation when the good news came that the awful tide had been turned back, that Paris and the world were safe, for a while, at all events.

Then for days we hoped for more news as good as this or better. Has Kluck been surrounded? Not to-day, but perhaps he will be surrounded to-morrow. But the days became weeks, the weeks drew out to months; the battle in the West seemed frozen. People speculated as to the reason of this inaction: the hopeful said that Joffre had a plan, that he was "nibbling"; others declared that we were short of munitions, others again that the new levies were not yet ripe for battle. So the months went by, and almost two years of war had been completed before the motionless English line began to stir and quiver as if it awoke from a long sleep, and began to roll onward, overwhelming the enemy.

* * *

The secret of the long inaction of the British armies has been well kept. On the one hand it was rigorously protected by the censorship, which, severe, and sometimes severe to the point of absurdity, became in this particular matter ferocious. As soon as the real significance of that which was happening was perceived by the authorities, an underlined circular was issued to the newspaper proprietors of Great Britain and Ireland. It warned each proprietor that he might impart the contents of this circular to one other person only, such person being the responsible editor of his paper, who was to keep the communication secret under the severest penalties. The circular forbade any mention of certain events that had taken place, that might take place; it forbade any kind of reference to these events or any hint of their existence. The subject was not to be referred to in conversation, it was not to be hinted at, however obscurely, in letters; the very existence of the circular, its subject apart, was to be a dead secret.

Now, a censorship that is sufficiently minute and utterly remorseless can do amazing things in the way of hiding what it wants to hide. Once one would have thought otherwise; one would have said that, censor or no censor, the fact of the murder at X— would certainly become known, if not through the press, at all events through rumor and the passage of the news from mouth to mouth. And this would be true of England three hundred years ago. But we have grown of late to such a reverence for the printed word and such a reliance on it that the old faculty of disseminating news by word of mouth has become atrophied. Forbid the press to mention the fact that Jones has been murdered, and it is marvelous how few people will hear of it, and of those who hear how few will credit the story that they have heard.

And, then, again, the very fact of these vain rumors and fantastic tales having been so widely believed for a time was fatal to the credit of any stray mutterings that may have got abroad.

Before the secret circular had been issued my curiosity had somehow been aroused by certain paragraphs concerning a "Fatal Accident to Well-known Airman." The propeller of the airplane had been shattered, apparently by a collision with a flight of pigeons; the blades had been broken, and the machine had fallen like lead to the earth. And soon after I had seen this account, I heard of some very odd circumstances relating to an explosion in a great munition factory in the Midlands. I thought I saw the possibility of a connection between two very different events.

It has been pointed out to me by friends who have been good enough to read this record that certain phrases I have used may give the impression that I ascribe all the delays of the war on the Western front to the extraordinary circumstances which occasioned the issue of the secret circular. Of course this is not the case; there were many reasons for the immobility of our lines from October, 1914, to July, 1916. We could undertake to supply the defects of our army both in men and munitions *if* the new and incredible danger could be overcome. It has been overcome,—rather, perhaps, it has ceased to exist,—and the secret may now be told.

I have said my attention was attracted by an account of the death of a well-known airman. I have not the habit of preserving cuttings, I am sorry to say, so that I cannot be precise as to the date of this event. To the best of my belief it was either toward the end of May or the beginning of June, 1915. The manner in which Western-Reynolds met his death struck me as extraordinary. He was brought down by a flight of pigeons, as appeared by what was found on the blood-stained and shattered blades of the propeller. An eye-witness of the accident, a fellow-officer, described how Western-Reynolds set out from the aërodrome on a fine afternoon, there being hardly any wind. He was going to France.

"'Wester' rose to a great height at once, and we could scarcely see the machine. I was turning to go when one of the fellows called out: 'I say! What's this?' He pointed up, and we saw what looked like a black cloud coming from the South at a tremendous rate. I saw at once it wasn't a cloud; it came with a swirl and a rush quite different from any cloud I've ever seen. It turned into a great crescent, and wheeled and veered about as if it was looking for something. The man who had called out had got his glasses, and was staring for all he was worth. Then he shouted that it was a tremendous flight of birds, 'thousands of them.' They went on wheeling and beating about high up in the air, and we were watching them, thinking it was interesting, but not supposing that they would make any difference to 'Wester,' who was just about out of sight. Then the two arms of the crescent drew in as quick as lightning, and these thousands of birds shot in a solid mass right up there across the sky, and flew away. Then Henley, the man with the glasses, called out, 'He's down!' and started running, and I went after him. We got a car, and as we were going along Henley told me that he'd seen the machine drop dead, as if it came out of that cloud of birds. We found the propeller-blades all broken and covered with blood and pigeon-feathers, and carcasses of the birds had got wedged in between the blades, and were sticking to them."

It was, I think, about a week or ten days after the airman's death that my business called me to a Northern town, the name of which, perhaps, had better remain unknown. My mission was to inquire into certain charges of extravagance which had been laid against the munition-workers of this special town. I found, as usual, that there was a mixture of truth and exaggeration in the stories that I had heard.

"And how can you be surprised if people will have a bit of a fling?" a worker said to me. "We're seeing money for the first time in our lives, and it's bright. And we work hard for it, and we risk our lives to get it. You've heard of explosion yonder?"

He mentioned certain works on the outskirts of the town. Of course neither the name of the works nor that of the town had been printed; there had been a brief notice of "Explosion at Munition Works in the Northern District: Many Fatalities." The working-man told me about it, and added some dreadful details.

"They wouldn't let their folks see bodies; screwed them up in coffins as they found them in shop. The gas had done it."

"Turned their faces black, you mean?"

"Nay. They were all is if they had been bitten to pieces."

This was a strange gas.

I asked the man in the Northern town all sorts of questions about the extraordinary explosion of which he had spoken to me, but he had very little more to say. As I have noted already, secrets that may not be printed are often deeply kept; last summer there were very few people outside high official circles who knew anything about the "tanks," of which we have all been talking lately, though these strange instruments of war were being exercised and tested in a park not far from London.

I gave him up, and took a tram to the district of the disaster, a sort of industrial suburb, five miles from the center of the town. When I asked for the factory, I was told that it was no good my going to it, as there was nobody there. But I found it, a raw and hideous shed, with a walled yard about it, and a shut gate. I looked for signs of destruction, but there was nothing. The roof was quite undamaged; and again it struck me that this had been a strange accident. There had been an explosion of sufficient violence to kill people in the building, but the building itself showed no wounds or scars.

A man came out of the gate and locked it behind him. I began to ask him some sort of question, or, rather, I began to "open" for a question with "A terrible business here, they tell me," or some such phrase of convention. I got no further. The man asked me if I saw a policeman walking down the street. I said I did, and I was given the choice of getting about my business forthwith or of being instantly given in charge as a spy. "Th' 'ast better be gone, and quick about it," was, I think, his final advice, and I took it.

It was a day or two later that the accident to the airman Western-Reynolds came into my mind. For one of those instants which are far shorter than any measure of time there flashed out the possibility of a link between the two disasters. But here was a wild impossibility, and I drove it away. And yet I think that the thought, mad as it seemed, never left me; it was the secret light that at last guided me through a somber grove of enigmas.

* * *

It was about this time, so far as the date can be fixed, that a whole district, one might say a whole county, was visited by a series of extraordinary and terrible calamities, which were the more terrible inasmuch as they continued for some time to be inscrutable mysteries. It is indeed doubtful whether these awful events do not still remain mysteries to many of those concerned; for before the inhabitants of this part of the country had time to join one link of evidence to another the circular was issued, and thenceforth no one knew how to distinguish undoubted fact from wild and extravagant surmise.

The district in question is in the far west of Wales; I shall call it, for convenience, Meirion. Here, then, one sees a wild and divided and scattered region, a land of outland hills and secret and hidden valleys.

Such, then, in the main is Meirion, and on this land in the early summer of last year terror descended—a terror without shape, such as no man there had ever known.

It began with the tale of a little child who wandered out into the lanes to pick flowers one sunny afternoon, and never came back to the cottage on the hill. It was supposed that she must have crossed the road and gone to the cliff's edge, possibly in order to pick the sea-pinks that were then in full blossom. She must have slipped, they said, and fallen into the sea, two hundred feet below. It may be said at once that there was no doubt some truth in this conjecture, though it stopped far short of the whole truth. The child's body must have been carried out by the tide, for it was never found.

The conjecture of a false step or of a fatal slide on the slippery turf that slopes down to the rocks was accepted as being the only explanation possible. People thought the accident a strange one, because, as a rule, country children living by the cliffs and the sea become wary at an early age, and the little girl was almost ten years old. Still, as the neighbors said, "That's how it must have happened; and it's a great pity, to be sure." But this would not do when in a week's time a strong young laborer failed to come to his cottage after the day's work. His body was found on the rocks six or seven miles from the cliffs where the child was supposed to have fallen; he was going home by a path that he had used every night of his life for eight or nine years, that he used on dark nights in perfect security, knowing every inch of it. The police asked if he drank, but he was a teetotaler; if he was subject to fits, but he wasn't. And he was not murdered for his wealth, since agricultural laborers are not wealthy. It was only possible again to talk of slippery turf and a false step; but people began to be frightened. Then a woman was found with her neck broken at the bottom of a disused quarry near Llanfihangel, in the middle of the county. The false-step theory was eliminated here, for the quarry was guarded by a natural hedge of gorse. One would have to struggle and fight through sharp thorns to destruction in such a place as this; and indeed the gorse was broken, as if some one had rushed furiously through it, just above the place where the woman's body was found. And this also was strange: there was a dead sheep lying beside her in the pit, as if the woman and the sheep together had been chased over the brim of the quarry. But chased by whom or by what? And then there was a new form of terror.

This was in the region of the marshes under the mountain. A man and his son, a lad of fourteen or fifteen, set out early one morning to work, and never reached the farm whence they were bound. Their way skirted the marsh, but it was broad, firm, and well metalled, and it had been raised about two feet above the bog. But when search was made in the evening of the same day, Phillips and his son were found dead in the marsh, covered with black slime and pond-weed. And they lay some ten yards from the path, which, it would seem, they must have left deliberately. It was useless, of course, to look for tracks in the black ooze, for if one threw a big stone into it, a few seconds removed all marks of the disturbance. The men who found the two bodies beat about the verges and purlieus of the marsh in hope of finding some trace of the murderers; they went to and fro over the rising ground where the black cattle were grazing, they searched the alder-thickets by the brook: but they discovered nothing.

Most horrible of all these horrors, perhaps, was the affair of the Highway, a lonely and unfrequented by-road that winds for many miles on high and lonely land. Here, a mile from any other dwelling, stands a cottage on the edge of a dark wood. It was inhabited by a laborer named Williams, his wife, and their three children. One hot summer's evening a man who had been doing a day's gardening at a rectory three or four miles away passed the cottage, and stopped for a few minutes to chat with Williams, who was pottering about his garden, while the children were playing on the path by the door. The two talked of their neighbors and of the potatoes till Mrs. Williams appeared at the doorway and said supper was ready, and Williams turned to go into the house. This was about eight o'clock, and in the ordinary course the family would have had their supper and be in bed by nine, or by half-past nine at the latest. At ten o'clock that night the local doctor was driving home along the Highway. His horse shied violently and then stopped dead just opposite the gate to the cottage. The doctor got down, and there on the roadway lay Williams, his wife, and the three children, stone-dead. Their skulls were battered in as if by some heavy iron instrument; their faces were beaten into a pulp.

It is not easy to make any picture of the horror that lay dark on the hearts of the people of Meirion. It was no longer possible to believe or to pretend to believe that these men and women and children had met their deaths through strange accidents. For a time people said that there must be a madman at large, a sort of country variant of Jack the Ripper, some horrible pervert who was possessed by the passion of death, who prowled darkling about that lonely land, hiding in woods and in wild places, always watching and seeking for the victims of his desire.

Indeed, Dr. Lewis, who found poor Williams, his wife, and children, was convinced at first that the presence of a concealed madman in the country-side offered the only possible solution to the difficulty.

"I felt sure," he said to me afterward, "that the Williamses had been killed by a homicidal maniac. It was the nature of the poor creatures' injuries that convinced me that this was the case. Those poor people had their heads smashed to pieces by what must have been a storm of blows. Any one of them would have been fatal, but the murderer must have gone on raining blows with his iron hammer on people who were already stone-dead. And *that* sort of thing is the work of a madman, and nothing but a madman. That's how I argued the matter out to myself just after the event. I was utterly wrong, monstrously wrong; but who could have suspected the truth?"

I quote Dr. Lewis, or the substance of him, as representative of most of the educated opinion of the district at the beginnings of the terror. People seized on this theory largely because it offered at least the comfort of an explanation, and any explanation, even the poorest, is better than an intolerable and terrible mystery. Besides, Dr. Lewis's theory was plausible; it explained the lack of purpose that seemed to characterize the murders.

And yet there were difficulties even from the first. It was hardly possible that a strange madman would be able to keep hidden in a country-side where any stranger is instantly noted and noticed; sooner or later he would be seen as he prowled along the lanes or across the wild places.

Then another theory, or, rather, a variant of Dr. Lewis's theory, was started. This was to the effect that the person responsible for the outrages was indeed a madman, but a madman only at intervals. It was one of the members of the Porth Club, a certain Mr. Remnant, who was supposed to have originated this more subtle explanation. Mr. Remnant was a middle-aged man who, having nothing particular to do, read a great many books by way of conquering the hours. He talked to the club—doctors, retired colonels, parsons, lawyers—about "personality," quoted various psychological text-books in support of his contention that personality was sometimes fluid and unstable, went back to *Dr. Jekyll and Mr. Hyde* as good evidence of this proposition, and laid stress on *Dr. Jekyll's* speculation that the human soul, so far from being one and indivisible, might possibly turn out to be a mere polity, a state in which dwelt many strange and incongruous citizens, whose characters were not merely unknown, but altogether unsurmised by that form of consciousness which rashly assumed that it was not only the president of the republic, but also its sole citizen.

However, Mr. Remnant's somewhat crazy theory became untenable when two more victims of an awful and mysterious death were offered up in sacrifice, for a man was found dead in the Llanfihangel quarry where the woman had been discovered, and on the same day a girl of fifteen was found broken on the jagged rocks under the cliffs near Porth. Now, it appeared that these two deaths must have occurred at about the same time, within an hour of one another, certainly, and the distance between the quarry and the cliffs by Black Rock is certainly twenty miles.

And now a fresh circumstance or set of circumstances became manifest to confound judgment and to awaken new and wild surmises; for at about this time people realized that none of the dreadful events that were happening all about them was so much as mentioned in the press. Horror followed on horror, but no word was printed in any of the local journals. The curious went to the newspaper offices,—there were two left in the county,—but found nothing save a firm refusal to discuss the matter. Then the Cardiff papers were drawn and found blank, and the London press was apparently ignorant of the fact that crimes that had no parallel were terrorizing a whole country-side. Everybody wondered what could have happened, what was happening; and then it was whispered that the coroner would allow no inquiry to be made as to these deaths of darkness.

Clearly, people reasoned, these government restrictions and prohibitions could only refer to the war, to some great danger in connection with the war. And that being so, it followed that the outrages which must be kept so secret were the work of the enemy; that is, of concealed German agents.

It is time, I think, for me to make one point clear. I began this history with certain references to an extraordinary accident to an airman whose machine fell to the ground after collision with a huge flock of pigeons, and then to an explosion in a Northern munition factory of a very singular kind. Then I deserted the neighborhood of London and the Northern district, and dwelt on a mysterious and terrible series of events which occurred in the summer of 1915 in a Welsh county, which I have named for convenience Meirion.

Well, let it be understood at once that all this detail that I have given about the occurrences in Meirion does not imply that the county in Wales was alone or specially afflicted by the terror that was over the land. They tell me that in the villages about Dartmoor the stout Devonshire hearts sank as men's hearts used to sink in the time of plague and pestilence. There was horror, too, about the Norfolk Broads, and far up by Perth no one would venture on the path that leads by Scone to the wooded heights above the Tay. And in the industrial districts, I met a man by chance one day in an odd London corner who spoke with horror of what a friend had told him.

"'Ask no questions, Ned,' he says to me, 'but I tell yow a was in Bairnigan t' other day, and a met a pal who'd seen three hundred coffins going out of a works not far from there.'"

Then there was the vessel that hovered outside the mouth of the Thames with all sails set, and beat to and fro in the wind, and never answered any signals and showed no light. The forts shot at her, and brought down one of the masts; but she went suddenly about, stood down channel, and drove ashore at last on the sand-banks and pine-woods of Arcachon, and not a man alive on her, but only rattling heaps of bones! That last voyage of the *Semiramis* would be something horribly worth telling; but I heard it only at a distance as a yarn, and believed it only because it squared with other things that I knew for certain.

This, then, is my point: I have written of the terror as it fell on Meirion simply because I have had opportunities of getting close there to what really happened.

Well, I have said that the people of that far Western county realized not only that death was abroad in their quiet lanes and on their peaceful hills, but that for some reason it was to be kept secret. And so they concluded that this veil of secrecy must somehow be connected with the war; and from this position it was not a long way to a further inference that the murderers of innocent men and women and children were either Germans or agents of Germany. It would be just like the Huns, everybody agreed, to think out such a devilish scheme as this; and they always thought out their schemes beforehand.

It all seemed plausible enough; Germany had by this time perpetrated so many horrors and had so excelled in devilish ingenuities that no abomination seemed too abominable to be probable or too ingeniously wicked to be beyond her tortuous malice. But then came the questions as to who the agents of this terrible design were, as to where they lived, as to how they contrived to move unseen from field to field, from lane to lane. All sorts of fantastic attempts were made to answer these questions, but it was felt that they remained unanswered. Some suggested that the murderers landed from submarines, or flew from hiding-places on the west coast of Ireland, coming and going by night; but there were seen to be flagrant impossibilities in both these suggestions. Everybody agreed that the evil work was no doubt the work of Germany; but nobody could begin to guess how it was done.

It was, I suppose, at about this time when the people were puzzling their heads as to the secret methods used by the Germans or their agents to accomplish their crimes that a very singular circumstance became known to a few of the Porth people. It related to the murder of the Williams family on the Highway in front of their cottage door. I do not know that I have made it plain that the old Roman road called the Highway follows the course of a long, steep hill that goes steadily westward till it slants down toward the sea. On each side of the road the ground falls away, here into deep shadowy woods, here into high pastures, but for the most part into the wild and broken land that is characteristic of Arfon.

Now, on the lower slopes of it, beneath the Williams cottage, some three or four fields down the hill, there is a military camp. The place has been used as a camp for many years, and lately the site has been extended and huts have been erected; but a considerable number of the men were under canvas here in the summer of 1915.

On the night of the Highway murder this camp, as it appeared afterward, was the scene of the extraordinary panic of horses.

A good many men in the camp were asleep in their tents soon after 9:30. They woke up in panic. There was a thundering sound on the steep hillside above them, and down upon the tents came half a dozen horses, mad with fright, trampling the canvas, trampling the men, bruising dozens of them, and killing two.

Everything was in wild confusion, men groaning and screaming in the darkness, struggling with the canvas and the twisted ropes, and some of them, raw lads enough, shouting out that the Germans had at last landed.

Some of the men had seen the horses galloping down the hill as if terror itself was driving them. They scattered off into the darkness, and somehow or other found their way back in the night to their pasture above the camp. They were grazing there peacefully in the morning, and the only sign of the panic of the night before was the mud they had scattered all over themselves as they pelted through a patch of wet ground. The farmer said they were as quiet a lot as any in Meirion; he could make nothing of it.

Then two or three other incidents, quite as odd and incomprehensible, came to be known, borne on chance trickles of gossip that came into the towns from outland farms. And in such ways it came out that up at Plas Newydd there had been a terrible business over swarming the bees; they had turned as wild as wasps and much more savage. They had come about the people who were taking the swarms like a cloud. They settled on one man's face so that you could not see the flesh for the bees crawling over it, and they had stung him so badly that the doctor did not know whether he would get well; they had chased a girl who had come out to see the swarming, and settled on her and stung her to death. Then they had gone off to a brake below the farm and got into a hollow tree, and it was not safe to go near it, for they would come out at you by day or by night.

And much the same thing had happened, it seemed, at three or four farms and cottages where bees were kept. And there were stories, hardly so clear or so credible, of sheep-dogs, mild and trusted beasts, turning as savage as wolves and injuring the farm boys in a horrible manner, in one case, it was said, with fatal results. It was certainly true that old Mrs. Owens's favorite Dorking cock had gone mad. She came into Porth one Saturday morning with her face and her neck all bound up and plastered. She had gone out to her bit of field to feed the poultry the night before, and the bird had flown at her and attacked her most savagely, inflicting some very nasty wounds before she could beat it off.

"There was a stake handy, lucky for me," she said, "and I did beat him and beat him till the life was out of him. But what is come to the world, whatever?"

* * *

Now Remnant, the man of theories, was also a man of extreme leisure. He was no more brutal than the general public, which revels in the details of mysterious crime; but it must be said that the terror, black though it was, was a boon to him. He peered and investigated and poked about with the relish of a man to whose life a new zest has been added. He listened attentively to the strange tales of bees and dogs and poultry that came into Porth with the country baskets of butter, rabbits, and green peas, and he evolved at last a most extraordinary theory. He went one night to see Dr. Lewis.

"I want to talk to you," he said to the doctor, "about what I have called provisionally the Z-ray."

Dr. Lewis, smiling indulgently, and quite prepared for some monstrous piece of theorizing, led Remnant into the room that overlooked the terraced garden and the sea.

"I suppose, Lewis, you've heard these extraordinary stories of bees and dogs and things that have been going about lately?"

"Certainly I have heard them. I was called in at Plas Newydd, and treated Thomas Trevor, who's only just out of danger, by the way. I certified for the poor child, Mary Trevor. She was dying when I got to the place."

"Well, then there are the stories of good-tempered old sheep-dogs turning wicked and 'savaging' children."

"Quite so. I haven't seen any of these cases professionally; but I believe the stories are accurate enough."

"And the old woman assaulted by her own poultry?"

"That's perfectly true."

"Very good," said Mr. Remnant. He spoke now with an italic impressiveness, *"Don't you see the link between all this and the horrible things that have been happening about here for the last month?"*

Lewis stared at Remnant in amazement. He lifted his red eyebrows and lowered them in a kind of scowl. His speech showed traces of his native accent.

"Great burning!" he exclaimed, "what on earth are you getting at now? It is madness. Do you mean to tell me that you think there is some connection between a swarm or two of bees that have turned nasty, a cross dog, and a wicked old barn-door cock, and these poor people that have been pitched over the cliffs and hammered to death on the road? There's no sense in it, you know."

"I am strongly inclined to believe that there is a great deal of sense in it," replied Remnant, with extreme calmness. "Look here, Lewis, I saw you grinning the other day at the club when I was telling the fellows that in my opinion all these outrages had been committed, certainly by the Germans, but by some method of which we have no conception. Do you see my point?"

"Well, in a sort of way. You mean there's an absolute originality in the method? I suppose that is so. But what next?"

Remnant seemed to hesitate, partly from a sense of the portentous nature of what he was about to say, partly from a sort of half-unwillingness to part with so profound a secret.

"Well," he said, "you will allow that we have two sets of phenomena of a very extraordinary kind occurring at the same time. Don't you think that it's only reasonable to connect the two sets with one another?"

"So the philosopher of Tenterden steeple and the Goodwin Sands thought, certainly," said Lewis. "But what is the connection? Those poor folks on the Highway weren't stung by bees or worried by a dog. And horses don't throw people over cliffs or stifle them in marshes."

"No; I never meant to suggest anything so absurd. It is evident to me that in all these cases of animals turning suddenly savage the cause has been terror, panic, fear. The horses that went charging into the camp were mad with fright, we know. And I say that in the other instances we have been discussing the cause was the same. The creatures were exposed to an infection of fear, and a frightened beast or bird or insect uses its weapons, whatever they may be. If, for example, there had been anybody with those horses when they took their panic, they would have lashed out at him with their heels."

"Yes, I dare say that that is so. Well?" demanded the doctor.

"Well, my belief is that the Germans have made an extraordinary discovery. I have called it the Z-ray. You know that the ether is merely an hypothesis; we have to suppose that it's there to account for the passage of the Marconi current from one place to another. Now, suppose that there is a psychic ether as well as a material ether, suppose that it is possible to direct irresistible impulses across this medium, suppose that these impulses are toward murder or suicide; then I think that you have an explanation of the terrible series of events that have been happening in Meirion for the last few weeks. And it is quite clear to my mind that the horses and the other creatures have been exposed to this Z-ray, and that it has produced on them the effect of terror, with ferocity as the result of terror. Now, what do you say to that? Telepathy, you know, is well established; so is hypnotic suggestion. Now don't you feel that putting telepathy and suggestion together, as it were, you have more than the elements of what I call the Z-ray? I feel that I have more to go on in making my hypothesis than the inventor of the steam-engine had in making his hypothesis when he saw the lid of the kettle bobbing up and down. What do you say?"

Dr. Lewis made no answer. He was watching the growth of a new, unknown tree in his garden.

It was a dark summer night. The moon was old and faint above the Dragon's Head, on the opposite side of the bay, and the air was very still. It was so still that Lewis had noted that not a leaf stirred on the very tip of a high tree that stood out against the sky; and yet he knew that he was listening to some sound that he could not determine or define. It was not the wind in the leaves, it was not the gentle wash of the water of the sea against the rocks; that latter sound he could distinguish easily. But there was something else. It was scarcely a sound; it was as if the air itself trembled and fluttered, as the air trembles in a church when they open the great pedal pipes of the organ.

The doctor listened intently. It was not an illusion, the sound was not in his own head, as he had suspected for a moment; but for the life of him he could not make out whence it came or what it was. He gazed down into the night, over the terraces of his garden, now sweet with the scent of the flowers of the night; tried to peer over the tree-tops across the sea toward the Dragon's Head. It struck him suddenly that this strange, fluttering vibration of the air might be the noise of a distant aëroplane or airship; there was not the usual droning hum, but this sound might be caused by a new type of engine. A new type of engine? Possibly it was an enemy airship; their range, it had been said, was getting longer, and Lewis was just going to call Remnant's attention to the sound, to its possible cause, and to the possible danger that might be hovering over them, when he saw something that caught his breath and his heart with wild amazement and a touch of terror.

He had been staring upward into the sky, and, about to speak to Remnant, he had let his eyes drop for an instant. He looked down toward the trees in the garden, and saw with utter astonishment that one had changed its shape in the few hours that had passed since the setting of the sun. There was a thick grove of ilexes bordering the lowest terrace, and above them rose one tall pine, spreading its head of sparse branches dark against the sky.

As Lewis glanced down over the terraces he saw that the tall pine-tree was no longer there. In its place there rose above the ilexes what might have been a greater ilex; there was the blackness of a dense growth of foliage rising like a broad, far-spreading, and rounded cloud over the lesser trees.

Dr. Lewis glared into the dimness of the night, at the great, spreading tree that he knew could not be there. And as he gazed he saw that what at first appeared the dense blackness of foliage was fretted and starred with wonderful appearances of lights and colors.

The night had gloomed over; clouds obscured the faint moon and the misty stars. Lewis rose, with some kind of warning and inhibiting gesture to Remnant, who, he was aware, was gaping at him in astonishment. He walked to the open French window, took a pace forward on the path outside, and looked very intently at the dark shape of the tree. He shaded the light of the lamp behind him by holding his hands on each side of his eyes.

The mass of the tree—the tree that couldn't be there—stood out against the sky, but not so clearly now that the clouds had rolled up. Its edges, the limits of its leafage, were not so distinct. Lewis thought that he could detect some sort of quivering movement in it, though the air was at a dead calm. It was a night on which one might hold up a lighted match and watch it burn without any wavering or inclination of the flame.

"You know," said Lewis, "how a bit of burned paper will sometimes hang over the coals before it goes up the chimney, and little worms of fire will shoot through it. It was like that, if you should be standing some distance away. Just threads and hairs of yellow light I saw, and specks and sparks of fire, and then a twinkling of a ruby no bigger than a pin-point, and a green wandering in the black, as if an emerald were crawling, and then little veins of deep blue. 'Woe is me!' I said to myself in Welsh. 'What is all this color and burning?'

"At that very moment there came a thundering rap at the door of the room inside, and there was my man telling me that I was wanted directly up at the Garth, as old Mr. Trevor Williams had been taken very bad. I knew his heart was not worth much, so I had to go off directly, and leave Remnant alone to make what he could of it all."

Dr. Lewis was kept some time at the Garth. It was past twelve when he got back to his house. He went quickly to the room that overlooked the garden and the sea, threw open the French window, and peered into the darkness. There, dim indeed against the dim sky, but unmistakable, was the tall pine, with its sparse branches, high above the dense growth of the ilex-trees. The strange boughs which had amazed him had vanished; there was no appearance of colors or of fires.

The doctor did not say anything about the strange tree to Remnant. When they next met, he said that he had thought there was a man hiding among the bushes. This was in explanation of that warning gesture he had used, and of his going out into the garden and staring into the night. He concealed the truth because he dreaded the Remnant doctrine that would undoubtedly be produced; indeed, he hoped that he had heard the last of the theory of the Z-ray. But Remnant firmly reopened this subject.

"We were interrupted just as I was putting my case to you," he said. "And to sum it all up, it amounts to this: the Huns have made one of the great leaps of science. They are sending 'suggestions' (which amount to irresistible commands) over here, and the persons affected are seized with suicidal or homicidal mania. In my opinion Evans was the murderer of the Williams family. You know he said he stopped to talk to Williams. It seems to me simple. And as for the animals, the horses, dogs, and so forth,—they, as I say, were no doubt panic-stricken by the ray, and hence driven to frenzy."

"Why should Evans have murdered Williams instead of Williams murdering Evans? Why should the impact of the ray affect one and not the other?"

"Why does one man react violently to a certain drug, while it makes no impression on another man? Why is A able to drink a bottle of whisky and remain sober, while B is turned into something very like a lunatic after he has drunk three glasses?"

"It is a question of idiosyncrasy," said the doctor.

Lewis escaped from the club and from Remnant. He did not want to hear any more about that dreadful ray, because he felt sure that the ray was all nonsense. But asking himself why he felt this certitude in the matter, he had to confess that he didn't know. An aëroplane, he reflected, was all nonsense before it was made.

But he thought with fervor of the extraordinary thing he had seen in his own garden with his own eyes. How could one fail to be afraid with great amazement at the thought of such a mystery?

Dr. Lewis's thoughts were distracted from the incredible adventure of the tree by the visit of his sister and her husband. Mr. and Mrs. Merritt lived in a well-known manufacturing town of the Midlands, which was now, of course, a center of munition work. On the day of their arrival at Porth, Mrs. Merritt, who was tired after the long, hot journey, went to bed early, and Merritt and Lewis went into the room by the garden for their talk and tobacco. They spoke of the year that had passed since their last meeting, of the weary dragging of the war, of friends that had perished in it, of the hopelessness of an early ending of all this misery. Lewis said nothing of the terror that was on the land. One does not greet with a tale of horror a tired man who is come to a quiet, sunny place for relief from black smoke and work and worry. Indeed, the doctor saw that his brother-in-law looked far from well. He seemed "jumpy"; there was an occasional twitch of his mouth that Lewis did not like at all.

"Well," said the doctor, after an interval of silence and port wine, "I am glad to see you here again. Porth always suits you. I don't think you're looking quite up to your usual form; but three weeks of Meirion air will do wonders."

"Well, I hope it will," said the other. "I am not up to the mark. Things are not going well at Midlingham."

"Business is all right, isn't it?"

"Yes; but there are other things that are all wrong. We are living under a reign of terror. It comes to that."

"What on earth do you mean?"

"It's not much. I didn't dare write it. But do you know that at every one of the munition-works in Midlingham and all about it there's a guard of soldiers with drawn bayonets and loaded rifles day and night? Men with bombs, too. And machine-guns at the big factories."

"German spies?"

"You don't want machine-guns and bombs to fight spies with."

"But what against?"

"Nobody knows. Nobody knows what is happening," Merritt repeated, and he went on to describe the bewilderment and terror that hung like a cloud over the great industrial city in the Midlands; how the feeling of concealment, or some intolerable secret danger that must not be named, was worst of all.

Merritt made a sort of picture of the great town cowering in its fear of an unknown danger.

"There's a queer story going about," he said, "as to a place right out in the country, over the other side of Midlingham. They've built one of the new factories out there, a great red brick town of sheds. About two hundred yards from this place there's an old footpath through a pretty large wood, most of it thick undergrowth. It's a black place of nights.

"A man had to go this way one night. He got along all right till he came to the wood, and then he said his heart dropped out of his body. It was awful to hear the noises in that wood. Thousands of men were in it, he swears. It was full of rustling, and pattering of feet trying to go dainty, and the crack of dead boughs lying on the ground as some one trod on them, and swishing of the grass, and some sort of chattering speech going on that sounded, so he said, as if the dead sat in their bones and talked! He ran for his life, anyhow, across fields, over hedges, through brooks. He must have run, by his tale, ten miles out of his way before he got home to his wife, beat at the door, broke in, and bolted it behind him."

"There is something rather alarming about any wood at night," said Dr. Lewis.

Merritt shrugged his shoulders.

"People say that the Germans have landed, and that they are hiding in underground places all over the country."

Lewis gasped for a moment, silent in contemplation of the magnificence of rumor. The Germans already landed, hiding underground, striking by night, secretly, terribly, at the power of England! It was monstrous, and yet—

"People say they've got a new kind of poison-gas," continued Merritt. "Some think that they dig underground places and make the gas there, and lead it by secret pipes into the shops; others say that they throw gas bombs into the factories. It must be worse than anything they've used in France, from what the authorities say."

"The authorities? Do *they* admit that there are Germans in hiding about Midlingham?"

"No. They call it 'explosions.' But we know it isn't explosions. We know in the Midlands what an explosion sounds like and looks like. And we know that the people killed in these 'explosions' are put into their coffins in the works. Their own relations are not allowed to see them."

"And do you believe in the German theory?"

"If I do, it's because one must believe in something. Some say they've seen the gas. I heard that a man living in Dunwich saw it one night like a black cloud, with sparks of fire in it, floating over the tops of the trees by Dunwich Common."

The light of an ineffable amazement came into Lewis's eyes. The night of Remnant's visit, the trembling vibration of the air, the dark tree that had grown in his garden since the setting of the sun, the strange leafage that was starred with burning, and all vanished away when he returned from his visit to the Garth; and such a leafage had appeared as a burning cloud far in the heart of England. What intolerable mystery, what tremendous doom was signified in this? But one thing was clear and certain: the terror of Meirion was also the terror of the Midlands.

Merritt told the story of how a Swedish professor, Huvelius, had sold to the Germans a plan for filling England with German soldiers. Land was to be bought in certain suitable and well-considered places, Englishmen were to be bought as the apparent owners of such land, and secret excavations were to be made, till the country was literally undermined. A subterranean Germany, in fact, was to be dug under selected districts of England; there were to be great caverns, underground cities, well drained, well ventilated, supplied with water, and in these places vast stores both of food and of munitions were to be accumulated year after year till "the Day" dawned. And then, warned in time, the secret garrison would leave shops, hotels, offices, villas, and vanish underground, ready to begin their work of bleeding England at the heart.

"Well," said Lewis, "of course, it may be so. If it is so, it is terrible beyond words."

Indeed, he found something horribly plausible in the story. It was an extraordinary plan, of course, an unheard-of scheme; but it did not seem impossible. It was the Trojan Horse on a gigantic scale. And this theory certainly squared with what one had heard of German preparations in Belgium and in France.

And it seemed from that wonder of the burning tree that the enemy mysteriously and terribly present at Midlingham was present also in Meirion. Yet, he thought again, there was but little harm to be done in Meirion to the armies of England or to their munitionment. They were working for panic terror. Possibly that might be so; but the camp under the Highway? That should be their first object, and no harm had been done there.

Lewis did not know that since the panic of the horses men had died terribly in that camp; that it was now a fortified place, with a deep, broad trench, a thick tangle of savage barbed wire about it, and a machine-gun planted at each corner.

One evening the doctor was summoned to a little hamlet on the outskirts of Porth. In one of the cottages the doctor found a father and mother weeping and crying out to "Doctor Bach, Doctor Bach," two frightened children, and one little body, still and dead.

The doctor found that the child had been asphyxiated. His clothes were dry; it was not a case of drowning. There was no mark of strangling. He asked the father how it had happened, and father and mother, weeping most lamentably, declared they had no knowledge of how their child had been killed, "unless it was the People that had done it." The Celtic fairies are still malignant. Lewis asked what had happened that evening; where had the child been?

"Was he with his brother and sister?" asked the doctor. "Don't they know anything about it?"

The children had been playing in the road at dusk, and just as their mother called them in one child had heard Johnnie cry out:

"Oh, what is that beautiful, shiny thing over the stile?"

They found the little body, under the ash-grove in the middle of the field. He was quite still and dead, so still that a great moth had settled on his forehead, fluttering away when they lifted him up.

Dr. Lewis heard this story. There was nothing to be done, little to be said to these most unhappy people.

"Take care of the two that you have left to you," said the doctor as he went away. "Don't let them out of your sight if you can help it. It is dreadful times that we are living in."

About ten days later a young farmer had been found by his wife lying in the grass close to the castle, with no scar on him or any mark of violence, but stone-dead.

Lewis was sent for, and knew at once, when he saw the dead man, that he had perished in the way that the little boy had perished, whatever that awful way might be.

It seemed that he had gone out at about half-past nine to look after some beasts. He told his wife he would be back in a quarter of an hour or twenty minutes. He did not return, and when he had been gone for three quarters of an hour Mrs. Cradock went out to look for him. She went into the field where the beasts were, and everything seemed all right; but there was no trace of Cradock. She called out; there was no answer.

She told the doctor:

"There was something that I could not make out at all. It seemed to me that the hedge did look different from usual. To be sure, things do look different at night, and there was a bit of sea mist about; but somehow it did look odd to me, and I said to myself, 'Have I lost my way, then?'"

She declared that the shape of the trees in the hedge appeared to have changed, and besides, it had a look "as if it was lighted up, somehow," and so she went on toward the stile to see what all this could be; and when she came near, everything was as usual. She looked over the stile and called, hoping to see her husband coming toward her or to hear his voice; but there was no answer, and glancing down the path, she saw, or thought she saw, some sort of brightness on the ground, "a dim sort of light, like a bunch of glow-worms in a hedge-bank.

"And so I climbed over the stile and went down the path, and the light seemed to melt away; and there was my poor husband lying on his back, saying not a word to me when I spoke to him and touched him."

* * *

So for Lewis the terror blackened and became altogether intolerable, and others, he perceived, felt as he did. He did not know, he never asked, whether the men at the club had heard of these deaths of the child and the young farmer; but no one spoke of them. Indeed, the change was evident; at the beginning of the terror men spoke of nothing else; now it had become all too awful for ingenious chatter or labored and grotesque theories. And Lewis had received a letter from his brother-in-law, who had gone back to Midlingham; it contained the sentence, "I am afraid Fanny's health has not greatly benefited by her visit to Porth; there are still several symptoms I don't at all like." This told him, in a phraseology that the doctor and Merritt had agreed upon, that the terror remained heavy in the Midland town.

* * *

It was soon after the death of Cradock that people began to tell strange tales of a sound that was to be heard of nights about the hills and valleys to the northward of Porth. A man who had missed the last train from Meiros and had been forced to tramp the ten miles between Meiros and Porth seems to have been the first to hear it. He said he had got to the top of the hill by Tredonoc, somewhere between half-past ten and eleven, when he first noticed an odd noise that he could not make out at all; it was like a shout, a long-drawn-out, dismal wail coming from a great way off. He stopped to listen, thinking at first that it might be owls hooting in the woods; but it was different, he said, from that. He could make nothing of it, and feeling frightened, he did not quite know of what, he walked on briskly, and was glad to see the lights of Porth station. Then others heard it.

Let it be remembered again and again that all the while that the terror lasted there was no common stock of information as to the dreadful things that were being done. The press had not said one word upon it, there was no criterion by which the mass of the people could separate fact from mere vague rumor, no test by which ordinary misadventure or disaster could be distinguished from the achievements of the secret and awful force that was at work. And since the real nature of all this mystery of death was unknown, it followed easily that the signs and warnings and omens of it were all the more unknown. Here was horror, there was horror; but there were no links to join one horror with another, no common basis of knowledge from which the connection between this horror and that horror might be inferred.

The sound had been heard for three or perhaps four nights, when the people coming out of Tredonoc church after morning service on Sunday noticed that there was a big yellow sheep-dog in the churchyard. The dog, it appeared, had been waiting for the congregation; for it at once attached itself to them, at first to the whole body, and then to a group of half a dozen who took the turning to the right till they came to a gate in the hedge, whence a roughly made farm-road went through the fields, and dipped down into the woods and to Treff Loyne farm.

Then the dog became like a possessed creature. He barked furiously. He ran up to one of the men and looked up at him, "as if he were begging for his life," as the man said, and then rushed to the gate and stood by it, wagging his tail and barking at intervals. The men stared.

"Whose dog will that be?" said one of them.

"It will be Thomas Griffith's, Treff Loyne," said another.

"Well, then, why doesn't he go home? Go home, then!" He went through the gesture of picking up a stone from the road and throwing it at the dog. "Go home, then! Over the gate with you!"

But the dog never stirred. He barked and whined and ran up to the men and then back to the gate. The farmer shook the dog off, and the four went on their way, and the dog stood in the road and watched them, and then put up its head and uttered a long and dismal howl that was despair.

Then it occurred to somebody, so far as I can make out with no particular reference to the odd conduct of the Treff Loyne sheep-dog, that Thomas Griffith had not been seen for some time past.

One September afternoon, therefore, a party went up to discover what had happened to Griffith and his family. There were half a dozen farmers, a couple of policemen, and four soldiers, carrying their arms; those last had been lent by the officer commanding at the camp. Lewis, too, was of the party; he had heard by chance that no one knew what had become of Griffith and his family, and he was anxious about a young fellow, a painter, of his acquaintance who had been lodging at Treff Loyne all the summer.

They came to the gate in the hedge where the farm-road led down to Treff Loyne. Here was the farm inclosure, the outlying walls of the yard and the barns and sheds and outhouses. One of the farmers threw open the gate and walked into the yard, and forthwith began bellowing at the top of his voice:

"Thomas Griffith! Thomas Griffith! Where be you, Thomas Griffith?"

The rest followed him. The corporal snapped out an order over his shoulder, and there was a rattling metallic noise as the men fixed their bayonets.

There was no answer to this summons; but they found poor Griffith lying on his face at the edge of the pond in the middle of the yard. There was a ghastly wound in his side, as if a sharp stake had been driven into his body.

It was a still September afternoon. No wind stirred in the hanging woods that were dark all about the ancient house of Treff Loyne; the only sound in the dim air was the lowing of the cattle. They had wandered, it seemed, from the fields and had come in by the gate of the farmyard and stood there melancholy, as if they mourned for their dead master. And the horses, four great, heavy, patient-looking beasts, were there, too, and in the lower field the sheep were standing, as if they waited to be fed.

Lewis knelt down by the dead man and looked closely at the gaping wound in his side.

"He's been dead a long time," he said. "How about the family? How many are there of them? I never attended them."

"There was Griffith, and his wife, his son Thomas, and Mary Griffith, his daughter. And I do think there was a gentleman lodging with them this summer."

That was from one of the farmers. They all looked at one another, this party of rescue, who knew nothing of the danger that had smitten this house of quiet people, nothing of the peril which had brought them to this pass of a farm-yard, with a dead man in it, and his beasts standing patiently about him as if they waited for the farmer to rise up and give them their food. Then the party turned to the house. The windows were shut tight. There was no sign of any life or movement about the place. The party of men looked at one another.

They did not know what the danger was or where it might strike them or whether it was from without or from within. They stared at the murdered man, and gazed dismally at one another.

"Come," said Lewis, "we must do something. We must get into the house and see what is wrong."

"Yes, but suppose they are at us while we are getting in?" said the sergeant. "Where shall we be then, Doctor Lewis?"

The corporal put one of his men by the gate at the top of the farm-yard, another at the gate by the bottom, and told them to challenge and shoot. The doctor and the rest opened the little gate of the front garden and went up to the porch and stood listening by the door. It was all dead silence. Lewis took an ash stick from one of the farmers and beat heavily three times on the old, black, oaken door studded with antique nails.

There was no answer from within. He beat again, and still silence. He shouted to the people within, but there was no answer. They all turned and looked at one another. There was an iron ring on the door. Lewis turned it, but the door stood fast; it was evidently barred and bolted. The sergeant of police called out to open, but again there was no answer.

They consulted together. There was nothing for it but to blow the door open, and some one of them called in a loud voice to those that might be within to stand away from the door or they would be killed. And at this very moment the yellow sheep-dog came bounding up the yard from the woods and licked their hands and fawned on them and barked joyfully.

"Indeed, now," said one of the farmers, "he did know that there was something amiss. A pity it was, Thomas Williams, that we did not follow him when he implored us last Sunday."

The corporal disengaged his bayonet and shot into the keyhole, calling out once more before he fired. He shot and shot again, so heavy and firm was the ancient door, so stout its bolts and fastenings. At last he had to fire at the massive hinges, and then they all pushed together, and at that the door lurched open suddenly and fell forward.

Young Griffith was lying dead before the hearth. They went on toward the parlor, and in the doorway of the room was the body of the artist Secretan, as if he had fallen in trying to get to the kitchen.

Up-stairs the two women, Mrs. Griffith and her daughter, a girl of eighteen, were lying together on the bed in the big bedroom, clasped in each other's arms.

They went about the house, searched the pantries, the back kitchen, and the cellars; there was no life in it. There was no bread in the place, no milk, no water.

The group of men stood in the big kitchen and stared at one another, a dreadful perplexity in their eyes. The old man had been killed with the piercing thrust of some sharp weapon; the rest had perished, it seemed probable, of thirst; but what possible enemy was this that besieged the farm and shut in its inhabitants? There was no answer.

The sergeant of police spoke of getting a cart and taking the bodies into Porth, and Dr. Lewis went into the parlor that Secretan had used as a sitting-room, intending to gather any possessions or effects of the dead artist that he might possibly find there. Half a dozen portfolios were piled up in one corner, there were some books on a side-table, a fishing-rod and basket behind the door; that seemed all. Lewis was about to rejoin the rest of the party in the kitchen, when he looked down at some scattered papers lying with the books on the side-table. On one of the sheets he read, to his astonishment, the words, "Dr. James Lewis, Porth." This was written in a staggering, trembling scrawl.

The table stood in a dark corner of the room, and Lewis gathered up the sheets of paper and took them to the window and began to read this:

> I do not think that I can last much longer. We shared out the last drops of water a long time ago. I do not know how many days ago. We fall asleep and dream and walk about the house in our dreams, and I am often not sure whether I am awake or still dreaming, and so the days and nights are confused in my mind. I awoke not long ago, at least I suppose I awoke, and found I was lying in the passage.
>
> There seems no hope for any of us. We are in the dream of death.

Here the manuscript became unintelligible for half a dozen lines. There was a fresh start, as it were, and the writer began again, in ordinary letter-form:

Dear Lewis:

I hope you will excuse all this confusion and wandering. I intended to begin a proper letter to you, and now I find all that stuff that you have been reading, if this ever gets into your hands. I have not the energy even to tear it up. If you read it you will know to what a sad pass I had come when it was written.

I have said of what I am writing, "if this ever gets into your hands," and I am not at all sure that it ever will. If what is happening here is happening everywhere else, then, I suppose, the world is coming to an end. I cannot understand it; even now I can hardly believe it.

And then there's another thing that bothers me. Now and then I wonder whether we are not all mad together in this house. Despite what I see and know, or, perhaps, I should say, because what I see and know is so impossible, I wonder whether we are not all suffering from a delusion. Perhaps we are our own jailers, and we are really free to go out and live. Perhaps what we think we see is not there at all. I wonder now and then whether we are all like this in Treff Loyne; yet in my heart I feel sure that it is not so.

Still, I do not want to leave a madman's letter behind me, and so I will not tell you the full story of what I have seen or believe I have seen. If I am a sane man, you will be able to fill in the blanks for yourself from your own knowledge. If I am mad, burn the letter and say nothing about it.

I think that it was on a Tuesday that we first noticed that there was something queer about. I came home about five or six o'clock and found the family at Treff Loyne laughing at old Tiger, the sheep-dog. He was making short runs from the farmyard to the door of the house, barking, with quick, short yelps. Mrs. Griffith and Miss Griffith were standing by the porch, and the dog would go to them, look into their faces, and then run up the farm-yard to the gate, and then look back with that eager, yelping bark, as if he were waiting for the women to follow him. Then, again and again he ran up to them and tugged at their skirts, as if he would pull them by main force away from the house.

The dog barked and yelped and whined and scratched at the door all through the evening. They let him in once, but he seemed to have become quite frantic. He ran up to one member of the family after another; his eyes were bloodshot, and his mouth was foaming, and he tore at their clothes till they drove him out again into the darkness. Then he broke into a long, lamentable howl of anguish, and we heard no more of him.

It was soon after dawn when I finally roused myself. The people in the house were talking to each other in high voices, arguing about something that I did not understand.

"It is those damned Gipsies, I tell you," said old Griffith.

"What would they do a thing like that for?" asked Mrs. Griffith. "If it was stealing, now—"

They seemed puzzled and angry, so far as I could make out, but not at all frightened. I got up and began to dress. I don't think I looked out of the window. The glass on my dressing-table is high and broad, and the window is small; one would have to poke one's head round the glass to see anything.

The voices were still arguing down-stairs. I heard the old man say, "Well, here's for a beginning, anyhow," and then the door slammed.

A minute later the old man shouted, I think, to his son. Then there was a great noise which I will not describe more particularly, and a dreadful screaming and crying inside the house and a sound of rushing feet. They all cried out at once to each other. I heard the daughter crying: "It is no good, Mother; he is dead. Indeed they have killed him," and Mrs. Griffith screaming to the girl to let her go. And then one of them rushed out of the kitchen and shot the great bolts of oak across the door just as something beat against it with a thundering crash.

I ran down-stairs. I found them all in wild confusion, in an agony of grief and horror and amazement. They were like people who had seen something so awful that they had gone mad.

I went to the window looking out on the farm-yard. I won't tell you all that I saw, but I saw poor old Griffith lying by the pond, with the blood pouring out of his side.

I wanted to go out to him and bring him in. But they told me that he must be stone-dead, and such things also that it was quite plain that any one who went out of the house would not live more than a moment. We could not believe it even as we gazed at the body of the dead man; but it was there. I used to wonder sometimes what one would feel like if one saw an apple drop from the tree and shoot up into the air and disappear. I think I know now how one would feel.

Even then we couldn't believe that it would last. We were not seriously afraid for ourselves. We spoke of getting out in an hour or two, before dinner, anyhow. It couldn't last, because it was impossible. Indeed, at twelve o'clock young Griffith said he would go down to the well by the back way and draw another pail of water. I went to the door and stood by it. He had not gone a dozen yards before they were on him. He ran for his life, and we had all we could do to bar the door in time. And then I began to get frightened.

But day followed day, and it was still there. I went to Treff Loyne because it was buried in the narrow valley under the ash-trees, far away from any track. There was not so much as a foot-path that was near it; no one ever came that way.

And now this thought came back without delight, with terror. Griffith thought that a shout might be heard on a still night up away on the Allt, "if a man was listening for it," he added doubtfully. My voice was clearer and stronger than his, and on the second night I said I would go up to my bedroom and call for help through the open window. I waited till it was all dark and still, and looked out through the window before opening it. And then I saw over the ridge of the long barn across the yard what looked like a tree, though I knew there was no tree there. It was a dark mass against the sky, with wide-spread boughs, a tree of thick, dense growth. I wondered what this could be, and I threw open the window not only because I was going to call for help, but because I wanted to see more clearly what the dark growth over the barn really was.

I saw in the depth of it points of fire, and colors in light, all glowing and moving, and the air trembled. I stared out into the night, and the dark tree lifted over the roof of the barn, rose up in the air, and floated toward me. I did not move till it was close to the house; and then I saw what it was, and banged the window down only just in time. I had to fight, and I saw the tree that was like a burning cloud rise up in the night and settle over the barn.

Another day went by, and at dusk I looked out, but the eyes of fire were watching me. I dared not open the window. And then I thought of another plan. There was the great old fireplace, with the round Flemish chimney going high above the house. If I stood beneath it and shouted, I thought perhaps the sound might be carried better than if I called out of the window; for all I knew the round chimney might act as a sort of megaphone. Night after night, then, I stood on the hearth and called for help from nine o'clock to eleven.

But we had drunk up the beer, and we would let ourselves have water only by little drops, and on the fourth night my throat was dry, and I began to feel strange and weak; I knew that all the voice I had in my lungs would hardly reach the length of the field by the farm.

It was then we began to dream of wells and fountains, and water coming very cold, in little drops, out of rocky places in the middle of a cool wood. We had given up all meals; now and then one would cut a lump from the sides of bacon on the kitchen wall and chew a bit of it, but the saltness was like fire.

And then we began to dream, as I say. And one day I dreamed that there was a bubbling well of cold, clear water in the cellar, and I had just hollowed my hand to drink it when I woke. I went into the kitchen and told young Griffith. I said I was sure there was water there. He shook his head, but he took up the great kitchen poker and we went down to the old cellar. I showed him the stone by the pillar, and he raised it up. But there was no well. Later I came upon young Griffith one evening evidently trying to make a subterranean passage under one of the walls of the house. I knew he was mad, as he knew I was mad when he saw me digging for a well in the cellar; but neither said anything to the other.

Now we are past all this. We are too weak. We dream when we are awake and when we dream we think we wake. Night and day come and go, and we mistake one for another.

Only a little while ago I heard a voice which sounded as if it were at my very ears, but rang and echoed and resounded as if it were rolling and reverberated from the vault of some cathedral, chanting in terrible modulations. I heard the words quite clearly, "Incipit liber iræ Domini Dei nostri" ("Here beginneth The Book of the Wrath of the Lord our God").

And then the voice sang the word *Aleph,* prolonging it, it seemed through ages, and a light was extinguished as it began the chapter:

"In that day, saith the Lord, there shall be a cloud over the land, and in the cloud a burning and a shape of fire, and out of the cloud shall issue forth my messengers; they shall run all together, they shall not turn aside; this shall be a day of exceeding bitterness, without salvation. And on every high hill, saith the Lord of Hosts, I will set my sentinels, and my armies shall encamp in the place of every valley; in the house that is amongst rushes I will execute judgment, and in vain shall they fly for refuge to the munitions of the rocks. In the groves of the woods, in the places where the leaves are as a tent above them, they shall find the sword of the slayer; and they that put their trust in walled cities shall be confounded. Woe unto the armed man, woe unto him that taketh pleasure in the strength of his artillery, for a little thing shall smite him, and by one that hath no might shall he be brought down into the dust. That which is low shall be set on high; I will make the lamb and the young sheep to be as the lion from the

swellings of Jordan; they shall not spare, saith the Lord, and the doves shall be as eagles on the hill Engedi; none shall be found that may abide the onset of their battle."

Here the manuscript lapsed again and finally into utter, lamentable confusion of thought.

Dr. Lewis maintained that we should never begin to understand the real significance of life until we began to study just those aspects of it which we now dismiss and overlook as utterly inexplicable and therefore unimportant.

We were discussing a few months ago the awful shadow of the terror which at length had passed away from the land. I had formed my opinion, partly from observation, partly from certain facts which had been communicated to me, and the passwords having been exchanged, I found that Lewis had come by very different ways to the same end.

"And yet," he said, "it is not a true end, or, rather, it is like all the ends of human inquiry—it leads one to a great mystery. We must confess that what has happened might have happened at any time in the history of the world. It did not happen till a year ago, as a matter of fact, and therefore we made up our minds that it never could happen; or, one would better say, it was outside the range even of imagination. But this is our way. Most people are quite sure that the Black Death—otherwise the Plague—will never invade Europe again. They have made up their complacent minds that it was due to dirt and bad drainage. As a matter of fact the Plague had nothing to do with dirt or with drains, and there is nothing to prevent its ravaging England to-morrow. But if you tell people so, they won't believe you."

I agreed with all this. I added that sometimes the world was incapable of seeing, much less believing, that which was before its own eyes.

"Look," I said, "at any eighteenth-century print of a Gothic cathedral. You will find that the trained artistic eye even could not behold in any true sense the building that was before it. I have seen an old print of Peterborough Cathedral that looks as if the artist had drawn it from a clumsy model, constructed of bent wire and children's bricks."

"Exactly; because Gothic was outside the esthetic theory, and therefore vision, of the time. You can't believe what you don't see; rather, you can't see what you don't believe.

"You must not suppose that my experiences of that afternoon at Treff Loyne had afforded me the slightest illumination. Indeed, if it had not been that I had seen poor old Griffith's body lying pierced in his own farm-yard, I think I should have been inclined to accept one of Secretan's hints, and to believe that the whole family had fallen a victim to a collective delusion or hallucination, and had shut themselves up and died of thirst through sheer madness. I think there have been such cases. But I had seen the body of the murdered man and the wound that had killed him.

"Did the manuscript left by Secretan give me no hint? Well, it seemed to me to make confusion worse confounded. You see, Secretan, in writing that extraordinary document, almost insisted on the fact that he was not in his proper senses; that for days he had been part asleep, part awake, part delirious. How was one to judge his statement, to separate delirium from fact? In one thing he stood confirmed; you remember he speaks of calling for help up the old chimney of Treff Loyne; that did seem to fit in with the tales of a hollow, moaning cry that had been heard upon the Allt. So far one could take him as a recorder of actual experiences. And I looked in the old cellars of the farm and found a frantic sort of rabbit-hole dug by one of the pillars; again he was confirmed. But what was one to make of that story of the chanting voice and the letters of the Hebrew alphabet and the chapter out of some unknown minor prophet? When one has the key it is easy enough to sort out the facts or the hints of facts from the delusions; but I hadn't the key on that September evening. I was forgetting the 'tree' with lights and fires in it; that, I think, impressed me more than anything with the feeling that Secretan's story was in the main a true story. I had seen a like appearance down there in my own garden; but what was it?

"Now, I was saying that, paradoxically, it is only by the inexplicable things that life can be explained. We are apt to say, you know, 'a very odd coincidence,' and pass the matter by, as if there were no more to be said or as if that were the end of it. Well, I believe that the only real path lies through the blind alleys."

"How do you mean?"

"Well, this is an instance of what I mean. I was talking with Merritt, my brother-in-law, about the strange things he had seen in a way that I thought all nonsense, and I was wondering how I was going to shut him up when a big moth flew into the room through that window, fluttered about, and succeeded in burning itself alive in the lamp. That gave me my cue. I asked Merritt if he knew why moths made for lamps or something of the kind; I thought it would be a hint to him that I was sick of his half-baked theories. So it was; he looked sulky and held his tongue.

"But a few minutes later I was called out by a man who had found his little boy dead in a field near his cottage about an hour before. The child was so still, they said, that a great moth had settled on his forehead and fluttered away only when they lifted up the body. It was absolutely illogical; but it was this odd 'coincidence' of the moth in my lamp and the moth on the dead boy's forehead that first set me on the track. I can't say that it guided me in any real sense; it was more like a great flare of red paint on a wall.

"But, as you will remember, from having read my notes on the matter, I was called in about ten days later to see a man named Cradock who had been found in a field near his farm quite dead. This also was at night. His wife found him, and there were some very queer things in her story. She said that the hedge of the field looked as if it were changed; she began to be afraid that she had lost her way and got into the wrong field.

"Then came that extraordinary business of Treff Loyne. I took it all home, and sat down for the evening before it. It appalled me not only by its horror, but here again by the discrepancy between its terms.

"It was, I believe, a sudden leap of the mind that liberated me from the tangle. It was quite beyond logic. I went back to that evening when Merritt was boring me, to the moth in the candle, and to the moth on the forehead of poor Johnnie Roberts. There was no sense in it; but I suddenly determined that the child and Joseph Cradock the farmer, and that unnamed Stratfordshire man, all found at night, all asphyxiated, had been choked by vast swarms of moths. I don't pretend even now that this is demonstrated, but I'm sure it's true.

"Now suppose you encounter a swarm of these creatures in the dark. Suppose the smaller ones fly up your nostrils. You will gasp for breath and open your mouth. Then, suppose some hundreds of them fly into your mouth, into your gullet, into your windpipe, what will happen to you? You will be dead in a very short time, choked, asphyxiated."

"But the moths would be dead, too. They would be found in the bodies."

"The moths? Do you know that it is extremely difficult to kill a moth with cyanide of potassium? Take a frog, kill it, open its stomach. There you will find its dinner of moths and small beetles, and the 'dinner' will shake itself and walk off cheerily, to resume an entirely active existence. No; that is no difficulty.

"Well, now I came to this. I was shutting out all the other cases. I was confining myself to those that came under the one formula.

"Then the next step. Of course we know nothing really about moths; rather, we know nothing of moth reality. For all I know there may be hundreds of books which treat of moths and nothing but moths. But these are scientific books, and science deals only with surfaces. It has nothing to do with realities. To take a very minor matter: we don't even know why the moth desires the flame. But we do know what the moth does not do; it does not gather itself into swarms with the object of destroying human life. But here, by the hypothesis, were cases in which the moth had done this very thing; the moth race had entered, it seemed, into a malignant conspiracy against the human race. It was quite impossible, no doubt,—that is to say, it had never happened before,—but I could see no escape from this conclusion.

"These insects, then, were definitely hostile to man; and then I stopped, for I could not see the next step, obvious though it seems to me now. If the moths were infected with hatred of men, and possessed the design and the power of combining against him, why not suppose this hatred, this design, this power shared by other nonhuman creatures?

"The secret of the Terror might be condensed into a sentence: the animals had revolted against men.

"Now, the puzzle became easy enough; one had only to classify. Take the cases of the people who met their deaths by falling over cliffs or over the edge of quarries. We think of sheep as timid creatures, who always run away. But suppose sheep that don't run away; and, after all, in reason why should they run away? Quarry or no quarry, cliff or no cliff, what would happen to you if a hundred sheep ran after you instead of running from you? There would be no help for it; they would have you down and beat you to death or stifle you. Then suppose man, woman, or child near a cliff's edge or a quarry-side, and a sudden rush of sheep. Clearly there is no help; there is nothing for it but to go over. There can be no doubt that that is what happened in all these cases.

"And again. You know the country and you know how a herd of cattle will sometimes pursue people through the fields in a solemn, stolid sort of way. They behave as if they wanted to close in on you. Townspeople sometimes get frightened and scream and run; you or I would take no notice, or, at the utmost, would wave our sticks at the herd, which would stop dead or lumber off. But suppose they don't lumber off? It was a quicker death for poor Griffith of Treff Loyne: one of his own beasts gored him to death with one sharp thrust of its horn into his heart. And from that morning those within the house were closely besieged by their own cattle and horses and sheep, and when those unhappy people within opened a window to call for help or to catch a few drops of rain-water to relieve their burning thirst, the cloud waited for them with its myriad eyes of fire. Can you wonder that Secretan's statement reads in places like mania? You perceive the horrible position of those people in Treff Loyne; not only did they see death advancing on them, but advancing with incredible steps, as if one were to die not only in nightmare, but by nightmare. But no one in his wildest, most fiery dreams had ever imagined such a fate. I am not astonished that Secretan at one moment suspected the evidence of his own senses, at another surmised that the world's end had come."

"And how about the Williamses who were murdered on the Highway near here?"

"The horses were the murderers, the horses that afterward stampeded the camp below. By some means which is still obscure to me they lured that family into the road and beat their brains out; their shod hoofs were the instruments of execution. The munition-works? Their enemy was rats. I believe that it has been calculated that in 'greater London' the number of rats is about equal to the number of human beings; that is, there are about seven millions of them. The proportion would be about the same in all the great centers of population;

and the rat, moreover, is on occasion migratory in its habits. You can understand now that story of the *Semiramis* beating about the mouth of the Thames, and at last cast away by Arcachon, her only crew dry heaps of bones. The rat is an expert boarder of ships. And so one can understand the tale told by the frightened man who took the path by the wood that led up from the new munition-works. He thought he heard a thousand men treading softly through the wood and chattering to one another in some horrible tongue; what he did hear was the marshaling of an army of rats, their array before the battle.

"And conceive the terror of such an attack. Even one rat in a fury is said to be an ugly customer to meet; conceive, then, the irruption of these terrible, swarming myriads, rushing upon the helpless, unprepared, astonished workers in the munition-shops."

* * *

There can be no doubt, I think, that Dr. Lewis was entirely justified in these extraordinary conclusions. As I say, I had arrived at pretty much the same end, by different ways; but this rather as to the general situation, while Lewis had made his own particular study of those circumstances of the Terror that were within his immediate purview, as a physician in large practice in the southern part of Meirion. Of some of the cases which he reviewed he had, no doubt, no immediate or first-hand knowledge; but he judged these instances by their similarity to the facts which had come under his personal notice. He spoke of the affairs of the quarry at Llanfihangel on the analogy of the people who were found dead at the bottom of the cliffs near Porth, and he was no doubt justified in doing so. He told me that, thinking the whole matter over, he was hardly more astonished by the Terror in itself than by the strange way in which he had arrived at his conclusions.

"You know," he said, "those certain evidences of animal malevolence which we knew of, the bees that stung the child to death, the trusted sheep-dog's turning savage, and so forth. Well, I got no light whatever from all this; it suggested nothing to me. You do not believe; therefore you cannot see.

"And then, when the truth at last appeared, it was through the whimsical 'coincidence,' as we call such signs, of the moth in my lamp and the moth on the dead child's forehead. This, I think, is very extraordinary."

"And there seems to have been one beast that remained faithful—the dog at Treff Loyne. That is strange."

"That remains a mystery."

* * *

It would not be wise, even now, to describe too closely the terrible scenes that were to be seen in the munition areas of the North and the Midlands during the black months of the Terror. Out of the factories issued at black midnight the shrouded dead in their coffins, and their very kinsfolk did not know how they had come by their deaths. All the towns were full of houses of mourning, were full of dark and terrible rumors as incredible as the incredible reality. There were things done and suffered that perhaps never will be brought to light, memories and secret traditions of these things will be whispered in families, delivered from father to son, growing wilder with the passage of the years, but never growing wilder than the truth.

It is enough to say that the cause of the Allies was for a while in deadly peril. The men at the front called in their extremity for guns and shells. No one told them what was happening in the places where these munitions were made.

But, after the first panic, measures were taken. The workers were armed with special weapons, guards were mounted, machine-guns were placed in position, bombs and liquid flame were ready against the obscene hordes of the enemy, and the "burning clouds" found a fire fiercer than their own. Many deaths occurred among the airmen; but they, too, were given special guns, arms that scattered shot broadcast, and so drove away the dark flights that threatened the airplanes.

And then, in the winter of 1915–16, the Terror ended suddenly as it had begun. Once more a sheep was a frightened beast that ran instinctively from a little child; the cattle were again solemn, stupid creatures, void of harm; the spirit and the convention of malignant design passed out of the hearts of all the animals. The chains that they had cast off for a while were thrown again about them.

And finally there comes the inevitable "Why?" Why did the beasts who had been humbly and patiently subject to man, or affrighted by his presence, suddenly know their strength and learn how to league together and declare bitter war against their ancient master?

It is a most difficult and obscure question. I give what explanation I have to give with very great diffidence, and an eminent disposition to be corrected if a clearer light can be found.

Some friends of mine, for whose judgment I have very great respect, are inclined to think that there was a certain contagion of hate. They hold that the fury of the whole world at war, the great passion of death that seems driving all humanity to destruction, infected at last these lower creatures, and in place of their native instinct of submission gave them rage and wrath and ravening.

This may be the explanation. I cannot say that it is not so, because I do not profess to understand the working of the universe. But I confess that the theory strikes me as fanciful. There may be a contagion of hate as there is a contagion of smallpox; I do not know, but I hardly believe it.

In my opinion, and it is only an opinion, the source of the great revolt of the beasts is to be sought in a much subtler region of inquiry. I believe that the subjects revolted because the king abdicated. Man has dominated the beasts throughout the ages, the spiritual has reigned over the rational through the peculiar quality and grace of spirituality that men possess, that makes a man to be that which he is. And when he maintained this power and grace, I think it is pretty clear that between him and the animals there was a certain treaty and alliance. There was supremacy on the one hand and submission on the other; but at the same time there was between the two that cordiality which exists between lords and subjects in a well-organized state. I know a socialist who maintains that Chaucer's "Canterbury Tales" give a picture of true democracy. I do not know about that, but I see that knight and miller were able to get on quite pleasantly together, just because the knight knew that he was a knight and the miller knew that he was a miller. If the knight had had conscientious objections to his knightly grade, while the miller saw no reason why he should not be a knight, I am sure that their intercourse would have been difficult, unpleasant, and perhaps murderous.

So with man. I believe in the strength and truth of tradition. A learned man said to me a few weeks ago: "When I have to choose between the evidence of tradition and the evidence of a document, I always believe the evidence of tradition. Documents may be falsified and often are falsified; tradition is never falsified." This is true; and therefore, I think, one may put trust in the vast body of folklore which asserts that there was once a worthy and friendly alliance between man and the beasts. Our popular tale of Dick Whittington and his cat no doubt represents the adaptation of a very ancient legend to a comparatively modern personage, but we may go back into the ages and find the popular tradition asserting that not only are the animals the subjects, but also the friends of man.

All that was in virtue of that singular spiritual element in man which the rational animals do not possess. Spiritual does not mean respectable, it does not even mean moral, it does not mean "good" in the ordinary acceptation of the word. It signifies the royal prerogative of man, differentiating him from the beasts.

For long ages he has been putting off this royal robe, he has been wiping the balm of consecration from his own breast. He has declared again and again that he is not spiritual, but rational; that is, the equal of the beasts over whom he was once sovereign. He has vowed that he is not Orpheus, but Caliban.

But the beasts also have within them something which corresponds to the spiritual quality in men; we are content to call it instinct. They perceived that the throne was vacant; not even friendship was possible between them and the self-deposed monarch. If he was not king, he was a sham, an impostor, a thing to be destroyed.

Hence, I think, the Terror. They have risen once; they may rise again. ❋

The Happy Children

A DAY after the Christmas of 1915, my professional duties took me up North; or to be as precise as our present conventions allow, to "the North-Eastern district." There was some singular talk; mad gossip of the Germans having a "dug-out" somewhere by Malton Head. Nobody seemed to be quite clear as to what they were doing there or what they hoped to do there; but the report ran like wildfire from one foolish mouth to another, and it was thought desirable that the whole silly tale should be tracked down to its source and exposed or denied once and for all.

I went up, then, to that North-Eastern district on Sunday, December 26th, 1915, and pursued my investigations from Helmsdale Bay, which is a small watering-place within a couple of miles of Malton Head. The people of the dales and the moors had just heard of the fable, I found, and regarded it all with supreme and sour contempt. So far as I could make out, it originated from the games of some children who had stayed at Helmsdale Bay in the summer. They had acted a rude drama of German spies and their capture, and had used Helby Cavern, between Helmsdale and Malton Head, as the scene of their play. That was all; the fools apparently had done the rest; the fools who believed with all their hearts in "the Russians," and got cross with anyone who expressed a doubt as to "the Angels of Mons."

"Gang oop to beasten and tell them sike a tale and they'll not believe it," said one dalesman to me; and I have a suspicion that he thought that I, who had come so many hundred miles to investigate the story, was but little wiser than those who credited it. He could not be expected to understand that a journalist has two offices—to proclaim the truth and to denounce the lie.

I had finished with "the Germans" and their dug-out early in the afternoon of Monday, and I decided to break the journey home at Banwick, which I had often heard of as a beautiful and curious old place. So I took the one-thirty train, and went wandering inland, and stopped at many unknown stations in the midst of great levels, and changed at Marishes Ambo, and went on again through a strange land in the dimness of the winter afternoon. Somehow the train left the level and glided down into a deep and narrow dell, dark with winter woods, brown with withered bracken, solemn in its loneliness. The only thing that moved was the swift and rushing stream that foamed over the boulders and then lay still in brown pools under the bank.

The dark woods scattered and thinned into groups of stunted, ancient thorns; great grey rocks, strangely shaped, rose out of the ground; crenellated rocks rose on the heights on either side. The brooklet swelled and became a river, and always following this river we came to Banwick soon after the setting of the sun.

I saw the wonder of the town in the light of the afterglow that was red in the west. The clouds blossomed into rose-gardens; there were seas of fairy green that swam about isles of crimson light; there were clouds like spears of flame, like dragons of fire. And under the mingling lights and colours of such a sky Banwick went down to the pools of its land-locked harbour and climbed again across the bridge towards the ruined abbey and the great church on the hill.

I came from the station by an ancient street, winding and narrow, with cavernous closes and yards opening from it on either side, and flights of uneven steps going upward to high terraced houses, or downward to the harbour and the incoming tide. I saw there many gabled houses, sunken with age far beneath the level of the pavement, with dipping roof-trees and bowed doorways, with traces of grotesque carving on their walls. And when I stood on the quay, there on the other side of the harbour was the most amazing confusion of red-tiled roofs that I had ever seen, and the great grey Norman church high on the bare hill above them; and below them the boats swinging in the swaying tide, and the water burning in the fires of the sunset. It was the town of a magic dream. I stood on the quay till the shining had gone from the sky and the water- pools, and the winter night came down dark upon Banwick.

I found an old snug inn just by the harbour, where I had been standing. The walls of the rooms met each other at odd and unexpected angles; there were strange projections and juttings of masonry, as if one room were trying to force its way into another; there were indications as of unthinkable staircases in the corners of the ceilings. But there was a bar where Tom Smart would have loved to sit, with a roaring fire and snug, old elbow chairs about it and pleasant indications that if "something warm" were wanted after supper it could be generously supplied.

I sat in this pleasant place for an hour or two and talked to the pleasant people of the town who came in and out. They told me of the old adventures and industries of the town. It had once been, they said, a great whaling port, and then there had been a lot of ship-building, and later Banwick had been famous for its amber-cutting. "And now there's nowt," said one of the men in the bar; "but we get on none so badly."

I went out for a stroll before my supper. Banwick was now black, in thick darkness. For good reasons not a single lamp was lighted in the streets, hardly a gleam showed from behind the closely-curtained windows. It was as if one walked a town of the Middle Ages, and with the ancient overhanging shapes of the houses dimly visible I was reminded of those strange, cavernous pictures of mediæval Paris and Tours that Doré drew.

Hardly anyone was abroad in the streets; but all the courts and alleys seemed alive with children. I could just see little white forms fluttering to and fro as they ran in and out. And I never heard such happy children's voices. Some were singing, some were laughing; and peering into one black cavern, I made out a ring of children dancing round and round and chanting in clear voices a wonderful melody; some old tune of local tradition, as I supposed, for its modulations were such as I had never heard before.

I went back to my tavern and spoke to the landlord about the number of children who were playing about the dark streets and courts, and how delightfully happy they all seemed to be.

He looked at me steadily for a moment, and then said:

"Well, you see, sir, the children have got a bit out of hand of late; their fathers are out at the front, and their mothers can't keep them in order. So they're running a bit wild."

There was something odd about his manner. I could not make out exactly what the oddity was, or what it meant. I could see that my remark had somehow made him uncomfortable; but I was at a loss to know what I had done. I had my supper, and then sat down for a couple of hours to settle "the Germans" of Malton Head.

I finished my account of the German myth, and instead of going to bed, I determined that I would have one more look at Banwick in its wonderful darkness. So I went out and crossed the bridge, and began to climb up the street on the other side, where there was that strange huddle of red roofs mounting one above the other that I had seen in the afterglow. And to my amazement I found that these extraordinary Banwick children were still about and abroad, still revelling and carolling, dancing and singing, standing, as I supposed, on the top of the flights of steps that climbed from the courts up the hillside, and so having the appearance of floating in mid-air. And their happy laughter rang out like bells on the night.

It was a quarter-past eleven when I had left my inn, and I was just thinking that the Banwick mothers had indeed allowed indulgence to go too far, when the children began again to sing that old melody that I had heard in the evening. And now the sweet, clear voices swelled out into the night, and, I thought, must be numbered by hundreds. I was standing in a dark alley-way, and I saw with amazement that the children were passing me in a long procession that wound up the hill towards the abbey. Whether a faint moon now rose, or whether clouds passed from before the stars, I do not know; but the air lightened, and I could see the children plainly as they went by singing, with the rapture and exultation of them that sing in the woods in springtime.

They were all in white, but some of them had strange marks upon them which, I supposed, were of significance in this fragment of some traditional mystery-play that I was beholding. Many of them had wreaths of dripping seaweed about their brows; one showed a painted scar on her throat; a tiny boy held open his white robe, and pointed to a dreadful wound above his heart, from which the blood seemed to flow; another child held out his hands wide apart and the palms looked torn and bleeding, as if they had been pierced. One of the children held up a little baby in her arms, and even the infant showed the appearance of a wound on its face.

The procession passed me by, and I heard it still singing as if in the sky as it went on its steep way up the hill to the ancient church. I went back to my inn, and as I crossed the bridge it suddenly struck me that this was the eve of the Holy Innocents'. No doubt I had seen a confused relic of some mediæval observance, and when I got back to the inn I asked the landlord about it.

Then I understood the meaning of the strange expression I had seen on the man's face. He was sick and shuddering with terror; he drew away from me as though I were a messenger from the dead.

* * *

Some weeks after this I was reading in a book called *The Ancient Rites of Banwick*. It was written in the reign of Queen Elizabeth by some anonymous person who had seen the glory of the old abbey, and then the desolation that had come to it. I found this passage:

"And on Childermas Day, at midnight, there was done there a marvellous solemn service. For when the monks had ended their singing of Te Deum at their Mattins, there came unto the altar the lord abbot, gloriously arrayed in a vestment of cloth of gold, so that it was a great marvel to behold him. And there came also into the church all the children that were of tender years of Banwick, and they were all clothed in white robes. And then began the lord abbot to sing the Mass of the Holy Innocents. And when the sacring of the Mass was ended, then there came up from the church into the quire the youngest child that there was present that might hold himself aright. And this child was borne up to the high altar, and the lord abbot set the little child upon a golden and glistering throne afore the high altar, and bowed down and worshipped him, singing, 'Talium Regnum Coelorum, Alleluya. Of such is the Kingdom of Heaven. Alleluya,' and all the quire answered singing, 'Amicti sunt stolis albis, Alleluya, Alleluya; they are clad in white robes, Alleluya, Alleluya.' And then the prior and all the monks in their order did like worship and reverence to the little child that was upon the throne."

* * *

I had seen the White Order of the Innocents. I had seen those who came singing from the deep waters that are about the *Lusitania;* I had seen the innocent martyrs of the fields of Flanders and France rejoicing as they went up to hear their Mass in the spiritual place. ❋

ABOUT S. T. JOSHI

A well known editor and literary scholar, S. T. Joshi's 1996 biography, *H. P. Lovecraft: A Life,* was widely praised and reviewed. Mr. Joshi edited the standard edition of Lovecraft's fiction, published by Arkham House, and also compiled the standard bibliography for Dunsany, published in 1993. In 1995 his critical study, *Lord Dunsany: Master of the Anglo-Irish Imagination,* appeared. His current interests include George Sterling and Ambrose Bierce. He lives in Seattle, Washington.

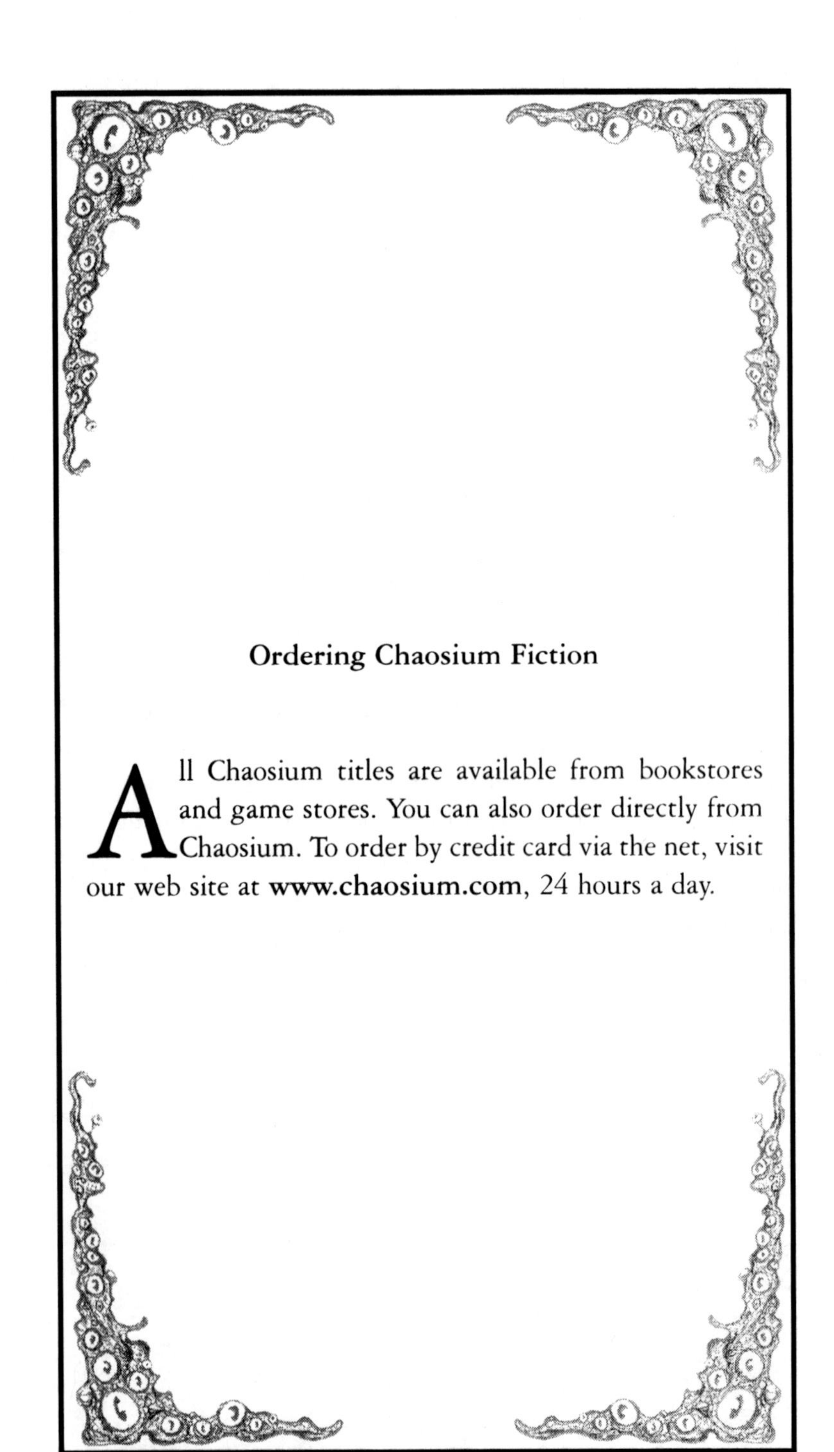

Ordering Chaosium Fiction

All Chaosium titles are available from bookstores and game stores. You can also order directly from Chaosium. To order by credit card via the net, visit our web site at **www.chaosium.com**, 24 hours a day.

ADDITIONAL CALL OF CTHULHU® FICTION TITLES

THE BOOK OF DZYAN

Mme. Blavatsky's famous transcribed messages from beyond, the mysterious *Book of Dzyan*, the heart of the sacred books of Kie-te, are said to have been known only to Tibetan mystics. Quotations from *Dzyan* form the core of her closely-argued *The Secret Doctrine*, the most influential single book of occult knowledge to emerge from the nineteenth century. The text of this book reproduces nearly all of *Book of Dzyan* that Blavatsky transcribed. It also includes long excerpts from her Secret Doctrine as well as from the Society of Psychical Research's 1885 report concerning phenomena witnessed by members of the Theosophical Society. There are notes and additional shorter materials. Editor Tim Maroney's biographical essay starts off the book, a fascinating portrait of an amazing woman.

5 3/8" x 8 3/8", 272 pages, $15.95. Stock #6027; ISBN 1-56882-198-0.

THE COMPLETE PEGANA

Lord Dunsany's fantasy writing had a profound impact on the Dreamlands stories of H. P. Lovecraft. This original collection is composed of newly edited versions of Lord Dunsany's first two books, *The Gods of Pegana* (1905) and *Time and the Gods* (1906). Three additional stories round out the book, the first time that all the Pegana stories have appeared within one book. Edited and introduced by S. T. Joshi.

5 3/8" x 8 3/8", 242 pages, $14.95. Stock #6016; ISBN 1-56882-190-5.

THE DISCIPLES OF CTHULHU
Second Revised Edition

The disciples of Cthulhu are a varied lot. In Mythos stories they are obsessive, loners, dangerous, seeking not to convert others so much as to use them. But writers of the stories are also Cthulhu's disciples, and they are the proselytizers, bringing new members into the fold. Published in 1976, the first edition of *The Disciples of Cthulhu* was the first professional, all-original Cthulhu Mythos anthology. One of the stories, "The Tugging" by Ramsey Campbell, was nominated for a Science Fiction Writers of America Nebula Award, perhaps the only Cthulhu Mythos story that has received such recognition. This second edition of Disciples presents nine stories of Mythos horror, seven from the original edition and two new stories. Selected by Edward P. Berglund.

5 3/8" x 8 3/8", 272 pages, $15.95. Stock #6011; ISBN 1-56882-202-2.

THE HASTUR CYCLE
Second Revised Edition

The stories in this book represent the evolving trajectory of such notions as Hastur, the King in Yellow, Carcosa, the Yellow Sign, Yuggoth, and the Lake of Hali. A succession of writers from Ambrose Bierce to Ramsey Campbell and Karl Edward

Wagner have explored and embellished these concepts so that the sum of the tales has become an evocative tapestry of hypnotic dread and terror, a mythology distinct from yet overlapping the Cthulhu Mythos. Here for the first time is a comprehensive collection of all the relevant tales. Selected and introduced by Robert M. Price.

5 3/8" x 8 3/8", 320 pages, $17.95. Stock #6020; ISBN 1-56882-192-1.

THE INNSMOUTH CYCLE

The decadent, smugly rotting, secret-filled town of Innsmouth is a supreme creation of Howard Philips Lovecraft. It so finely mixes the carnal and the metaphysical that writers continue to take inspiration from it. This new collection contains thirteen tales and three poems tracing the evolution of Innsmouth, from early tales by Dunsany, Chambers, and Cobb, through Lovecraft's "The Shadow Over Innsmouth" to modern tales by Rainey, Glasby, and others.

5 3/8" x 8 3/8", 240 pages, $14.95. Stock # 6017; ISBN 1-56882-199-9.

THE ITHAQUA CYCLE

The elusive, supernatural Ithaqua roams the North Woods and the wastes beyond, as invisible as the wind. Hunters and travelers fear the cold and isolation of the North; they fear the advent of the mysterious, malignant Wind-Walker even more. This collection includes the progenitor tale "The Wendigo" by Algernon Blackwood, three stories by August Derleth, and ten more from a spectrum of contemporary authors including Brian Lumley, Stephen Mark Rainey, and Pierre Comtois.

5 3/8" x 8 3/8", 260 pages, $15.95. Stock #6021; ISBN 1-56882-191-3.

THE NYARLATHOTEP CYCLE

The mighty Messenger of the Outer Gods, Nyarlathotep has also been known to deliver tidings from the Great Old Ones. He is the only Outer God who chooses to personify his presence on our planet. A god of a thousand forms, he comes to Earth to mock, to wreak havoc, and to spur on humanity's self-destructive urges. This volume of stories and poems illustrates the ubiquitous presence of Nyarlathotep and shows him in several different guises. Among them, his presence as Nephren-Ka, the dread Black Pharaoh of dynastic Egypt, dominates. The thirteen stories include a Lin Carter novella. Selected and introduced by Robert M. Price.

5 3/8" x 8 3/8", 256 pages, $14.95. Stock #6019; ISBN 1-56882-200-6.

SINGERS OF STRANGE SONGS

Most readers acknowledge Brian Lumley as the superstar of British horror writers. With the great popularity of his *Necroscope* series, he is one of the best known horror authors in the world. Devoted fans know that his roots are deep in the Cthulhu Mythos, with which most of his early work deals. This volume contains eleven new tales in that vein, as well as three reprints of excellent but little-known work by Lumley. This book was published in conjunction with Lumley's 1997 trip to the United States.

5 3/8" x 8 3/8", 256 pages, $12.95. Stock #6014; ISBN 1-56882-104-2.

TALES OUT OF INNSMOUTH

Innsmouth is a half-deserted, seedy little town on the North Shore of Massachusetts. It is rarely included on any map of the state. Folks in neighboring towns shun those who come from Innsmouth, and murmur about what goes on there. They try not to mention the place in public, for Innsmouth has ways of quelling gossip, and of taking revenge on troublemakers. Here are ten new tales and three reprints concerning the town, the hybrids who live there, the strange city rumored to exist nearby under the sea, and those who nightly lurch and shamble down the fog-bound streets of Innsmouth.

5 3/8" x 8 3/8", 294 pages, $16.95. Stock #6024; ISBN 1-56882-201-4.

THE XOTHIC LEGEND CYCLE

The late Lin Carter was a prolific writer and anthologist of horror and fantasy with over eighty titles to his credit. His tales of Mythos horror are loving tributes to H. P. Lovecraft's "revision" tales and to August Derleth's stories of Hastur and the *R'lyeh Text*. This is the first collection of Carter's Mythos tales; it includes his intended novel, *The Terror Out of Time*. Most of the stories in this collection have been unavailable for some time. Selected and introduced by Robert M. Price.

5 3/8" x 8 3/8", 288 pages, $16.95. Stock #6013; ISBN 1-56882-195-6.

All titles are available from bookstores and game stores. You can also order directly from **www.Chaosium.com**, your source for Cthulhiana and more. To order by credit card via the net, visit our web site, 24 hours a day. To order via phone, call 1-510-583-1000, 9 A.M. to 4 P.M. Pacific time.

CALL OF CTHULHU® FICTION TITLES

THE NECRONOMICON

Although skeptics claim that the *Necronomicon* is a fantastic tome created by H. P. Lovecraft, true seekers into the esoteric mysteries of the world know the truth: The *Necronomicon* is a blasphemous tome of forbidden knowledge written by the mad Arab, Abdul Alhazred. Even today, after attempts over the centuries to destroy any and all copies in any language, some few copies still exist, secreted away. Within this book you will find stories about the *Necronomicon*, different versions of the *Necronomicon*, and two essays on the blasphemous tome. Now you too may learn the true lore of Abdul Alhazred. Selected and introduced by Robert M. Price.

5 3/8" x 8 3/8", 334 pages, $12.95. Stock #6012; ISBN 1-56882-070-4.

THE YELLOW SIGN AND OTHER STORIES

This book contains all the immortal tales of Robert W. Chambers, including "The Repairer of Reputations," "The Yellow Sign," and "The Mask." These titles are often found in survey anthologies. In addition to the six stories reprinted from *The Yellow Sign* (1895), this book also offers more than two dozen other stories and episodes. These narratives rarely appear in print. Some have not been published in nearly a century.

This is a complete collection of Robert W. Chambers' short weird fiction—his published horror, science fiction, and fantasy/supernatural, as well as some self-conscious whimsy. The writing can be facile and out of fashion, of interest to collectors and those desiring to comprehend the writer. But other stories are as delicate and durable as those wrought by Lord Dunsany, and worthy of every reader's time.

5 3/8" x 8 3/8", 652 pages, $19.95. Stock #6023; ISBN 1-56882-170-0.

THE ITHAQUA CYCLE

The elusive, supernatural Ithaqua roams the North Woods and the wastes beyond, as invisible as the wind. Hunters and travelers fear the cold and isolation of the North; they fear the advent of the mysterious, malignant Wind-Walker even more. This collection includes the progenitor tale "The Wendigo" by Algernon Blackwood, three stories by August Derleth, and ten more from a spectrum of contemporary authors including Brian Lumley, Stephen Mark Rainey, and Pierre Comtois.

5 3/8" x 8 3/8", 260 pages, $12.95. Stock #6021; ISBN 1-56882-124-7.

SINGERS OF STRANGE SONGS

Most readers acknowledge Brian Lumley as the superstar of British horror writers. With the great popularity of his *Necroscope* series, he is one of the best known horror authors in the world. Devoted fans know that his roots are deep in the Cthulhu Mythos, with which most of his early work deals. This volume contains eleven new tales in that vein, as well as three reprints of excellent but little-known work by Lumley. This book was published in conjunction with Lumley's 1997 trip to the United States.

5 3/8" x 8 3/8", 244 pages, $12.95. Stock #6014; ISBN 1-56882-104-2.

TALES OUT OF INNSMOUTH

Innsmouth is a half-deserted, seedy little town on the North Shore of Massachusetts. It is rarely included on any map of the state. Folks in neighboring towns shun those who come from Innsmouth, and murmur about what goes on there. They try not to mention the place in public, for Innsmouth has ways of quelling gossip, and of taking revenge on trouble-makers. Here are ten new tales and three reprints concerning the town, the hybrids who live there, the strange city rumored to exist nearby under the sea, and those who nightly lurch and shamble down the fog-bound streets of Innsmouth.

5 3/8" x 8 3/8", 294 pages, $13.95. Stock #6024; ISBN 1-56882-127-1.

THE BOOK OF DZYAN

Mme. Blavatsky's famous transcribed messages from beyond, the mysterious *Book of Dzyan,* the heart of the sacred books of Kie-te, are said to have been known only to Tibetan mystics. Quotations from *Dzyan* form the core of her closely-argued *The Secret Doctrine,* the most influential single book of occult knowledge to emerge from the nineteenth century. The text of this book reproduces nearly all of *Book of Dzyan* that Blavatsky transcribed. It also includes long excerpts from her *Secret Doctrine* as well as from the Society of Psychical Research's 1885 report concerning phenomena witnessed by members of the Theosophical Society. There are notes and additional shorter materials. Editor Tim Maroney's biographical essay starts off the book, a fascinating portrait of an amazing woman.

5 3/8" x 8 3/8", 272 pages, $13.95. Stock #6027; ISBN 1-56882-114-X.

CPSIA information can be obtained at www.ICGtesting.com
Printed in the USA
LVOW07s0611141115
462406LV00002B/5/P